The Weaving

of A Warrior

Also by K. C. Mitchell

The Tapestry of A. Taylor

Coming Soon

Slaves

For Spicier Novel…

check out the following by Kasey Mitchell

The Uncommon Waiter

The Weaving

of A Warrior

Second Book in

The Tapestry Series

Edition 2014

K. C. Mitchell

A Create Space Publication

All characters in this book have no existence outside the imagination of the author and have no relation to anyone bearing the same name or names. Any resemblance to individuals known or unknown to the author are purely coincidental.

ISBN 978-1-500-67675-9

For my children- *Brittney, Christopher, & Kyle*,
who boldly seek to fulfill their dreams thus inspiring
me to go confidently in the direction of mine.

Contents

Preface

Life is But a Weaving (The Tapestry Poem)
Attributed to Corrie Ten Boom

My life is but a weaving
Between my God and me.
I cannot choose the colors
He weaveth steadily.
Oft' times He weaveth sorrow;
And I in foolish pride
Forget He sees the upper
And I the underside.
Not 'til the loom is silent
And the shuttles cease to fly
Will God unroll the canvas
And reveal the reason why.
The dark threads are as needful
In the weaver's skillful hand
As the threads of gold and silver
In the pattern He has planned
He knows, He loves, He cares;
Nothing this truth can dim.
He gives the very best to those
Who leave the choice to Him.

The Weaving

of A Warrior

~ *1* ~

Broken Pieces

It began as an ordinary day except that I decided that I was not going to hide out in my office eating lunch alone again; instead, I ventured to a nearby restaurant to enjoy my soup hot for a change. I should have known better. Just as I finished and looked up from the printout I brought with me, I spotted him. My heart jolted as if a thousand-watt plug had struck it. He did not see me yet. I immediately hid my face behind the sheets of work I brought to distract me. I had managed to hide from Seth for over four years since I fled our home that last fateful night. I hoped I would never see him again. The outrageous plan of moving to the opposite side of this large city worked beautifully and would have worked even better had I not gotten pregnant from Seth raping me that last night. I had followed my new boss back to the very business district I wanted to stay away from because I found my dream job and was finally making enough money to support my two children. After over a year of eating at my desk and keeping myself from gatherings outside of the office, my plan has now failed. I thought surely that I could manage to miss Seth with all these precautions. The consequences of him finding me were too great. I had fled in the night, as he lay passed-out beside me. I had unearthed his secret of homosexuality that he kept from his affluent friends and family. I felt he would do anything to keep that secret. The stakes were high for him. And yet now I also had a secret- his son.

The waitress came and slid my sales ticket onto the table announcing that I could pay the cashier on the way out.

"Could you please take it for me?" I pleaded handing her a ten. She looked at me indignantly. "I'm begging you. There is a man over there who has been stalking me. I don't want him to see me." She looked around expectantly as if a stalker would be obviously dressed. "I'll double your tip." I added, taking out a five from my wallet and placing it on the table. "No change needed." Her demeanor changed then and she nodded, not saying a word. She slipped the money and ticket into her apron as if to be inconspicuous and walked away. I took leave as well and walked directly to the door, too afraid to look up, praying every step of the way that he had not noticed me.

Just before stepping out of the door, I glanced back. He was by himself as well and my hesitation at the door must have caught his eye because, at that moment, he looked directly at me. The recognition in his face was evident. The few seconds of us staring at each other made the unmistakable identification all the more obvious. I fled as if a bomb had just detonated. I walked swiftly in the direction of my office only a few blocks away.

After a moment, I looked behind me, hoping to see only strangers going about their own day. I was horrified to see him come out of the restaurant door, glancing both ways and spotting me. He headed toward me and I fled. I no longer cared about walking inconspicuously. I ran as quickly as my rubber legs would move. I looked back and he was following me. I had never seen him run when we were married and the site frightened me into a paralyzed state. My head began to swim. I glanced again to see if he was gaining on me and he was. I turned the corner, now heading in the opposite direction of my office. I craved the safety of my office but knew that if he saw me enter our building then he could easily find me. As soon as I turned the corner, I knew I must dash into one of the shops before he could turn the same corner and could see me again. I dove into the first one I saw, which happened to be a quaint ice cream shop.

"Where's your restroom?" I barked at the young man scooping ice cream from under the clear freezer. His eyes looked toward the short hall and I ran before he had a chance to speak. Once I entered the restroom, I immediately locked the door behind me.

"Breathe. Breathe." I whispered to myself. My heart pumped frantically and yet my lungs screamed for air. My head spun and I looked around the room for a place to sit before my legs gave out. There was only the toilette so I placed a toilette paper seat cover over it and sat, fully clothed. I waited, expecting at any moment to hear a pound on the door and Seth screaming for me to get out. Flashbacks of our marriage assaulted my brain and I felt my insides constrict. Then I waited a moment longer. I did not hear anything and was not sure what I should be listening for. I looked at my watch. Fifteen minutes had gone by. Apprehensively, I opened the door peeking out to see if he stood waiting for me. I did not see him. I slowly went to the front of the store and scanned the shop. He was not here. I went to the window and looked outside-nothing. I waited, watching to see if any movement would alert me to his presence. All appeared normal. I took a deep breath, knowing I must proceed to my office. I said a silent prayer and then I opened the door to walk out onto the sidewalk. I stood, transfixed, looking around and fully expecting him to ambush me. People walked around me and there was no reason I could find not to head toward my office. Then I walked slowly, turning around every few feet to scan the area. My heart's beat matched the rhythm of my fast pace as I walked.

Once I finally entered into my office building, I stood at the door and looked out, again insuring that he was not following me from a safe distance to see where I went. I did not see him at all so

I went on to my office. I stayed there the rest of the day barely breathing and constantly expecting him to walk in.

"What's up?" Rick responded in his usual casual manner. Rick was a terrific boss but, more importantly, he had become an indispensable friend. We rarely had time to talk of personal matters during tax season. I was thankful that we had time now as the hot sun rose in the July sky.

"Do you have a minute?"

"Sure. Come in." I entered Rick's messy office and closed the door behind me. He gave a suspicious look, somehow knowing I needed privacy.

"I saw Seth at lunch today." I waited for him to react with horror as I had when I saw Seth but Rick's cool character revealed nothing but relaxed interest. I needed to talk to Annie Mae, my confidant from my hiding place on the opposite side of town. She would have immediately drilled me with questions and shown unabashed curiosity. Rick continued to look at me as if he wondered what I was waiting on so I continued to answer his unasked questions. "We didn't speak but he definitely recognized me. He chased me until I was able to ditch him." Rick still gave no response.

"Rick, it terrified me. What should I do?" I knew Rick's lack of enthusiasm did not reflect lack of concern for me. Rick and his wife, Tracy, had practically adopted my children and me since our move to the north side of town. Rick had helped me to locate an apartment that I could afford. Tracy helped me to get Katie enrolled into school and find a nursery for Josh. In fact, she watched Josh for me for several weeks during the transition until I was settled. They were the only family I had left. It was painful to leave Annie Mae, Poppa, and Ezekiel when I moved. Their presence these past four years made this significant difference in my life. I owed them everything. I wanted to call Annie Mae now to get her take on this incidence but I had not talked to her in months and it seemed the only time I called was when I needed something. I thought of calling Kayla since we had remained close even though we were not able to get together any longer. She was trying to get on as a student at University of Georgia in Athens. I knew she was feeling overwhelmed herself, jumping through all the hoops the university demanded to be a part of their post-graduate program. I felt guilty even thinking of taking up her time.

"I don't know that you need to do anything. It sounds like you handled the situation." Rick's response reigned in my wandering mind.

"But, what if he finds me? Now that he saw me, he knows I'm here!" I yelped.

"Well, Brie, 'here' is a big place. Atlanta is an easy city to get lost in and just because he saw you at some restaurant doesn't mean he knows you are here. For all he knows, you were passing through. I wouldn't worry about it if I were you; just go on about your business as normal." I was not sure what I expected from Rick. His response was typical for a man, I supposed. Of course I couldn't go on as usual because my usual was hiding, looking over my shoulder, and being a loner. I had spent the last four years of my life running from Seth and, now that I lived in his area, it would only get progressively worse. Rick could tell I was disappointed in his advice. "Brie, I know you worry about this constantly but, well, to be honest, I sometimes think it may be better to get it over with. I mean, seriously, what can he actually do to you?" Yep, just like a man. My mind blurred with all the things he could do to me, had already done to me.

"You're right, Rick. I do worry about this all the time. Thanks for talking with me." I got up to leave trying very hard not to let the disappointment show in my voice but I knew that Rick saw it. He knew me too well.

"Brie, why don't you call a lawyer and see about getting a divorce? Maybe if you were proactive in meeting Seth right where he lives, then you'd feel more in control of the situation and it wouldn't disturb you so much. Face it head on!" Right, like that's going to happen.

"You're probably right. I'll think about it." I smiled weakly at him and left. When I got back to my office, I picked up the phone to call Annie Mae but something kept me from it and I hung up the receiver. I must learn to stand on my own two feet.

That night I dreamed of Seth. It was the first time in over a year but I awoke with the same shaky limbs and beating heart that I always did after those dreams. The next day was uneventful and the next.

"Good morning beautiful." Joe's voice met me the next morning. Joe was one of the stockbrokers who occupied the neighboring office units and our proprietor. There was certainly chemistry between us but I kept him at bay. There were too many reasons to remain single and anonymous now and besides, with two children, a career, and a truckload of baggage from my past, I didn't have the energy or inclination to be in a relationship.

"Good morning, Joe," I responded coolly as I continued toward my side of the office park. Joe often arrived at exactly the same time that I arrived and we would greet one another. Occasionally, he would come by our office to chat or bring goodies for our office staff. Every woman within our office cooed over him and several single ladies leached onto him when he would walk in the door. If I heard him from down the hall, I would usually close my door. He was tempting, to be sure, but I did not need the distraction. Moreover, if I were honest with myself, I knew he was way out of my league. I learned my lesson once before with Seth to not overshoot myself. If I ever fell in love, it would be with an "average Joe", not this Joe who was rich, successful, and sinfully handsome.

"You free for lunch today?" he called as I walked away from him.

"Oh, sorry- busy day, won't have time. Thanks any way," I called back behind me.

"Why don't I bring lunch to you then?" He didn't give up easily. I had to give him that much.

"I brought my lunch, thanks," I responded as I tried to unlock our office door. The key was always somewhat difficult and every single morning that I unlocked it, I remembered the very first time I had tried. Rick had wanted to see the office I rented on his behalf while he was out of the country with his wife. Joe met us there and the infatuation between us was thick. I had arrogantly insisted I needed no help but could not unlock the door. Joe came up behind me and placed his hand over mine to guide the key into the correct position. The electric current that passed between us had shocked us both. The remembrance of that moment made me blush even now, especially with Joe standing watching me.

"Need some help?" He asked as he walked toward me.

"I've got it," I announced too quickly. Joe was only a few yards away from me when the key finally gave and clicked. I waved at him as I entered the building. His face fell and he walked away. The blood pounding through my veins rang in my ear and I proceeded to the break room to start the morning coffee.

Several days went by after seeing Seth at lunch and my mind fixated on trying to find a solution. I felt I could not sit idly by and wait for Seth to discover me. I knew him too well to hope that he would not try to find me now that he had witnessed my return. I finally conceded to calling Annie Mae. It was early and I knew her day at the beauty shop would still be quiet before her endless line of patrons began to demand her time.

"Hello," her familiar voice rang through the phone lines and felt like a warm hug.

"Hi, Annie Mae, it's Brie. How are you doing?"

"Hey baby! Whut you doin', chille?" She always seemed so glad to hear from me and the miles between us felt nonexistent.

The truth of the matter was that the miles that separated us were nothing compared to the worlds apart from which we came. My moving to her doorstep was not a coincidence. It had been a divine act of God to place this angel in my life. She and her family took us in, supported me, encouraged me, helped me, and showed me genuine love. Even though everything about her world was the polar opposite of mine, she was more a mother to me than my own had ever been.

"I was just thinking about y'all this morning and thought I'd check on you," I lied.

"Well, ain't that sweet. Yeah, me an' Jessie doin' jus' fine. 'Zekiel had a bit of a cold but nuttin' serious. How the babies doin'?" It was just like Annie Mae to skim over her own life and ask about mine.

"They're doing very well. Katie enjoys her daycare for the summer and has a little boyfriend. Josh has grown so much. I need to get out there so y'all can see them." We both knew I would not. I finally bought a car but it was not the most dependable breed. I supposed I could borrow one from someone, perhaps Rick, but except to see Annie Mae and the group, I had no desire to return to that neighborhood. Just thinking about going made me uneasy. I considered myself lucky to have managed no harm by the time I moved away from there and I was in no hurry to return, not even for a visit. I had begged Annie Mae and Jessie to sell their properties and move with me but they insisted that this was their home. As unimaginable as that seemed to me, I was powerless to change them.

"Oh, honey chille, I'd love that so much!" The yearning in her voice made me feel guilty and I decided that, regardless of my trepidation, I would find a way to visit with them soon.

"So, any gossip?"

"No, chille, it's been a slow season 'round here. What's goin' on with you? I knowed you got some reason for callin' Annie Mae out the blue. Rick ok?"

"Yes, Rick is fine. But, as usual, you are right about my having a reason to call. I saw Seth the other day, my husband. We didn't speak," she interrupted me abruptly.

"Lord, chille, you what? Oh my goodness, tell me everythang. Don't leave nuthin' out, you hear?" I could hear her excitement and could tell she was pulling a chair up to get comfortable.

"Well, it turned out to be nothing really but it scared the you-know-what out of me." I continued telling her my version of the story and even told her what Rick had suggested. "What do you think, Annie Mae? What should I do?"

"Oh, chille, I don' know. Lemme think for a minute. 'Zekiel, get momma a drank will ya?"

"Tell Ezekiel I said, 'hi'" I interjected.

"Miss Brie says, 'hi' 'Zekiel" she quoted. I could hear Ezekiel in the background telling her to tell me, "hey" back. "Ok. You ain't gone like this none but I'm gone tell ya what I think. Rick's on ta somthin'. Seth done seen ya so tha cat's out a tha bag. You should get you a lawyer and slap him upside the head with divorce papers before he has a chance to find ya, if'n he's even lookin'." She was right. I didn't like this advice. I had run away from my problems in the past and I was not fully prepared to meet them head on now. "Sooner or later, you gots ta git a divorce, ya know? One day you gone meet someone an wanna git married but ya won't be able to cause you already married. Just bite the bullet an git it over with." I didn't respond at all and the momentary silence between us let her know what I was thinking. "Chille, you asked me what I think. Now I done told ya. Don't mean you gotta do it but that's just what I think."

"Oh, Annie Mae! You and Rick make it sound so simple. In reality, I feel that I would only be opening up a can of worms to contact him. I don't know what the consequences would be but I'm sure it wouldn't be good."

"You right, baby, you don't know but I guarantee ya there is also consequences ta not movin' on with yo life. An', you already know I think he outa be payin' ya some child support for that baby. You an' that baby both deserve that much!"

"I'll think about it Annie Mae." I felt suddenly nauseous and wished I'd eaten a little something before I called her.

"No you won't, chille. You gone keep right on ignorin' this here problem like you done been doin' for the past four years till somethin' blows up in yo face and forces ya to deal with it. I knows you." I had to laugh. She certainly did know me well.

"Well, Annie Mae, I do appreciate your advice and concern. I may not always take it, but I do always appreciate it." I laughed, trying to soften the blow of the truth.

"Well, chille, I gotta go. I see Mrs. Wilson comin' in the door. You know she ain't got no patience. Give them kids a kiss from Momma Mae, ok?"

"I sure will. Annie Mae?" I softened, "It's good to hear your voice."

"O.K., Chille, you, too." Annie Mae was never one for sentimental words or emotions although many occasions had shown me that she did have an enormous love for all those around her. Hearing her voice made me long for those days again of working with her. There was something in her presence that made the environment feel safe and comforting. I paused for several minutes to enjoy the sense of peace from talking with her. I did not want to meet this problem head on. The risk of the outcome was just too great. I would put off dealing with Seth for as long as possible. I could avoid Seth; however, I could not avoid the foreboding feeling that I would live to regret this decision.

~ 2 ~

Revving Up

A month passed by and I was beginning to relax again. A day or two would go by and I would not even think of Seth. My life resumed to business as usual. The summer wound down and fall was around the corner. As Rick's wife did each year, Tracy began to frequent the office. One day she came into my office and closed the door.

"Do you have a minute?" she asked me.

"Of course," I always enjoyed talking with Tracy and we hadn't caught up in a while.

"Well, I want to plan a surprise party for Rick. As you know he's been in business for just over forty years." I immediately panicked that she was about to tell me he was going to retire. Where would I be without this job? "I'd like it to be very big and at a venue that can cater it. Will you help me to plan it?"

"I'd be honored to help you, Tracy. Um, is he planning to retire?" There, I got it out.

"Oh, dear, no! I don't think he'll ever retire. You know him. No, I just want him to see how much his staff, his clients, everyone, and me all appreciate him. I really want this to be special for him." With a sigh of relief, I zealously jumped in to help her plan the party. It would be the first of many meetings Tracy and I would have to insure the party was perfect. We decided to schedule it around the first of December and to tell Rick it was the company's annual Christmas party, surprising him once he was there with the fact that it also encompassed an appreciation party for him. The date allowed us ample time to plan it well without stress. The Christmas party façade would help to disguise its purpose.

The company had grown since our move to this bigger office on the north side of town. We added seven accountants to fill the empty offices bringing the total to thirteen including Rick. Sandy, the office manager and I also had executive offices and the secretaries had their own offices, leaving the receptionist to work up front, as she greeted clients. The increase in people within our office brought with it an increase in income and Rick had put Sandy and me in charge of making everything run well so he was free to continue his accounting duties as he had for decades. Of course, I was still Rick's personal assistant/apprentice so most of the day-to-day responsibilities fell on Sandy. Rick compensated both of us generously as his revenue picked up from the increase in business. I felt confident in my duties at last and Rick spent many hours teaching me all that I needed to know to one day be a full-fledged accountant.

For the first time in my life, I felt self-assured that my children and I would be financially secure. I realized as I reflected back on a conversation I had enjoyed with Kayla that I was living my dream of self-reliance. I no longer depended on the government, my mother, or a husband for help. I knew there was no way I would have made it this far without good friends to help me along the way.

Throwing a surprise party, even though we incorporated it into the Christmas party, for so many people was a much bigger undertaking than anything I had ever done. Tracy arrived to each meeting exuberant with anticipation and always had completed several tasks necessary to insure the party's success. I gathered names of all of our clients, around seven hundred, and personally sent notes asking for RSVP's from them. To my amazement, five hundred and thirty-five responded! After Tracy added eighty-six of their friends and family and we counted on the twenty of us from the office and our families, we were looking at almost six-hundred and fifty guests. I was overwhelmed. It seemed a daunting task and yet, Tracy, who was usually a reserved homebody, came alive. Her organizational skills amazed me and I learned so much from her.

"Oh, it's not so bad when you break it down," she consoled me as I voiced my qualms to her one day over lunch. I convinced her to come to my office for lunch most days saying we had access to computers and printers here if needed. "It's just like planning a wedding. In fact, it's exactly like it but without the added stress of having the perfect dress," she laughed.

"I think we should keep it simple, with only hors d'oeuvres since we have so many people coming," I suggested.

"Oh, no, Brie, We must do this properly with a meal. Although I do feel a buffet may make feeding them easier and more affordable. I was thinking the country club would be the perfect place to have it." No! I wanted to scream to her. Seth was a member there and I could not risk seeing him. If we had it there, we would need to go several times for various necessities, not to mention the actual party.

"I didn't think y'all were members there," I slyly interjected.

"Oh, honey, we are not. Rick doesn't take time for such frivolous activities but our son, Kyle, is and he could get the reservation for us" She beamed with pride. I did not have the heart to burst her bubble but I felt that I must be honest with her.

"Tracy, I have to tell you something," I began and I filled her in on the entire story, even telling her Seth's name, which I rarely did. I went so far as to tell her that I had recently seen him and how the ordeal had petrified me. I wanted her to understand how difficult this was for me and, even if she did not change the venue, to at least understand my trepidation. She came across as such a meek person that I was not prepared for her response.

"Abriella Taylor! Be ashamed! You struggled all these years and continue to struggle because you haven't the courage to stand up to a bully! What are you teaching your children?" I was stunned. I opened my mouth to respond but had no response. "I'm sorry, dear. I didn't mean to blurt that out but, seriously, what are you thinking?"

"It's not that simple, Tracy. You don't understand," I started to tell her all my reasons for not standing up for myself.

"You're absolutely right that I don't understand," she interrupted my answer, "I don't understand how you can allow your children to do without because you're afraid some man will intimidate you. You have to know that their lives would be better with the financial assistance he owes you, not to mention having a mother that lives fearlessly rather than cower behind her desk each day." I had never witnessed Tracy's full disapproval before and I did not like it at all. She had no idea what it was like to live the way I had. She had a loving husband who worshiped her. The rebellion welled up in my throat and it was all I could do to sit there and listen to her reproach me.

"I am sorry, dear. I don't usually voice my opinion but since you shared your problem with me, I assume you want me to be honest with you." She reached over the desk and placed her hand over mine. I wanted to move it but knew I could not. "Sweetheart, this man took years of joy from your life. Don't let him have another day." The meeting was obviously over for the day and she made up an excuse why she had to run, to my great relief. It was only two in the afternoon but I could not focus on work any longer so I decided to leave early.

My intention when I left was to go home and wallow in my self-pity. When I got in my old car to head that way, something changed inside of me. As I sat on my torn seats, looking out the window at all the luxuries that money could buy, I asked myself, "how would our lives be different if Seth had to pay child-support?"

Immediately, I thought, "I'd buy a better car so I didn't have to worry about this wretched car cranking every day. We could take a vacation, which we had not had since I left Seth. I could shop at a real store and not have to depend on Goodwill having something I liked or sales at the area discount stores. It would change our lives exponentially. I could start a college fund for the kids. Katie would be going to high school in only three more years and, before I knew it, she would need funds for college. We could move into a better place, maybe bigger. Seth's income was tremendous and with the laws mandating twenty-three percent of his income towards child-support, I would literally have more money from his support than I made at my job. He lives as a king, with his every whim catered to by servants. Why should my kids have to live so poorly?

Why had I put this off so long? What was I so afraid of? Seth could not hurt me any longer. He would try, of course, to intimidate me but, honestly, what could he do to me now? I would face him and, furthermore, I would put him on the defense for a change. I had the element of surprise on my side and I would use it.

As if the heavens opened up to predict that my new resolve would not insure an easy journey, my car sputtered to a slow death. I made it to the side of the road and into a parking lot before it completely conked out.I was on the corner of Maple and Turner streets. I was only about five blocks from the office so I decided to walk back. The exercise would do me good and the fresh air would help me think clearly. I knew I needed a plan- an ironclad, foolproof plan. I would need help, too. For sure, I would require an attorney, but also I knew I needed emotional support. When I got to the office, I went directly to Rick's office.

"Hey. Do you have a minute?" It looked like I had caught him at a good time. He nodded to confirm this and motioned with his hand for me to come in as he finished writing something. I sat opposite him and waited. When he finished he revved back in his chair.

"I've made a very difficult decision, thanks, in part to your wife." I tried to smile so I would not look upset but the grimace that graced my lips left no doubt that I wasn't the happiest I'd ever been.

"Yeah, Brie, about that, Tracy called me. She's worried she upset you. She can be very headstrong sometimes. I'm sorry about that, she didn't mean," I held up my hand for him to stop. I had to cut him off.

"No, Rick, you don't need to explain. In fact, I owe her sincere thanks for giving me the kick in the butt I needed. All this time, I've been thinking I was the one suffering from my bad decisions so, I guess, I kinda felt like I may even deserve what I was having to deal with but, my kids, well, they definitely do not deserve to have to live the way they do. You, Annie Mae, and Tracy are all right! I need to get child-support from Seth. But, I'm not going to lie, it is very intimidating. I need a plan. Can you help me?"

"Brie, you're going to need an attorney first." Rick said as if I had not thought of that. "I have a client, Mr. Brennon, you may remember him. Do you want me to give him a call?"

"Please, thank you," I sat looking at Rick intently. He pulled his rolodex over in front of him and slipped his reading glasses on, thumbing through the old-fashioned contact system as he had done a million times. When he finally reached the correct card, he leaned over, picked up the phone on his desk, and punched each number on the phone with his index finger, double-checking each digit as he hit the corresponding digit on the phone. The whole process seemed terribly slow as I waited.

"This is Rick Mallott. Is Ken in? Yes, it's important. Thank you," he covered the phone with his hand and looked at me, "Do you want to talk with him or make an appointment?" Before I could answer him, Ken must have answered. "Hey Ken, Rick. How are you doing? Good, yes, we're fine, too. Look, I have a friend in need of a divorce but it's sort of a different situation. They've been separated for several years and there's a child involved. Do you handle these type cases? Uh, huh. Yes, I believe so. I see. No, it will be a pretty tough case, I believe. Well, it's kind of a sticky situation and will be a high-profile case as well. We need an attorney who can really be tough, you know, not intimidated by some of the toughest attorneys in town. I see. Well, who do you recommend then? Morgan? I thought he retired. Well, yeah, that would be great. What's his number? Oh, ok, call me back then. Thanks so much." I was dying on the inside to know what Ken's answers had been and was glad when Rick finally hung up. "He's going to see if old man Morgan is still practicing. He'll make an appointment if he is and call me back either way."

"What did he say? Does he not do divorces? Is this Morgan guy going to be touch enough if he's that old? What was Ken saying?" I had a million more questions but knew Rick was not one to fill in all the gaps so they would go unanswered. This was very frustrating.

"Ken's not doing divorces so much anymore. He recommended Morgan. Said he was the best in his day." That scared me. I didn't want to have to push my lawyer into the courtroom in his wheel chair and wake him up from time to time. I wanted someone who would make Seth shake in his boots at the very mention of his name, not laugh in mockery. "He's going to call me back when he knows more."

"Rick, how old is this Morgan, anyway?"

"Not sure. But if Ken says he is the best then that's irrelevant." Hm. That's not how I saw it. "He'll call back. Meanwhile, did you see the case file for the Stamper's? I can't find it anywhere." I just made one of the toughest decisions in my life and all he can say is, "where's the Stamper's file?" I leaned over to the chair beside me, which stayed full of paperwork. Yep, the Stamper's file was the second from the top. I stood up, handed the file to Rick, and turned and walked out of the door and went back to my office to call a mechanic.

I Googled Roger Morgan and after reading about him, I decided that even if he is retired, I hoped he would come out of retirement for my case. His reputation was beyond reproach and his track record was unbelievable. He had actually represented several truly high-profile cases of pop stars and politicians, many of which were much more tangled and complicated than my divorce looked comparatively. The only drawback I could see was that there was no way I could afford him. I knew that the good attorneys would be expensive- that was the very reason that Seth was so rich. He was just that good.

I assumed he would have one of the attorney's in his family take the case, or possibly handle it himself, although most of them would probably feel my measly divorce was beneath them. I hoped they would underestimate me. My heart was beating wildly at the thought of confronting him. I reminded myself that court officials and other people would surround us. The worst he could do to me now would be to give me a dirty look. I could handle that. I had already handled much worse.

The day was almost over when Rick popped into my office to say that Ken had made an appointment with Mr. Morgan for the following Tuesday.

"Really? That far off?" I responded, disappointment evident.

"That's only three business days, Brie. He's actually working you in as a favor to Ken. Here's the address and his phone number." He said this as he laid the paper on my desk with the information scribbled on it.

"Thanks, Rick. Sorry. I guess I'm just scared I'll lose my courage by then." Rick turned to look at me before he walked out of the door and, in a rare moment for him, looked me straight in the eye.

"Brie, you're doing the right thing. Stay focused on that." Then he was gone. I pulled my calendar up on my computer and put the appointed time on it. Then I straightened my desk and left a few minutes early. I was fortunate that a bus stop was right in front of our office park and as I waited, watching the other workers get into their cars, I couldn't help but feel relieved. It was a matter of time now before I would have a dependable car. I would sleep better at night knowing that I had money to pay my bills each month or to handle an emergency. It was just a matter of time, now. How naïve I was to believe this.

~ 3 ~

A Simple Plan

Tuesday arrived finally and by the time I stood at Mr. Morgan's entrance, my stomach felt tied into a thousand knots. Rick had even offered to come with me Monday before I left work. I think he was afraid I would not go through with it. It was a legitimate fear. I was unsure myself.

I was temporarily taking the bus everywhere until I could get my car fixed so I arrived a few minutes early. Mr. Morgan's receptionist was an older lady, probably late sixties at least. I wondered if she had worked for him for decades. I was too nervous to make small talk so I just gave her my name and sat down. Mr. Morgan's office was an old house, not the fancy, tall office buildings that attorneys now liked to boast. The house, renovated long ago to be an office, had a smell of old books. The furniture was plush but of an outdated style and, again, I wondered how long Mr. Morgan had practiced from this very office. Did he never see the waiting area, did he not see how outdated the ambiance was or did he not care- since, no doubt he would be retiring soon? My mind continued to wander in this manner until at last, the receptionist opened the door and called me back.

"Hello, Mrs. Taylor," Mr. Morgan walked into the conference room soon after I was seated. He shook my hand and looked me square in the face. I returned the shake and the look and immediately felt a warm connection with this old-timer. I assumed we would jump right into the proceedings but he began with small talk and asked several questions that seemed to have nothing to do with the case, presumably, getting to know me. “Ken tells me you work for Rick Mallott. He’s a fine business man.” I nodded my head agreeably. How long have you worked for him?” We went on this way for probably fifteen minutes and I was getting a little anxious because I knew I couldn’t afford small-talk if I was paying him for his time.

“Mr. Morgan, I don’t know what your fee schedule is but I am a single mother and will need to probably work out some type of payment plan if that is satisfactory.” Probably? That was optimistic.

“Mrs. Taylor, normally I charge a three-thousand dollar retainer but, between Ken and Rick, I know you’re of good stock so I’ll only charge you one-thousand. You can work that out with my bookkeeper.” I gulped. One-thousand dollars? And that was one-third less than he usually got up front? My mind raced as I wondered how I would come up with a thousand dollars. “Mrs. Taylor? Did you hear me?” Huh?

“Yes, I heard you- one thousand. Thank you so much for reducing your fee but Mr. Morgan, I don’t think I can do that either.” I leaned forward to get out of my chair to dismiss myself when he placed his hand over mine on the mahogany table.

“No, Mrs. Taylor, I asked you to tell me about your situation. Your mind must have wandered.” Oh, yeah, I guess it did, right after you dropped the bomb on me. “Don’t worry about the retainer today. We’ll work something out. Now, tell me about your situation. What is so complicated that you required my services?” Wow! He must only take the hard ones. I proceeded to tell him the whole story, leaving nothing out. I told him about Seth’s treatment of me when we were married, the distance he kept from me, the shock of his homosexuality, the rape later the same night, my escape to Annie Mae's neighborhood, my surprise pregnancy, and ultimately my move back to north Atlanta with Rick. I left nothing out. Mr. Morgan would need to know every detail in order to represent me well. Mr. Morgan sat quietly, taking notes the entire time I talked, only giving me an, "uh huh" or "alrighty" every now and then.

"And, that's about it." I finished. Mr. Morgan put his pencil down on his tablet resting in front of him, leaned back, and looked at me intently. The quiet pause in the room was deafening and I waited for him to tell me that this was too complicated and he would not be able to help me. His aged eyes inhabited a deep wisdom that I recognized. I looked at him then for the first time since he walked into the conference room. He looked in his seventies, maybe even late seventies. He was tall and very lean, sitting a little stooped over as if the weight of his statue had grown too much to bear upright. His skin appeared paper-thin and I could see the blue of his veins beneath. He had a habit of leaning his head back and looking at me from his bifocals. He certainly did not seem in a hurry and, I supposed, felt there was little left in his life that required his haste. When he spoke, his voice sounded confident yet with a hint of strain from his years of litigating.

"So, you're telling me that Seth Taylor is your husband?" Didn't I say that in the beginning? I thought.

"Yes, that's what I said." I was perplexed at his question.

"Huh," he responded to himself.

"Mr. Morgan, what am I missing?" He looked at me as if trying to read a complicated book.

"I don't know how to break this to you, Mrs. Taylor, but," ah, here we go; now he would give me all the reasons why he couldn't help me. "You are supposed to be dead."

"What?" I was stunned. Surely, I had not heard correctly.

"Yep, I don't know the whole story but I know he is engaged to be married and you are dead." My mind was reeling with this new information. How? I was confused and the room seemed to shrink before my eyes. "I'm going to have to look into this to get to the bottom of it. In the meantime, I want you to keep a low profile. As long as he thinks you're dead, we have all the time we need." He continued to scribble on his notepad.

"He knows I'm not dead," I whispered.

"What's that you say?" He stopped writing and looked up at me.

"He saw me about a month ago, in a restaurant on Twentieth Street. He chased me and I hid in a little ice cream shop. But, without a doubt, he knew it was me." Mr. Morgan laughed a pitiful, almost fake laugh.

"Well, this is just getting better and better, isn't it?" I looked up at him then, recovering from my dazed state. How could he think this was funny? "Mrs. Taylor, I'll take your case. This will be the most interesting one I've had in a while. Let me get more information from you and I'll need the boy's birth certificate and a copy of your marriage license. Don't speak with anyone about all this. We need to be discreet. Let's meet back next Tuesday to continue this, shall we?"

I left Mr. Morgan's office completely bewildered. Seth must have told everyone I was dead? How did he play that off? Did I have a funeral? I went directly back to the office and asked Rick if I could borrow his car. In the past, my car had been sufficient to get back and forth from work but anytime I had to go far, I would find alternate means of transportation. Thankfully, he was tied up and handed me the keys without asking any questions. I headed straight toward downtown. I would get a copy of my death certificate and see what had killed me.

The courthouse had me fill out paperwork and show my identification. The woman looked at me oddly when she saw that my name and the name of the deceased for which I wanted the certificate were one and the same. I would have loved to know what she was thinking. After waiting for a while, she finally brought a certificate. It was not what I expected. I guess I had assumed it would resemble a diploma but it was just a piece of paper, like a file. I immediately looked at the "immediate cause of death" section and discovered that I died from an intracranial injury. Listed below that was the "underlying cause of death" and I found I was injured in a motor vehicle accident. Wow! How did he pull this off? I sat on one of the benches in the hall to absorb this new information. I looked at the certificate more closely. It was dated September of the year I had left Seth. He waited only two months before he decided to kill me off. So, while I was finding out I was pregnant with Josh, Seth was pretending to be a grieving widower. Well, he was right about one thing- his wife is dead. On the other hand, I resurrected as a very different woman, one I hoped he would not find quite as easy to dismiss.

When I returned to the office, I showed Rick the certificate and caught him up to speed. As he looked over it, he scratched his head, as was his customary habit when he was in deep thought.

"This says you died in Spain."

"What? I didn't see that. Let me see." I was on his side of the desk before he could continue. His finger pointed the way for my eyes to look for the information. "What the heck. I've never been to Spain." Rick handed the paper back to me and I proceeded to sit back in the chair across from his. "What is going on?"

"It appears that Seth concocted a story when you disappeared that you'd gone to Spain. I guess when you didn't return, he got creative. You may want to fax that over to Morgan's office."

The rest of the afternoon, I walked around in a stupor, my mind a whirl and trying to make sense of this new labyrinth. Did I have a grave site here? Did I have one in Spain? Where was Katie supposed to be during all this? After hours of contemplation, I only came to more questions. Who was Seth engaged to? I felt sorry for the poor girl. When was he supposed to be married? I went on line, knowing that there would have been a huge engagement announcement in the paper. It took me several minutes but I finally came across it.

Mr. and Mrs. Bryan Berkett of Jacksonville, Florida, announce the engagement of their daughter, Tiffany Berkett, to Seth Taylor, son of Mr. and Mrs. Robert Taylor of Atlanta, Georgia. The future bride graduated from Florida State University with a Bachelor of Arts degree. She is employed as a court reporter at Atlanta Consolidated Government. The future groom received a Bachelor of Arts degree and a Juris Doctorate from University of Georgia. He is an attorney in Atlanta, Georgia. A June wedding is planned and the couple will reside in Atlanta, Georgia.

I printed the announcement and began a file with the documentation I had accumulated thus far. I wish there had been a photo of the happy couple. I pictured Tiffany as being a young, naïve girl. I guessed that it seemed Seth's style. I decided to fax the wedding announcement to Mr. Morgan as well. It was extremely difficult to concentrate at all the rest of the day. I was thankful it was not the busy tax season. Hopefully, this would all be over before I was crucially needed at work. My mind drifted to a beautiful church ceremony covered with flowers and I waited until the minister asked if anyone present had any objection why Seth and Tiffany should not be joined and I stand up and announce loudly to the crowd that I am Seth's wife, resurrected from the dead.

By that afternoon, my head throbbed with anxiety. I was just about to go to the bus stop when my phone rang.

"Ms. Taylor," my mechanic always addressed me by my last name although I had asked him repeatedly to address me by my first, "I'm afraid I have bad news for you. Turns out your transmission is shot. I've looked ta try ta find a overhauled one since it wouldn't make sense for ya ta buy a new one for this ole car but there ain't one available I can find." I sat numbly in my chair. How could this all be happening to me at the same time? "I'd say it'd take more ta fix tha car than it's worth. Sorry."

Over the next few weeks, Mr. Morgan and I began to piece together the puzzle, albeit most of the information was hearsay that he was able to glean from gossip. Seth's story was that Katie and I had gone on vacation to Europe and I had sustained substantial injuries in an auto accident. Seth went to Europe to take care of my arrangements and to get Katie, who he supposedly took to my mother to raise. My body was never brought back to the states. Seth returned with an overseas death certificate, which he filed locally. After several months of mourning, he returned to the social scene. I was flabbergasted. It all appeared so clean and tidy. How dare he?

"Mrs. Taylor, until he saw you in July, he had thought you were out of the picture for good. This could turn the situation in our favor. He has much more at stake than you- his homosexual secret, his felony of faking your death certificate, and his engagement. He has a lot to lose. I would think he would rather keep this all hush-hush." I was still in too much shock to respond. "I think, given his money, he would be willing to settle out of court, pay restitution, back child-support, and set up on-going child support. This would be the fastest, cleanest he could hope to get out of this situation. He'd be stupid not to sign the documentation on sight." Mr. Morgan's confidence was unbridled. I had my serious doubts. Seth was too controlling and prideful to let this go that easily. "What are you thinking, Mrs. Taylor?"

"Please don't call me Mrs. Taylor." The sound of it sickened me. My voice sounded pitiful even to me. "Brie is fine."

"Very well, I understand. If this route is satisfactory with you, I'll draw up the paperwork. Why don't you come back next Tuesday and we'll go over it?" My stupor did not wear off for several days. It was all just too easy. I would not even have to confront him. My attorney would meet with his attorney. Seth would sign the papers. I would get a check. I would never have to see him. Then I would get a check every month until Josh grew up. It was too much to hope for and I knew this fantasy of an idea would not be fulfilled. The generous, kind Seth that I had met that fateful day would easily write the check. Money was no issue. Nevertheless, the mean, vindictive Seth I had lived with for five years would never allow my victory to be that easy.

As we planned for Rick's party, Tracy single-handedly completed the arrangements for the most part. I refused to accompany her to the country club to meet with the planning committee there but I did help on the back end. Our meetings were always at the office now. My nerves could just not take chancing running into Seth by accident. Tracy seemed content that I was filing for divorce and asking for child-support and rarely brought the subject up.

"I ordered the cake yesterday from Patty Cakes. I wish you could have gone with me because they all looked like wedding cakes and we had to improvise to feed the expected guests and yet not make the cake seven feet wide." Tracy laughed as she said this like it was the funniest thing she had ever heard.

"I wouldn't have been much good to you if I had gone, Tracy. My mind is just a big bag of mush lately."

"Why don't you and the kids come over this weekend? It would do you all good to get out of that apartment, play in a yard, and get some sunshine."

"That actually sounds wonderful," I heard myself respond and my insides cringed. I loved Rick and Tracy but I did not feel up to smiling and acting as if I was happy right now. My thoughts were worried about one thing- Seth's reaction to the news that I was suing him for divorce and child-support once he received the papers. He did not even know he had a child. As fearful as I was, I also wished I could see his reaction when he received the papers.

"Good. We can put the finishing touches on the party then." She added gleefully.

"What about Rick?"

"Oh, dear, Rick usually settles back in his recliner to read on Saturday afternoons. Plan on staying for dinner, ok?" I nodded as she left. Immediately, my mind returned to Seth. Perhaps Mr. Morgan was right. It did make sense that Seth would want the quickest and quietest way out of this predicament. Maybe I might catch a break and it would all be over by Christmas. Even as my thoughts voiced this idea, my gut screamed of another outcome.

Rick and Tracy had bought a home on the north side immediately after our office moved. They had downsized somewhat but the house still seemed big compared to my little apartment. The backyard was equipped with a swing set for their grandkids and made a perfect area for the kids to play while Tracy and I talked about the party. As Tracy had predicted, Rick dismissed himself to read shortly after we arrived.

"I'm getting very excited. Aren't' you?" Tracy began as soon as we pulled the patio chairs from under the back patio and onto the grass by the swing set. The days were still hot but not too bad for mid-September. The kids were oblivious to the heat but Tracy and I wanted to stay out of the sun to keep cool. The small backyard had a privacy fence and quaint landscaping with evergreens around the edges. The swing set sat toward the back of the property about thirty feet or so from the back patio. Tracy had brought out a pitcher of lemonade and cookies she had just baked before we got there. After the initial conversation about looking forward to cooler weather, our thoughts turned to the party.

"Yes, I'm getting excited, too," I lied. It infuriated me when I thought of it because under normal circumstances, I would be excited. I was very proud of Rick and knew that he deserved this party. But every time I pictured the party, I saw myself looking up and down the enormous hallways of the cold and impersonal country club. Of course, Seth and I had been there for dinner many times. I even had to go without him for several ladies luncheons and charity events but all those memories seemed like an old movie reel I had seen when I was a child. None of those memories seemed real at all to me now.

"I didn't have a chance to tell you about the cake. It will be rectangle and three layers high with each layer getting smaller. The icing will be simple white with the decoration on the top layer looking like an adding machine!" She said this with such excitement that I did begin to get excited with her. "We decided to keep the food a buffet with two meats, baked chicken breasts and prime rib, and an assortment of vegetables. Do you think we should have a band? I was thinking since we are going all out and it is also the Christmas party, that a band would be a nice touch."

"Does Rick know you're doing all this?" I had to ask because I could not imagine him approving spending this much money. He tended to be very conservative when it came to finances around the office.

"Well, dear, he doesn't know about all of it, of course but, yes, I did tell him about the buffet and having it at the club. He wasn't too fond of the idea but I have my ways of persuasion." I envied their relationship. It seemed so easy, so comfortable. Perhaps one day, I could find someone to be so happy with and we could enjoy one another. "Anyway, all the kids are going to be there but Rick doesn't know that. He would be too suspicious if he thought they were coming to our company Christmas party. By the way, what are you and the kids going to wear to the party?" Huh? I had not even thought of that.

"I have no idea. I hadn't thought about even bringing the kids."

"Of course you will! What else would you do with them?" She had a good point. I did not exactly have a list of babysitters to watch them. "I tell you what, why don't we go shopping next weekend? I'd like to get Katie a Christmas dress and Josh a little Christmas suit. That way they could wear them for the rest of the season. Perhaps you could get family portraits made. You've never done that, have you?"

"No, Tracy, that's not necessary. I can get the kids something."

"I want to. Please, let me do this for you and your family. Y'all mean the world to me. It can be my Christmas present to you." The way she lit up, no one could refuse her.

"Alright."

"Yea! Next Saturday morning then; I'll pick you up at ten. Will that give you enough time to get the kids up and breakfast out of the way?"

"Yes, of course. That is very sweet of you, Tracy."

"Oh, honey, I love buying clothes for children. I'll get more joy out of it than you will," she beamed.

"Will Christmas clothes even be out yet?" I did not usually shop at the malls and, despite how stores always sold pre-season items; I doubted we would have luck this much in advance.

"Of course, dear, I have a couple of boutiques that I love and I happen to know they will be getting in most of their Christmas wardrobes next week! Even if they don't have them on display, they'll let me see them." The more I thought of it, I realized that it really would help me so much. I desperately needed to get another car and every little bit of help would get it for me sooner. Besides, I hadn't considered what we would wear to the party but now that she brought it up, I knew we would be better dressed if she helped me to pick it out. Since she was going to buy the kids something, I thought I might be able to swing getting myself a new dress.

The afternoon proceeded as it had started with Tracy interjecting information about the party as she thought of it while we talked of other things, including my situation with Seth. I would say something and it would trigger a thought for her about the party. She would tell me what came to her mind and then we would resume the conversation.

As the afternoon wore on, we convened in the kitchen while the kids watched television in the living room where Rick read. Tracy made pulling a meal together look simple and effortless. We talked and laughed as I helped her season chicken breasts with spices, stuff them with dressing, and roast them in the oven. She deep-fried green beans, saying it was the only way she could get her boys to eat them when they were growing up. Then she whipped up cream potatoes and created a fresh salad for each of us complete with carrots cut with faces on them and celery made to look like a scarecrow. She put one broccoli floret on top of each of their salads, decorating it with two small dots of dressing as eyes and a half cut black olive for a smile. I watched fascinated as she perfected her food art.

"You really enjoy that, don't you?" I finally had to ask her. Her focus was on the creations and she was oblivious as I watched.

"Yes, I do," she sighed as she stood back to admire her work. "I love the grandkids. I'm so glad that we are closer to them now."

"How old are they?" It suddenly dawned on me that I did not really know much about their sons or grandkids.

"Well, Haley is nine and J.R. just turned seven. I keep hoping I'll get another grandbaby but Kyle and Elaine say they are finished and Josh just got engaged so they need to wait a while."

"What about Mark?" I somehow remembered their third son's name and was thankful it came to me at just that moment.

"Well, Mark lives in California." She smiled as she said this and seemed to remember something in her subconscious. "He's our wayward son, not that he's bad, mind you. He just marches to the beat of a different drum. He had never seen the ocean by the time he was in middle school but he said that one day, he would move to California and become a surfer. Rick was adamant that he had to go to college so Mark finally conceded but the day after he graduated, he was gone. He loves it out there, too, so, even if he does get married and have a baby, I wouldn't get to see them very much."

"Well, don't rush them. Kids can be very consuming." I smiled as I said this to lighten my words but the truth was, I stayed exhausted.

"Yes, they are but, honey, they grow up so quickly. Katie's in middle school now, right?"

"Yes, she'll be twelve on her birthday in February and Josh will be four in April. And you're right. The time, in one sense anyway, has flown by."

"Mom! Josh just broke my pencil!" Katie screamed from the other room.

"Speaking of consuming… I'll be right back." I told Tracy. The kids were getting tired and I knew I had to go right after dinner or it would just get worse. Josh had not gotten his nap today and that could only spell trouble. As soon as I got them settled again, I came back to the kitchen and Tracy was taking all the food to the table. I helped her get it set and we all sat down to eat.

"Would you say grace, dear?" Tracy said as she looked at Rick.

"Sure," he bowed his head and we all followed suit, "Dear Lord, thank you for the food we are about to eat. Bless the hands that prepared it. May they be a comfort to me in my old age and a source of strength to our grandchildren as they grow. Amen."

"Ricky, you didn't bless our guests!" Tracy scolded. Rick bowed his head again quickly and added.

"Sorry Lord, please be with Brie on her journey and give her courage and wisdom for each new phase of her life. Amen." He peeped up at Tracy then, "That ok, momma?" Tracy smiled deeply.

"Much better, dear, much better, thank you." It all seemed so odd to me to see Rick in this personal setting. I had seen him and Tracy together at the office, which seemed strange at first, too. But to see Rick lounging in his recliner, saying grace, and exchanging pet names with Tracy in his own home made me feel suddenly like I had intruded upon them. The food was all as fabulous as it looked and smelled. I remembered Rick telling me what a great cook Tracy was the first time we had a personal conversation in his office at the old place. He had patted his belly with a proud thump as if it were a trophy for her award-winning meals. The kids devoured the vegetables and Katie even ate some of her chicken.

As soon as we finished the dishes, I told Tracy we had to get home. She did not try to stop us, which surprised me, but I could see from her face that she was fatigued also. Rick drove us home so I would not have to take a cab. Neither of us spoke much on the way. It was one of the things I liked about our relationship. Neither of us felt we had to fill up the empty spaces with noise unless there was something we needed to say.

"So, you really are going through with this?" Rick asked just before we got to my apartment. He did not have to say what "this" was- we both knew.

"Seems that way," I sighed, sounding unsure of myself. "According to Mr. Morgan, it won't be as complicated as I had feared."

"Is that what you think?"

"That's what I hope," I answered, unconvinced. No one knew Seth as I did. The façade he put up was for show and only a few knew the other man I had seen. The more I thought of it, the more I knew in my heart that there was no way it would end up as simple as we all hoped.

~ *4* ~

Unforeseen Circumstances

The following Tuesday came, Mr. Morgan and I sat at the same conference table we had shared for many weeks in a row now. He spelled out each page of the lawsuit and the déjà vu from sitting at Major Whitcomes' office looking over the adoption papers to give up Josh came flooding back to me. The flashback was so intense that I had to ask Mr. Morgan for a break. Suddenly, sweat ran down my back profusely. I rushed to the bathroom. I thought I was going to puke but after splashing cold water on my face many times, I was able to get a hold of myself. I could still feel the fatigue of the visit to Dr. Carnes', the doctor who wanted to adopt Joshua, just before the scheduled meeting with his friend and attorney, Major Whitcomes. They had manhandled me in a way so that I was too exhausted to understand the papers or ask the appropriate questions. The strange thing was, if they had not been so immoral the way they went about it, I probably would have gone through with the adoption. It was the uneasy feeling they gave me that made me ultimately have the courage to keep Josh. I was so thankful now that it had turned out the way it did.

"Are you alright, Brie?" Mr. Morgan asked upon my return.

"I'll be okay." I answered weakly. I did not want to get into that saga with Mr. Morgan. There was no need for him to know all about the almost-adoption. Mr. Morgan explained that the papers laid out my charges that Seth had been abusive resulting in my abandonment of the marriage. Then proceeded to unearth Seth's plan to forge my death certificate in order to get out of the marriage and demanding to discover whether Seth had received monetary gain from a life insurance policy. I had not even thought of that possibility. The last matter exposed my secret of our son and explained that, due to the terms of our marriage, I felt too traumatized then to face Seth in regards to support for the child but now sought full back pay as well as the maximum child-support allowed by law. Mr. Morgan stopped reading to tell me that would be twenty-three percent of his gross monthly income, which includes all sources of income such as wages, disability, unemployment insurance payments, monies paid from rental properties and money received from retirement plans or benefits. I had no idea what Seth's income was but I knew that twenty-three percent of it was a substantial amount.

"Do you think I will really get this?"

"Well, Georgia law has changed to include consideration of both parent's income; however, given that yours is substantially lower and that you have a second child who is not Seth's, I feel you'll easily receive twenty-three percent. Most certainly, in the end, you will; however, I must warn you that Seth will probably demand a paternity test." This was the first I had heard of this but I did not put it past Seth.

"That's fine. I'm not worried about that. He is definitely the father." Mr. Morgan seemed satisfied with this answer and proceeded. The papers also laid out that I requested full custody of Josh and that visitation rights would be set up after a psychological evaluation of Seth determined he was fit to care for Josh.

"No! He is not seeing Josh- ever!"

"Brie, the court will allow him to see his son unless they determine he is unfit. Seth may be a scoundrel but I have serious doubts they will mandate that a prominent attorney is unfit to visit with his own son. Frankly, the request for evaluation may very well be dismissed."

"No!" My eyes stung with tears. The thought of sharing Josh with Seth was overwhelming. "Forget it. Forget everything. I'm not letting Seth see Josh. He can keep his stupid money. No!" Mr. Morgan looked at me slightly annoyed but mostly concerned.

"Brie, it's altogether possible he would have no desire to see him. Besides, even if he does, it may not last. He may get him once or twice and then move on with his life." I was shaking my head the whole time he spoke.

"No." I touched my heart and realize that it literally ached at the thought of Josh alone with Seth unsupervised. I choked out a plea, "No, please, I can't do this. I didn't realize, no, just, no." Mr. Morgan stood up and crossed the room bringing back a box of tissue to me. I sobbed quietly for a few minutes and finally looked up at him. "You don't understand. I don't trust Seth. He would hurt Josh just to spite me."

"Brie, Seth is an affluent businessman in our community. He has a reputation to uphold and I really don't think he would jeopardize all that to hurt a child-let alone his own son."

"You don't know him!" I spat, "You only know the 'businessman Seth'. I know the man behind the scenes. He is cold and uncaring and can be cruel when he wants to be." I was coming undone at the seams and I could tell by the look on Mr. Morgan's face that he was having serious doubts about the validity of my sanity. I tried to calm down but felt powerless against the panic that threatened to choke me. Mr. Morgan looked on as I got control of my emotions. "Look, I'm sorry, but I guess I didn't think this through very well. No amount of money in the world is worth having to let my son go with him for any period of time. As things stand, Seth doesn't even know he has a son. So, let's just leave it at that. I'll get you your thousand dollars. We are through here." I stood up and walked out of that conference room.

I did not go back to work that Tuesday. I went home and cleaned the apartment. It is amazing how much you can get done when you're upset. I had been trying to get the apartment clean to prepare for the upcoming holidays for over a week but could not find it within myself to start. Now, today, I had the entire apartment clean within two hours. I pulled a few fall decorations out of the storage. I was not in a decorating mood but I sprinkled a few things in with the ones the kids had made at school and daycare. I thought briefly that I would get them out of school to enjoy them but I just felt too tired. I sat down to thumb through a magazine but my mind couldn't even focus enough to look at the pictures. I needed to talk to a friend- and not just any friend. I needed a friend who would participate in my feelings. I decided to call Annie Mae.

Ezekiel and I managed to catch up before Annie Mae got to the phone. It was strange how our lives were separated by insurmountable odds and yet, the connection was so profound between us.

"Hey baby chille!" Annie Mae chimed when she finally made her way to the phone, "how you doin'?"

"I'm okay Annie Mae but I do need a friend. Do you have a minute?" It was late in the afternoon and I knew her having free time was a long shot but I really needed to hear her voice.

"Yeah, I gotta minute. What's wrong, honey chille?" I spilt my guts to her, catching up the story she was unaware of up to this point. "I see."

"Annie Mae, you know first-hand how I feel about Seth. How can I let him see Josh?"

"Yeah, I can understand yo feelin's, chille. That man done you harm sho nuff. What the lawyer say?"

"Well, of course, he wants me to go through with it. It'd probably mean more money in his pocket."

"Yeah, an' what about Rick? What he say?"

"I haven't told Rick all this yet but he and Tracy both feel I should confront Seth. Annie Mae, please stand with me on this. I need a friend."

"Chille, once again, you gotta go with your gut. Do you really think Seth would hurt the boy?"

"I don't know Annie Mae, but I'm not willing to take a chance."

"Well, chille, you gotta do what you feel good 'bout. If'n you thinkin' Seth ought not see the boy, then you his momma, it's up ta you to keep the chille safe. I sure wish y'all could get out this way, just for a minute. I bet Josh done grown somethin' fierce."

"Yes, he has, Annie Mae. I promise I'll see if I can borrow Rick's car and get out there soon."

"I thought you got yourself a car."

"I did, Annie Mae, but, like everything else in my life, it went to pot, too."

"Oh, no, I be so sorry. You think Rick may let ya borrow his car?" Annie Mae was nothing else, if not persistent. I felt guilty asking Rick to borrow his car to go and see Annie Mae. He was so generous already. I decided to go and look for a nice used car. I had ridden the bus for years when I lived with Annie Mae and Poppa but having a car again had spoiled me, even if it had been an old run-down car.

That Saturday morning, the kids and I were giddy with anticipation of shopping with Tracy. She picked us up at ten sharp and we headed toward the most northern part of the city. I had dressed the kids in some of their cutest outfits so they would appear to fit in with the boutique crowd once we were there; however, as we pulled up and I saw the adorable clothes in the window, I knew I had failed. We dressed efficiently but there was something about these specialty clothes. They exuded wealth.

Once we were inside, Tracy went directly to the attendant while the kids and I looked around. Katie immediately found several dresses she loved but when I saw the enormous price tag, I scolded her and told her not to touch anything else. Tracy came back to us and instructed us to follow her. The attendant led the way to a back room where long rows of clothes hung on poles with wheels, most still wrapped in plastic.

"These are the boy's size and these," she pointed to another row of dresses, "should be within the size range for the young lady." Katie beamed at being called a young lady. She really was growing up so quickly. Then the attendant dismissed herself and Tracy told us to look through to see if there was anything we liked.

"Tracy, please don't take this the wrong way but, well, these clothes are enormously expensive. Why don't we just go to the mall? I'm sure we could find something more than suitable."

"You're right, dear. You could find something suitable but I'm not looking for suitable. I want you and your precious little family to feel special. This night is going to be magical and I want you all to feel special." I knew from her tone that she was determined. I decided to find one of the least expensive dresses there so we could all be satisfied.

"Oh, mommy! Look at this!" Katie almost screamed. I shushed her. Katie held up a crushed red velvet dress trimmed in black ribbons and white chiffon lace. It really was the most beautiful dress I had ever seen. Tracy insisted Katie try it on even though, after looking at the price tag, I protested. When

Katie came out of the dressing room, I knew she must have this dress. Katie was gushing as she looked in the mirror. Tracy insisted on getting the hair bow, tights, and shoes to match it. I felt quite guilty but even more grateful.

Josh was oblivious to the shopping allure so Tracy picked out a miniature suit that made him look like a little man. It was a dark color, almost black and had a red shirt and even a tiny tie to go with it. When he had the entire outfit on, he looked like a little Seth. Seeing my two children look so grown up tugged at my heart. I really must begin to enjoy every day more.

Not only did Tracy insist on getting the kids beautiful outfits but she also insisted on getting me a new dress. I knew that she did not normally shop at such expensive places but she insisted on spoiling us. This shop was rather larger than most boutiques and seemed to carry every size needed. Their selection was enormous and very elite. I tried to pretend I could not find anything I preferred but, of course, Tracy saw right through my ploy.

"Ah, what about this, dear?" Tracy asked me as she lifted a particular dress off the rack. "It'll bring out your brown eyes and hair." The dress was a deep green satin. The top was fitted and only slightly low-cut. The length was a tad short but not unfashionable. As I looked in the mirror, I knew it was the one I wanted. I tried to get Tracy to let me give her at least some money toward our plunder but she was adamant.

After the shopping extravaganza, Tracy took us to a quaint restaurant for lunch. The kids did not eat much and were more interested in playing in a small play area to the side of the bistro. Tracy and I sat in the shade and caught up. I told her about my visit with Mr. Morgan and my decision not to pursue the case any longer.

"I see," she stated softly. "I understand your reservations, Brie. Perhaps down the road you may feel differently."

"I don't think so. Having Seth hurt Josh is never going to be an option," I tried to sound matter-of-fact but realized, even as I talked, I lacked confidence.

"Do you really think Seth would hurt his own son?" I grimaced. Everyone assumed that Seth was a normal man. I had seen his worst side and I was not taking any chances with my son. "Brie, if Seth is getting married next spring and he knows you're alive, don't you think he will continue to look for you until he finds you? After all, he can't get married if he is still legally married to you, regardless of the fake death certificate." I had thought of that, of course, probably a million times. "And furthermore, you will never be able to remarry either, as long as you are married to him." I had not thought of that. There was no relationship in my near future that I could see so that had not crossed my mind. I vaguely replied to Tracy with answers and she quickly saw that I did not want to mar this day with conversation about Seth. Therefore, we changed the subject to the party and any other safe topic.

A month went by with nothing good or bad happening. I was having no luck on finding a car that was any better than the last one with a down payment and payment plan I could swing, especially given my attorney's bill and Christmas around the corner. I decided I would pull the bus routine until after the first of the year.

As November tarried on, the cool air was a welcome change. I grew anxious for no apparent reason. It seemed now that I had ventured to consider the option of confronting Seth, I could not get it out of my mind. I knew everyone was growing weary with my whining. I had to admit, I was tired of it myself. Yet, each side of the argument, whether to continue the divorce or not, bounced from one side of my brain to the other like balls in a tennis match.

Katie was having a wonderful year at her new school. She took on the role of preteen as if it were a destination of prestige. I envied her ability to thrive regardless of where she lived. It had taken her no time at all to adjust last fall when we first moved here. After the first week of school, she had as many friends as she had left in the ghetto. She could converse about matters that amazed me such as fashion, technology, and social circumstances. When I asked her where she learned so much, she would simply answer, “I just listen, mom.” I wasn’t sure whether to be proud or worried. Her constant companion at home was her cat, Sparks, whom we had gotten before we moved after Josh was born.

Josh, while never becoming a very happy child, enjoyed most days with a complacent and yet nonchalant character rare for a four-year-old. He would pick a flower from a bush and bring it to me on the playground and then, as I made over it, he would turn and walk away. He was a complex person and, I knew, as he grew older, he would be a force with which to be reckoned. I could see Seth in him a lot. I truly hoped I would have the skills to help him as he grew to be a man.

The week before Thanksgiving, I called Annie Mae to check on them. It seemed I rarely talked to them except when I needed them and I wanted them to know I really cared about them, not only as a source of advice but for their friendship.

“What about Thanksgivin’ next week? Ya think ya could make it for our annual dinner? I sho would love to see them kids.” I cringed inside. I really did not want to go out there for Thanksgiving. As nice as they had been in the past, I just did not want to go there.

“We’ll see. I’d have to borrow Rick’s car. I’ll call you and let you know, okay?”

“What if Poppa come an’ gits ya?” Oh, no. I really did not want Poppa to drive all the way here to get us, back for dinner, then all the way here to bring us here, and back to his home again. I would feel awful if anything happened to him

"No, Annie Mae. Let me ask Rick about his car. I'll call you back. I promise." Slightly pacified, Annie Mae and I talked small talk until she had to go. On the one hand, I longed to be there with her and the rest of the group. I had not talked to Kayla in so long and I missed her. I could really use a hug from Poppa and Annie Mae and Ezekiel but the thought of driving all the way down there and spending Thanksgiving in that neighborhood again was not appealing. I was thinking that I may mention the idea to Katie and if she really wanted to go then maybe, I would work it out.

"Oh momma, please! I'd love to see Ezekiel again and I miss Gabby so much!" Katie's exuberance was overwhelming so I decided I would ask Rick if I could borrow his car. I figured he probably would not need it on Thanksgiving Day anyhow. After I thought about it more, I decided it may not feel very much like Thanksgiving in our little apartment with just the kids and me, anyway.

Rick did not mind me using his car but did seem slightly concerned about me returning to the old neighborhood. He is so laid-back though that he really did not object, only gave a warning to be careful. I called Annie Mae back and told her that we would be there. I had to move the phone receiver from my ear to keep from going deaf from her scream.

"Oh, chille! I cain't wait! I'm gone let everybody know you an' tha kids are comin'. I know Kayla, Gabby, and Gail gone be here. They'll be so glad ta see ya all." I had to admit, it did seem like fun. As we started talking about it, I grew excited.

When Thanksgiving finally arrived, I was a little nervous. Rick had let me take him home the day before so I could keep his car for Thanksgiving morning. I had planned to go early but the kids and I were not having a good morning. It was midmorning before we got out of the door. The drive was quiet for Atlanta traffic and yet, because I was not used to driving this far, it still made me a little uneasy. It took longer than I remembered to get there and when we finally arrived, everything seemed so different. I had only been gone a little more than a year and yet the neighborhood had gone downhill so much, or had it? Maybe I had just forgotten how bad it had been. My mind had apparently blotted out the run-down buildings and the dingy sidewalks. I was beginning to think I was lost when I saw the store. I pulled Rick's car to the side of the store, and nervously looked around to see if it was safe to get out. Katie appeared to be more apprehensive, too. When we walked in to the front of the store, a loud squeal assured me that at least the warm reception had not changed.

"Chille, I was jus' beginin' ta think you done changed yo mind," Annie Mae said as she squeezed us individually. She looked exactly the same and the store still had the same at-home feeling. Poppa was right behind her, beaming as if we were his children coming home. Just as we finished hugging them, Ezekiel came out of the back with his hands full of chairs. When he saw us, he dropped all the chairs on the floor, making a terrible clatter and ran toward us.

"Miss Katie!" he oozed love. When he finally reached her, he picked her up and swung her in the air. Josh clung to me as if to insure he would not be next. He didn't remember any of these people and he was not so sure he wanted to get to know them.

"Where's Kayla and them?" I asked Annie Mae when things finally settled down.

"They comin'. Gail called an' said the casserole takin' a little longer ta cook but they'd be here directly." There were many new faces but a lot of familiar ones, as well. I tried to make my way around to say, "Hello" to everyone but Josh was uncomfortable and was making visiting difficult. Finally, Kayla,

Gabby, and Gail arrived. Kayla looked radiant and Gabby had grown so much. Katie and Gabby were not the same excitable friends they had been when we left. They both acted somewhat shy for the first ten minutes or so but finally warmed up to one another. Kayla and I found a quiet corner to catch up.

"So, how is school going?" I asked immediately. I was so envious that Kayla was able to finish school. I would have loved to be able to go.

"I graduated last spring!" She was beaming.

"Really? I was thinking you were still in your last year. I am so very proud of you," I sounded so maternal even though we were very close in age, I felt so much older than she.

"That's because you've been gone for a year," she replied emphatically. She was right. For some reason, it seemed to me that time stood still in this forgotten neighborhood but their lives had continued upon their own paths just as mine had changed and continued upon my path.

"So are you in graduate school?" I asked with hope, knowing that was her plan.

"Well, I just missed the scholarship. It's harder to get those for graduate school. So, I'm working full time trying to save up my money. Actually, I'm working close to sixty hours a week! I plan to get my graduate degree in psychology, or counseling. I'm meeting with the school counselor in January to help me lay out the next step of my education but it looks like I may have to work a year and go to school for a year. At this rate, it'll take me forever!"

"Where will you go to school?" I knew she would have to move to pursue the next level of education.

"I'm looking at several different schools. I'd love to go to University of Georgia but I'm sure I could never afford tuition there. I guess I'll find out more after I meet with our career counselor. How are you doing? Are you enjoying living in your new apartment?"

"I do. I like it a lot but, honestly, it's not the same as living here. I have several friends but none that I feel like I really connect with like I do you and Annie Mae. I miss y'all so much!" It was true. I did. This homecoming felt good and I was so glad I came.

"Let me give you my cell number. I have a cell phone now. Can you believe it?" Kayla said as she wrote her number on a scrap piece of paper. "I'll come visit you. Maybe we can go shopping or something."

"That would be wonderful. I'd really like that." We continued to catch up. Kayla was still working for Annie Mae. She worried about giving up her job once she moved on to get her graduate degree. She was also very worried about leaving Gabby and her mother behind in this neighborhood.

"I wish so much I could take them with me wherever I end up going. Everything is so up-in-the-air right now."

"I know," I agreed and then I told her about all the news concerning Seth and how I had seen him and what all I had found out. She was astounded. Before long, Poppa was calling everyone to order around the table. As was customary, we went around the table as we ate, each telling what we were thankful for this year. I had so many blessings to be thankful for that it was difficult to pick only one. Annie Mae and Poppa always made everyone who gathered around the table feel special and it was truly a Thanksgiving meal. I was able to ask Poppa at one point if my little cottage was rented out. I would have liked to see it but he said they did have a tenant living there.

"Did y'all not invite them to Thanksgiving dinner?" I asked. That seemed odd to me that they would not have included them.

"No, baby. It's an old man and he don't want no company.

We wouldn't know if he dead or alive 'cept when he walk over ta pay tha rent and git a few supplies on the first of each month." I was surprised that Annie Mae let him get by with that but could tell by Poppa's description that they had not warmed up to him yet. I felt sure Annie Mae would have him here by next year.

The time flew by and as the guests dwindled down to the last few, I felt it was time to go home.

"Chille, it was so good ta see you an' the kids. Josh don't even remember me. Please git by every now and then so they don't forget me, will ya?"

"I know Annie Mae. I'm sorry. It's just so hard with all the hours I normally work, now with no car, and then all that drama with Seth. I promise I will try though, okay?" We all hugged good-bye as if it was the last time we would see one another. The kids both fell asleep on the way home and the drive seemed to take forever but, alas, we drove up to my tiny apartment. I carried Josh to his bed then lay him down, and tucked Katie in her bed. Sparks jumped up to snuggle with her as he did most every night. When I finally sat down to reminiscence about the day, I had a full, satisfied feeling. It was not the same as it had been when I lived there, but it was a good day. I put Kayla's number where I would remember to put it in my computer at work. Everything would be in high gear beginning Monday because the party was only a week away. I imagined Tracy was probably tweaking it as I sat in my chair relaxing.

Tracy and I spent enormous amounts of time on the phone and getting last minute plans in order. She had every minute detail in order and I admired her tenacity. The week of the party, Joe happened over to the office. I had not heard him come in because I was on the phone with Tracy when he popped his head into my office.

"Whatcha doing?" he tried to sound casual. Because Tracy heard him in the background, she cut me off and said for me to call her when I was not so busy. I wanted to continue talking with her to hint to Joe that I was too busy but once Tracy hung up, I felt obligated to invite Joe in to sit. "I didn't mean to interrupt," he told me once I hung up.

"No, its fine. What's up?" I always tried to be right to the point with him. I could not put my finger on why I wasn't more interested in him. He was attractive but I just seemed to lack enough interest in him to make me want to get to know him better.

"Well, Rick invited me to the Christmas party y'all are having this weekend at the club." Oh, no, I thought. "And I was wondering if I could pick you up to take you."

"Oh, how sweet," I was stalling while I tried to think of some way to get out of it, "but I may have to get there early to help Tracy."

"That's fine. I can get you early and help y'all out."

"Well, I'll have my kids with me."

"It's okay. It's not like I'm going to eat them or anything." He laughed.

"I just don't think it's a good idea." I finally managed to say.

"Brie, you don't have a car. What are you going to do? Take a bus to the country club? Let me pick you up and take you home. If you don't want to make it a date, fine, but at least let me give you a ride." He had a valid point.

"I wouldn't feel right about that. I don't want to," I started before he cut me off.

"Don't want to what? Lead me on? I think it's pretty obvious you're not interested in me. I'm a big boy. I can take it. But I can't take the idea of you dragging your two kids across town in a bus or taking a cab so," he sighed deeply, "what time should I pick you up? Five, six?" I could not think of anything else to say.

"Six, I guess."

"Six it is. Text me your address. You've got my number, right?" I nodded. "Okay. See ya Saturday." He got up and left although it seemed to me that his shoulders drooped a little and I felt guilty seeing him act so ordinary when there was nothing about him that was ordinary. He really is a nice guy. At first, my attraction to him was evident but the more he tried to get close to me, the less attractive he was to me. I figured that was a character flaw on my part. All the other women in the office swooned over him and yet I was beginning to find him almost annoying. Although I had to admit, it was a load off my mind to know he would drive me to the party this weekend. I just hoped he did not try to make it into more than it was.

The week sped away as Tracy and I made final adjustments to the plans. She had managed to find a decent band to play even given the last minute decision to have one. Planning the party had not been as stressful as I had feared, although admittedly, Tracy had done most of the planning. I was not sure how much money she had spent on it but I was sure it was more than Rick would have liked. Saturday began lazily. The kids and I slept late; a rare treat in my household. I took it as a sign that it was going to be a good day and looked forward to the party that evening. I could not have been more wrong.

~ 5 ~

A Lovely Night

As I looked in the mirror, I could not help but smile. I must thank Tracy once more for spoiling the kids and me. The deep green dress accentuated my dark features, although my skin was fair and looked milky against the dark color. I put my hair up in a high bun with ringlets falling slightly around my face.

As I looked at the finished product, I felt more confident and proud than I had my entire life. I had a glow about me now that I had never possessed, even with the expensive clothes and best make-up that I had worn when I was married to Seth.

My happiness with my new life seemed to exude itself from inside of me. This dress and these accessories only proved to make my confidence more obvious.

The kids looked equally picture perfect. I braided Katie's hair into a round circle on the top of her head that looked like a beautiful crown. Then I weaved ribbon between the braids, which made it look even more so. She wanted to wear make-up but I flatly refused. Just before Joe was to arrive, I put a tad of lip-gloss on her and the smile she returned warmed me. We had painted both our nails earlier in the day and she twirled around in the living room as if she were a ballerina.

Josh had been especially pleasant all day. Even dressing him was quickly completed and he stared at himself in the mirror as if wondering who the little boy staring back at him was. Looking at him all dressed up in this suit, it was obvious he looked just like Seth. I had seen it before, of course, but dressed like a little lawyer, he was unmistakably Seth's son. As handsome as Seth is, I hoped Josh would outgrow his resemblance. When we were all dressed, I looked at us and knew that we must get a family portrait together. It would be our first.

Joe arrived a few minutes early and put Josh's car seat into his Mercedes. Joe's car was gorgeous, shiny and black on the outside and the inside appeared without dust or debris of any kind. The leather seats felt so soft and smooth. I was almost afraid for us to ride in it. It had been a long time since I had enjoyed such luxuries.

"Wow! You look beautiful!" Joe said when he first saw me. I could not help but blush. After introducing him to the kids, he began to talk to them. At first, the kids were shy but Joe quickly warmed them up to him. He carried Josh to the car but I had to put him in the car seat because Joe could not figure out its complicated contraption. We talked small talk all the way to the country club and the awkwardness I had feared never happened. It was almost as if I was with a friend. Once we arrived, Joe came around, opened my door, and helped me get the kids. Again, he carried Josh into the country club and I felt a bit uneasy with us walking in like a little family together.

Joe helped us get our coats checked in and find the appropriate ballroom. Tracy was already there, making sure each table's centerpieces were perfect. She said that she had sent Rick to the lounge on the second floor for a drink. I suggested for Joe to join him but he declined. As it turned out, Joe made a great babysitter while I helped Tracy with the final touches.

"Follow me dear," she instructed, "I want to show you the cake." We went into the kitchen entrance and she walked directly to one side of the room. No one questioned her authority to be there and she walked as if she owned the place. I was seeing a completely different side of Tracy than the mellow lady I thought I had known all this time.

"Oh my goodness!" I exclaimed sincerely. The cake was magnificent. They had it on a huge cart on wheels, presumably to push it out to the banquet room at the perfect time to surprise Rick. The bottom layer covered the entire top of the cart and the top two layers were almost as big. As promised, the top layer realistically resembled Rick's adding machine. The other two layers had icing in the shape of pencils, pens, account reports, and print outs pleasantly scattered about the cake. It was truly unbelievable. "That is absolutely perfect!" Tracy was so proud of it.

It seemed like only a few minutes went by before some of the guests started to arrive. When Rick's son, Mark, arrived, Tracy introduced us and then instructed him to make himself scarce.

"If Rick sees you, he'll know something's up. Don't go to the lounge, though because that's where your dad is."

"Where am I supposed to go, mother?"

"There's another bar on the lower floor. Go down there and come back precisely at seven ten. I'll send the others down to join you. Lord, I hope your dad doesn't see them."

"Mother, calm down," Mark put his arms around Tracy, "I'll text them and tell them to meet me there and not to go through here." Tracy immediately relaxed.

"Thank you, baby. I just want everything to be perfect." Mark left and Tracy and I resumed greeting the other guests. Before we knew it, the room filled and grew loud because everyone was talking and the music began lowly over the speakers. I looked up from talking to one of our clients and saw Rick and Tracy with another couple, laughing and having fun.

Then I looked around to find Joe and my children. They were sitting at our table, well, Joe was sitting and Josh was on his lap while Katie stood before him talking his ears off. I could see by her expression that she was totally crushing on Joe. I did not want them together again. The last thing I needed was for my kids to grow attached to him.

"Everything is just lovely, isn't it?" Tracy had snuck up behind me and slipped her arm around my waist.

"Yes, it is. Everything is perfect. How did you want to surprise Rick? You can't make your boys hide out in the bar all night." I teased.

"I'm glad you asked, dear. They are all in the kitchen and prepared to enter, pushing the cake, on queue. Will you do the honors?"

"What? What do you mean?"

"I was hoping you could do a little welcome speech on stage to our guests. I'm going to join the boys in the kitchen. When you say something like, 'We would like to surprise Rick tonight for forty years of great service' the band will strike up *For He's a Jolly Good Fellow* and out we'll all come from the kitchen pushing the cake."

"You've got to be kidding! I can't speak in front of all these people. Why didn't you tell me your plan earlier? I could have told you I can't do that!" I was close to panic. Tracy smiled a knowing smile.

"That is precisely why I didn't. I knew you'd get all worked up about it. Now, go. I'm headed to the kitchen." She turned away from me and was gone. I stood, transfixed, breaking out into a sweat. I could not do this. I had to do this. Tracy would kill me if I didn't. She was depending on me to do this. My legs, weak as they were, made my way up to the stage.

Once I was at the top step, the leader of the band gave me a wink, letting me know he was ready. I turned and looked at the myriad people who began to quiet as they noticed I took the stage. I stood, staring back at them as if I was waiting on them to speak. The room began to hush. The bandleader stepped forward and brought the microphone to me.

"Um," I stumbled, "Thank you all for coming tonight." My voice cracked and I sounded as weak as I felt. I was making an idiot of myself and my contempt for Tracy was profound at the moment. Now the room was completely silent as everyone waited for me to continue.

"As you all may know, we don't usually celebrate Christmas in such extravagant style. This is a first for us and we appreciate each of you supporting our effort to make it a memorable Christmas this year." Okay, I was feeling slightly less nauseous now. "We are all fortunate to be able to commemorate in such grand style- fortunate for our jobs, our friends, but mostly for our families." I saw several people acknowledging me. Their encouragement gave me confidence to go on.

"These past few years, Christmas has taken on a new meaning to me. First off, I finally discovered the true meaning of Christmas when I found Christ. He has changed my world. In addition, I found people who represent the Christ-like spirit for which we are all called. Rick and Tracy are two of those people. They love without hesitation, give without reservation, and generally provide an excellent example for the rest of us." I took a deep breath.

"So, I'd like to take this opportunity to thank them publically for all they've done for me and my family." The audience smiled back at me and I wondered how many of them really knew my story.

"Of course, the reason we are here is to celebrate Christmas but, there is another reason. Rick has been in business for forty years this year. Rick, where are you? I'd like you to join me on stage, please." I could use the company to stop my legs from shaking, I thought.

"Rick?" I could hear the crowd murmuring and finally saw several people pushing Rick toward the stage.

Once Rick finally stood beside me, I looked at him but spoke into the microphone, "Rick, you have taught me so much about business. Not only how to crunch the numbers but, more importantly, how to conduct business with integrity, principles, and respect for everyone. The knowledge you've so generously shared with me has changed me as a person. The service you've provided for your clients these forty years is beyond reproach. You are diligent, honest, kind, and authentic." Rick looked at me and his eyes were slightly wet. I had to go on before I teared up myself.

"More importantly than all this, you love your family beyond words. Your love has shown them how to lead successful lives. Your love has completed your wife, children, and grandchildren and they are blessed indeed. Because of the man you are, the example you have provided, and the service you have so freely given- Tracy, your sons, your grandchildren, and all these hundreds of people would like to honor you."

I looked at the band director and the band struck the first chord, the audience erupted into applause, and the kitchen's double doors were opened as Tracy, their three sons, Kyle's wife, Elaine and their two sons, and Josh's fiancée, Trish all came out of the door with the cake before them. Rick let out a burst of tears and practically ran to Tracy. They hugged openly and I could tell Rick was touched in a powerful way. At last, Rick let Tracy go and hugged each of his sons. Then the grandkids jumped into his arms.

I was in tears as were most of the guests by now. As the band played, people began to sing and by the end of the chorus, the entire room rang out in a jubilant celebration. Tracy's smile lit the room and I was glad that she had hired a photographer to capture this magical moment. I stepped down from the stage and Joe came up with the kids in tow.

"Wow! I didn't know you were so well spoken." The admiration was evident in his eyes and I wondered briefly if he must be in love with me to be so blind to think I had done well. I felt like I had stumbled through every word. Nonetheless, I blushed as he peered down at me. We made our way over to Rick and Tracy to offer our personal acknowledgments to them.

"Oh, thank you dear. That was beautifully spoken. Just perfect." Tracy said when I hugged her.

"If you ever do that to me again, I will strangle you," I laughed when I said this to lighten the words but I hoped she could tell that I truly did not appreciate being put on the spot.

"Don't be silly. You were stupendous. I knew you would be."

"Thank you, Brie. That really was all very nice." Rick added. They finally got around to introducing me to their sons and grandbabies. As could have been expected, they were all just as sweet and humble as Rick and Tracy. The night progressed beautifully. The buffet was exquisite. The band played a blend of old and new music and most everyone danced. I took Josh out onto the dance floor while Joe danced with Katie. The excitement in the air was tangible.

The photographer had set up a gorgeous Christmas scene towards the front side entrance of the ballroom complete with a mall-worthy Christmas tree in the foreground and a portrait scene of a roaring fire in the fireplace in the background. Katie, Josh, and I had our photos made, of course. The photographer had me sit in the large upright chair. Josh stood beside me with his hand on my knee and Katie sat on the chair of the arm on the other side. I could hardly wait until we would be able to get them weeks from now.

The evening continued so beautifully. Tracy orchestrated everything so beautifully. As the night wore on, I made my way to as many guests as I could, introducing myself to those I did not know by face and saying salutations to those I knew well. The magic of the perfection of it all grew as the night progressed. I could not think of anything that could possibly make it any better.

"Could I have one dance?" Joe asked as he held out his hand for me to take. I did not want to dance with him. The proximity of our dancing would be too uncomfortable. More importantly, I did not want people to begin to assume we were now an item. It was enough that he brought me and was helping so much with the children all night. I felt sure the rumors would solidify by Monday morning and every girl in the office would hate me now. Nevertheless, I could not tell him, 'no'. He had been a true friend to me since I had met him and especially tonight. All he asked in return was one dance. I could not find it in my heart to refuse him.

"Of course," I smiled up at him. "Kids, y'all stay here. Katie, you watch Josh for a minute, okay?"

"I'll watch them. You kids go on, my goodness," Tracy spoke up. Our round table consisted of Joe, my kids, Rick, Tracy and their three boys and their families.

"Thank you," I replied. Once Joe and I were on the dance floor, the band changed to a slow song. I cringed. Dancing with him was bad enough but to actually dance in his arms was excruciating. Joe immediately took my hand with his and put his other arm around my waist.

"Brie, you have been wonderful tonight." He said quietly in my ear.

"Thank you," I mumbled, "so have you. Thank you so much for helping with the kids all night." My head was close enough to lie on his chest but I held it erect, not wanting to lead him on. We danced and as the song played, I begin to relax a little. Joe led smoothly and never tried to pull me closer. He was always the perfect gentleman. I wondered if I might like him better if he was not. When the song finally finished I assumed we were done.

"Thank you," I looked up at his face to complete our dance. Our faces were much too close though and the same chemistry that had created a spark as I tried to unlock that door so long ago, fired between us. From the look he gave me, I could tell this was painful for him. I did not want to cause him pain but I knew I was not ready for this. We looked at one another for a few seconds more then I turned my head, released his hand, and walked back to the table.

"Mommy, I have to go to the bathroom," Josh said when I reached for him.

"Okay," perfect timing baby, I thought. Katie, Josh, and I left the ballroom and walked down the long hall toward the restrooms around the corner. The noise from the ballroom faded as we walked further and further away. The quiet difference in the hall and restroom was a welcome change. I was getting tired and hoped that it would be time to go soon. As wonderful as the night had been, the moment between Joe and I had started something that I wasn't sure would stop easily. After our business was done and I had straightened up Katie's hair and my make-up, we headed back toward the ballroom.

"Momma, are you and Joe dating?" Katie asked me just as we stepped into the hall.

"No!' I answered quickly. "No, honey, we're just friends." I softened my answer.

"So it's okay if I dance with him?" her innocent face looked at mine with expectation. I smiled at her. The hall was somewhat crowded as patrons from another party found their way toward the bathrooms so I focused on navigating Katie by the hand and picked Josh up to get through them and head back to our banquet room. Once we were successfully on our way, I responded to her question.

"Katie, don't you think Joe is a little old for you?"

"Mom, it's not like we're going to get married or anything," she said pitifully. I had a feeling if he asked her she would say, "Yes".

"Well, okay, as long as you understand he's just our friend." Once we got back to our table, everyone was gone. I turned around to look on the dance floor to find them and stopped in my tracks as I saw Seth standing across the room staring at me.

~ 6 ~

Whirlwind

I froze. My heart stopped and yet beat wildly at the same time. I panicked. All I could think of was how to get out of here. I grabbed Katie's hand, pulled Josh up closer to me, and turned to run- literally run away. I had no plan, just operated on an instinct to get away from him and hope he had not seen Josh. If he had, the resemblance between them would be undeniable. Because I was looking in Seth's direction and running in the other direction, I stumbled over a chair that someone rudely left pushed away from their table. When I did, I fell over the chair and barely grabbed Josh securely enough to keep his head from hitting the floor. The commotion caused the entire room to go quiet and several people ran to my aid. There I lay, sprawled out, trying to get up so I could run again, Josh stunned, and Katie lying beside me. My loss of balance had caused her to fall, as well, and we made a sore sight for everyone to witness. I scanned the room looking for Seth and did not see him. My mind ignored my pain and embarrassment for the time being. I scanned the room quickly hoping that maybe Seth had left. Joe was at my side instantly, trying to help me up. Instinctively, I allowed him to take Josh so I could get up. I continued to scan the crowd.

"Mommy, are you okay?" Katie's voice sounded shaky so I put my arm around her as I stood up. My legs were trembling, I was not sure I could continue to stand. Someone pulled a chair up behind me so I sat. It was not until they put their hand on my shoulder that I turned, looked up, and saw that it was Seth. Again, I froze.

"We need to talk," he said quietly, locking my eyes in his. I hadn't heard his voice in so many years and had forgotten how deep it sounded. I could not speak. I could not look away. I could not breathe. "Not here of course." Our eyes still locked upon one another and to any onlooker I supposed they might think we were in love. It could not have been further from the truth, with my senses heightened from adrenaline, I felt the weight of his hand on my shoulder as if it were a lead plate. "Can we go into another room, with privacy?" The sentence was technically a question; however, his authoritative meaning made it sound more like a demand. I felt numb but automatically began to shake my head. "You can't keep running from me forever." I felt like a trapped animal. My escape was ruined. My fate appeared sealed. My mind tried desperately to figure a way out of this predicament.

His hand slipped off my shoulder then and reached out to Josh's face and he cupped his chin looking intently into Josh's eyes. Joe was holding him and instinctively moved Josh away from Seth for which I was grateful. Two things happened simultaneously. First, Joe's movement caught Seth's attention and Seth turned his gaze to Joe, obviously trying to put the pieces together. Secondly, I regained my composure enough to stand up to protect my son from Seth's grasp. I took Josh from Joe's arms and grabbed Katie's hand. When I turned to leave, I realized for the first time that the entire room's eyes were upon us. Immediately, I felt the crush of the moment pierce my heart. I took a step to move and Seth grabbed my arm.

"Where do you think you're going?" Seth spoke as if he still had any say-so over me. Before I could speak, Joe intervened.

"Look, I don't know who you are but you need to let her go," Joe growled at Seth.

"I'm her husband," Seth stated matter-of-factly as he stared at Joe. Seth appeared completely unabashed by this turn of events as if he had planned the entire situation. I knew, of course, that that was impossible. The sting of Seth's statement had the exact reaction for which he had hoped. Joe's brow crinkled and he looked completely perplexed.

"No, you're not," came another male voice. Rick had found his way to the front of the crowd and stood erectly before Seth as if to challenge him. "And, I think you need to leave." Seth took in the situation- hundreds of people starring at us, two men standing up for me, and a hush on the crowd that was deafening.

"This isn't over," he said directly to me. Then he looked at Josh again, turned, and walked away bumping into Joe purposefully. It almost looked like Seth said something to Joe but it was much too quick an exchange. I collapsed into the chair that I had sat in before I grabbed Josh.

"I need to get home," I said to no one in particular. "Take me home." I repeated. When no one moved, I looked directly at Joe. "Joe, now, please." I demanded. Joe stood dazed, starring at Seth's back as he walked away. Rick helped me stand up and Tracy took Katie by the hand. "I'm so very sorry I ruined your party," I told Tracy as I hugged her good-bye.

"Nonsense, dear. You just get home and relax." When Joe and I finally got into the car, there didn't seem to be anything to say. I wanted to explain everything to him but not in front of the children. He deserved an explanation. The relaxed atmosphere we had enjoyed on the way to the party was gone, replaced by this awkward, thick melancholy.

"Will you come in for a minute?" I asked when we arrived at my apartment.

"No," he said flatly. The passion I had heard in his voice for the past year was absent and, for some reason I could not explain, my heart hurt. "I'll help you get the kids in but then I have to go." He carried Josh's car seat and walked behind us as we all proceeded to my door.

"Joe, I want to explain," I tried before he cut me off.

"You don't have to. I understand now."

"No, you don't, Joe, its"

"Brie," he sounded emphatic, "I couldn't understand why for this past year you could not warm up to me when every other woman I've pursued in my life chased me. Tonight, my eyes were opened. I'm sorry if I've been a nuisance. You won't have to worry about me any longer."

"Joe, seriously, you're not even going to listen?" I tried.

"Brie, you're not into me anyway. Why do you care what I think now?" It was a reasonable question. He had understood more than I realized so I let him walk away. I watched him get in his car and drive away and I knew, somehow, that I would never have his attention again.

I was exhausted- physically, mentally, and emotionally. Josh was nodding off so I undressed him, put his pajamas on, and laid him straight into his bed. Katie, on the other hand, was wide awake from the excitement and full of questions. I told her for us to get ready for bed and then I would talk with her. I hoped the few minutes that it took us to change clothes would give me the time to come up with answers for her.

"Momma, who was that man? Was that Seth?" I had half hoped she would not remember him. After all, it had been four years since she had seen him and she was only seven when we left. I wanted to protect her, to lie and tell her it was some estranged man I did not know and that we would never see him again. I decided to go with the truth.

"Yes, baby, you remember him?"

"Sort of. I remember him being mean. Why was he there?"

"I don't know exactly. Maybe he was at another party."

"But, how did he find us?"

"Again, I don't know, Katie. I don't have all the answers. I'm sorry if he scared you."

"I thought Joe was going to beat him up like Randy beat up Travis on the playground that time." I smiled at her youth.

"No, honey, grown men don't handle their differences that way. Besides, Joe has no reason to harm Seth."

"He would have beat him up to save you." She stated as if she knew. I felt like she may have been right before tonight but not anymore.

"I'm sorry you had to see all that. I don't want you to worry about this."

"I'm not worried. Can we go to the park tomorrow?" That was one of the greatest things about kids, their ability to finish talking about the troubles and move on. I envied Katie's ability not to worry about anything. I, on the other hand, found that sleep eluded me until the wee hours of the morning and then the nightmares I had escaped for so long ago invaded my dreams.

The next morning came too soon and the kids were in full force, wanting to go to the park that our apartment complex offers. As much as I wanted to lie in bed, I finally got the energy to take them to the park. I could not wait until Josh was old enough to play without my help as Katie does. As it was, I had to follow him carefully from one gym set to the other to insure his safety. To top it all off, I kept looking at the parking lot half expecting Seth to drive up and join us on the playground. By the time we went back to our apartment, my nerves were shot and I felt mentally and physically exhausted.

The day had been chilly and windy and I felt cold all the way to my bones. All I wanted was to soak in a hot tub but that was not possible.

I was glad when Monday morning finally arrived and I was able to get back to the office. I was never meant to be a mother who stayed home with her babies. There was something in me that felt restless at home and even when I was busy with the kids or cleaning the house, I felt bored. I figured I had inherited my own mother's selfish side or we were missing the maternal gene. I loved my children, of course, and knew I would never treat them as my mother had done me. I would give them the support and protection they deserved; I just was not the cuddly, fun mom I envied in so many other women.

I thought it was strange that Joe, for the first time I could ever remember, did not arrive at the same time I arrived. I wondered briefly if he had somehow strategically planned to get to the office at the same time each morning to see me. I was not sure if I was so conceited that I was thinking I was worth all that trouble or paranoid that he had been stalking me. Either way, I knew those days were over and, again, I felt a dull pain in my chest. Joe would have been perfect for me. What was wrong with me that I could not reciprocate his affection? He was gorgeously handsome and my heart definitely skipped beats when he was around but, somehow, our being together just did not feel right in my gut. Maybe I would never be able to trust a man. Maybe I was destined to be alone. My heart ached at the thought of it.

Rick found me right away, hiding in my office.

"Hey, you okay?" he said casually.

"Just embarrassed," I admitted. "I think I'll stay in my office for, well, for the rest of my life." I tried to smile.

"Yeah, I'm sorry that happened. Boy, I do see what you mean about being intimidated by him, though." Oh, *now* you see my point! I thought. "What are you going to do?"

"About what? He doesn't know where I am."

"Brie, he knows you're here. He knows you work here. It would have been too easy for him to ask whose party was there Saturday night and find out. Anyway, he also saw himself in Josh's face. He's not going to passively ignore this." He gave me a minute for this to sink in. I was shocked that, as much as I had thought and thought about this since Saturday night, none of what Rick just said had hit me. Now that it did, I realized instantly that I was trapped. "Brie, you're going to have to go forward with your plans now."

"I know," I replied quietly as I hung my head. "I wish I had just stayed with Annie Mae and Poppa."

"You can't mean that," Rick's response sounded very paternal. "You're doing so much better here."

"Yeah, financially but, Rick, this is going to be a nightmare. Mr. Morgan said I'm going to have to let Seth see Josh- like visiting days and stuff."

"Well, of course, Brie, why wouldn't you?"

"Rick, you just said Seth even intimidated you. Do you think Josh can take care of himself? He's only three-years-old!" My blood pressure rose and I felt immediately furious.

"Brie calm down. Do you really think Seth would hurt his own son?"

"I don't know. Mr. Morgan asked the same thing. All I know is that Seth is a selfish, abusive man and I don't trust him. How am I supposed to hand my son over to someone like that? What kind of a mother would I be if I felt that the money I would gain from Seth was worth putting my son in harm's way?"

"Brie, if Seth does anything to Josh you can have an injunction to stop the visitation. Until then you may want to consider the possibility that this may be a good thing. A boy needs a father." Rick was pushing me this morning and I was not up to it after my sleepless and worrisome weekend. I was at the breaking point.

"A real father, a caring and nurturing father- yes but not a control-freak, lying, manipulating father! No! Josh is just fine without him."

"Now, yes, he's just a baby. However, one day he's going to grow to be a young man who'll need a father's advice and help. Then he's going to ask questions about his father and want to get to know him. If he finds out then that you stood in the way of their relationship, he will never forgive you. Look, I'm not saying you have to do it today but I would say sooner rather than later. It would probably be the smartest thing you could do at this point." My eyes stung with tears that threatened to escape but my will stopped them in their tracks. No more tears! I was tired of my emotions getting the best of me. "Why don't you talk to Tracy about all this? Maybe another woman can understand your feelings better than me." I nodded. It was a good idea.

The workday dragged on and I continually had to force my mind to focus on the accounts I worked on. I skipped lunch, too afraid to venture out of my office. That afternoon, there was a knock at my door. I jumped instinctively. I had not talked to a soul since this morning and had kept my door closed to avoid everyone. The sudden noise startled me and made me realize I had been breathing shallowly all day. My first thought was that it was Seth but then, I realized, he would not knock.

"Come in," I announced. Tracy came in sheepishly.

"I hope I'm not interrupting," she spoke quietly. I physically relaxed seeing her kind face.

"No, not at all," I stood up then as if to help her in. She carried a small picnic basket, proceeded to set it in the empty chair, and hugged me tight.

"Are you okay?" she whispered in my ear as she continued to hug me. It felt odd but, at the same time, exactly the remedy I needed today. I could not remember anyone hugging me this tight except my kids and Annie Mae. The security of her embrace calmed me in a way I had not felt since I left Annie Mae and Poppa.

"I don't know," I told her honestly.

"I brought you some food. Rick said you've walled yourself up in here and I know you well enough to know that means you didn't eat lunch." She released me as she said this and proceeded to take the items out of the picnic basket. "I brought you some loaded potato soup and a half a turkey sandwich." She laid the food out on the side table as if preparing it for a king. She had thought of everything- utensils, napkins, and even a thermos of sweet tea. She made the best sweet southern tea I had ever had. I sat down and proceeded to eat although I had no appetite. Once I began eating the soup, my stomach let me know that it had been hungry and my tongue appreciatively accepted every bite with joy.

"This is delicious," I complimented. "Thank you so much for thinking of me. You shouldn't have gone to so much trouble."

"Dear, I didn't mind. I'm so worried about you and the babies." We smiled at one another then and I began to relax as I ate. "What are you going to do, Brie?" I did not really want to talk about it. I wanted to pretend we were just two friends enjoying a light lunch albeit at three o'clock in the afternoon.

"I'm not sure. Everyone is telling me to face him head on but, Tracy, you saw him. Even Rick said he was intimidating.

How am I supposed to face him? I'm petrified of him. I'm no fighter."

"Brie, everyone is a fighter given that circumstances require it. For most people, fighting is not a preferred choice. Why, you can look at the history of war and know that there are those who provoke it and then there are those who respond to it. Even the ancient Amazon warriors responded to male subjugation by creating an entire empire of female warriors. I'm not saying you have to become a man-hater but, let's face it dear, you're going to have to gird your loins and put on your armor. Once this battle is won, then you can learn to trust a good man who can protect you." She looked intently into my eyes as if by sheer will to invoke me with the right genes necessary to rise up and fight.

"Tracy," I looked down at my lap, unable to articulate exactly what my feelings were, "I," I took a deep breath, "I just can't". She cut me off abruptly, standing to make her point.

"Abriella Taylor," she had a fierce ring to her voice that I could have never imagined she possessed, "stand up." It was not a request and I obeyed. We now stood face to face and I was perplexed to what her next move would be. She raised her hand quickly as if to slap me across the face and my arm flew up instinctively to protect myself.

"There you have it," she said adamantly. "You know how to protect yourself physically. You've proved that many times already. You have survived many situations that would have crushed lesser people. You are tough as nails to the point of others having a hard time getting to know you. You are the most independent woman I've ever met for your age. Why, your name even comes from a Hebrew origin that means, 'strength of God'. You *are* a warrior so why do you insist on acting like a wimp?" My face stung as if she had succeeded in slapping me and I opened my mouth to rebuttal. "No, I did not come here to listen to more of your excuses. You have cowered behind Annie Mae's skirt, and now within the walls of this office long enough. Stand up and face the man. My goodness, you have enough on him to send him to his own corner shaking." She turned from me then, walked to the window of my office, and looked out. I wanted to respond to all of her accusations but I did not trust my own judgment right now. I was so mad that I knew if I spoke, it would be unkind so I just watched her. After only a moment, she began to talk again but this time her demeanor was different.

"Brie, you know I had cancer, right?" she began softly.

"Yes," I said quietly.

"Well, I never had to fight in my life like I had to fight then. I never thought of myself as strong, or brave, or able before that battle. I had to reach deep within my soul to grasp the fight within me. I had to find every reason I could think of to take the next step. I labored over the plan of action I was to take to live. In the end, God gave me the reason I needed most- a grandbaby for which to look forward. I had a goal. My sights were set on living to see that baby, not only born, but to read stories to him, to make sure that baby knew his grandma. Once I had that goal firmly implanted in my mind, I made a plan of action to succeed. I got three opinions from various doctors, holistic and oncologists. I changed everything about my life- my diet, my routine, my personal time. I began to meditate, do yoga, and read my Bible more. I prayed but I put legs on my prayers."

"Legs on your prayers?" I had never heard that expression.

"Yes, Brie. That means I didn't sit back and wait for a miracle. I worked as best I could by participating, actively and aggressively, in my recovery. No one could do those things for me. Rick would have gladly laid down his own life to spare mine but he could not. My children tried to protect me but they were helpless. The doctors advised me but could not cure me." She turned from the window then to face me.

"What I'm trying to tell you is- only you can save yourself. We, your friends and confidants, can only advise or help you, hide you, and protect you for so long. At some point in your life, you are going to have to fight for the life you want. It pains me to see you settle for mediocrity when you're capable of so much more. I'm here to help you, Brie, but the battle's victory is going to be up to you." She crossed the room and packed up the picnic basket. I knew I should respond somehow to all she had said but stood transfixed, unsure of what my response should be.

"Brie, Rick and I love you. We don't have a daughter of our own. Our daughter-in-law is the closest we've had to a daughter but we consider you part of our family now. I hope I haven't overstepped my bounds by speaking plainly to you. I've talked to you like I would one of my own children." Then she raised her hand slowly to my face and patted my cheek. "We're here for you, dear. Believe in your ability. God does not allow a battle to come into our lives for which He has not given us the ability to fight it." Then, before I had a chance to hug her, she turned and left.

~ 7 ~

A Startling Crisis

That night I could not stop thinking about what Tracy had said. I felt humiliated by my running from Seth and then tripping over the chair in the banquet room and envisioned many different outcomes. I wished I had walked across the room when I saw him and stood boldly before him demanding for him to leave the room because he was not invited.

I thought about slapping him across the face in front of the huge crowd. I even imagined going to the stage microphone and announcing to everyone that Seth Taylor, renowned attorney, was a fraud- while he appeared to be an upstanding citizen, he secretly abused those in his life; micro-controlled everything around him, and slept with men while pretending to be happily married.

I visualized a magnificent plan where I tortured him by making his life as miserable as he had made mine. I thought about so many ways I wish I had handled the situation and in every plan, I arose from courage within me rather than spinelessly running away. It was early in the morning before I finally drifted off to sleep and the alarm scared me to death when it went off.

When I finally arrived at work, Rick was already there. It was unusual for him to beat me to the office this time of year.

The tax season was the only time he usually came in so early so I went directly to his office.

"Hey boss. Everything okay?" I tried to sound chipper.

"Hey Brie. Good morning. Yes, everything's fine. I'm meeting with another accountant today about coming on board. I was going to ask you to sit in on it but I got a call from Annie Mae this morning. Poppa's had a heart attack." My heart stopped and I opened my mouth to ask a thousand questions. Rick stopped me short by continuing with the explanations that he knew I wanted. "He seems to be fine but he is in the hospital. I figured you'd want to get down there so, here are my keys. Go on down and see to them. Please let them know why I couldn't come and if they need anything to let me know, will you?"

"Of course, Rick. Thank you so much. Which hospital?"

"Saint Joseph's" he replied. My heart lurched. The thought of returning to the southern side made me nervous. Again, I wondered how I had found the courage to walk into Annie Mae's store that dreadful day. I left immediately and went straight to Saint Joseph's. I knew it would take a while to get through downtown traffic at this time of day but was ill prepared for the bumper-to-bumper headache to follow. It took me well over an hour to get there and I prayed the entire way that Poppa would be all right. I could not imagine their life without him. Poppa was the strong, silent type and, while he did not add a lot verbally to Annie Mae's and Ezekiel's lives, he was the secure foundation of their existence.

When I finally arrived at the hospital, the parking garage was filled nearly to capacity and I had to park on the top floor. It took several minutes to walk the length of it and I started running towards the elevator, partially to hurry and get to Poppa and partially because I was afraid of being in this parking garage by myself.

Once I found out Poppa's room number and began my way up the hall, I felt a flood of emotions, taking me back to the night I had sat with Annie Mae waiting to hear if Ezekiel would survive his gunshot wound after the botched robbery attempt at the store. I found Annie Mae and Poppa quickly and felt immediate relief when I walked into their room and they were laughing.

"Well, I didn't know y'all were having a party," I said spryly as I opened the door, "I heard someone was sick."

"Lord have mercy!" Annie Mae jumped up from her chair and headed toward me encompassing me into her gigantic arms as if I were a small child. "Chille," she pushed me away at arm's length and examined me. "Lord, chille, you gettin' skinnier and skinnier. You need ta come by tha store and let me fix ya some real food, put some meat on your bones." I laughed at her thinking.

"Awe, Annie Mae, you're so silly. I just saw you at Thanksgiving. It's still so good to see you. What happened to Poppa?" I looked at Poppa then, lying in the hospital bed. He appeared tired but, other than that, unchanged.

"Yeah, chille, Poppa had a litt' attack this mornin'. I told 'im ta take out the trash and he knelt down on tha floor like I had whooped 'im. I knowed right away what was going on cause he ain't never been sick a day in his life and if'n he cain't take out the trash, I knowed he was sure nuff sick. I called the ambulance right away and God sent us some good paramedics who got my Poppa here fast-like. Doctor did some kinda procedure, they called it a procedure, I call it a surgery, and now Poppa's good as new!"

"Wow!" I had forgotten how animated Annie Mae could be. "I'm so glad they fixed it in time. Where is Ezekiel?"

"He's gone back ta tha store. Once we got Poppa settled, I sent him back with ole Miss Ruth. You remember her? She the one who come in every Tuesday an' was always late." I shook my head although I knew I probably should remember her. "Don't matter no ways. Ole Miss Ruth brought me an' 'Zekiel up behind the ambulance and stayed till they got Poppa situated. I asked her could she open the store on up and I'd be there directly soon as I make sure they gone feed my Jessie."

"Who's taking you back to the store?" I asked.

"Oh chille, I don't rightly know now. I figure it out when it's time." Just then a hospital staff person came in with a lunch tray for Poppa. "There you is. Y'all starving my Jessie ta death round here." Annie Mae took over the room, pulling Poppa's elongated tray over his hospital bed and uncovering the various parts of the lunch tray. The staff lady took the hint and made an easy escape. "Lawd have mercy. Looky here at this mess they call food. How's my Jessie supposed to git better if'n all they gonna feed him is bird food?" I could not help but laugh at Annie Mae's description of the tray. Certainly, the diet they had Poppa on was one to encourage a healthier heart and probably a lighter portion considering his morning activities but Annie Mae's idea of a meal was probably one reason Poppa was in need of medical care in the first place. "I'm gone hafta git him some real food ta help him git well."

"Annie Mae, maybe the doctors are on to something by feeding him a special diet. You don't want to aggravate his heart condition."

"Ha!" she spat loudly. "Them doctors know how ta save lives, alright, but they don't know how ta eat. Have you ever seen them? Why, they fatter than me an' Poppa put together. If they really thought a rabbit's diet would save their own lives, they'd be eatin' that way themselves." I laughed a weak laugh but had to admit to myself that she had a point. Annie Mae fed Poppa like a child despite Poppa trying to get her to sit down and let him feed himself. "You might as well stop your fussin' old man, cause you knowed I'm gonna take care of ya long as I'm here." Annie Mae told him. Poppa finally conceded and allowed her to feed him and I detected a small smile as he looked up into her eyes. I had forgotten how profound their love shown. I envied them that, if nothing else. After Annie Mae finished feeding Poppa, she settled down in the chair opposite him. We talked for several minutes but, despite Annie Mae's questioning, I didn't reveal my plight for fear of upsetting Poppa.

"Annie Mae, if you need a ride back to the store, I can take you," I offered after a while.

"I stay here with my Jessie," she spoke emphatically.

"No, you won't," Poppa spoke up in a rare authoritative way. "You need ta git back to thu store. You knowed Ezekiel cain't run that store and Miss Ruth probably done gone and laid down for a nap. I'm fine here. If'n I need anything, I'll hit that button thu nurse said ta hit." Annie Mae opened her mouth but Poppa beat her to the punch. "Annie Mae, I ain't fightin' 'bout this. I need ta rest anyways and I cain't rest knowin' you over there watchin' every twitch I make. Go home, eat, and take care a thu store."

"Annie Mae, I think that's a good idea," I interjected on Poppa's behalf. "You can always come back this evening. Maybe you could sneak in some turnip greens for him." I jested. Annie Mae's eyes lit up when I said this and I took it that she thought I was serious.

"Alrighty then. If'n y'all gone gang up on me, I'll just go. You sure you can take me all the way down there?" She asked me.

"Of course, it'd be my pleasure. It will give us some time to talk." I thought Annie Mae was going to give out by the time we arrived at my car.

"Lawd, chille, did ya hafta park so far from the place?" she huffed as we finally came up on Rick's car. She was clearly out of breath and I began to worry about her having a heart attack as well. Once we were headed in the right direction, Annie Mae began her usual interrogation of my life. For once, I was glad. I felt that maybe she was a good person to help me figure out what to do so I explained the whole situation to her.

"You know what you remind me of?" she asked me when I finished my story. I shook my head and kept my eyes focused on the road. "You like ole Gideon in the Bible. He was hidin' out in thu wine presses from the Midianites. Hidin', just like you doin' and have been doin' ever since I met ya. He was too afraid ta take on those persecutin' him. Well, when God was ready, he sent an angel ta tell Gideon ta git up an' fight but ole Gideon didn't think he was strong enough and he didn't trust the Lord enough ta believe that he could win."

"Annie Mae, I appreciate your analogy but we're not talking about the Bible days. I'm talking about the here and now." I interrupted her. I was not in the mood for a Sunday school lesson. "I'm not some warrior in the Bible."

"Hear me out, missy," she continued. Why did I think that my interjection would change her train of thought? "The first thang Gideon told that angel was that he wadunt no warrior either. He said he was from the poorest of the poorest tribe. He didn't have no courage either so he even asked for a sign, you know, that he was really the right man for tha job, as if God may have made a mistake or somethin'. So, God was patient with 'im and showed Gideon without a doubt that He would be with 'im in the fight. Well, I guess I ain't gotta tell ya that tha good Lord knowed what He was doin' and Gideon led the fight ta victory. Missy, you just like Gideon. You keep tellin' yo'self that you cain't but the battle lay before ya that keeps callin' yo name. Seth may have started the battle but it's gone be up ta you ta finish it. You been runnin' and hidin' for too long, chille. Now, I'm 'bout ready ta find that Seth my own self and kick his butt for hurtin' you and those babies. But ain't no angel give me no sign that it's my battle."

"Annie Mae, I haven't seen any signs either."

"Yes, you have, chille. You seen Seth at that restaurant and you ran jus' like you ran from 'im at your house. Then he showed up at your own party an' you ran again. Its high time you stopped runnin' and turned round and met him face ta face. Put him on the defense for a change."

"Ha, that's easy for you to say. I have nothing to put him on the defense with. He's bigger, stronger, richer, and smarter than I am."

"Chille, chille, you gots information enough on that man that would put him on his knees ta keep it from gittin' out. You got the best weapon any warrior could have- knowledge. You knowed he's secretly homosexual. You knowed he don't want no body ta know it. You knowed he falsely claimed you was dead an' probably got all yo life insurance money. I'm the last person ta wanna blackmail somebody but if'n you down ta the last straw, then you got ta use what ya got. You smarter than you give yourself credit for. I bet once ya git started, the heavens will open up and your path will be clear. Maybe you won't even hafta use the secret information ta make him behave but if'n you do, well, then you do." We pulled up to the store just as Annie Mae declared her stance. The store boasted a fresh coat of paint on the front porch since Thanksgiving. The windows beamed with the same Christmas decorations we had helped her put up years before and, even though it all seemed so foreign to me, I still felt the faint nostalgic feeling of home as we went inside.

"Miss Brie," Ezekiel came running to me when I walked in. I hugged him tightly and we exchanged salutations. "Where's Miss Katie?"

"I'm sorry, Ezekiel. She is at school. I couldn't bring her." His expression fell and I felt guilty, knowing that Katie would probably love to see him also. "I'll try to get down here with her soon, I promise." He beamed then as if I'd given him an awesome Christmas present. I knew that I must make good on my promise. I stayed a while, visiting with some of the ladies shopping in the store, the men around the old pot-bellied stove, and Ezekiel. I finally got back to the beauty shop, but instead of the busy place I had remembered, it was dormant. One lady was sweeping up the place.

"Hi, I'm Brie Taylor. I used to work here. Do you know where Kayla is?" She stopped sweeping and looked at me with skepticism.

"Kayla ain't working taday." She stated unemotionally.

"Do you know where she is?" The woman went back to sweeping robotically.

"She had ta take her momma to the doctor." I knew I would get nowhere with her so I went to find Annie Mae, who was just returning downstairs from her home where she had gone to change clothes when we arrived.

"Yeah, chille, Kayla doin' real good. I'm surprised she hasn't called ya. Maybe she don't know your new number. Here, lemme give ya hers." She scribbled a number on a small paper she ripped off an order tablet from the sideboard café. As I looked at the number, I remembered that Kayla had given me her number at Thanksgiving but I had misplaced it. I put the paper in my purse with resolve that I would call her this time. "I knowed she'd love ta hear from ya." Annie Mae went behind the café serving bar and made herself and me a large plate of food. She didn't even ask if I was hungry. We went to the small lunchroom we had enjoyed so many times and sat down to eat. She caught me up on Kayla's life. "Kayla's momma been a little sick lately. You know she always down and out. I hope she gone be okay. Poor little Gabby'd be lost without her."

"What's wrong with her?"

"Don't no doctors seem ta know. She been real sick-like for 'bout ten years. She used ta work two, sometimes three, jobs. Then one day, she just quit. Ever since then, she don't seem ta be able ta do much without gettin' down and out again."

I sat in the beauty shop talking for an hour or so after lunch. It seemed awkward to stay any longer. I had seen and talked to everyone and the store seemed to be back to business as usual. I hugged Annie Mae and Ezekiel and made my departure. The ride home took even longer because I had waited too late to leave in order to miss the rush hour of traffic. My only solace was that the worst of it seemed to be exiting the city rather than heading into it. On the upper side of Atlanta, though, the traffic jam brought me to an abrupt halt. I sat in the traffic, moving slowly toward my destination. When I finally arrived at the office, I was exhausted. It had ended up being a good day despite how it had begun. I said a silent prayer thanking God for keeping Poppa healthy.

I hoped that Rick did not mind my visiting while I was so close to Annie Mae. I did not intent on being gone all day and worried slightly that Rick may be frustrated waiting on me. It was nearly five in the afternoon and I would be hard-pressed to get to the nursery and the after-school program to get the kids before they closed. I wondered briefly if Rick would be willing to give me a ride to save time from waiting on the bus. When I turned the corner and pulled into our office park, my heart stopped abruptly. I saw Rick on the sidewalk in front of our office talking with Seth.

~8 ~

An Unexpected Visitor

My first response was to keep driving, just to drive past them as if I had not seen them and come back later. Yet, I knew that was impossible. Not only was I already late getting the kids, but I had Rick's car. In addition, Rick and Seth spotted me as I drove up. As I parked the car, my heart flew into a frenzy. My hands were shaking so badly I had a hard time putting the car in park. Afraid my legs would give out if I stood up, I pretended to gather papers on the seat of the car and check my purse for an imaginary necessity. Alas, I knew I could not postpone the inevitable any longer. At least Rick was here with me, I sighed. For that, I was thankful.

"Brie," Rick opened his arm toward me as if to beckon me to him, "Seth and I have been talking." I walked slowly toward Rick not taking my eyes off him, afraid to look at Seth. When I finally reached Rick, he put his arm around me, no doubt for comfort. "Seth came by and apologized for the other night." Yeah, sure, he did, I thought. "He would like to settle your issues amicably." Please, tell me that you did not fall for that! I was talking to myself now. I looked in Rick's face to see any hint that he knew better, that he understood that Seth's ploy was to appear the good guy, that he secretly planned to hurt me. Instead, Rick seemed imperviously bent on swallowing Seth's story. No! No, no, no! I looked at Seth then, not for direction

but in an accusatory way. How dare he infringe upon my friends and turn them against me.

"Brie, I realize how you must feel," Seth began confidently, "but".

"No, Seth, no, you couldn't possibly realize how I must feel. You treated me like your personal slave for years, all the while living a lie, and then you raped me. I fled like a scared child in the night but I am not that child any longer. I have been to the depths of hell because of you and I have run scared for the last time. You," I pointed my finger in his face unabashedly, "You will never intimidate me again. I have run from you for the last time. You are a bully who tries to control everything and everyone around you because inside you feel so out of control. But I am no longer under your jurisdiction." I was astounded at my bravado even if my voice shook as I spoke the words. Seth appeared only slightly surprised. I felt Rick's strong arms holding me and, at the moment, I felt his strength must have been the charge that flowed through me giving me courage.

"We have unfinished business," Seth stated astutely.

"Yes, I guess we do. Maybe if you hadn't killed me off and collected my life insurance it wouldn't be so complicated for you now to remarry with a wife surprisingly alive." Now I caught him off-guard. Apparently, he had no idea I was so well informed. Immediately, I realized in my arrogance, I had crippled our surprise factor in the case.

"Yes, well, there is that, too but I was referring to my son." I gasped, scared of how to proceed.

"He's not your son," I spat, unsure of where I was going with this.

"Of course he is. He is identical to the portrait of me at his age hanging over the mantle in my study. You remember that photo, don't you?" I did. I had forgotten it until he mentioned it just now, because I had only been in his study half dozen times in the years I was married to him but, now that he mentioned it, there was no doubt that Seth was certain that Josh was his flesh and blood son. My hesitation left no mistake.

"He's not your son," I repeated less sure of myself.

"Yes, well, we'll have to see about that," Seth looked back to Rick. "Thank you for talking to me, Rick. Again I offer my apologies for disturbing your Christmas party." Then Seth looked back at me. "Brie, it is obvious you're disturbed by my presence. I hope we can settle our matters amicably. I'll give you some time to think about how you'd like to handle this. Please call me at this number when you're ready to talk." He held out his business card but I only looked at it as if it would bite if I accepted it. Rick took it for me. Seth turned away, got into his new Mercedes and drove away. I stood, staring at Seth's car until it was out of sight then my legs gave out and, had it not been for Rick's arm still around me, I would have fallen to the ground. Rick helped me into the office and sat me in the receptionist's chair.

"Brie," Rick spoke quietly as he handed me a glass of water he had retrieved, "you okay?"

"Rick, how could you let him stay here?"

"It wasn't like that. He came into the office looking for you. We talked only briefly and he was leaving when you pulled up." I drank the cold water and felt it flow all the way down my esophagus to my stomach. It soothed me somehow. "Brie, I have to say, you surprised me. If it hadn't been for your shaking, I would have sworn you were not afraid of him at all." He tried to make light of it but I could not find it in myself to laugh. "Come on. You're late. Let me take you to get the kids then y'all can eat dinner with us." I rose and obeyed his instructions, getting in the car without saying a word. After we had picked up both kids and drove to Rick's house, Tracy fixed us a drink. The kids went to the living room with Rick while Tracy and I put the finishing touches on dinner.

"I am so proud of you," Tracy acknowledged. "I knew you had it in you."

"Tracy, you're so funny. I didn't even know I had it in me." I whipped the potatoes as she started the gravy on the stove. "I see now that the ball is rolling and I'd better get ahead of it or I'm going to get run over."

"So, what's your plan?" she whispered.

"Not sure yet, first, I guess I need to see my lawyer, Mr. Morgan." I was embarrassed about how I had walked out on him but, without a doubt, he was the attorney I wanted to represent me. I hoped he would take me back.

"Well, that sounds lovely, dear." She smiled as if I had presented her with a wonderful idea. The rest of the evening was delightful. We didn't discuss Seth anymore but enjoyed lively conversation as we ate. Tracy had made roast beef and gravy with mashed potatoes, curried carrots, and Italian green beans. She even made an impromptu dessert by pouring heated raspberries over French vanilla ice cream. It was delicious. Rick drove us home after I helped her clean the kitchen and helped me get the kids in the apartment. I locked the door behind him, still leery of Seth and worrying that he may be following me.

The next day, I called Mr. Morgan's office and made an appointment. Disheartened that the quickest appointment available was over a week away, I went to Rick's office to see if he could pull some strings. Rick didn't think it was necessary to push the appointment.

"Rick, what if Seth comes back?"

"What if he does?" Rick could be so obscure sometimes. I continued about my business as best I could, yet looking over my shoulder anytime I ventured out, always jumping when I heard the bell ring for a visitor's entrance, and jumping whenever the phone rang. My nerves were just about shot and if it had not been for Christmas, I probably would have completely lost my mind. The necessary distraction of the holidays proved to help my psychosis. I took off work early one afternoon to go with Tracy, who had insisted on taking me shopping for the kids. I got Katie a new bike because she had long out-grown the one that Annie Mae and Poppa had bought her. I got Josh a small riding toy that resembled Fred Flintstone's car. It would be the perfect combo for them to ride together. Along with their rides, I got them each new clothes, winter coats, a few games for us to play as a family, and stuffed teddy bears. I even got Katie's cat, Sparks, a new toy to chase. This would be our best Christmas yet, as far as presents went. I couldn't wait to see the look on Katie's face come Christmas morning.

"And what are you getting yourself for Christmas, dear?" Tracy asked as we took a break for coffee.

"Oh, nothing." What a silly question, I thought.

"What do you need?" she persisted.

"I don't know. A miracle." I forced a laugh.

"Dear, I know you're worried about all this trouble. But when you get my age, you find that trouble has a way of working itself out. Stay focused on the wonderful blessings in your life." She patted my hand across the table as she said this.

"Thanks Tracy. That means a lot."

"What about a cell phone?" she said.

"What?"

"Could you use a cell phone? I worry about you taking that bus every day without a way to get help if you need it."

"Oh, no, that is so sweet of you but I'll be fine." We finished the shopping and took our loot to their house to hide until Christmas Eve since I had no room at my apartment. Christmas was only a week away and I found, once again, I was praying for a Christmas miracle. It was one tradition I would be happy to forego.

My appointment with Mr. Morgan could not come quickly enough and yet it seemed the time flew and then I was sitting at his conference table once again. I was relieved that Seth had not tried to make contact with me anymore.

"Good afternoon, Brie," Mr. Morgan's soft yet confident voice filled the room. We shook hands and he sat catty-corner from me at the large table, placing my file in front of him. "So, I presume you've had a change of heart?"

"Honestly, no, but there's been a change of circumstance now and I don't seem to have a choice any longer." I proceeded to catch him up to date.

"Ah, so the cat's out of the bag, huh? Yes, those things do have a way of happening." He eyed me warily as he twirled his glasses in one hand. "So what would you have me do, Brie?" I was flabbergasted. I had hoped he would tell me what to do.

"Mr. Morgan, this is your area of expertise. I have no idea how to continue."

"I see. Well, as previously discussed, you'll have no option but to allow him visitation once parentage has been established."

"I know. I agree. I realize now that I have no choice."

"It appears so."

"I told Seth that Josh is not his son. Couldn't I buy some time by pressing the issue and forcing a paternity test? How long does a paternity test take? What does that involve?"

"Well, you could, yes; however, a DNA test is a simple procedure of swabbing the inside of his cheek and the results can be back in as little as two days, possibly sooner if he pays more. So, that wouldn't really help, time wise. Seems to me, that Seth is not opposed to the idea of Josh being his son so he may not require one. Once he assumes responsibility, under Georgia law, he is then obligated for the duration of Josh's life to continue monetary support. So, a paternity test may not be necessary unless you have doubts." I gave Mr. Morgan a look to let him know I didn't appreciate the insinuation.

"There is no doubt whatsoever. In addition to my own knowing, the resemblance between them is unmistakable to anyone who sees them both."

"Well, then my dear, I would suggest we go forward with the original papers I drew up. Let's ask for the maximum, arrears, and get this done, shall we?" It all sounded so simple and I had to admit to myself that I seemed to be the only one complicating it.

"Sure. Let's do this." I agreed. Mr. Morgan presented the papers he had already gone over with me previously, only briefly reminding me of their intent. I signed where he directed and we shook hands before I parted. When I walked out of his office, I felt elated, lighter somehow, and felt that I stood taller. Could I dare to hope that this would be as cordial as Rick and Mr. Morgan tried to convince me it would be?

I went back to the office and told Rick I had filed the paperwork. Mr. Morgan advised that the papers probably would be served to Seth by the end of the week. Then it was just a matter of waiting for Seth's response. That was my biggest fear-Seth's response. I told myself once more that Seth's power over me was rendered harmless now. He could no longer hurt me. He was powerless. My gut wretched as if in direct response to my wishful thinking.

The end of the week drew near and as each day passed; my nerves grew more and more fragile. By Friday, I was a basket case, jumping at every noise or motion. I was relieved when the end of the workday came and Seth had still not shown up. I stepped on the bus to go home and worked my way back to my usual seat. As I looked out of the window, I could not help but wonder what it may be like to have some financial freedom. If Seth paid me child support, I would no longer have to ride the bus each day to and from Katie's school, Josh's daycare, and my work. If he did pay me arrears up front, I could easily pay cash for a nice, dependable car. I would not, of course, but at least it would give me a nice down payment so the monthly payments would be small. I would not miss the time spent on a bus now or the extra time I had to allot for transportation.

After the bus dropped us off close to our apartment, Katie, Josh, and I walked the remaining half block. It was getting dark by the time we arrived and the silhouette of the playground shown through the streetlights beyond. I got my keys out as usual just before we reached our building and froze in my tracks when I recognized Seth's car parked directly in front of our apartment.

~ 9 ~

Strangest Turn of Events

Seth leaned casually against the hood of his Mercedes as if this was our usual routine, him waiting for me after work. He had already spotted me so I knew there was no escape. I decided instead to meet this new challenge head on. I walked directly up to him.

"Seth, what are you doing here?" He smiled a lazy smile, the subtle light from the street lamp giving him a more menacing look. Katie squeezed my hand and I squeezed hers in return. He pushed himself away from the car slowly and sauntered toward us. "Seth, I swear before God if you lay a finger on any of us, I will have you arrested. I don't think that would do your practice any good."

"Brie, Brie, Brie. What makes you think I would want to hurt you?"

"Well, you certainly seemed to take joy in it for years." I was impressed with my ability to appear calm.

"I just came to discuss the terms of your proposal."

"Call my attorney." I stated firmly. I turned toward my door, unsure if I should open the door, afraid he would force himself into the apartment. I decided I had to take the chance. I was not going to stand in the parking lot and argue with him. Maybe if I walked away, he would leave.

"Oh, I already have, sweetheart. You're in for a rude awakening if you think I'm going to be played like a puppet."

"I'm not trying to play you, Seth. I wouldn't stoop to your level." I continued to walk toward my door with key in hand. Once I got to my door, I attempted to put the key in but fumbled in my haste and dropped my key chain. Before I could retrieve it, Seth reached down and picked it up. I reached for it but he brushed my hand away and easily opened my door for me, pushing it wide for us to enter. I held my hand out for him to return my key and he placed them in my palm. "Don't even think of coming in here." I stood between my doorframe and Seth as if I could block his entrance was he determined to push his way in. Katie and Josh went in and I could see from the corner of my eye that Katie had Josh's hand guiding him deeper into the safety of our apartment. Seth leaned toward me, his face only inches from mine but I stood my ground, unwilling to let him know I was still terrified of him.

"Watch your step, sweetheart. If you think I was harsh with you when we were on the same team, you will not like me when we are on opposing teams."

"We were never on the same team, Seth. Our marriage was a farce. You were always on an opposing team. Don't think I've forgotten that." I could see his cheek twitch. I could smell his sweet cologne. I could feel his breath on my face. Our eyes locked and I would not allow myself the ability to look away. I met him eyeball to eyeball.

"You will never be able to prove it." He leaned even closer and I thought for a split second that he was going to kiss me.

"Seth, I don't care about your sexual orientation. I don't need to prove anything; however, I would imagine there are those in your click who do care and have serious doubts about you. I imagine one claim would be all the evidence they need. You may find yourself on the other end of being judged for a change."

“No one gives a damn about anyone’s sexual orientation anymore, stupid. This is the twenty-first century. Don’t try to blackmail me.”

“No? Then why do you hide it, Seth? You are right that no one cares but you seem to, ah, and I presume that Tiffany Berkett may have an opinion about it.” The words hit their mark. Seth backed away from me, too stunned to reply. It was the first time I could ever remember having the upper hand in our relationship. Apparently, he had not considered the idea that I would tell her.

“You’d better keep your mouth to yourself,” his voice took on a deep, low tone.

“Maybe, if you had done that, we wouldn’t be in this mess, Seth.” He raised his hand to strike me and, although I flinched, I did not move.

“Mommy!” Katie screamed. Seth stopped dead in mid-stride, barely stopping in time before his palm reached my cheek.

“Get out,” I said emphatically.

“You haven’t heard the last of me,” he spat. Then he turned and walked away. When he was finally in his car, I closed and locked the door. My breath was shallow and I felt faint.

“Mommy, are you okay?” Katie ran up to me and held me. “I thought he was going to hit you.” I made my way to the couch to sit down.

“I’m okay, Katie. Thanks for screaming. That’s probably what saved me.” Katie and I both felt shaken and held each other closely for a few minutes. Josh played with his toys a few feet from us, oblivious to the drama. It took several minutes before Katie regained her composure. I would not be able to relax for the rest of the evening.

The next day, after telling Rick all that had transpired he told me to call Mr. Morgan who promptly suggested I file a restraining order.

"Brie, I want you to have this," Rick said in a weird shy way I had not seen from him. He reached in his desk and handed me a cell phone box. "Tracy suggested it and we were going to give it to you for Christmas but after last night's incidence, I think you need it now." I was touched.

"Wow. Thank you so much, Rick. This is so thoughtful of you both. You'll have to show me how to use it though." Rick then showed me how to program numbers that I would frequently call and he put his home number and the numbers for the office in it. I told him I would put the kid's schools in later. It did give me a sense of security knowing that I could call for help at any time from any place. "Rick, thank you so much. This is, well, very generous of you."

I borrowed Rick's car and spent the entire morning going through the procedures necessary to file the restraining order. First, I went to the city clerk's office to file a petition for a temporary restraining order. The tiny elderly lady behind the partition told me to wait outside the judge's chambers and after only a moment, I was escorted in to a small office. My nerves were on edge. This was Seth's stomping ground, not mine. While I was waiting for the judge to get to me, I decided to call Tracy and thank her for the phone. I had secretly hoped that they were going to get me one after she had mentioned it the day we shopped but I would never have assumed it. Just having it with me made me feel safer. I dialed Rick's home number and was waiting for Tracy to answer when I heard the door close firmly and looked up to see Judge Miller, the very same judge who Seth was with the day I discovered he was homosexual. My mouth went dry and I broke out into a hot sweat. I shoved the phone in my lap and covered it with my hand.

"Good afternoon," Judge Miller appeared unraveled. "I understand you're filing for a temporary restraining order." He seemed to either not recognize me or was doing a great job of ignoring the fact that I was in on his little secret. Was I supposed to go along with his charade?

"Yes," I answered aloud.

"Ms. Taylor, you understand that in so doing, you will bring scrutiny to yours and Mr. Taylor's reputation, don't you?"

"I'm more worried about my safety." Judge Miller looked much older than I remembered him.

"Under what circumstances do you propose this claim necessary?"

"Judge Miller, with all due respect, I think you know most of the circumstances. But, most immediately, Seth showed up at my apartment last night and threatened me verbally and almost slapped me."

"Almost slapped you, Ms. Taylor?" He half-spat the sarcasm evident in his voice.

"Yes. My little girl screamed when she saw him raise his hand to me. He stopped just short of his intended goal."

"I see," he said hesitantly. I could see the wheels turning in his mind, looking for a solution that would both appease me and protect his lover. "Would it be suitable to you if I spoke with him? I think I could prevent any future occurrence without this extreme measure." I did not know what to say. I most certainly did not feel that it was suitable but to say I was not willing to work with him would make me appear uncompromising, wouldn't it? "You see, Ms. Taylor," Judge Miller revved back in his overly large chair, "Mr. Taylor is in a state of shock right now. He believed you to be dead. Then, unexpectedly, you arrive on the scene after years of absence and, strategically, before his forthcoming nuptials, and with his son, no less. Any man would be in shock. Perhaps if you give him a few days to absorb the situation, he will revert to his usual self." It was too much! This was too much to endure. I did not want to cross the line and get arrested but I could not sit here and listen to this malarkey. I stood up barely grabbing my phone in time, preventing it from falling on the floor.

"Judge Miller, you and I both know that Seth's story of my death was his poor attempt to explain why I would flee from him out of fear in the middle of the night, the night of the very day that I found him in his office engaged in sexual misconduct with *you*! You and Seth can try to play this off as a hysterical woman but we both know the truth. I will not sit here and pretend that this is normal. Seth abused me and my daughter for years and that is one of the many reasons why I ran from him. Now, he is trying to intimidate me again. I am not the same little girl who was so easily scared away. I intend to carry this through. I had no intentions of dragging you into this but if you refuse to do your job of approving this restraining order and giving me the peace of mind I deserve for my children and myself, then I will have no choice but to ask for another judge and explain the entire circumstances to him in order to have justice."

"Ms. Taylor, sit down," Judge Miller raised his voice. I instinctively obeyed. "You will do no such thing. I am the only judge you will see regarding this case. I have the authority to see to it that I will oversee your divorce case as well and insure that Seth will have the sympathy of a jury, if need be, to assure his wishes are fulfilled. You may think you know all the details because you witnessed Seth and I in a compromising position; however, our history goes back much further than his façade of a relationship with you." He leaned back in his chair without pausing.

"I told Seth not to marry you that it would only complicate the matter but people were beginning to talk. He felt a marriage to a simpleton like you would be ideal. Admittedly, it did seem ideal for a few years. You were more a slave than wife. Then you had to make trouble by pushing your way into his life." He hit his finger on his desk to emphasize his point.

"If you had just looked the other way, you would still be married to him, enjoying his money, and wouldn't have to resort to such extreme measures to take it. Honestly, a baby? I do not even know how you worked that out. Now, you have Seth thinking he wants a relationship with a son he thought he would never have. Well, I am neither a simpleton like you nor a sentimental fool like Seth. I will not be blackmailed by the likes of you." I had been so proud of myself for standing up and voicing my rights. Now I sat as scared as I had ever been in my life, unsure of how to proceed. After only a moment's silence, he continued. "Now, I'll sign this piece of paper if that's what you want but don't come into my chambers and threaten me again. Do you hear me? You want a divorce and Seth's money, fine, but you will not ruin him and most especially, you will not repeat anything you saw or think you know about me. Got it?" I nodded. He signed the petition and practically threw it at me, then turned and walked out. I felt stupid- like a reprimanded child. What had gotten into me? Had I gotten so cocky after my win against Seth that I now felt I could talk to anyone, even a judge, as if I were someone important? I sat in a stupor for a few minutes, shaking slightly. At last, I stood up and picked up the petition he had thrown toward me.

When I returned to the office, I told Rick everything. I did not really mean to but I was about to burst and felt I had to get it off my chest. Rick suggested I call Mr. Morgan so I did but had to leave a message with his receptionist since he was in court. I only asked him to return my call because I did not want to tell her what needed to be said. It was later that afternoon when Mr.

Morgan finally returned my call. By then I had a headache and was seriously thinking I may drop the whole case.

"I see," Mr. Morgan said quietly after I relayed the entire scene within Judge Miller's office. "Unfortunately, Judge Miller is one of the most respected judges in town and you have no proof of what you saw in Seth's office or what transpired in Judge Miller's chamber today. Brie, I'm not sure what we should do at this point. I can request a different judge, but, again, without substantiated evidence, we are at his mercy."

"Then what is the point of moving forward? He is not going to rule in my favor. This will basically be another rape. Seth will get everything he wants and according to Judge Miller, Seth has decided he now wants a son." I was already at a breaking point and we had just begun. I knew in my heart there was no way I was tenacious enough to see this long, drawn-out ordeal to the end. My worst nightmares were coming true. More than ever, I wished I had stayed with Annie Mae. On so many levels, my life was simpler.

"Brie, now is probably not a good time to tell you this but I received an answer from Seth's attorney concerning your petition for divorce. Are you sitting down?" No! No! No! I couldn't take any more. Mr. Morgan took my lack of a verbal answer as affirmation and proceeded to explain the terms of Seth's counter offer to me. "Seth is filling for sole custody of Joshua on the basis of you being emotionally unstable and financially unable to care for him. With this proposal, you would also receive no child support, of course. In addition, he claims spousal abandonment and arrears from you for damages due to your abandonment."

"What? This is crazy! How can that be?" I was screaming into the phone. Even though I somehow knew it was wrong, I took all my frustrations out on Mr. Morgan. "You didn't say anything about this possibility. You sounded so sure of yourself. You said it would end in my favor. What about all that crap about Seth forging my death certificate?" I was hysterical and realized this was not helping Seth's claim of my being emotionally unstable. Mr. Morgan allowed me to wind down.

"Brie, just because Seth makes these claims and demands, doesn't mean he will succeed in making them stick. You're going to have to trust me. We will win." Admittedly, I did not trust Mr. Morgan, or anybody for that matter, where Seth was concerned. Everyone seemed to underestimate him. Now, I was fighting Seth and Judge Miller. How could this possibly turn to my favor? "Brie, are you there?"

"Yes, I'm here," I felt spent. "Mr. Morgan, I told you from the beginning that Seth was vindictive, that he would never let me win easily. I never imagined he would actually want Josh in his life but apparently, he has decided he does which only gives him one more reason to make sure he buries me. I know it is too late to undo this but, with every fiber in my body, I have a bad feeling about this whole situation. What do we need to do for me to keep my son? Because I'm telling you right now, I will kill Seth before I let him get custody of Josh."

"Brie, don't say that. You don't mean it," Mr. Morgan apparently underestimated me as well.

"Yes. Yes, I do. Seth may have to get visitation rights but if he dares to take my son I will kill him and move to Spain for real."

"Don't think like that. I am not surprised that Seth appealed this. This isn't my hardest case, by far. We should meet tomorrow and go over the options you have. That will help you to feel better. Is two o'clock a good time for you?"

"Sure," I answered automatically and hung up on him. I had no way of knowing at the time, that by tomorrow, everything would have changed.

~ *10* ~

The Reprieve

I was sound asleep when the phone rang. I had taken two sleeping pills to get my brain to shut down after my horrendous day but, even in my fog, I knew that if the phone was ringing at this time of night, it must be important.

"Hello," I said groggily.

"Brie, its Rick. Did I wake you?" I looked at the clock and it was only eleven-fifteen, not the middle of the night as I had thought. For some reason, I felt guilty being asleep already.

"No, well, yeah, I guess I dozed off. You okay?"

"I'm fine. Wake up. I've got important news for you." I sat up in the bed and cut the nightstand lamp on trying to get the cobwebs out of my head.

"What is it?" I still sounded asleep.

"Brie, apparently you called the house while you were at the courthouse." Was that a question or statement? I tried to remember way back to this morning when I was at Judge Miller's chambers.

"Yeah, I think I did. Yeah, seems like I tried to call Tracy but she wasn't home. Why?"

"Brie, wake up! This is important!"

"Okay, okay, I'm awake," I lied.

"The conversation you had with Judge Miller is on our answering unit." He waited for a reaction from me but I still didn't understand the point.

"So?"

"Brie, you have Judge Miller admitting to many wrong doings on tape now. Your entire conversation with him is on my answering machine. Don't you understand what this means?" I shook my head as if he could see me. "Brie, this will be your Holy Grail, your salvation. Everything you discussed with him damns him and Seth. That was brilliant of you to do." Brilliant? Me? I still did not understand.

"Rick, how? What do you mean?"

"Brie, are you okay?"

"Yeah, I just took some sleeping pills to help me get to sleep and now I can't seem to wake up."

"Alright. Go back to sleep. I'll bring the tape and explain everything in the morning. Sorry I woke you but this is pretty important."

"Thanks, Rick. I'll see you in the morning." I fell back to sleep immediately.

The next morning I vaguely remembered he had called when I awoke. He had said something about Judge Miller and it being important but the rest of the conversation escaped me. As luck would have it, Rick did not come in until almost lunchtime.

"Where have you been?" I asked when he popped his head into my office. He wore the biggest smile I had ever seen on him.

"Saving your butt," he looked so sneaky and his enthusiasm was infectious. I smiled back at him and had no idea about why I was smiling. He came in, closed the door behind him, and sat down. "I've been all over town this morning- got copies made of the tape, dropped one by Morgan's office and talked to him, and brought you some lunch." He placed a to-go box on my desk.

"What are you talking about?" I asked, as I looked into the box of Chinese noodles that he had brought me. "And thanks for lunch."

"Do you remember any of our conversation last night?" he asked me incredulously.

"Vaguely, I was pretty tired."

"But you do remember the conversation you had with Judge Miller yesterday, right? All about his and Seth's affair, your demise, his making sure he gets your case, all that? You do remember all that, right?"

"Of course," I was confused.

"Brie, you called my house. Thanks to my wife keeping our old-fashioned answering machine, your entire conversation with Judge Miller is taped. He just hung himself with his own words." Suddenly, it all came to me- what Rick had meant last night about this being important.

"Rick, are you serious?" He smiled bigger, understanding that I finally got it.

"Yep! I took a copy to Morgan and we listened to it. He said he wants to postpone your meeting until tomorrow. He has a plan."

"No. I want to meet with him today and know what his plan is," I interrupted.

"Brie, he has to work out all the details first. Give him until tomorrow. Meanwhile, I'd say your worries are over." Again, everyone underestimated Seth. No tape, no matter how damning it may be, would force Seth into a corner.

"Rick, this is wonderful news. If you hadn't given me that phone yesterday, I would have never been able to do that."

"At first, I thought it was brilliant of you but, after hearing your surprise last night, I'm guessing you didn't plan it this way?" It was a rhetorical question and we both laughed.

"So, what did Mr. Morgan say when he heard it?"

"He was ecstatic. He couldn't stop smiling. Although he did say that it wouldn't be admissible in court because neither of you were aware you were being recorded; however, if you had been aware of it, then it would have been. He also said that, even though it's not admissible in court, it will be a most powerful tool to subjugate Judge Miller and Seth. Judge Miller will definitely not be able to reside over your case, if it even goes to court."

"Wait- you mean it may not go to court now?" That alone made me happy.

"Not sure. Guess we'll wait and see what Morgan's plan is." Rick stood up then and I knew this conversation was over. I still had a million questions but they would have to wait.

The next day, I asked Rick if he would go with me to Mr. Morgan's office but he had already promised Tracy that he would go Christmas shopping with her.

"There won't be any need for me today, anyway," he added to lessen my disappointment. "Morgan's probably just going to lay out his plan for you. You can fill me in later." Rick had never been one to get as excited about drama as most people but it still surprised me that he would not want to know the plan today. I was about to burst from anticipation. Since Rick and Tracy were shopping, he had Tracy pick him up at the office so I could borrow his car again. Mr. Morgan's office was much too far to take a bus and a cab would be quite expensive. I decided that if I ever did get money from Seth, the first thing I was going to do was buy a car.

"Good afternoon, Brie," Mr. Morgan said as he entered the conference room. I was beginning to feel at home in this room and Mr. Morgan's smile today made me feel even more comfortable. I smiled back. "Well, isn't this a rare turn of events?"

"Yeah, I guess so," I added. Mr. Morgan took his time laying out several papers in front of him. At last, he sat down and cleared his throat.

"I've considered several plans of action and, after consulting with colleagues and knowing your anxiety level is maxed out, have decided we will use this evidence to force them to settle out of court."

"Oh, good!" I exclaimed. He smiled his wrinkled smile at me, satisfied that I was happy with his decision.

"I will advise an informal hearing. This will be as intimidating as possible for them and less stressful for you. Also, the element of surprise will be on our part as I fully expect them to think we are requesting such because of our own fear of a trial."

"Okay, sounds good," I repeated. I did not understand all of his legal jargon but not having to go to court sounded good to me. "When will we have it?"

"I've already requested it for the first of the year. We are on the docket for January twelfth, which is a Tuesday."

"That far away?"

"That is actually pretty quick. I do expect Seth to request temporary visitation rights, especially in light of the holidays. I pushed for the earliest possible date. That's the only reason you got it that close. I suggest you enjoy the few days left before Christmas and then New Year. We'll reconvene before the date to go over everything so we're best prepared."

"Wait! I can't possibly forget about all this until then. At least give me an idea what a hearing entails."

"Briefly, we will meet at the court house. Judge Miller will probably reside but," he raised his hand when he saw me about to object, "we will immediately request a new judge to be appointed pending evidence to be presented. After that is settled, we will allow them to present their claims about your incompetency, lack of income, etc. Basically, we'll give them enough rope to hang themselves. When it's our time, we'll present Judge Miller's affair with Seth, Seth's physical, mental, and verbal abuse, Seth's forgery of your death certificate, etc. When we are finished, the verdict will go in your favor. To be honest, we could probably push this to have Seth and Judge Miller disbarred but, that wouldn't help your child-support income any." He seemed so confident. It gave me a sense of wellness that I hoped I could maintain until after this was over.

I took Mr. Morgan's advice and focused on Christmas. I did not want to infringe on Rick and Tracy's family plans and it just did not feel right to go back to Annie Mae and Poppa. We had usually spent Christmas morning separately anyway. So, I decided to enjoy my two babies with a quiet day. As expected, the children were very excited with their new toys. Since the weather was not too bad, we ventured outside after a quick breakfast so they could ride their bike and push-car. We were outside a little over an hour and, completely by accident, I happen to look up just as Seth rode by in his car. My first thought was to run inside. Then, I decided I would not. If Seth were stupid enough to try something, I would call the police. I patted my cell phone securely tucked in my coat pocket. As of yet, we had not even established his paternity to Josh so he had no believability to argue his right to see his son on Christmas day. He did not ride by anymore and we enjoyed another hour or so outside before we went back in so I could start dinner. I knew the kids could not care less about what we ate but I did want to have at least some traditional fanfare so I had planned a roasted chicken breast, new potatoes, green peas, and baby carrots. The vegetables were the only ones that Josh would eat and one breast was enough for all of us because Katie still was not a fan of meat.

As the kids played with their other toys inside and I was busy in the kitchen cooking, my mind wandered. I loved my kids beyond comprehension but there was a lonely pang of emptiness inside me. I did not spend much time thinking about male attention but every once in a while, like today, I wished I had someone to wrap their arms around me and present me with a surprise gift. My mind then wandered to Seth. Gifts were one area in which he did not falter, minus the arms around me, of course, but he was generous to a fault with his money. He would often claim it was to, "keep up appearances", that any family of his necessitated the best clothes, toys, vacations, etcetera. I had never been in-love with him, but I had to admit, now that we had a great distance between us, that there was a part of him that I loved. I wondered if there was a part of him that loved me, even if it were not the way I needed to be loved. I wondered what he was feeling today. What would compel him to ride by our apartment on Christmas day? Did he yearn for a child? Was he hurting?

"Mom, Josh broke my doll!" Katie screamed from the other room, breaking my daydream. I went to the living room and Katie presented her new baby doll with one arm.

"Where's the other arm?" I asked somewhat impatiently. She looked around her on the floor and found it, handing it to me quickly. I snapped the doll's amputated arm back in place and gave it a good push, securing it in its former position then handing her the now intact doll.

"Thanks, mom!" Katie exclaimed as if I had surgically saved the arm. I turned and went back to the kitchen to put the finishing touches on our holiday meal. If only adult life could be so easily fixed. Again, I thought of Seth and wondered what had driven him to seek out his son. Was it just the sentimentality of Christmas? Was he spying? Perhaps I had painted the portrait of him unfairly in my mind. Admittedly, he had done many wrongs to Katie and to me but maybe I had focused only on the negative. After all, it is human nature to remember the traumatic and forget the pleasantries of everyday life. Maybe I had handled the negativity poorly, running away like a spoiled child in the night with no word, no trace of where I had gone. Without a doubt, Seth knew why I had fled. Perhaps he wished to apologize or explain or, better yet, make amends for his behavior.

I was relieved when dinner was complete. It is the curse of housework that it occupies one's hands but not their mind. Skeletons that haunted a person could always sense when the mind was empty.

"Dinner's ready. Y'all wash up." I called to the living room as I headed that way knowing full well that announcing dinner would not start a stampede toward the table. "Come on. It's time to eat. Go wash your hands- now."

"But we're playing. It's Christmas!" Katie announced as the spokesperson for them.

"Well, you still have to eat on Christmas. Come feed Sparks and then go on and wash up." Reluctantly Katie stood up and came to the kitchen to feed Sparks and Josh, as usual, followed her. After I got them in their seats and plated up their food, I sat down. "Let's say grace." I took their hands and bowed my head. We were not in the habit of praying at every meal. In fact, we often sat in front of the television while we ate. It was a habit that I did not like but seemed powerless to break. By the time I got home from work and fixed them dinner, I just wanted to collapse and relax. "Dear Lord, thank you for this meal we are about to eat. Thank you especially for this year, for bringing us through a hard time, and for blessing us abundantly. Amen."

It had been a quiet Christmas, no big ordeal, no visitors, no extended family but, as I lay down that night, I felt a sense of calm and peace. It had been a terrific day and yet, again, I missed the absent arms that I longed to hold me as I fell asleep that night. It will be nice to get past the holidays so that all this emotional upheaval would retreat from whence it came.

The week between Christmas and New Year's Day was hectic. Katie was out of school so I had to take her to the office with me. She found it exciting for a while but within the first few hours, she was bored. We had brought many of her toys, even a puzzle and coloring book, but she had whizzed through them all and demanded my attention. Because it was the off-season, I was able to give her some attention that would have been impossible the following month. Yet, it was not enough. She was eleven now, almost twelve, and her ideas of quality time with her mother were changing so fast that I could not keep up.

"Can I go to a friend's house or something?" she finally asked.

"Baby, not today- maybe you could find somewhere to play tomorrow." I told her absent-mindedly as I continued to look over the end-of-year reports.

"I shoulda brought Sparks," she mumbled. After lunch, a picnic basket I made to try to dress-up the fact that we were not going out, Katie grew particularly bored. I finally conceded to let her walk the halls for a bit just to get her out of my office. When she had been gone for some time, I decided I had better check on her. I popped my head into each office as I went. No one had seen her. I began to grow apprehensive. Then I went to Rick's office. Katie was there bombarding Rick with questions.

"Katie, Mr. Rick has work to do. Come on." I tried to sound nonchalant but I was embarrassed. The other employees who had small children put them in daycare when school was out. I did that in the summer, but if it was only a few days or a week, like the holidays, I brought her with me. I had never officially asked Rick if that was all right. Since he had never voiced otherwise, I assumed it did not bother him but I did not want to push my luck by having her intrude upon him.

"She's fine," Rick stated, "I'm putting her to work."

"Oh, and what do you have her doing?" I smiled.

"She's cleaning my office, putting these papers in the correct file, and then I'm going to have her put them in alphabetical order in the cabinet."

"Wow! That's pretty enterprising, isn't it?"

"Not really. She's a smart girl."

"Are you sure you don't want me to take her back?"

"No, she's fine. You're always telling me to clean my office. Now, I am." He forced a fake smile that looked more like a chipmunk than human. I laughed aloud.

"Alright then, let me know if it gets to be too much." Rick waved his hand at me as if to shoo me away so I turned and retreated to my office. The rest of the afternoon went by quickly since I was able to focus on my work and by five o'clock. I had finished the year-end reports. Tomorrow I could begin entering the last figures into the computer so I could issue tax reports. Katie and I left the office a few minutes early. I had a terrible headache so we grabbed hamburgers on the way home for dinner. I put the kids to bed a little early and took medicine before I went to bed.

The next morning, the phone startled me awake. It was Tracy insisting that Katie spend the day with her since she was watching her grandkids. Katie could play with them and give me a break. Rick was already on his way over to get her. I jumped up and got her dressed and peeled an apple for her breakfast. I knew Tracy would feed her well all day so I was not too worried about her eating such a light breakfast. After Rick left with Katie, I got Josh up to begin his day. I still felt somewhat frazzled from the quick start and as I rushed out of the door, I forgot my cell phone. I had only used it twice, not counting the day I accidently taped Judge Miller's conversation, so I was not yet in the habit of taking if off charge and carrying it. As Josh and I got on the bus, I realized I'd left it. It would be all right, I surmised. After all, I had been without one for years. It was a decision I would live to regret.

~ *11* ~

Confrontation

When Josh and I got off the bus nearest his nursery, I proceeded as I had many mornings before to walk the block to his school. Just as I came upon it, I saw Seth's car parked in the front of the daycare. My heart skipped a beat but my feet managed to continue toward the front door. If I could just get Josh in and safe, I felt I could take care of myself.

"Brie," Seth called to me as I turned away from his car to move towards the door. He had stepped out of his car. He was dressed in a casual way, unlike the usual suits he wore. He was still just as handsome as ever and I had to admit it was no wonder I had fallen for his charms that first fateful sunny day.

"Go away, Seth. You're not supposed to be anywhere near me." I called back, stepping up my pace.

"Brie, I just want to talk, please." I kept walking and tried to hurry up Josh. I would have picked him up but my hands were full with his bag and my work and purse. "Brie, we can work this out without all this legal red tape. I don't want to hurt you." Oh, how I wish I could believe that, I thought. Could I? "Brie, I know Josh is my son. I want to be a father to him. You know I love kids. I could help you if you'd just stop and listen.

Just five minutes. What have you got to lose?" I turned to look at him and he looked more pitiful than I had ever seen him. Maybe he was sincere. My glance at him served as a nonverbal affirmation to him and he began to walk towards me- not in his usual self-assured way but more like a puppy shimmying shyly towards the pack. I looked at his face and he looked tired. I was almost at the front door so I decided I could talk with him here. If things went south, I could easily get into the front door of the daycare.

"What do you want, Seth?" I tried to sound forceful. He was about ten feet from me now and my heart beat rapidly. He slowed slightly and looked me straight in the eyes.

"Brie," he spoke softly as if I were a frightened child he did not want to startle, "I know we've had our differences but we have a son now. I never thought I'd have a son and I want to be a father to him." He looked directly at Josh then and I could see his eyes were misty. Had I really misjudged him that much?

"Seth," I stammered, unsure of what I was about to say, "I'm not trying to keep you from your son but I will not let you hurt him."

"Hurt him?" he seemed genuinely astonished. "I want to love him."

"Like you loved me?" I didn't mean to say it aloud. He turned back to me and stared at me intently.

"I did love you, Brie. Maybe not in the way a woman wants a man to love her but I did love you. I cannot help that which I am not capable of feeling." He actually seemed so vulnerable that I believed him.

"No, I suppose you couldn't help that but you could have been honest with me about it." That was really the basis of my hurt, wasn't it- that our entire relationship seemed to be a lie?

"I couldn't even be honest with myself, Brie. I was living a lie; how could I be honest with you when I couldn't be honest with myself?" That seemed a fair estimation of his dilemma. "Can we just talk? Not here," he looked around as if we stood outside a prison. "Let's just go somewhere and sit down and talk."

"No, Seth. You're not even supposed to be here."

"Why do you keep saying that?"

"Because of the restraining order," I answered.

"Restraining order? I haven't been served with a restraining order." His countenance changed then, not back to the harsh one I was familiar with but not the gentle one I had witnessed this morning either. "You took out a restraining order on me?" He sounded hurt.

"Seth, what do you expect? You keep showing up, uninvited, even riding by my apartment. Then, the night you actually came, you almost slapped me. I'm not the same child you abused for so many years. I'm not going to stand by and let you terrorize me." I was so proud of myself for being honest and forthright.

"Brie, I promise, I am not trying to terrorize you. It's just that, well, you frustrate me to a point, like no one has ever done. Sorry, I know that is no excuse. What can I say? You've made up your mind." He looked back at Josh who was getting antsy and trying to pull his hand out of mine. "Can I hold him?" Intuitively, I pulled Josh to me. "Brie, you act like I'm a monster. My god, I just want to touch my son for the first time." Maybe I was being paranoid. What did I expect him to do, run away with him?

"Okay," I shocked myself. Seth leaned down in front of Josh getting on his level.

"Hey, little buddy," Seth said kindly. He held out his hand to Josh and Josh looked up at me.

"It's okay," I urged. Josh didn't move.

"Josh, my name is Seth. I'm your daddy," Seth sniffed slightly and I could tell he was tearing up. My heart hurt for him and for the first time, I could sympathize with his plight. Josh moved slightly forward then and put his hand in Seth's extended hand. "Can I pick you up?" he asked Josh. Josh did not answer. My nerves kicked into high gear, ready to snatch Josh at any moment I felt he was threatened. Josh stepped another step closer to Seth and Seth picked him up as if he were an expensive and fragile china doll. As Seth stood up erectly, his eyes never looked away from Josh and Josh returned the stare. "Brie, thank you so much?" Suddenly, I felt like an intruder upon this intimate moment- a father's first connection with his son. After a few minutes, Josh seemed to relax and Seth pulled him to his chest, hugging him tightly. Josh put his arms around Seth and returned the gesture. Tears slipped down Seth's closed eyes and, for the first time, I felt genuine love from him.

After a few silent minutes, Seth asked Josh a few superficial questions that Josh did not answer. Josh had never been a very verbal child but he could talk in complete sentences so I was surprised he did not speak to Seth at all. Finally, Seth put him back down and turned to me.

"Brie, I want us to settle this affably. There's no reason for us to create an expensive and messy divorce. You know as well as I do that the only winners in such cases are the attorneys."

"I'm a little confused, Seth. You seem genuine now but I need answers. Why did you kill me off? You say you couldn't be honest with yourself when we were married, and yet, you're engaged to another poor girl who, I assume, is clueless about it. You say you only want to love Josh but you have your lawyer claim I am an unfit mother. I feel like you know better than that so why would you try to claim it?" I tried to look him in the eyes but he looked so helpless and it made my resolve to be tough more difficult so instead I looked down at Josh.

"You're right, Brie. I'll talk to my lawyer. Are you open to resolving this matter so we can just get on with the business of building a relationship that works for Josh's best interest?"

"Of course," I answered. Was that too much to ask for? Could Seth actually put all this behind him? Could he concede? Was my judgment that misguided?

"Okay, well, I'll let you two go. How are you getting to work?" He asked as he turned slightly to leave. I did not want to tell him but, after I thought about it, I knew he already knew the answer so I told him by bus.

"Your office is on the way to mine. You want a ride?"

"No, Seth. I'm fine, thanks," I could not understand this new man standing before me.

"Brie, that's silly. I'm driving right past it. Take Josh on in and I'll wait for you. I can take you. I won't hurt you, I promise." My instinct screamed a resounding, "no". My mind scolded me for being so negative. After all, hadn't he changed? "I'll wait while you check him in. If you decide to take the bus when you come out, that's fine." Then he waved to Josh and with a voice I had never heard him use, said, "Bye, bye little buddy," to Josh. Josh waved good-by to Seth and we went in the building. I felt safe in here. Josh kept looking back at Seth as if he knew. Once I got Josh settled in his classroom and headed back toward the front door, I noticed by the clock on the wall that I was now late. I had missed my usual bus and would have to wait forty-five minutes on the next one. I started to call Rick from the nursery for a ride but I knew he was probably already at work. Maybe I should just let Seth take me. I did not honestly think he would hurt me now.

Seth sat in his car on the street in front of the daycare. I walked up to the car and he rolled down the passenger's side window with his electric button.

"So?" was all he said.

"Alright," I reached for the door handle just as I heard Seth click the unlock button. The car was obviously expensive with soft leather seats and all the luxuries of wealth. He turned the radio off once I was in and buckled up and he looked at me. I was not sure what his expression meant. It was almost an affectionate glimpse and he smiled so I smiled back at him.

"Just like old times, eh?" he said. I hope not, I thought but managed to keep my thoughts to myself. Seth looked behind him for traffic then pulled out slowly. The silence was awkward and I wished he had left the radio on. Finally, I could stand it no longer and made an attempt at conversation.

"So, what brought on this big change?" I tried to sound casual as if we were discussing the weather.

"What do you mean?"

"Well, you know, you seem so happy now." Seth took his eyes off the road and peeked at me sideways.

"I was always happy, Brie. You were the one who walked around as if your world consisted of gargoyles and witchery." Seriously? Surely, he did not think that.

"Huh, I guess we were just poor communicators then. I always thought you hated me."

"I didn't hate you, Brie. I resented you sometimes. I mean, you only wanted to be around Katie. I needed you to take on some responsibility around the house and you seemed, well, miserable, like I said."

"I wasn't miserable exactly, just lonely, I think. You were never home. You would not allow me into your life. Even though we were married, we were like strangers." He kept giving me side-glances as if I spoke heresy. "What? You don't agree? Surely, you couldn't have been content."

"You know, Brie, you really haven't changed much."

"Ha!" I spat, "I've change completely. I had to grow up quickly and in the worst way."

"Well, you brought it on yourself. No one told you to run out like an idiot. You could have stayed and continued to be treated like a queen. Josh could have had an appropriate welcoming into the world. You lacked for *nothing* and you threw it all away." Something about his emphasis on "nothing" made me sense the old Seth.

"Nothing?" I repeated, "I lacked for everything that matters- love, affection, companionship, even sex. The only basic needs you fulfilled for me was food and shelter. For that I was grateful but there is more to life than survival, Seth."

"I tried to give you all those things and more. You were a spoiled brat who didn't appreciate anything I did for you or your brat daughter." His voice rose slightly as he went on. I could see this conversation escalating into one of our old arguments and I was beginning to regret accepting the ride. I decided I needed to back off from this confrontation and keep the atmosphere cordial.

"Seth," I intentionally softened my voice while taking a mental note of how much further we had to go before we reached my office, "I'm sorry. I didn't mean to rile your anger, I just,"

"Anger? You leave me after all I did for you with no trace, no word, not even so much as a freaking note and *now* you worry that you've roused my anger?" Uh, oh, I was beginning to sweat. I pulled my purse closer thinking I could grab my phone if need be and remembered I had forgotten it. "You have no idea what you put me through! I was humiliated. At first, I made up a stupid lie, thinking you'd come home as unexpectedly as you left after you got hungry. But, no. Then, I made up some elaborate story so I could save face, worrying every day that, after I had announced your death, that you would then show up and I'd have to explain *that*. You left a huge mess, Brie, which I had to clean up! You are a selfish, narcissistic bit". I cut him off.

"Stop it!" I screamed. "I thought you had changed but I was obviously wrong. I'm not going to listen to your abuse any longer. Stop the car. I want out." I demanded.

"If I let you out, it will not be because you want out. It will be because I'm ready to *put you out*. I tried to be nice to you but you won't let anyone be nice to you. I guess, deep inside, you know you're a worthless piece of crap." I was getting very nervous. I looked around, trying to get my bearings. We could not be more than two or three blocks from my office. Seth had gone a different route than I took and I felt a little disoriented.

"Seth, let's not do this. We were doing well. Just let me out and let's forget about this conversation." I felt panicky. All I could think about was getting away but I knew I was trapped. I was at his mercy. I knew that regardless of what Seth wanted to do to me, I would be powerless to stop him. He could beat me, rape me, or even murder me and no one would know. No one knew I had not taken the bus this morning. No one would find me if he did not want me found. I had been a fool for falling for him the first time and downright stupid for believing him this time. Seth began to smile a wicked smile and forced a laugh.

"Oh, yeah, now you want to forget about it. The little bird wants to fly the coop again, eh?"

"Seth, please, let's not do anything we'll regret," I realized I was begging. In a last ditch effort to subdue him I decided to pull out my only ammunition. "If you hurt me, I'll tell Tiffany what you are." Seth pulled over in a parking lot that was empty. It was a shopping area and it was still too early for them to be open. I reached for the door handle to get out and Seth leaned over grabbing my hair on the back of my head and pulled me back to him. I gasped.

"You little snitch. You will not ruin my life with all your lies. I am to be married in a few months and you will not repeat to anyone what you think you know. I am not going to be blackmailed by the likes of you." It seemed odd that he chose the same words that Judge Miller had said to me. "Do you understand?" his voice was low, throaty, and menacing. I had no choice but to nod my head. His grip loosened then and I reached once again for the door handle but before I could get out of the car, Seth interjected. "Get out." I got out of the door and stepped away from his car just in time before he sped off.

A sense of relief flooded over me. I was safe. I had learned a valuable lesson without enduring any real harm. He could be as diabolical as he could sweet. I must never forget this again. I looked around and realized I was only one block from my office so I began walking. The cold, fresh air and exercise helped to calm my nerves. It only took me about five minutes to reach my building. I went straight to my office and collapsed. This was a nightmare, possibly bigger than I could have imagined. All the sentiment I had felt on Christmas day was gone. Seth was a bully, an egotistic, selfish bully. I had accused everyone else of underestimating him and, in a strange turn of events, once again, I had underestimated him myself. Well, no more! I had been bullied my entire life, from my mother, from Lonnie who had taken me against my will, from Dr. Carnes and Major Whitcomes, and from Seth. I was not a child any longer and there was no gym teacher to tattle to about this. I would do what every underdog must do at some point if they are to gain their self-respect. I must fight back. I would fight with every fiber of my being. Seth may have won another battle but I was determined he would not win the war.

~ *12* ~

A Welcome Distraction

I was afraid to tell Rick what had happened because I realized in retrospect that I had been stupid to get in Seth's car; however, I also knew the truth would come out so I decided to confess.

"You what?" Rick was more upset than I had imagined he would be.

"I know, I know," I tried to defend myself.

"Brie, for heaven's sake, what were you thinking?"

"I don't know. It was late. I missed the bus. I forgot my phone. He was being so nice. I thought maybe he had changed." There, my guts spilt.

"Don't you ever do that again! And go call Morgan and find out why Seth hasn't been served those papers yet." I hesitated. Were we finished? "Go." I turned and left. Mr. Morgan was out of the office until after the holidays so at least I did not have to deal with his anger also. Rick insisted on giving me a ride to get Joshua and then to his house to pick up Katie.

"You'll stay for dinner, dear," Tracy stated rather than asked. I obeyed daughterly. I didn't want to upset Rick twice in one day. Dinner conversation was good and, of course, Tracy's culinary skills were superb. As I helped her finish the dishes, I told her about my morning.

"Yes, Rick told me. I won't lie, Brie. That was very foolish of you. I'm quite surprised. You always seemed so afraid of him and then you just go and jump in the car with him? I don't understand."

"If you could have seen him with Josh, you may understand. He was like a completely different person- so gentle, sweet, and caring."

"A man will be different with his baby son than with a former lover," she stated matter-of-factly.

"Yes, I suppose you're right. Well, I learned my lesson and no harm was done, so…"

"No harm done, eh?" Tracy gave me a look I could not read.

"No, I'm fine, a little shaken for a while but I'm fine." I could tell from the look she gave me that she was not convinced. Rick drove us home after we finished the dishes. Once we arrived, he told me he would pick us all up in the morning and take Katie back to his house, Josh to the nursery, and I could ride in with him. He seemed pretty adamant and, again, I did not want to rile him for a second time today, so I agreed.

The next morning, Rick arrived as planned. We dropped Katie off with Tracy and then Josh. Seth was nowhere to be found. Then Rick headed in a different direction than our office.

"Where are you going?"

"You'll see." We did not talk much in the car and I figured he was still upset with me for yesterday's infraction. I tried to make small talk but Rick had never been one to feel like he had to fill the silence so I finally gave up. A few minutes later, we arrived at a used car dealership. When Rick got out of the car, a tall gentleman came up and held out his hand.

"Top of the morning to ya," he said in a loud, boisterous voice. Rick shook his hand but cut right to the chase.

"I have an appointment with Peter," he told the loud man, whose face shown all the disappointment a salesman could show.

"Sure, sure, right this way," he turned his back to us and began walking into the glass showroom.

"Rick, what are you doing?" I asked as we trailed behind the salesman. I was getting a bad feeling of his intentions and I absolutely refused to allow Rick to buy me a car. He ignored me and kept walking. "Rick?" No answer.

"Hey Rick," a voice from the back of the showroom called as we entered the door. "I saw you pull up and was getting the keys. Here you go. Wanna take her for a spin?" Rick held out his hand and took the keys, shaking Peter's hand with the other. The tall salesman who had greeted us was already heading back to the parking lot.

"Peter, this is Brie, the girl I was telling you about. Brie, this is Peter McCarthy." The name sounded familiar. "He's one of my old friends and a client for twenty years or so." Oh, that is where I had heard the name. I had seen it a hundred times. Peter was pretty well off. He had several car dealerships and dallied in a few other businesses as well. "Where is it parked?" Rick asked Peter.

"Come with me. I'll show you," Peter turned and headed back to the parking lot we had just come from. "She's a few years old but a beauty, like I told you on the phone- low miles, clean record, a real find," he explained as we walked. How was I going to get through to Rick that, if he was doing this for me, it was unacceptable? I decided to wait until we were in the car alone. After a long walk, we came up on a small Honda Civic. It was white and had four doors. My heart sank as I thought of the possibility of owning it. It would simplify my life so much but I knew, there was no way I would accept a gift this big from anyone, most especially my boss. "Okay, y'all take it around the block. When you come back, I'll have the paperwork ready." Wow! He sure was presumptuous. To my surprise, Rick got in the driver's seat. I was embarrassed. All this time, I had thought Rick was looking at a car for me. Now who was being presumptuous? We rode about a block away from the dealership and Rick gunned it. The pick-up the car possessed surprised me. Rick made a few more risky maneuvers and his ability to handle himself impressed me. I would not have thought it from an accountant who sits behind a desk all day.

"Handles pretty good. Top safety rating, too." He spoke but not in a way that expected an answer. "Do you like it?"

"Yeah, it's nice. Are you getting it for yourself or Tracy?" He gave me an odd look. "What? One of your sons?"

"Brie, I'm not buying it for anyone. You're buying it for yourself."

"Rick, I wish. I couldn't possibly afford this."

"Yes, you can. I know what I pay you and about what your bills are and I've done the math. You can afford it. Peter's giving it to me at costs. You won't find a better deal."

"Well, that's really nice of him but I'm sure the payment would still be more than I could do. I don't have a down-payment. Then, I'd have to get insurance. Rick, it's a very nice gesture to try to help me but I'm not quite ready. Maybe once I'm getting child support in a few months."

"Brie, did you notice you didn't get a bonus this Christmas?"

"Yeah, but that's okay. I know you've had extra expenses on you in this new office. Its okay, Rick. You aren't responsible for me. I'll get by…"

"Brie, good grief you can be a chatty-patty when you want to be. Listen, your Christmas bonus is the down payment. The payments will be barely over a hundred dollars a month. I know you can do that. The insurance premium will be low because it's a safe car and therefore at a good rate. Plus, I'm assuming since you haven't had a car that went over fifty miles an hour since I've known you that you have a pretty good driving record, right?"

"Rick," I was at a loss for words.

"Don't get all mushy on me now." He pulled over into a shopping parking lot. "You drive back and see if you like it." Then he jumped out and began walking around to my side. I got out, stunned, and walked to the driver's side. After adjusting the seat to accommodate my shorter legs, I looked around. It was spotless, practically new looking.

"How old is it?" I knew it was not new but it was in excellent condition.

"Three years old, which is perfect because you never wanna buy a brand-new car. They lose most of their appreciation the first couple years but, it has low miles so, it's perfect." I ran my hands across the cloth seats, then the dash. It was overwhelming to think this would be mine.

"Rick, tha…" He raised his hand to stop me, "No, Rick. I am going to thank you."

"I haven't done anything, except decide for you what you'll spend your Christmas bonus on." He winked at me. I drove back to the lot and Rick instructed me to park right up front. We walked back to Peter's office and, as promised, Peter was waiting.

"Coffee?" he asked.

"No, thanks," I replied. Rick just shook his head.

"Peter, can you fill it up with gas? Also, looks like it's going to need an oil change in about a thousand miles, how about a freebee for her first one? I could not believe Rick. Peter was giving him the car at costs and he was asking for more? I expected Peter to refuse but, instead, he laughed and patted Rick on the back.

"Always one for a bargain, aren't you?" Then Peter walked out of his office with the keys. Rick and I looked over the paperwork while he was gone. I was surprised how low the price was after Peter's discount. Then I scanned down to see how much Rick had put down as a down payment. I was stunned. It was twice what he had given me last year. Rick had me sign the paperwork, that already had my name, address, and pertinent information typed. Apparently, Rick had all the details worked out. Finally, Peter came back and sat down, looking over the paperwork.

"Alright, miss," he handed me the keys. "Here you go."

"That's it?" It all seemed so simple.

"Yep. Rick handled everything when he came over yesterday. You've got yourself a new car with a full tank of gas." He eyed Rick when he mentioned the gas. When we walked outside, Rick moved Josh's car seat into my new car for me and I followed him to the office. I drove on in disbelief that I would never have to worry about the bus route or getting a ride again.

This would be a short week since we were off for New Year's Eve. The kids had been ecstatic about the new car and insisted we drive somewhere. We got up early New Year's Eve, packed a picnic lunch and headed to Stone Mountain. I had never been there and decided it was high time we did something exciting. It was only about a thirty-minute ride from Atlanta and the views on the way were exciting to see. Just riding in our new car was exciting to us, regardless of where we headed.

The day was a magical experience. Stone Mountain Park was still celebrating the Christmas season and had the characters of Rudolph the Red-Nosed Reindeer and Bumble the Abominable Snow Monster greeting the kids. At first, Josh was scared, but after he saw Katie's enthusiasm, he warmed up long enough for me to get a picture on my new phone. Throughout the day, they had many shows like “Forever Christmas” and “Holly Jolly Cabaret, Toyrific!” We had never seen anything like it before and none of us could stop smiling. We had our picture taken with a beautiful Snow Angel along a stunning tunnel of lights. Later, we went aboard the “Sing-along Train”, saw the story of the first Christmas, and listened to carols. After lunch, we sat long enough to watch “The Polar Express 4-D Experience”. Finally, that night we stood in amazement as we watched the Christmas Parade with its whimsical floats. Just when we thought it was all over, there was a magnificent celebration of fireworks. It was a day like no other we had ever experienced. I had spent more money than I planned but decided on the way home that it was worth every penny. It was a day we would never forget.

It was late when we got home. Katie and Josh were both sound asleep. I had to wake Katie but carried Josh. I was glad it had been dark when we left so that I remembered to leave our porch light on so I could see. We were all so very exhausted and Katie went straight back to sleep when I lay her down. Josh never even budged as I put on his pajamas for the night. Finally, I lay down, dog-tired yet happy. Tomorrow would be a new year. It seemed to me that each year had gotten better and better with this past year being the best I had ever had in my life. I could not help but hope that, once I was getting child-support and had this case behind me, that this year would be the best yet. I fell asleep with a smile on my face and hope in my heart. It did not occur to me that night that every privilege comes with a price.

I slept particularly well that last night of the year. So well, that it was Josh who woke me up the next morning. The cold, winter air of the previous day’s exercise had worn us all out. Josh and I sat cuddled up on the couch when Katie came from her room rubbing the sleep from her eyes.

"What are we gonna do today, momma?"

"Rest!" I laughed. Just then, the phone rang. Tracy wanted us to come for her traditional New Year's Day lunch with greens and black-eyed peas to insure prosperity for us all in the following year. I could not resist. The kids and I showered and dressed quickly and drove to Rick's house.

I knew when I pulled up and saw Kyle's car that he, Elaine, and the kids were here. Shortly after we arrived, Josh and his fiancée, Trish, arrived. Mark, Tracy told me later, did fly home for Christmas Eve and Christmas day but had flown back the day after.

"I hate I missed Mark," I told Tracy, "I didn't get a chance to get to know him at the party." Remembering the party brought a blush to my cheeks that I hoped no one noticed.

"Yes, well, he can't stay in one place for too long, dear. He gets antsy." She laughed but I could see the pain behind her smile. She must miss him terribly despite having her other two sons and her grandkids here. "If we could tie him down long enough, I'd fix him up with you." She laughed again.

"No, you wouldn't," Kyle said as he walked into the kitchen, "Brie deserves better than Mark."

"Oh, now, you behave yourself. Your brother's not here to defend himself," Tracy scolded. Elaine, Trish, and I helped Tracy finish up the meal and set the table. Once we all sat, the conversation never ceased. I never felt like an intruder in this close family. Haley and J.R. played well with Katie and Josh, who I called, "my Josh" when I was at their house to differentiate from Tracy and Rick's son, Josh. After dinner, the kids reconvened outside as the men folks watched them play and we women cleaned up. It was an old-fashioned arrangement but no one had any complaints.

"Brie, have you met Hazen Thatcher?" Rick asked me as we joined them on the back porch.

"No, I don't believe I have. His name sounds vaguely familiar. Where would I know him from?"

"He's been a client of mine for years. Nice guy. Pretty well off, too." Rick always seemed to talk in short choppy sentences when he bothered to talk at all. "He's been traveling the world for a while and he's finally decided to settle down in Atlanta. He'll be here on Tuesday to go over his paperwork. I'd like you to sit in on the meeting."

"That's fine. What time?"

"Oh, I'm not sure. It's on my calendar. In the morning sometime."

"Sounds good." It was a simple conversation. I forgot it almost as soon as we changed the subject and yet, I would never forget its impact.

~ 13 ~

Strange Turn Of Events

Tuesday morning came quickly enough and I dressed slightly better than normal, remembering at the last minute that Rick and I had a meeting with a very important client. I was not one to doll over my wardrobe or dally with a lot of make-up so I still wasn't as up-to-par as most of the women in our office. I knew one day that I would probably want to spend a little time on a makeover if I were ever going to attract a man. Right now, I knew romance was not in the cards for me. After I dropped the kids off and arrived at the office, I made coffee, turned on the lights, and all the usual day's routine I had done for so long now. Then I went to my office and looked up Hazen Thatcher's record to become familiar with his file before he arrived.

"Hey, you ready?" Rick asked as he popped in before I had a chance to read Hazen's file.

"Oh, sure. I thought it was at ten?" I had looked at Rick's calendar the previous day to confirm the time.

"It was but he got in town early and came straight here from the airport so, we'll just get started." I felt a little uneasy going in unprepared but I knew that Rick was very familiar with all his clients so I would probably have very little to do with the meeting other than taking notes to post in the computer later. Rick headed to the conference room. We could never meet anyone in his office because it stayed such a mess.

Our conference room was beautiful. Tracy had decorated it. The conference table was white wood with a high-gloss sheen.

The chairs were simple with white leather seats and backs and trimmed in a shiny silver metal. The pictures on the wall had an eclectic range. Two large paintings on one wall were free form with multiple colors splashed against the blank canvas. The other wall had character silhouettes in black and white of various sizes and shapes. Tracy had decorated it all very tastefully and it gave an elegant appeal.

I walked in the conference room behind Rick, not thinking anything other than this was a regular meeting with another client I had not met.

"Hazen, this is my assistant Brie Taylor. Brie-Hazen Thatcher," Rick introduced us as he walked into the room but he still stood positioned between the two of us. Once Rick and I were both entirely in the room, Rick moved to the right to sit down. That is when I saw Hazen for the first time. He was like no one I had ever seen before. He appeared several years older than I, probably mid-thirties. His eyes were black as coal and I was immediately mesmerized. His hair, shiny and very dark brown, was slightly longer than his shoulders but pulled neatly back in a ponytail. His side-burns came down slightly in a manly way but not overpowering. His skin, oh, his skin was olive and tanned. I assessed his physique and swallowed hard. His build was like a man who worked hard outside every day. I had no idea what he did for a living or anything about him; for all I knew, he was married with a dozen children but if he asked me to marry him right here and now, I would accept.

"Uh, hi," I stammered. What an idiot I was around handsome men. He held out his hand and I was afraid to take it, afraid I would not let it go.

"Hello Ms. Taylor." His voice was deep and smooth and had a slight accent that I could not distinguish. He was like a fairy-tale hero, no, more like a trash-novel hero. I felt I was dreaming. I reached out my hand to accept his but our eyes never looked away from one another. I leaned forward slightly to meet his hand and, because I was not looking in front of me, I tripped over the chair leg and fell forward- right into him. He caught me quickly and helped me back on my feet. My face burned crimson with embarrassment and I looked down to avoid his gaze. I was never good around men. My inexperience made me self-conscious and klutzy.

"Oh my gosh, I am so sorry," I managed to get out as I frantically tried to regain my equilibrium.

"It's quite alright, Ms.Taylor. I don't know how you ladies ever walk in those high-heels." His arms embraced me firmly and our faces were only inches apart. Although I had looked down when I fell into his arms, I made the mistake of looking back up at him. We were close enough to kiss. I could not breathe. There was something about his eyes, a magic that cast a spell. The odd sensation that our souls had just merged came over me and the intensity of it made me close my eyes. His scent was heady and I inhaled deeply to grasp more of it into my lungs.

"Eh hum," Rick cleared his throat and it broke the moment's spell. I realized I was still in Hazen's arms and, with my eyes closed so close to him, I was painfully aware that it appeared I was about to kiss him. The blood rushed to my face for the second time in the thirty seconds since I met him. Although I was on my feet now, I still felt unsteady.

Yet, I knew I had to stand on them and move away from this Greek god-like creature and his magic. I reached over and held the back of a chair tucked under the conference table for support. "Shall we sit?" Rick offered, taking my elbow to guide me to the chair. I felt I would never be able to look Rick in the face again. I was humiliated. I was acting like a middle-school girl who had a crush on her physical education coach. With

Rick and Hazen's support, I managed to sit in the chair. The effort left me breathless.

"Okay, I've brought all your paperwork for us to go over," Rick tried desperately to act as if nothing had just transpired- an effort for which I was grateful. "I made copies for you so we could all go over them together. Hazen, Brie has my full confidence so, if it's alright with you, she'll be handling most of the changes you want to make."

"Of course," Hazen's clear, deep, liquid voice filled the room and, despite my best efforts, I looked up at him. He was sitting directly across from me. Rick had taken the seat at the end of the table between us. "I've no doubt she is capable if you trust her." His declaration took me aback and I felt more confident just because he believed in me. What was it about his eyes? The trance between us was just too powerful. I was still breathing shallowly and did not trust my voice to speak.

"Isn't that right, Brie?" Rick intervened. Had he asked me a question?

"What?" I managed to get out.

"You've handled most of my high-profile cases with confidentiality for over two years now?" he prompted.

"Yes," I spluttered but could not think of anything else to say. Rick proceeded to spell out for Hazen the issues they had come to discuss. I could hear him speaking but it was as if he spoke a foreign language, or spoke from the bottom of a deep well. The words were there but my mind did not absorb their meaning. I listened half-witted until Hazen spoke.

"So, Rick, what you're saying is I need to restructure my various organizations in order to get the best tax advantage?" Hazen's voice was hypnotic. Regardless of what he said, it came out exuding warmth.

"Yes. That's one of the reasons I wanted Brie to come in on this. She is sort of an expert at restructuring and organizing divergent businesses under one umbrella to maximize earnings. She's done it for several other clients and they have profited greatly." I knew Rick was waiting for me to say something. I could not think of one intelligent statement to add. "Um, you know what? I just realized we have a conference call in ten minutes. It won't take long." What? No, we did not. What was Rick talking about? "Hazen, why don't you look over these reports and we'll come back in about twenty minutes. That'll give you a chance to think about how you'd like to handle things and then Brie can give you some ideas. Is that alright?"

"Of course," Hazen smiled. "Can I get a coffee?"

"Yes, Brie will, never mind, I'll get the receptionist to bring you one." Rick seemed perturbed for some reason. He stood up and I knew I was supposed to follow him. Why wasn't I getting up? Rick pulled my chair out and the trance was broken enough that I managed to get up and follow him out of the room.

"What is wrong with you?" Rick said after we were several feet away from the door.

"I don't know. He," He what? "He's,"

"Brie, get your head out of your butt! He is a very wealthy client and I do not want him thinking you're incompetent. Restructuring all his businesses is going to be a huge undertaking and I just don't have the time for it with tax season upon us. You're going to have to spend some time with him to get all this right and I don't want to have to worry about this." I'm going to spend time with him? "Do I need to pull one of the other accountants in instead?"

"No!" I did not mean to say it so forcefully. "I'll be fine." I hoped. "Is he married?" Rick sighed heavily.

"No, but you are," he spat. "Go put some cold water on your face or something. When you come back, try to act your age." Rick had never been cross with me, not in the beginning when I was so ignorant of all he was teaching me, not when I lacked enough confidence in myself to make a decision without his approval, not all these years of being so needy, not all the times I depended on him for transportation. It hurt me to know that he was angry with me now. I nodded my head and went to the ladies room. I looked in the mirror. Whom was this silly person acting like a schoolgirl? I wet a paper towel and dabbed it on the back of my neck, then my face and arms. It did help me to retain a normal heart rate but I wasn't sure if that would last once I was in Hazen's presence again. I stretched my arms up and to the side. I bent over almost to the floor to stretch my spine. I turned left and then right trying to shake off this crazy dream-like state of which I seemed to be stuck.

"Okay," I told myself in the mirror, "I'm not sure what that was but if it returns when you go back, you will be oblivious to it. You are a professional! You are a grown woman, with kids for God's sake. Grow up!" There, that should straighten me out. I headed back to the conference room, fully hoping between Rick's reprimand and mine that I would be able to hold myself together. Maybe the magnetism I had toward Hazen was in my imagination. Maybe when I go back, I will feel perfectly normal.

"Okay, I'm back," I said as I entered the room, avoiding Hazen's magnetic eyes just for good measure. I took my seat, looked at Rick, and smiled.

"Alright," Rick proceeded, "Brie, we are looking at the west coast businesses that Hazen's family started initially." I looked at the paperwork before me and focused on the figures I saw. The dozens of businesses located from California all the way up to Washington showed enormous profits; however, they were in so many various types of enterprises and levels of profit that it was difficult even to grasp the entirety of it all. Rick waited for me to inspect the printout before continuing. The dilemma of the mess in front of me forced me to transition from schoolgirl with a crush to business professional with a challenge. "Just off the top of my head, I'm thinking Brie will probably reorganize the businesses by tax bracket, and"

"No, actually Rick," I interjected, "I'm thinking otherwise. He has so many hugely profitable businesses in the same category with these other less profitable ones. I'm thinking, after a thorough analysis of course, that we could leverage the lesser ones in similar categories with those that are paying tremendous taxes because of their level of success. Let's balance the power to play down the profits of these," I pointed to the notation on my printout to show which ones I meant. I felt like Rick probably already knew this and was possibly prompting me to rise to the occasion.

"That's why I wanted her on this," he addressed Hazen, who I had still not looked at since I had reentered the room. "Then, these closer to home appear to be a little better situated, as far as organization, so I am thinking only minor adjustments there. What do you think, Brie?" I pulled the separate paper work to view another couple dozen businesses located from Florida up to Maine. These were younger companies and, like the west coast properties, varied from restaurants to manufacturing. It was an amazing spread of industry, a smorgasbord of commerce. I was curious how any one family could obtain such wealth in so many varying ways.

"Mr. Thatcher," I resorted to my business voice, "I'm curious. What is your long-term business plan?" I leaned back in my chair from the position I had maintained of stooping over the reports on the table. When I did, I made the mistake of eye contact with him. Immediately, I knew my error.

"Good question, Ms. Taylor," I detected a smile beneath his use of my surname. Looking at him again, coupled with the sound of his voice saying my name and the smirk on his face when he replied, proved to be a grave blunder. "My father and his father before him have built an empire with which I now find I must run. Their interests were not only different from one another but also changed as they did. My grandfather passed recently and my father is not handling it well. He has asked me to oversee this, this, well, this empire." His voice, his demeanor, his countenance were all dope to my senses. I had to tell myself to focus on his words rather than his voice in order to follow his story.

"I have spent the past few decades abroad, studying, learning, and enjoying our small planet. I find myself in unfamiliar territory. My father and I have not always agreed on how we should spend our time on this Earth. You see, these businesses, this wealth, mean nothing to me." I was stunned but at the same time, I now understood how his appearance opposed the stereotype of a man with these assets.

"Having said that," he went on after giving me a moment to take in his declaration, "I fully realize that it is because of these businesses that I have enjoyed the pleasure of travel and change I've been able to make in the world."

"Change?" My voice actually sounded half-way normal and I was proud of myself for being able to regain my composure, even if only for one word.

"Yes. You see, while my father and grandfather worked to build wealth, I established schools, orphanages, and churches in Africa. I sponsored children's programs in Romania, Bulgaria, the Ukraine, and Poland. I have been all over the world and the destitution I never knew existed because of my sheltered upbringing struck me. So, I set out to help where I could and to change young people's lives by teaching and enabling them to care for themselves and their communities." I stared at this man, this dream, this angel and the longer I stared, the more in awe I became. It took a moment before I realized there was silence in the room and Rick and Hazen were waiting for me to break it.

"I see," my voice was back to the trance-like state of whispering. I looked away from Hazen and cleared my throat, trying to gather my wits again. I looked back at the spreadsheets on the table. "And did you use these expenses as tax deductions?"

"No, Ms. Taylor," again with the smile, "My father may have. I don't think so though because I didn't send paperwork back to him for most of it."

"Well, then that would be the first place I would start," I looked back at him. I felt so numb. Perhaps he had picked up some witchery in a foreign country that he was using to put a spell on me now. "It sounds possibly like you have millions of dollars of deductions you could use to offset your profits. I'll need detailed reports on each of these endeavors you've undertaken. This is going to be a long and tedious process."

"Not really," his mellow voice spoke. "I don't have many detailed reports. In fact, I don't have any reports at all." I choked.

"You mean you've spent hundreds of thousands of dollars and you have no record of it?" I was incredulous. How could anyone be that irresponsible?

"I admit, it now seems unbelievable but, you see, my mind was never taught to worry about records or reports. My father, despite his not understanding my way, patiently allowed me to grow up as I saw fit. After I completed my education, my way was to travel and see first-hand what the world was really like. I did not want to only read about the Soviet Union. I wanted to see it, feel their arctic breezes, and race sled dogs in Kamenushka. I wanted to taste Almas caviar from the Caviar House & Prunier in London and walk the Great Wall of China. In essence, I wanted to live fully. So, various friends of mine and I travel extensively. It is my life." Okay, now I was thinking he was just weird. Who really wants to do all those things?

"So have you done all you set out to do?" I asked.

"Yes, and then some. I see you think it odd that I have such ambitions, Ms. Taylor." That was an understatement. "I was not raised with the same inhibitions that most Americans are taught. I traveled abroad even as a child, therefore, the natural tendency as an adult was to expound upon my already vast experiences. My parents took me and five of my friends to the Olympics in what was then Yugoslavia for my fourth birthday party. They felt it was important to show me that the world did not revolve around me. It was a message I took to heart. I was intrigued then and my thirst for hands-on knowledge has never been quenched."

"Wow! What an interesting life! And I thought I'd done something when I took Tracy to Europe." Rick laughed. He had been so quiet until then that I had almost forgotten he was there.

"I don't tell you this to brag." Hazen said and he leaned forward in his chair and looked directly at me. "I want you to understand me. Most people assume I am but a spoiled man who lacks responsibility. They do not know me." He then leaned forward in his chair and looked to Rick. "My family never called on me to accept the responsibility of our fortune. Now that I am, I am, not only capable, but also quite willing to pull my weight." Now he turned and looked me in the eye.

"But, as I said, I want you to know that I am not the man some profess me to be." I gulped.

"Hazen, uh, Mr. Thatcher,"

"Please, call me Hazen. I like the way you say my name." What? Was he flirting with me? Oh, no. His voice, he was torturing me.

"Hazen," I realized I had whispered his name, "I have no idea what anyone professes you to be. I'm not a judgmental person anyway. I've learned that few people are what they appear to be." Hazen and I intently looked at one another. Time stood still. We did not move. No one spoke. It was as if we were caught in a bubble, floating in our own universe.

"So, Brie," Rick interrupted the atmosphere and burst our bubble, "Do you think you can help Hazen?" I broke my gaze away from Hazen and looked at Rick, which returned the business atmosphere to the room. How would I ever be able to focus on business once Rick was out of the picture and Hazen and I were alone?

"Of course," I said matter-of-factly. It would be an enormous undertaking but I was determined that I, and no one else, would insure that this statuesque man would be treated honestly. Given the wrong person, Hazen's lack of interest in his family's business could be used against him. Rick stood up then.

"Well, I'll leave you two to it then. Obviously, we'll need to meet on numerous occasions but I will only intercede as needed if that's okay with you?" He directed his question to Hazen who answered with only a nod. Rick quietly slipped from the room without as much as a good-bye. Hazen and I had not taken our eyes off one another.

"Hazen," I began, still fruitlessly trying to act like this meeting was only about business. "I've never undertaken anything of this magnitude before. I will need help, professional help, to navigate all of this."

"Brie, I will buy you a university if it is required to further your knowledge in order to help."

"I don't think I'll need quite that much but I may need to employ a few specialists."

"Name it and it is done."

"I'll need more information from these businesses and also your own benevolent excursions. There is a vast amount of data that needs to be collected before I can begin to reorganize it."

"I'll see to it that you have authority to access anything you need. Will you also need me?" Need you? I just met you and already feel that I can't live without you! Yes, unequivocally, I need you. I need to be able to hear your voice. I need to stay lost in your eyes. I need to smell your musky sent. I need this sensation of, what? What was this strange feeling that has overcome me?

"Yes," thankfully was the only word that came out of my mouth.

"Here is my cell number then. Call me anytime. I'm staying at St. Regis. I'm in suite two." He wrote his phone number on a piece of paper and slid it over to me. I was relieved I did not have to touch him to retrieve it and yet, disappointed I had no excuse to touch him again.

"You don't have a business card?" I asked as I looked at his number scribbled on the small scrap paper. He laughed lightly.

"Brie, a man doesn't need a business card who is not in business." How apt. The meeting's purpose had concluded and yet we sat, staring at one another. "What is Brie short for?"

"Abriella."

"Abriella, would you like to go to lunch with me?" What? Seriously? I'd like to go to Russia with you, and China, and Africa, and, well, anywhere, the moon perhaps!

"Sure. Let me get my purse. I'll be right back." I stood up and gathered the paperwork spread out in front of me, not even bothering to organize it. I shoved the papers into a file folder and headed toward the door trying to stay erect all the way. Once out of the room, I breathed a deep cleansing breath. I went to Rick's office and told him we were going to lunch.

"Lunch? Its only ten-thirty in the morning." I shrugged. I did not care if it was ten-thirty at night, I would eat lunch with this man. "You want me to go with you or will you be alright?" Rick responded to my shrug.

"Do you want to go with us?"

"No, not particularly. The electricity between the two of you is disconcerting." Apparently, it was not just me. Rick had noticed it, too.

"Rick, how well do you know him?"

"Well, I've known him for years but only from a distance. I've done his personal taxes but usually it's all done over phone or electronically."

"Why did he need taxes done? Wouldn't his family have handled all that?"

"You'd think. No, his father put a few businesses here locally in his name- to try to settle Hazen down, I think- nothing all that consuming; more of a write-off for them. I trust him, if that's what you're asking. He's a good man and comes from good stock."

"I'll be fine then," I answered his first question.

"Call me if you need me. And take your cell phone!" He called to my back as I exited. Hazen was waiting for me in the lobby and we walked out of the door without either of us saying a word. The sun was shining today although it was chilly. I had forgotten my jacket but the fresh air felt so good that I did not return for it.

"Do you need me to drive?" I asked him.

"Why would I need you to drive?" he asked whimsically.

"Well, I thought if you're staying at a hotel, you may not have a car."

"I have a car. Come with me." He headed toward a strange looking car, a deep brown color that looked like melted chocolate and had an interesting swerve to the body. I really felt

I could take a potato chip, swirl it on the car, and eat it. When we got a little closer, I could see Maserati scribbled across the back. It was the most beautiful car I had ever seen in my life.

~ *14* ~

Electrifying Ecstasy

Hazen opened my door for me and I reluctantly sat in the plush leather, cream-colored seats. As he walked around to his side, I quickly stroked the leather of my seat. It felt like satin against my fingertips. Then I looked toward his door anticipating his entrance. The emblem on the back of his seat was embossed in a contrasting deep brown stitch that matched the exterior color. The car appeared small on the outside but as I sat, waiting for Hazen to join me, it felt quite comfortable from the inside and even had a nice size back seat. The bucket seat formed perfectly to my body and I felt as if it was hugging me. Hazen finally entered and immediately cranked up the car without glancing at me. I was relieved he did not because of our close proximity.

"Mind if I put the top down?" He asked almost sheepishly, "You look like a convertible kind of girl." Convertible? I did not see how this car could be a convertible. It looked like any other car, except for the fact that it was ridiculously gorgeous.

"Sure," I answered with a smile, "I've never ridden in a convertible before."

"Well, then, you're in for a treat," he returned my smile as he pushed a button. Suddenly, the top began to lift off. I felt like I was in a transformer vehicle and I waited for the car to turn into a large robot. It took only a few seconds and the entire top of the car tucked neatly into the trunk area. It seemed a little chilly to drive with the top off to me but the idea of riding in this exquisite car excited me and I snuggled into the soft leather to enjoy the ride. He reached up and turned the heater on and the warm air on my feet and arms assured me I would be fine. "I guess it's a little cold for the top down, but I just returned from the Soviet Union so it doesn't seem so to me. Here, I'll put your seat heater on, too. If you get cold, just let me know and I'll put the top back up."

"No," I spoke too quickly, "this is great." I was relieved that the close proximity between us felt less intimate with the top off. Maybe I could breathe now.

"Where would you like to go for lunch?" he asked. My first thought was that I did not want to run into Seth.

"Somewhere far away from here." He eyed me inquisitively so I added, "so we can ride longer." He smiled then.

"I guess it's not exactly lunch time but I just got off a long flight and I'm starved."

"Actually, I missed breakfast this morning, so an early lunch sounds good to me, too." I felt like I was being too agreeable but I bet this man was used to everyone always agreeing with whatever he wanted.

"Okay, any suggestions?" I had to think for a minute. I was not used to eating out at all; much less deciding where would be an acceptable place for this idol. Besides, I felt that anything Atlanta had to offer would seem subprime to this worldly man. Then I remembered a spotlight article I had just read on a little restaurant called St. Cecilia. It was a place that featured European food and I hoped it would measure up to the authentic European food that Hazen enjoyed.

"I'm not sure where exactly it's located but I've heard good things about a restaurant called St. Cecilia in Buckhead." I tried to sound knowledgeable and yet I felt like he could see right through me.

"Alright," he smiled, "sounds good. Let's just plug it in here," he spoke as he hit a screen on the dash. The dark screen sprang to life beneath his fingertips. "I'd like directions to St. Cecilia Restaurant in Buckhead, Georgia." He was talking to the car. In only seconds, the car responded.

"St. Cecilia restaurant is located at 3455 Peachtree Road north east, Atlanta, Georgia. Would you like directions or a map?" the robotic woman answered.

"Map, please."

"Right away," the car obediently responded. Quickly a GPS navigation picture came up on the screen. Hazen turned to back out of the parking lot and we were on our way. I sat in awe. Seth and I had enjoyed many luxuries but I had never seen anything like this. I wondered if Seth's car boasted all these extras. Perhaps they were not available when we were married. As if my mind responded to my thoughts, Rick's voice resounded in my mind when I had asked him if Hazen was married, "No, but you are!" He was right, of course. That was a situation I knew I had to resolve quickly now.

"So, tell me about yourself," Hazen broke my concentration.

"I'm afraid I am quite boring compared to you," I admitted.

"Nonsense, I have a feeling you've lived a very interesting life." I would have thought that carrying on a conversation would be difficult with the top off a car but it was remarkably quiet. I deliberated about how much to tell Hazen. I did not want to scare him off. I decided to be vague.

"Not much to tell, really," I tried to think as I spoke. "I've been Rick's assistant for a couple of years. I love what I do." I shrugged my shoulders as if that was my whole story. He glanced at me from the side, obviously waiting for me to go on. When I didn't he took the reign again.

"Well, from what I can see, you're much more than an assistant. Rick seems to depend on you pretty heavily." I knew I should respond but since it was not a question, I decided to take this opportunity to turn the conversation elsewhere.

"So, tell me about this car," I started enthusiastically.

"Ah, alright," he smiled. He knew exactly what I was doing but thankfully allowed the transition, "I used to own a similar Maserati but sold it when I lived abroad. I do not usually stay in one place long enough to warrant buying a vehicle so I normally rent. I figure I'm going to be in Atlanta for a while, at least until we can get a game plan with these corporations so, I ordered this one a couple months ago."

"You ordered it?" I wondered. He made it sound like take-out.

"Yes, well, I was still in the Soviet Union but knew I must return soon so, I ordered it online." I choked.

"You ordered a car online." It was an incredulous statement, not a question. He smiled.

"I realize how I must seem to you, to everyone, Abriella, but, I assure you I don't take such benefits lightly." So he preferred my whole name?

"No, that's fine. Cool, actually." I had felt impervious to wealth after I left Seth, equating it with evil and manipulation. Hazen did not seem to fit that description but, then again, I had to admit, Seth did not seem to at first either. I had to remind myself that I knew nothing about Hazen except what he had told me. As much as my heart screamed, my mind insisted I slow down until I could get to know him.

"So, what else do you order online," I asked to keep the conversation away from me. He laughed aloud.

"Not all that you would probably think," he continued to laugh.

"So, this car, I know it's a Maserati but what makes it so special?" I was not a car kind of girl but anyone with eyes would have admired this vehicle.

"Well, it can go from 0-60 in 4.8 seconds."

"Oh my, and how often do you do that?" He laughed again.

"Only a few times to test it. It has a horse power of four-hundred fifty four and a V8 engine." I was lost now but kept my mouth shut since I was the one who had asked him about the car. "It can go 180 miles an hour."

"And where do you drive that fast?"

"No where. I haven't actually tried that yet."

"Yet?"

"I may enjoy some risky hobbies but I am not suicidal. Anyway, I do like a fast car for when I want to ride for sport but I would never drive recklessly on a public road." I wanted to ask him how much a car like this costs but would never, of course. I'd wait until I returned to the office and Google it.

"So, no more about you, eh?" oh, no, he was turning the tables on me. "You prefer to remain an enigma?" Now, I laughed.

"No, not an enigma but I guess I just have a harder time talking about myself than most people."

"Yes, especially most women," he chuckled to lighten his insult. "Alright, I won't pry. So tell me about this restaurant we're going to."

"I'm sure it won't compare to the places you've been but I read an article about it recently. The menu is supposed to feature seafood and pasta specials that had great reviews."

"Are there no good restaurants around here?" it was a reasonable question for which I had to think quickly to answer.

"Oh, sure, I just get tired of the same local ones, though, you know." That sounded nonchalant enough, I decided. We proceeded to make small talk all the way to St. Cecilia's. I loved the outdoor experience of the convertible and I easily pulled the conversation back to the car when Hazen started to ask questions about my life. The restaurant was lovely and the atmosphere was less than intimate, which was perfect for our first lunch. Our *first* lunch? I heard myself think this silly thought. I had to stop. The inside of the restaurant was bright and clean. The lunch crowd filled the place up and Hazen and I were seated at a table that was smaller than most. It was by the window as all the seats in the front were because the entire front of the building was windows. After we were seated, a young lady introduced herself as Amelia, our server.

"Would you like wine?" Hazen asked me.

"Oh no, just water for me, thanks," I did not drink alcohol often at all and didn't trust myself to drink it around this gorgeous model of a man.

"Two waters," Hazen told Amelia.

"You can have wine if you like," I told him after she had walked away.

"No, I usually drink water at lunch." I wondered if this was entirely honest. We talked about the menu. It looked inviting with everything from chilled oysters to several items I could not pronounce. When Amelia returned with our drinks, Hazen told her we were in no hurry to order and asked her to come back later. We continued to make small talk, about the menu, the atmosphere, other places that Hazen had enjoyed abroad that were similar to this one. He was a very interesting conversationalist and I knew I could listen to him all day. He told me how he and his friends would go on an excursion, like the dogsledding he had just returned from in the Soviet Union. After a few weeks or so of fun, they would undertake a 'project' as he called them. Apparently, he had many friends who shared his own interests as well as his concerns.

Amelia continued to check on us every few minutes and at last, Hazen ordered the dishes upon which we had decided.

"We'd like to try the salt cod beignets for an appetizer. The lady will have Agnolotti and I'll take the Block Island swordfish." He sounded as confident as if he had written the menu himself. Amelia asked all the usual questions about which sides we desired and how we liked our meat cooked but did not write anything down. I would be curious to see if she got our order entirely correct. Shortly, she brought the salt cod beignets appetizer. I did not know what to expect since I had never heard of beignets. The plate sat, beautifully displayed as a work of art with many small pieces of the cod battered and fried. It was delicious.

Shy at first, I ate small portions cutting the small pieces in half before dipping them. By the time we had finished the plate, I was already almost full. As soon as Amelia took our empty appetizer plate, she brought our meals, presenting a beautiful meal with red wine braised beef short ribs lying amongst roasted mushrooms and Parmigiano on top. Hazen's was equally discriminating and served with olives, garlic and tomato. We both ate heartily as if we were famished. The food smelled as wonderful as it looked.

"Here, try mine," Hazen extended his fork toward me, full of fish and the sides. Self-consciously I opened my mouth to allow him to place his fork inside my mouth. Our eyes locked as I took it in and my cheeks flushed red. Just when I thought I was getting a little comfortable he would have to go and create more intensity. I looked down immediately and wiped my mouth with my napkin.

"It's delicious." I finally got out after I had swallowed his fish almost whole. "Here, try mine," I offered in return. As he had done, I put a nice bite on my fork and extended it to him. He placed his hand over mine and brought the fork to his mouth. The combination of his touching me and his opening his mouth to take my fork struck another chord in my heart and, again, I looked away.

"Hm, very good," he said. "Brie, can I ask you a question?" he added after swallowing his bite.

"Of course," I tried to sound casual.

"How old are you?" I was not expecting that.

"Um, haven't you ever heard that a woman who will tell her age will tell anything?" I dodged. He laughed so loudly that several tables around us looked to see what they had missed.

"No, I have never heard that, but obviously you do not tell strangers *anything* so I guess I won't expect your answer."

"I'm just kidding. I'm twenty-nine," I admitted. I had evaded so many of his questions that I felt I could at least be honest about this one.

"How is it that a woman as beautiful, smart, and funny as you is still not married?" I froze. Should I tell him the story of my wretched life? Should I lie?

"I was married," I gave him a half-truth but did not go on to explain. I averted his look by concentrating on my meal. I hoped with all my heart that we could change the subject again. I guess, he realized that I did not want to talk about it so he graciously changed the subject for me this time.

"Would you like dessert?"

"No, please. I won't be worth anything back at the office as it is," I stated as I rubbed my stomach. When Amelia came with the ticket, Hazen laid a shiny silver credit card on the table. Amelia looked a little astonished at first but quickly regained her composure as she walked away with it. I could not contain my curiosity any more. This man was introducing me to more new luxuries than I would be able to remember to Google once I was back at the office.

"That was a very pretty card. What's so special about it?" I knew I sounded bold but at this point, I felt Hazen and I would probably never be an item. I was kidding myself to think it was possible. So, I figured, what did I have to lose?

"My father likes for me to put everything on the card. You know, for tax purposes." He smirked at me and then looked away. Now he was the one being evasive.

"Yes, that is very smart. What kind of card is it?" I did not really mean for that to come out and regretted it instantly. "I'm sorry. I do not mean to pry. I just noticed our server's look; as if she knew it was prestigious. I was curious. Forgive me."

"It's alright, Abriella. I am not one to boast," he looked down for a second when he said this. "You will find out soon enough as you will be doing my taxes now. It is a JP Morgan Palladium Card." I didn't want to sound as ignorant as I was but that didn't really mean a lot to me. I guess he could tell from my reaction so he explained. "It is actually made of metal, a palladium and twenty-three karat gold alloy." He made this sound as normal as he could but it was apparent I was missing pertinent information.

"So, I guess that's a pretty high spending limit, huh?" I tried to play off this awkward moment by making a joke and it was the only perk I could think of that would warrant such a pricy card.

"You could say so." Hazen looked embarrassed. "You have to be a JP Morgan client with substantial assets. There is no limit." He said this quietly as if he had told me he lived in a box under a bridge.

"Oh," I answered. The atmosphere was more discomfited now and to make it worse, Amelia returned with the card and a much friendlier smile.

"Thank you for visiting St. Cecilia's. Here's my card. If you ever come back, please ask for me." She suddenly seemed very seductive toward him although Hazen did not seem to notice.

The ride back to the office was quieter than the one going had been and I wondered what Hazen was thinking. Had he seen that I don't measure up to him? Was he questioning my ability to handle his wealth amass? It would not surprise me if he changed his mind about who he wanted to handle his affairs and I thought, momentarily, that our entire lunch might have been a test. Did I fail it? By the time we pulled into my office parking lot, I was a bundle of nerves.

"Well, thank you for lunch," I told him as I reached for the door handle, eagerly awaiting my escape.

"One moment, please," he spoke lowly. I hesitated but did not remove my hand from the door handle. "Abriella, I'm not sure what I have done to offend you. I apologize if anything I've said or asked has hurt you." What? Me offended?

"No, Hazen," I looked him in the eyes then, dubious that he could truly think he had offended me. "I'm not, you didn't," I blubbered like an idiot. Our faces were inches apart in this small space and even the infinite area of the sky seemed smaller as we gazed into one another's eyes. "Hazen," I repeated, "you're a very intense man. I'm not used to," To what? My mind went completely blank. No adjective came to mind that could accurately describe what I felt when I was around him.

"What, Abriella?" he was almost whispering. "You're not used to what?" I could not speak.

My mouth went dry and my imagination took over. As I looked into his eyes, I envisioned myself leaning forward and kissing him full on the lips. It was not like me to be so forward and the only reasoning I could justify in my mind was that I felt it would be my only chance to kiss his beautiful mouth. My mind allowed only a brief kiss, only a few seconds, and not a deep kiss but, even though it was in my imagination, the tension between us definitely changed from awkward to intense. My mind's eye continued this scenario as if it were a movie playing out in my mind.

"I am so sorry," I whispered as I drew away. Then, as my fantasy continued in my thoughts, he put his hand behind my neck and drew me back to him, kissing me passionately. This kiss, his kiss, was beyond intense. A few minutes later, he pulled away gently, while I, on the other hand, leaned forward, not wanting the moment to end even though it was not real.

"Please don't be sorry, Brie," his breath against my face was like a hypnotic gas assaulting my senses with a passion that ignited my being. He was the loveliest creature I had ever witnessed and his kiss felt like the first to me. In so many ways, it was. "You are mesmerizing." Me? I stared at his face, with my mind lost in my fantasy. Then I realized my mistake in prolonging this daydream as Hazen stared at me, waiting for my answer. Suddenly, my daydream evaporated before my eyes.

"Um, I'm not used to taking so long for lunch" I stammered as I tried to acclimate my senses to the reality before me. Oh, no, it *had* been a daydream. Immediately, I was embarrassed as if he could somehow know my thoughts and had seen us kissing in my vision. Hazen just smiled a lazy smile and his eyebrow rose slightly as if to try to read my mind.

I reached for the door handle trying to escape before he succeeded. I could not help but look back, hoping that my fantasy would come true.

~ 15 ~

Here We Go

began to put together a spreadsheet of all of Hazen's family usinesses. It required a lot of phone calls, emails, and tax searches nd consumed most of my time at work now. Rick and I rarely saw ach other except for him popping his head into my office and sking if I needed help. I would call Hazen a few times a day with uestions or instructions of paperwork I needed. He made all the ecessary arrangements for me to have access to his businesses ıcluding other accountants around the country and, even several f his friends who had accompanied him. Indeed, the vastness of apital required a certain detached attention. If I stopped to think of ıis as actually being real money, it could be paralyzing. 'herefore, my mind processed it like a game of Monopoly, where ıoney exchanged from one line to another on my spreadsheet as nly a number, not actual dollar amounts.

I had hoped that Hazen and I would be able to see one another more because of my work for him but had to admit that it was probably easier this way. Since my vision of his kiss, it was difficult not to think of him. I had become so engrossed in my work that my case with Seth took a welcome back burner. The phone ringing this morning changed my priorities.

"Happy New Year," Mr. Morgan's voice proclaimed, even though it was already a week into the New Year. After our formalities, he told me that we had a date set for February twenty-seventh, almost two months away. "I'm afraid that Seth and his attorney have declined our offer to settle out of court. I imagine they consider themselves as having the upper hand. We will not be able to use the tape in the court of law unless one party knew they were being taped." This was not good news to me. "They have us residing under Judge Miller. We will have to get a continuance to allow time to change judges and we'll have to have a good reason. Brie, have you considered that if you claimed that you taped Judge Miller purposely, that it may be admissible?"

"But, I didn't," I stated.

"Yes, I know, but it may be your saving grace if you were willing to claim it."

"You mean, if I were willing to lie under oath?"

"Brie, I get that you are a woman of integrity but what we are dealing with here may call for drastic measures. The simplest way would be to allow the tape to stand as evidence that would, not only dismiss Judge Miller from this case, but expose him for the crooked way he has handled you." I thought about it. It was tempting. Then I knew that I could not ignore what was right, and legal, by making a false claim.

"I'm sorry, Mr. Morgan. I can't do that." He sighed heavily.

"Alright, Ms. Taylor. We'll work with what we have. I'll call you next week." He hung up the phone on me, out of exasperation, I presumed. I went to Rick's office and told him the update of information.

"What do you think I should do, Rick?" Rick looked at me for a few minutes. I loved that he always thought about an answer rather than spouting off the first thing that came to him.

"I agree with you, Brie." I breathed a deep breath of relief for his support. "If you compromise your principles now, you will not be able to live with yourself. We'll figure something out." He looked out of his window briefly then turned back to me. "How's the Thatcher case going?"

A week went by and I tried intently to focus on my work but the more I thought about actually having to go to court, the harder it became. I wanted desperately to ignore that Seth was fighting me for my son. The thought of losing Josh seemed ridiculous but I knew that, with Seth's skill of manipulation, it was possible.

"Hi beautiful," Hazen's deep voice flowed through the phone and touched my heart. We had grown into a more relaxed, and even flirtatious, manner. It was easier over the phone, not looking into his eyes or smelling his heady scent. "I'm going to be in town tomorrow. Can I take you to lunch?" My heart stopped. I had not seen Hazen since that first day I met him and the thought of being with him, close to him in his car, eating off of his fork again caused me to drop the phone.

"Sorry," I said sheepishly once I retrieved it. "Um, lunch, yes, that'll be fine."

"Great! I'll pick you up at noon. Maybe I could stay after lunch and go over your work so far."

"I'm far from ready but if you'd like, that would be fine." I was glad he had given me notice so I could better prepare the paperwork and wear something a little more appealing tomorrow. I tried on at least a dozen outfits that night, trying to find the perfect blend of professional and sexy. There was no ideal combination in my wardrobe. I wished I had picked up a new dress but there was not time now. It was hard to go to sleep that night because my thoughts kept fantasizing about Hazen's eyes, his voice, his intensity.

The next morning started out a little crazy. Because of my lack of sleep, I hit the snooze button too many times, which made us all late. Thanks to my new car, I did not have to worry about missing the bus. Josh chose this morning, of all times, to spill his cereal all over himself and I had to wash and redress him quickly. Katie, who usually fixed her own hair, insisted I braid it today. It seemed quicker to braid it than to argue with her about it. I decided to wear one of my old-faithful skirts, a navy one that hit just above my knee. I paired it with a white blouse that had an over-lay in the front. I did not have excess jewelry, so I decided to wear the simple diamond studs that had been a gift from Seth. I would usually wear my hair back at work to keep it from falling in my face while bending over reports and I had planned to put it up in a bit of a bun or French-twist, but because I was short on time, I just brushed it and let it flow loosely down my back.

I spent the entire morning making the work I had finished thus far look more advanced than it actually was in reality. I had made a great deal of progress but I wanted everything to be as perfect as possible. Organizing my work helped to keep my mind off the fact that I would see Hazen today. I freshened up about eleven-thirty in preparation for his arrival. It was then that my heart began to beat uncontrollably. Just before noon, the new receptionist, Therese, knocked on my door. I expected her to announce Hazen's arrival.

"Can I talk to you for a minute?" she said.

"Of course," I wondered what she could possibly want.

"I need to ask you something but I don't want to offend you." She seemed nervous and for the life of me, I could not imagine why.

"I know that you and Joe Fitzpatrick were seeing each other. I'm not sure what happened at the Christmas party but he asked me out and," oh, so this is where she was going. I had to let her off the hook.

"You have my blessings, Therese. He's a nice guy. We were never seeing each other. It was never like that. Don't worry about my feelings at all. Please." There, I made that pretty clear .She smiled at me then but looked a little confused about my response.

"Well, thank you, Ms. Taylor, I,"

"Please, call me Brie." I interrupted her.

"Okay, thank you Brie," then she turned and walked out. Something seemed odd about the conversation but I was too preoccupied with anticipation of seeing Hazen to worry about Joe and Therese right now. I looked at my clock. It was twelve-ten. I begin to wonder if Hazen was going to stand me up when my buzzer cracked and Therese announced I had a visitor in the lobby. I decided I would make him wait a few minutes since he was late. After exactly five minutes, I headed for the lobby. Hazen sat on the far side of the room and I had to walk a ways toward him as he watched me. His stare made me very nervous and I had to concentrate to keep from tripping in my high-heels. He did not make an effort to meet me half way and he only stood up once I approached him. My old-fashioned, southern side told me that it was rude for a man not to stand up when a lady entered the room.

"You look stunning," he whispered in my ear as he hugged me and then kissed my cheek once I arrived in front of him. Okay, all is forgiven. "I had hoped in part that you were a figment of my imagination at my last visit. I was assured the allure would not be equal today but I was wrong." He stood back and kept looking at me. I blushed like a teenager. He took my hands in his and held them out, looking at my outfit. "Abriella, you are a magnificent woman." How could this statuesque man possibly think that about me? I felt so damaged, so used up. I could not respond except to bow my head to avoid his intense stare. He released one of my hands and placed his hand under my chin, raising it to look him in the eyes. "You don't even see it, do you?"

"See what?" my voice squeaked.

"How poised, graceful, and beautiful you are," he was not smiling as he said this. In fact, his gaze was so passionate, his compliment so sincere, that tears stung my eyes. I turned my head again, releasing his hold on my chin. "I don't know how you don't see it, my lovely, but you will. You will when I'm finished." Even though Hazen and I had enjoyed many personal conversations on the phone and we flirted as if we had known one another a long time, I was not expecting him to treat me in this new, intimate way. It was perplexing to have this magnificent man treat me so personally.

"Eh, um," I heard Therese clear her throat at her desk. I had completely forgotten she was in the room. Oh, well, I figured. At least now she would know for sure that I was not interested in Joe any longer.

"Are you ready to go?" I asked Hazen.

"Yes," he led the way to his car. It was drizzling a little today so he did not take the top off. It made the small interior of his car seem much more personal. I had Googled his Maserati and knew that it costs almost two-hundred-grand. It amazed me that anyone would spend that kind of money on an automobile. "If you don't mind, I did some research to find a lunch place today."

"Of course, so where are we going?" I enquired. Secretly hoping it was far from this district.

"It's a surprise," he announced proudly. He wound through the streets of Atlanta like a veteran citizen. We made small talk but it was too obvious that neither of us felt our meeting was casual or business. The atmosphere in the car felt very personal and to make matters worse, my skirt rose up somewhat as I sat in the perfectly formed bucket seat. Hazen glanced over, noticing this, but did not look that way again the duration of the trip. I focused on him so intently that I was surprised when we rode up to the country club- the very same country club that Seth frequented and where the scene had taken place not two months ago. I froze.

"The country club?" I said aloud. Hazen smiled. No doubt, he thought he had done a good thing by bringing me here and mistook my stunned question as pleasant surprise rather than the horrific fear that overtook me.

"Yep, I figured if I am going to live in Atlanta, I might as well jump in with both feet." I did not know how to tell him or if I could tell him but I was not sure I could walk in without my legs literally giving out on me. He drove right up to the portico where several valets stood waiting. One attendant opened my door while another headed toward Hazen's side. I managed to get out and, once Hazen joined me on my side, I accepted his arm to escort me inside the dining hall.

I scanned the area as we entered, looking for Seth or any of his family or colleagues. I saw no one but knew that was not assurance no one would not come. Hazen pointed me toward a table almost in the center of the huge dining room and I panicked.

"Um, could we sit somewhere a little less conspicuous?" I asked him as I continued to search the room.

"Of course, we can sit anywhere you'd like." He looked around the room and saw a small table in the corner. "Would that be alright?" he pointed. I just nodded my head, too afraid to trust my voice. Once we sat down, a waiter came and asked if we would like a menu or would we like the buffet.

"We'll both take the buffet," Hazen spoke for both of us.

"Oh, I think I'd rather look at a menu," I interjected. There was no way I was going to risk cruising across the room several times and increasing my risk of seeing anyone that would know me. The waiter looked at Hazen as if to confirm my choice. He nodded.

"I'm sorry, Abriella," he looked sincerely apologetic; "I didn't mean to offend you. Of course, have whatever you'd like. I just thought you'd like the variety of food choices on their buffet. I hear it's quite a smorgasbord." The waiter then handed me a menu and walked away.

"It's fine, Hazen. I'm just not that hungry today so I thought I'd have a salad." I was lying, of course, but it seemed like a likely enough reason to skip the country club's famous buffet. We talked a few minutes and after I ordered my salad, Hazen excused himself to fill up at the buffet. I continued to scan the dining room while he was gone and the entire time we ate. It would be impossible to relax here. The waiter brought my salad about the same time that Hazen returned with a full plate from the buffet.

"Wow! The choices they have here are amazing. Next time, you'll have to give it a try," he said when he returned. I had eaten their buffet many times in my past life and wanted to agree with him but the last thing I wanted to do was pique his interest about my life. I knew I must come forth about my impending divorce. Hazen seemed to be a man of great integrity. I knew instinctively that he would not approve of moving forward in a relationship with a married woman. The thought of having to tell him about Seth made my stomach flip and even eating the salad became difficult. I consoled myself by reminding me that a man like Hazen Thatcher would never be seriously interested in a woman like me so, ultimately, it did not matter. He could have any woman he wanted- models, debutants, actresses, anyone. Why would he settle for me?

Lunch finally concluded. Our conversation was minimal and I was relieved we were ready to go. I was immensely relieved that I had seen no trace of Seth or any of his family or friends. My only thoughts were of escaping this place without an incident. As Hazen and I headed toward the door, I finally began to relax slightly. Just as we reached the portico door, I happen to glance outside and saw Seth walking up with a beautiful young lady, who I presumed must be Tiffany. If we were to walk out the door right now, we would run directly into them.

"Oh, Hazen, you don't mind if I slip off to the ladies room do you? Why don't you have the car brought around and I'll be right out?"

"That's fine, I'll wait. You go ahead." He gave me a strange look. I was momentarily thankful that men were oblivious to women's emotions so he wouldn't pick up on the fact that I was not myself today. I looked again and Seth was only a few feet from the door. I turned and walked quickly toward the back hall where the restrooms were located. I would not make it around the corner before Seth walked in but the odds of him recognizing my backside seemed small enough. I stayed in the restroom for as long as I could without making Hazen wonder. I hope that it was long enough for Seth to get to the dining area and out of the hall.

Before I came out, I glimpsed down the long hallway and it appeared clear. Even Hazen was gone. I assumed he grew tired of waiting and decided to have the car pulled around after all. I walked the hall toward the door and my heart beat wildly with every footstep. The consequences of running into Seth while I was with Hazen were just too great. I needed to tell Hazen my story at least, just in case we did run into Seth in the future. I walked right by the huge dining room's open door and to the portico entrance expecting to see Hazen waiting in the car. He was gone. I thought he must have gone to the restroom himself so I sat on the bench outside and waited. Ten minutes must have gone by and Hazen peeked out of the door.

"There you are," he announced as if I were a child hiding from her parent. "I ran into someone who I wanted you to meet but we somehow missed you." He gave the valet our ticket and sat on the bench beside me. "He's a prominent attorney in town and I was thinking of securing his services for our legal matters, Seth Taylor. Have you ever heard of him?" I felt paralyzed. My head quickly snapped at him and my mouth fell open. "What? What is it?" Hazen's gorgeous car purred up right at that moment and he opened my door for me. Once he got in, I knew I had to fess up.

"Um, Hazen, there's something I need to tell you." I began shaking my head and trying to figure the best way. My hands fidgeted in my lap from the nervous tension that filled me.

"Yeah, I could tell you were distracted today. Are you okay?" I looked back at him and saw nothing but concern.

"No, not really," I took a deep breath. How much did he need to know? Would this be our ruination? "To be honest, I don't want to tell you this but I feel like you need to know." I kept looking at him and he reached over and put his hand over mine, which I held clinched in my lap. I relaxed instantly. "Look, I don't know where our," no, I couldn't say relationship, "this, this is going but you asked a few questions about me last time we were together and I evaded the answers because my life is a little complicated right now."

"Abriella, you don't have to,"

"Yes, I do." I did not want to but I knew I had to tell him. "That man, Seth Taylor, is my ex-husband. We've been estranged for years and are in a bit of a custody battle now. It's pretty ugly and I'll understand if you don't want to see me again, except professionally, of course." I hoped I would at least see him about work-related issues.

"Abriella, it's alright. I understand. Okay, no retainer for Seth Taylor. I'll find another lawyer to keep in my pocket." He smiled at me and squeezed my hand. "So, you have a child?"

Wow! I couldn't believe I had been so secret as to keep that from him.

"Two, actually, but only my son is Seth's. I had my daughter just after high school. I was unwed at the time." When I painted the picture like this, I had to admit it made me look bad. I held my head down, suddenly wanting to hide.

"Abriella, it's okay." He compressed my hand in his again. His assurance flowed throughout my entire body.

"Thanks," I responded. It did not take us long to get back to the office and, for once, I was glad. My nerves felt frazzled and my head was beginning to hurt. Hazen and I went to my office and I laid out the paperwork on the side table in the corner of my office. We sat beside one another and I went over all the notations I'd taken on his various businesses and the projection, which wasn't complete yet, of how I saw reorganizing his empire. Hazen didn't say much as I explained my plan and I realized towards the end of my presentation that I hadn't given him much time to talk.

"Do you have any questions?" I finally concluded.

"Yes, one," he looked from the paperwork spread before us and turned to face me. "Will you have dinner with me tonight?" I couldn't help myself. I smiled and looked down at my lap.

"Hazen, that's sweet but dinner is more difficult because I've got the kids and all."

"Great! I'd like to meet them."

"Oh, no, I don't think,"

"Abriella, I know you don't know me well but I like you and I think you like me." Could he really be unsure of this? "So, how about just a casual dinner?" Hazen had learned just today that I had two children and had met my ex-husband and yet, he still wanted to get to know me more? I could not speak but I nodded my head. "Great! Give me your address. Is seven alright?" I thought that was a little late for the kid's bedtime.

"Is six okay with you?"

"Six is fine." He stood as if to leave after I gave him the paper with my address on it.

"Wait! What about all this?" I motioned to the spreadsheets in front of us with my hand. "What do you think?" He smiled down at me and cupped my chin in his hand.

"Everything looks fine, Abriella. I trust you. You're a very intelligent woman." Then he walked toward the door. "I'll see you at six." Then he was gone.

~ 16 ~

The Dream Continues

As I lay down that night, exhausted but exhilarated, I thought back over the day. Hazen had met Seth, found out about me, seen my business proposal, and spent the evening with my children. His easy manner and laid-back personality made life seem so easy, flow so smoothly. Yeah, I guess if you have no worries life can be easy, I thought as I relaxed. Hazen had been perfect all night. He conversed with Katie and opened the car door for her. I could tell that Katie was smitten with him already. Josh took to him quickly as well and Hazen did not even seem to mind when Josh wanted him to read a book to him while I finished Katie's hair before we left. Hazen's car thrilled Katie even though it was too cool at night to have the top off. I hoped he would still be around come summer so the kids could experience that joy.

Hazen took us to a pizza place where there was a buffet of dozens of types of pizza and a few games to the side to play after we had eaten. He kindly helped to get Josh in and out of his car seat and then his booster seat at the restaurant. He selflessly played a few games of air hockey with Katie as Josh and I watched. It was a perfect evening- the best night I could ever remember. Everything felt so easy with Hazen. Was it real? Did I dare believe?

"Brie, can I see you in my office for a minute?" Rick called me on my desk phone first thing the next morning. Something was not right in his voice so I went immediately, worried there

was a new revelation in my case with Seth. "Yeah, so Hazen called me at seven this morning," he looked at me sternly. What could possibly be the problem with that? "He feels that you're doing a good job but," oh, no, my house of cards was about to crumble, "he thinks you could benefit from touring some of his places and he wants his father to meet you since his approval would be necessary to proceed." Tour his places? Father? Approval? Proceed?

"What? Um, I don't understand. What do you mean?" I stammered.

"It's not unreasonable. He likes what you're planning but if daddy ain't happy then all this is a moot point. Also, I agree that a hands-on approach for these businesses would be beneficial. Remember how you reorganized Annie Mae and Poppa's businesses so well?" I nodded. "Well, same thing here. You were able to do such a good job because you saw first-hand how the businesses ran. So, go with Hazen. Check out the ones he feels are most important. Meet his dad. Then get back here and wind this up so we can get the entirety of the account." My mind was astir. How could I?

"Rick, you know I can't just up and go off like that. Those businesses are located all over the country. I've got the kids."

"Oh, yeah, he did mention he met them last night." Rick smiled a secret smile. "He said it's fine if you need to bring them along."

"What? I can't. Katie's in school. She can't. Rick, I think," I was babbling.

"Brie," Rick held up his hand, "You can come up with a thousand excuses but bottom-line, if you want to stay on this account, you're going to have to work it out."

"When? When do I need to let you know by?" Now I sounded panicky. Rick stopped writing something on his notebook and looked up at me.

"Brie, this is a good thing. Don't screw it up by over thinking it. I'm sure he'll be flexible on the dates. You may wanna call Mr. Morgan and see if that court date is still for end of February before you put this on your calendar."

"Good idea," I said over my shoulder as I left his office. Mr. Morgan assured me the court date still stood and I was fine to go on a business trip as long as I was back by the week prior to the court so we could go over any last minute preparation. So, I called Hazen that afternoon.

"Hi beautiful!" he answered the phone as if he was truly glad to hear from me.

"Well, I got your message," I replied to him with a smirk in my voice.

"I hope you don't mind," I could tell he was smiling through the phone.

"It's not that I mind, there is just so much that needs to be done before I can commit to going. How long do you think it will take? I'll need to get with Katie's teacher at school to make sure she doesn't fall behind. Plus, we have a cat. I can't just leave him by himself for that long."

"Oh, I'm so sorry, Brie. I hadn't thought of that. I'm not used to having to worry about kids and such. Why don't I bring a tutor to help her with her studies while we are gone?"

"No, Hazen, that won't be necessary. I can help her. I just need to know about how long you think we'll be gone."

"Brie, there's no agenda. I was hoping to take you to the wineries and quarries in California and then a few of the factories there including the ship factory. I'd like you to see the farm in Washington as well as the Boeing plant and we could slide over to Colorado to meet my father. He's at his mountain home right now. After that, I was hoping we could proceed to Maine so you could tour our ship building plant there. I know it's asking a lot but I was hoping we could also squeeze in a trip to our biomedical facility and the resorts there. Now that I spell it all out, I guess it sounds like a lot to take in on your first tour." He paused a moment. "Abriella? You still there?"

"Uh," what was I supposed to say? "Hazen, how long did you anticipate we would be gone?"

"I don't know. I guess a month maybe more."

"Hazen, I can't, how, um, I," I literally could not think of words to express what I was thinking.

"Too much, huh?"

"Uh, yeah, I guess you could say that. I have a home here and kids in school. Well, technically only Katie in school but, still. I can't just up and go off for that long. Plus, how could I tour all these plants and wineries and quarries and ship-builders with two kids in tow?" My heart began to see what only my mind had understood since I first met Hazen; I did not fit into his world and never would. "Hazen, I can't do this. I'm sorry." I felt a distinctive stab in my heart as I heard my words and I felt as if I was about to cry.

"Woe, Brie, don't go there. Let's talk about this. Okay, how about a week and only a few of the west coast businesses? I can get my father to fly to the California winery for a day to meet you. He loves that place anyway and it may do him good to get out of the house since my granddad died." My mind calmed somewhat.

"Um, that would probably be doable but, Hazen, can I ask you something?"

"Of course, you can ask me anything."

"Are you having me do this because of the job I'm doing for you or for another reason?" There, I had said it. There was silence on the phone for a few seconds. I waited impatiently for his answer.

"I won't lie, Abriella," his voice seemed deeper and subdued, "I'd like you to see some of the places and meet my father but, mainly, I just want to spend time with you and your children. I like what I see so far and I want to know you better."

"Hazen," I checked my words before speaking them, "I am flattered but we can get to know one another right here in Atlanta. We don't have to go all over the country to do that."

"Yeah," he laughed, "I guess we could but you know me; I don't do normal."

"I'm beginning to get that," I laughed back at him to keep this new, lighter mood. "Okay, how about this," I breathed deeply, "how about one week, two- maybe three places and that's it for a first excursion? I'll board Sparks, our cat, I guess."

"The cat can travel with us. That's no problem. The rest sounds good and I'm sorry if I overwhelmed you for a moment there."

"Hazen, you overwhelmed me the first minute I met you." Oops! I did not mean to say that aloud. Hazen laughed heartily.

"Was that the moment before or after you fell into my arms," he was stoked now. Despite the fact that he could not see me, I turned a crimson red, again.

We talked on the phone for almost two hours that afternoon. If I had not had to pick up the kids from school, I felt I could have talked to him the rest of the day and into the night. We decided to leave the following Friday. This would give me time to prepare, Hazen time to find a suitable tutor for Katie of whom he insisted upon, and for me to complete my projections. I had a lot of preparations to do both personally and at the office. It turned out to be a whirlwind of a week. Before I had time to get nervous, it was time for us to go.

The kids, especially Katie who understood better than Josh, were intensely excited. I had gotten us each a few new items of clothes, such as winter coats appropriate for Washington. Tracy had insisted I borrow their luggage to keep from purchasing my own. As I packed on Thursday evening, I realized that I might just as well have kept the kids out of school on Friday because there was no way that Katie would be able to pay attention anyways. However, my maternal instincts had me drop them off on Friday morning as planned. I only worked half the day so I could get the kids as soon as school was out at three, rather than wait until five-thirty as usual. Hazen picked us up in a limousine from our apartment. He had brought it, he said, because we would not all fit into his small sports car with our luggage. He and the driver loaded our luggage and off we headed to the airport- or so I had thought.

I knew Atlanta airport's location was well on the far south side of this great city so when Butch, the driver, headed north, I was confused.

"Where are we going?" I asked Hazen as he read Josh a book in the car. He looked up as if he was just as confused as I was and replied.

"The airport."

"No, the airport is south," I answered thinking his driver must be confused.

"No, it's above Atlanta." He sounded so confident.

"No, Hazen, you're mistaken. It is south. In fact, it is many miles south of Atlanta. I've been there many times."

"Oh, you must be thinking of Hartsfield International Airport," he acted surprised and it all made no sense to me.

"Of course, I am, what other,"

"I'm sorry, Brie. I should have explained. We're taking the corporate jet. We're going to a private airstrip. This way avoids the check-in, security, and standing in line delays- cuts out several hours. I should have told you. I didn't think about it because I'm so used to this way." Of course he was, because he is rich. I could not stop staring at him speaking of this immense luxury as if it were a small detour. It did help me understand why bringing Sparks had not been a problem, though. I didn't need to worry about his crate being shoved somewhere or him while flying. No doubt, Hazen intended for Sparks to fly in the cabin with us. Hazen went right back to reading Josh's book as if no big deal. I had the sensation of being transported into another universe, one that made even Seth's lifestyle seem meager. I had resented Seth's money, felt it unnecessary and shallow. Now, I realized, my resentment had more to do with the way that Seth used his money. His money serviced his need to be in control, to use as a tool for his own selfish, power-hungry needs. It was not the money, per se, that I had resented. The use of it is what sickened me.

As I watched Hazen gently reading to my sweet boy, I knew. I knew that he lacked the same twisted need to rule over others that consumed Seth. I knew he would never use his money, or any situation, to try to control me. After having seen a glimpse of how he had used some of his money to help those in need all over the world, I knew that he would use his wealth for good. Yes, his luxuries were extravagant and yet, given his budget, they were not as absurd as would be expected. A two-hundred thousand dollar car was extravagant; however, that was no different to his budget than my cheap car was to mine. There are many in the world who possess not only one, but also several cars that cost millions of dollars each, I thought. Maybe I was just trying to justify my feelings toward Hazen. I hoped with all my heart that he is the honorable man I envisioned. I prayed that he is.

When we finally arrived at the airport, I imagined we would ride right up to the airplane as the rich people do in the movies. Instead, the limo took us to a terminal and we checked in at the office. Our luggage was unloaded from the car and loaded onto the plane. Then a golf cart picked us up and took us down the hangers a ways until we reached Hazen's plane. I was not sure what I had expected, a small plane that sat four or five people, I guessed. We rode up to a plane that seemed far too big for just the four of us.

The kids were giddy with excitement as we walked up the stairs to embark. The inside was plush but not over the top. The interior boasted a simple yet well-decorated interior. The seats were much nicer than normal airplane seats. Seth and I would always ride in first-class commercial and these seats were almost identical to those. There looked to be about twenty seats but several sets of seats had small tables between them. Hazen helped me get the kids settled and buckled. Hazen buckled Sparks' crate in the seat beside Katie. Just as he and I were about to sit, the pilot came back to greet us.

"Good afternoon Mr. Thatcher." He shook Hazen's hand. "We'll be ready for take-off in approximately twelve minutes if that's alright with you."

"That'll be perfect. Chad, may I present Abriella Taylor. Abriella, this is Chad Bishop." We said our salutations quickly. "We're ready when you are Chad." Hazen said as he sat next to me.

"Very good, sir." Chad responded as he retreated into the cockpit.

"Once we are in the air, I'd like to take the kids up to the cockpit for a moment. It's very exciting up there. I think they'd like it. Is that alright with you?" Hazen asked me.

"Only if I get to go, too," I smiled.

"You didn't think I would let you stay behind, did you?" he answered demurely. Then he took my hand, pulled it into his lap, and gently clutched it. He was so gentlemanly. We had not even shared a kiss, yet, except in my mind. I really hoped this trip would be the magic to make it happen. The kids giggling broke my reverie. They were looking at Hazen and me snuggling. It occurred to me that neither of them had ever seen a man be affectionate to me. I beamed back at them.

"Mr. Thatcher, we'll be taxiing to the runway in less than one minute." The intercom blasted. A beautiful young woman came in from behind the curtain then and asked Hazen if we were comfortable.

"Of course, Patti. We're good. Take a seat."

"Very well, sir." She said as she disappeared behind the same curtain. The kids let out small screams as the plane's engine grew louder and we began to move. Within minutes, we sped down the runway and rose into the beautiful sky. Once we were airborne and steadied again, Chad announced that we were free to get up if we needed.

"I could go to the restroom," I announced quietly.

"I wanna go," Katie said excitedly. Hazen laughed and gave us directions. As soon as we stood up, Josh motioned that he wanted to go as well.

"I'll take him," Hazen volunteered.

"Oh, that's okay. I can."

"I know you can but you and Katie are already going. I don't mind." Such a simple gesture Hazen offered yet it meant so much. After our bathroom breaks, Hazen took us up to the cockpit. He held Josh in his arms; presumably, to keep him from hitting a button and Katie asked a million questions. Josh said a few words, as well, letting us know he had questions, too. After the cockpit visit, Hazen showed us several interesting facts about this plane including the small kitchenette that housed the ability to serve full meals.

"Can we eat on the plane?" Katie enthusiastically asked.

"No, sweetie," I began.

"Well, we can have a snack but I have something very special planned for us for dinner once we arrive in California," Hazen added. We all took our seats and soon Patti brought drinks, muffins, pretzels, and a variety of fresh fruits from which to choose. She laid the array of snacks on the small table along with napkins and utensils. Then she poured drinks for each of us. The four and a half hour flight went quickly. To our disappointment, we landed too soon. It was dark by the time we arrived and the children's noses pressed against the windows to see the lights of the airport as we landed. A limousine awaited us and we watched from the airplane windows as the men loaded our luggage from the plane to the car's trunk. Then we disembarked and got into the back of the car. Hazen joined us almost immediately with a big smile on his face.

"What is it?" I inquired.

"You'll see," his smile resembled an impish boy. Hazen's masculine demeanor sometimes contradicted his boyish charms. His features were dark and mysterious in appearance and yet, as I was getting to know him, he was open and down-to-Earth.

"Where are we?" It occurred to me I did not even know where we had landed.

"San Francisco but we're not staying here." His grin let me know he was not giving any information away. We drove through San Francisco and the lights shown beautifully. The kids were beginning to get tired but their eagerness to take in every detail of this trip kept them asking questions and pointing to various points of interest. Hazen shared information that amazed us as we rode through the streets of San Francisco.

"San Francisco is Spanish for Saint Francis. During the California Gold Rush of 1840, it grew to be the largest city in California at the time. In 1906, a great earthquake almost destroyed the city. It took years to rebuild but it was rebuilt better than it had started." We continued to ride and Hazen told interesting stories about Alcatraz and its notorious residents of old. "You can't see it as well at night but out in that bay is an island where a famous prison for terrible prisoners was built."

"Are they still there?" Katie's curiosity piqued.

"No, in fact, it's a visitor attraction now. The Army built it as a military fortification and lighthouse but it later became a prison. Maybe we could see it next time we come to California. It is pretty cool even in the summer months and would probably be too cold for us this trip. But it sits on an island just out there." He pointed to the blackness where a sole light shown over the waters. I noticed he inferred that we would be back to California with him again and my heart swelled with anticipation. "Alright, we are about to go over the famous Golden Gate Bridge. Look ahead kids!" We all looked and saw the iconic structure with awe. "This bridge had to overcome enormous odds to be built. Just as the financing for it was coming together, the 1929 crash hit and so a thirty-million-dollar bond measure was approved to begin construction." The kids wowed this statement as if they understood what Hazen meant.

"It was finally completed in 1937. When it was opened, over two-hundred-thousand people crossed the bridge on foot before it was allowed open to traffic a week later." He told the stories in such an animated way that we all got caught up in them. Learning about the bridge as we crossed it made an impact on us all. We looked up through the sunroof of the limousine at the enormous towers and cables that ran across the skyline.

"It's so beautiful," I expressed.

"Yes but sometimes the fog is so great that the bridge literally disappears in it." It was impossible to imagine. We continued on this way until all the lights of the city were behind us. The kids were getting tired and a little hungry.

"It's not much farther," Hazen instructed as I laid Josh's head in my lap. "They'll have our dinner ready when we arrive."

"Who are 'they'?" I asked. Hazen smiled, shook his head, and touched my nose with his finger, never saying a word. About twenty minutes later, we saw lights again as our car made several turns off the main highway. These were not magnificent lights of a large city but rather a lit path toward an illuminated area ahead. At last, we turned onto what looked like a very long driveway, perhaps two or three miles long with antique street lamps on both sides of the road. As the lighted area ahead grew closer, Katie and I became more and more excited. Josh, who had been almost asleep, arose and looked out of the window to see the excitement.

"What is it, mommy?" he asked.

"I don't know." I looked at Hazen who was still not divulging any information. Finally, we came to the source of the lights and our excitement. My eyes and mind could barely take it all in.

A mansion spread before us with two-story high columns amass across the front. It was white and resembled the old antebellum homes of the Deep South. As we got close to it, the street changed from the cement of the driveway to a beautifully constructed cobblestone with a tiered water fountain in the middle of the circular way. We drove around the fountain all "oohing" and "ahhing" as we went. The car stopped at the front door and several attendants joined us from within the house.

"What is this place?" I asked Hazen, no longer content to be kept in the dark.

"Do you like it?"

"Like it? My gosh, it's the most gorgeous place I've ever seen in my life."

"This is Mi Paz." The name sounded vaguely familiar and I knew it was because I had probably seen it on the spreadsheets. "It means, 'my peace' in Spanish." My grandfather renamed it when he bought it in 1929. He raised my father here, for the most part. We used to spend summers here when I was a kid." I could not imagine enjoying a place like this as a kid.

"Wait. You said 1929? That was the year of the market crash. How in the world did your grandfather buy a place like this while everyone else," I let the words fade away.

"Yes, he was a very wealthy man who invested in real estate rather than the stock market. While the hit naturally affected him as well, he was a keen businessman. He got this in foreclosure at a remarkable price, of course. He opened it to many people for no rent except to work his vineyards. He saved many families from demise. He even built shacks along the outskirts of the fields for those he could no longer fit into the house so they would have homes. He also turned some of the wine gardens into vegetable gardens in order to insure everyone ate. Our family will miss him terribly." The attendants had our luggage out and disappeared into the house as Hazen, the kids, and I stood on the deep porch and admired the view.

"I'm hungry, momma," Josh reminded us.

"Ah, my little one, a dinner fit for a king awaits." He picked Josh up and we headed into the house. "Maria, how are you darling?" Hazen addressed an older, Spanish woman approaching us quickly.

"My Hazen!" she exuded enthusiasm to see him. They embraced and then he introduced us all to Maria, the mansion's chief caregiver.

"Maria has been with my grandfather since I was a little boy. She and her husband live here and take care of everything, even my grandfather until he passed."

"Oh and we miss him so," she expressed with her thick Spanish accent. "But come, you must all be starving." She led the way into a large banquet room. It was after dinnertime, she explained, but she had made sure the kitchen kept everything warm for us. "Sit, sit. I get Clara to bring out your dishes, eh?" Hazen helped me get the kids settled and held out my chair. Then he walked over to a large bar area, pouring out two glasses of wine and brought them to our table.

"Here, I want you to try this," he said as he placed one of the glasses in my hand. I sipped it. It was delightful. "This is one of our signature wines. We export it to all areas of the world. Some think it is more of a summer wine but I like it year round."

"I agree. I could drink this every night." I was not much of drinker but this light golden wine was delicious. Just then, several ladies came from the kitchen, all smiles and heavy handed with plates already filled. Pot roast with mashed potatoes covered about half of our plate. Assorted vegetables including carrots, green beans, and cauliflower filled the other half. The staff put gravy boats filled with a rich, brown liquid by each plate. Then they placed a separate plate by each of us with soft yeast rolls and pats of butter in the shape of a flower. Josh and Katie got small glasses of milk. Maria poured more wine for Hazen and me. We all ate heartily because it was all so wonderful. As stuffed as we were, when Clara brought out coconut cake, no one declined to eat it.

"More wine, my sweet?" Hazen asked just as they placed the cake in front of me.

"No, please. I'm starting to get a little tipsy."

"You are a light weight, my dear." Hazen teased.

"Would you like coffee?" Clara asked.

"That would be lovely, if it's not too much trouble." She was gone and back in just a moment with coffee cup and saucer in hand. "Oh my. This coffee is as good as the wine."

"Ah, yes, we have it flown in green, roast it ourselves, and grind it just before brewing."

"Amazing!"

"I know you are all tired but we need to walk off this dinner. How about a small tour of the place? We'll have the big tour in the morning."

"Yay!" the kids shouted before I had a chance to protest. After we freshened up, Hazen took us outside. We walked around the area immediately surrounding the huge mansion as he told us stories of its past and his childhood here.

"See that small building there?" he pointed into the darkness and I could faintly see the silhouette of a small building in the distance. "That is the shed behind which I received my first correction as a mischievous boy."

"What do you mean?" Katie asked innocently.

"My grandfather had me pick out a switch from a nearby tree and he spanked my behind with it- right behind that shed."

"What?" Katie was alarmed. "That's terrible!" Hazen laughed aloud.

"Yes, my little one, I guess you would think it was but, you know what?" Hazen leaned down to look Katie in the eyes and she shook her head. "I never lied to him again." I could see the respect in Hazen's eyes and realized his grief must be great. He had recently lost the patriarch of his family- a loss so great that it had crippled his father and now, Hazen was being called upon to change his life forever from the free-spirited philanthropist to astute businessman. Yes, his loss was emotional as well as literal.

"You must miss him terribly." I tried to console.

"Abriella," I loved it when he called me by my full name, "no one could ever understand. He was not only a grandfather. He was my mentor, spiritual advisor, confidant, and hero." He looked back toward the shed that housed the memory.

"I wish I could have met him."

"Me, too. He would have loved you."

"Are you and your father not as close?"

"We've had our differences for sure but, he is also a great source of strength to me. He made me stronger by pushing me and, once I finally began to grow up, I appreciated his will. He will like you also." He looked at me and the illumination from the moon and the lights sprinkled around the yard shone on his dark face. "He will love you." There, between us, that magnetism that had struck us so passionately from the first moment we met crept back into our eyes as we stood gazing at one another. I wanted to kiss him, longed to taste him and feel his embrace. The kids squealing nearby as they chased Sparks reminded me that this was neither the time nor place for our first romantic interlude. I assured myself that it would happen, though. I would insure that it would happen before we left this gorgeous setting. I would give him another memory to think of every time he returned to this haven.

~ 17 ~

Better Than Better

Maria showed the kids and me the suite that she prepared for us. It had only one bed but it was a king size and I felt better knowing the kids would stay with me. There was a small sitting area and a private bath. Katie, Josh, and I snuggled up in the big bed and giggled until we finally gave out. Josh fell asleep first and Katie had many questions.

"Do you like him, momma?"

"Yes, I do, but sweetie, Hazen and I are only friends." I didn't want Katie's imagination going wild. I didn't ever want her to be hurt if things didn't work out.

"But you want him to be your boyfriend, don't you?" She has always been very persistent.

"We'll see. Now, go to sleep, Katie. We have a big day ahead of us again tomorrow."

"What are we doing tomorrow?"

"I have no idea. Go to sleep." I could hardly hold my own eyes open. Katie quieted and sleep finally came.

The next day began early. We enjoyed breakfast in the dining room. The kids and I moved slowly this early but by the time we finished our meal, the conversation and anticipation had us all wide-awake.

"I thought we'd take a tour on horseback. Katie can ride by herself but Josh can ride with me." Hazen suggested.

"Oh yes, mommy, please," Katie started immediately. My children on horses made me very nervous.

"I don't know. Maybe Katie should ride with me." I prompted.

"Mommy, please! My birthday is in a few weeks. This can be my birthday present! You know how much I miss my horse! For my birthday, p l e a s e !" I felt cornered. Katie had ridden well then but that was years ago.

"Alright, but Hazen, I want her on a gentle and small horse."

"Of course, madam," he jested in a mock English accent.

We rode all morning. Hazen showed us the rows and rows of grapes all supported by trellises that adorned the property beautifully. He explained the irrigation system to me and Katie asked many intelligent questions. There were several small lakes on the property and we rode the horses to them. Hazen had asked Maria to pack a picnic lunch for us. Around eleven-thirty he led us to a beautiful spot beside one of the lakes that overlooked a particularly gorgeous orchard.

"This is my favorite spot on the entire plantation," Hazen shared after we had eaten. Maria had packed sandwich cold cuts, potato salad, cookies, water, and of course, wine. It was obvious this was not the first picnic she had packed and I wondered how many women Hazen had brought here. "You see how the rows are all planted in north-south directions?" I nodded. I had not noticed that until he mentioned it. "We do that because both sides of the vine need to be exposed to the sun to prevent frost. Come with me." He insisted as he held out his hand to help me up. The kids naturally followed.

He walked us up to the vines and held a vine in his hand. "See how we've pruned the vines back for winter? They must rest. In a few months, small buds will appear and soon the entire field will be aflame with beauty."

"When is harvest season?" I asked, suddenly interested in this art form.

"Well, here in northern California, it is usually in the fall. We must watch the grapes though to insure they are ripe. The exact time of year varies."

"I didn't know you were so knowledgeable of all your family's affairs." I said honestly.

"Yes, well, growing up I was forced to help during harvest most years. Once the grapes ripen, we must harvest them quickly so they are suitable for wine. Now we use machines to do some of the harvesting, depending on the type of grape and wine it is to become. When I was a boy, we harvested all fields by hand. People would come from all over to help. Some would pitch tents for the night. We paid well, so finding enough help was seldom a problem.

"I'm tired, mommy," Josh pulled my shirt and I picked him up.

"Why don't we take the kids back to the house? There is more I would like to show you." Hazen suggested.

"But I don't wanna go back? Why should I have to go back just because he's tired?" Katie argued.

"I tell you what, little one," Hazen consoled Katie as he lifted her up to reach the horse's stirrup. "Why don't you help the others in the stables? There are several horses in need of exercise."

"Really?" Katie expressed as she snuggled into the saddle. We all rode back and Hazen held Josh tightly because the rhythm of the horse's gallop had almost lulled him to sleep by the time we reached the house. Hazen carried Josh up to our room and laid him on the bed. I followed close behind.

"Hazen, I can't leave him. He'll be scared if he wakes up alone." As much as I wanted to follow Hazen anywhere, my maternal instincts would not allow me to do it.

"My dear, I'll have Genevieve sit with him. She is Maria's granddaughter and a very trusted baby-sitter." After we got Katie to the stables and introduced her to several of the caretakers, Hazen took us to the crush areas. The buildings were massive and divided into areas that included crushing the grapes, extracting the juice, discarding the grape skins, and preparing the juice for making wine.

"Mr. Thatcher, may I use your horse to run back to the house for a bit?" one of the caretakers asked after we had toured the area for about thirty minutes.

"Take hers and leave it there. I'm going to take her over to the winery next. She can ride with me." The thought of riding on a horse with Hazen excited me. Maybe this would be my chance to steal that kiss of which I could not stop thinking. Once we finished the crush area and went outside, Hazen helped me onto his horse, which was much larger than mine had been. He mounted behind me and wrapped his arms around me to hold the reigns.

Our bodies folded intimately together. Hazen and I had never touched like this. We had never been this close. My senses screamed at me to lay back on his chest, to pull his arms closer to me. We galloped at a steady pace a little ways away to a more distinguished building. I was disappointed when we arrived. Hazen got down and reached up effortlessly to take me by the waist and help me. When I slid down from the horse, Hazen and I stood face-to-face and almost touching. I was mustering up the courage to get on my tiptoes to reach him when he turned away.

"Shall we go inside?" he said gruffly. I felt rebuffed. Could it be that I had read more into his actions than he intended? Maybe this grand trip was truly only a business arrangement to him. Yet, he had implied, I thought, that there may be more to us than strictly business. Had I misconstrued his words? Could I possibly be that wrong? Once inside, Hazen began again with the explanation of how the juices are fermented.

"See these vats?" He pointed at the obviously humongous vessels erected back to back within the warehouse-like room.

"They house the juice for primary fermentation. These tanks are stainless steel, which we use to make Riesling. For some wines we use open wooden vats, wine barrels, and sometimes even inside the wine bottle itself."

This was all very fascinating but I really wanted to kiss this man. I felt I would burst if I did not know his intentions. Was he interested in me at all? He was always calling me sweet names like, 'beautiful', and 'sweetheart', and 'dear'. Maybe he did that to all women. I begin to fade out, partially because my brain was overfilling with information from the day, but mostly because I could not stop thinking of kissing his beautiful lips. "So that's how we do it in this facility. Would you like to see the others?" No, I would like to close my eyes and fall upon you as I did the first time I met you.

"Actually, Hazen, I'm a little overwhelmed. Can we sit a bit?"

"Of course, here." He took me by the elbow as if I could no longer walk and led me to the side of the huge tanks. "Sit here," he pointed to some cement steps. "If you'd like, we can go to the lounge where we host wine tastings. You would be more comfortable there and we could sample a few wines." No, I want to sample you, I thought.

"Actually, Hazen," I stood back up and we faced one another again. A position we had been in several times now but he appeared oblivious to noticing. "I have a question."

"Great! About the winery or fermentation process, or,"

"No, about us." Hazen looked me in the eyes then, understanding immediately where I intended to go with this.

"Abriella," his voice changed to the soft deep one that I had first noticed about him. "You are a beautiful woman." Ah! Here it is. The reason he has not made a move. He took my hands and looked me straight in the eyes. "I find you very attractive but," here we go. "I," get it out already. This was just too painful. I had to let him off the hook and even as I thought this, my eyes begin to sting with tears.

"It's alright, Hazen," I interjected, "I have a lot of baggage. I get it." I moved away and turned my back on him so he would not witness my humiliation. "Two kids, poor single mom. Don't feel bad. You are a good man. I…"

"Abriella, you're mistaken," he grabbed my arm and turned me back to him. I tried to hide my face but it was too late. I was not openly crying, thank goodness, but my eyes defiantly betrayed me. "Abriella, don't cry."

"I'm not," I lied, "Look, um, Hazen, can I just go to the restroom or something for a minute. I'm not mad, really."

"You are a stubborn woman, you know it? I'm trying to tell you something and,"

"You don't have to explain. You're way out of my league. I get it, you," his mouth was upon mine instantly, kissing me deeply. His hands cradled my face forcefully and his strength pulled me to him. His body pressed upon me. His tongue devoured me. The flame that had begun the moment we saw one another had grown over these past few weeks. The anticipation of this moment had increased our intensity. His hand released my face and he pulled my body up to his with a gentle force as the kiss deepened.

I felt he engulfed me and I reveled in this raw vehemence. It was like no other kiss I had felt. I was not a teenager experimenting, or a begrudging wife fulfilling a duty. I was a woman following her instincts to respond to a man who had awakened in me the ancient beast of passion.

Time had no meaning to us at this moment. My hands reached up to embrace his arms and they felt like steel beneath my palms. He was strong, physically and mentally. His mouth barely allowed me to breathe as he continued to caress mine with a skill that I never knew existed. His hands pressed my body's full length to him and I could feel that his chest and legs exceeded his arms in power. I surrendered to the moment, to him.

"Oh Abriella," he breathed heavily, "I have wanted you since the first moment you fell into my arms." His mouth took mine again before I could think to respond. I put my hand behind his head to pull him into me. I did not want us to ever separate again. The gesture seemed to enliven him. He crushed me to him with a magnetic force that seemed impossible to break. I wanted him, no doubt about it. I needed him.

"Hazen," I grunted breathlessly. I did not recognize my own throaty voice. "I want you." I was powerless.

"Oh Abriella," he stopped for a moment to look at me. His hands held my face again softly but with an obvious intent of keeping me at a distance. I tried to push towards him, to continue this magnificent dance we had begun but his hands held me firmly away.

"What's wrong?" Could he not see how much I wanted him? Abruptly, he laughed so loud that it echoed from the huge room.

"My dear, nothing is wrong except we cannot do this, not here, not now, not like this." His beautiful smile looked down upon me to soften this blow.

"Why not?" My instincts spoke up.

"Because I treasure you," he was still smiling, "I respect the hell out of you and I will not cheapen you by taking you in the middle of this winery." I wanted to scream, "Take me! I don't mind!" but somewhere in the back corners of my mind, I knew he was right. At the moment, I did not care about respect, his or mine, but I knew that his judgment and self-restraint would make me admire him all the more. Still, I tried to lean forward to kiss him again, not wanting this sensation to stop. It was dope to my blood.

"Abriella, please, if you have any care for me at all, please stop. I respect you, yes, but I am a man." This sobered me a little and I stopped pushing against his hands that were trying to hold me back. He relaxed a smidgen then and his hands fell to my shoulders as if he could no longer hold their weight. "You tempt a man beyond reasonable measure." He was not smiling any longer. Instead, his countenance was somber, still, and intense.

"There will be a day that you will be mine, Abriella. But it will come in time, after we have grown into each other's lives, after we understand our future," he continued. My breath was returning to normal and my heart finally began to slow to a normal pace. I felt spent and exhilarated at the same time. His hands fell from my shoulders and his right hand took mine as he led me outside.

The sun shone brightly after being in the low lighting of the winery and it took a moment for us to adjust. Hazen helped me back atop the horse and joined me. Our stance had changed. No longer did I feel the self-conscious frigidity of trying not to lean upon him. No longer was he erect in the saddle. Now, I leaned back upon his strong body and he melded into mine. The sharp gallop we had enjoyed all day turned to a slow methodical trot and we headed back toward the house, neither anxious to arrive.

The evening and the next morning went too quickly as Hazen continued to show us the vineyard and its facets. This vineyard that had produced grapes for centuries had not changed but Hazen and I had. We held hands at times. He became even more courteous, opening doors, helping with the kids, and pulling my chair out for me at the table. The waltz we danced was age old and yet, to us, felt new. The staff seemed to take notice as well sharing knowing smiles. The kids took to Hazen as if he had been in their lives since birth. I could not imagine anything more heavenly than this feeling. Never had I felt it. I was incapable of describing it. All I knew was that I never wanted it to end.

"Hazen, can I talk to you for a moment?" I asked after lunch as he read Josh a book before his nap.

"Just a moment," he whispered, "we're at the best part." It had bothered me that I did not tell Hazen that my marriage to Seth was not completely dissolved. I justified it because I knew the truth- that we had never been a truly married couple, and we had not lived together for years now. Nevertheless, I understood that legally I was still married to Seth and that needed to be resolved if Hazen and I were to build this relationship further. I did not want to tell him on the trip. I had planned to tell him upon our return. I did not want to ruin this trance that we both operated under now.

"Alright, my sweet," he answered softly as he closed the door, "what can I do for you?"

"Well, I know that you had quite an agenda for our travels and we've been here for two days."

"Ah, yes, I was going to speak with you about that. I stayed a little longer hoping my father would join us but he said he is just not up to it yet. I know you are enjoying this immensely but I was hoping either this afternoon or, at the latest, in the morning, if we could move on to Washington. The Boeing plant up there does not project the same aesthetic response as the winery but it is equally beautiful in its own way."

"That's fine," a sense of melancholy fell over me but I knew we must move on. "Today is fine." I knew if we stayed, our time left would only feel sad now. I would rather move on and leave on a high note.

"Are you okay?" he asked as he brushed my cheek.

"Yes, but I'll miss this place. It oddly feels like home." Hazen smiled a knowing smile.

"Yes, for me as well. We can return anytime you like." That sounded like a terrific idea to me. He leaned down and kissed me, not the deep intense kiss we had shared before but a sweet and gentle assuring kiss. It ignited my passion all the same and I pressed upon him wanting more.

"Abriella, we have to be careful," he whispered. He was right. He was always right. Josh was in the next room sleeping and Katie could be anywhere near. They could easily walk in on us. "I exercise as much self-control as I can with you but I am not a man who has long appreciated delayed gratification. If we are not careful, we could go too far. Then there would be no undoing it." Oh, that is not what I thought he had meant. I did not want to undo anything with him. Yet, he was being smart, and taking a higher moral ground than I felt capable of when I was around him. I needed to learn to think at a higher level as he did.

"Okay," I whispered back to him, "but know that it is against my will that I walk away."

"One day I will be at a weak moment and then you will be in trouble," he said as I turned to leave.

"Promises! Promises!" I cooed to him over my shoulder as I begin to walk away. Hazen grabbed my arm and twirled me back into his arms. With one swift movement, his mouth found mine and he began kissing me deeply, passionately. I melted into him with no resolve to pull away. The kiss escalated quickly and I faintly noticed that I pulled him closer to me, pressing my body against his. Hazen's strong arms held me tightly to his chest and I could feel his passion growing. My brain began to tell me to back away but I immediately told it to keep quiet. Hazen abruptly let me go and I had to grab his arm to steady myself.

"Do not tempt fate," he said as he walked away and left me standing there.

~ 18 ~

A Strong Foundation

We arrived in Washington around four that afternoon. The rplane made moving from location to location almost as easy as ɔpping in the car. Seattle seemed bigger than San Francisco to me ut probably only because we saw more of the city here. Because it ıd already been a full few days, Hazen asked if the tutor, who 'as meeting us in Seattle, could watch the kids while he and I ıecked out the Boeing plant.

"I know the kids are getting tired," he explained. "It won't ıke more than a couple of hours then we'll come get the kids for inner."

"That'll be fine. The tutor can work with Katie while Josh plays." Hazen had a limo take us for the thirty-minute drive to Everett, where the Boeing plant is located. It was nice to have him all to myself for a change. He grew animated as he talked of the Boeing plant and expressed his zeal to show it to me.

"This building is the largest in the world, by volume at four-hundred seventy-two million cubic feet of space," he began explaining before we had gotten far from the condominium his family owned in Seattle for just such trips. "They have a visitor's tour that lasts about four hours but we are going to skip the PR films and what not. One day I would like to bring the kids. It is a fascinating place but Josh would probably get too tired. If we had more time, I could take them on the commercial tour; it's better equipped for children. Yes, definitely, we'll have to bring them back for that one day." I loved how he kept referring to our futures as if it were a sure thing that we would always be together. I had learned my lesson about getting married too soon with Seth. As much as I felt that I could trust Hazen, I wanted us to enjoy a dating relationship for a long time, except when he kissed me.

The plant was indeed a massive building, resembling a small city in itself. Even as we pulled into the parking lot, I was awe struck. Once we entered, Hazen talked to several men and introduced me to them as his business advisor, which made me feel more important than I knew I actually was to his company. His family had been successful for generations before me and, no doubt, would continue to be for generations to come regardless of any contribution I did or did not make. We began the tour by quickly going through the visitor's center that displayed Boeing's history. Then we moved on to the actual tour of seeing the gigantic planes as the workers assembled them.

"Boeing began in Everett during World War II. They gave subassembly support for the B-17. This plant didn't actually open until May of 1967. My father is the one who took interest in this branch of business. He became a partner in the late seventies when they expanded to accommodate more sales. Since then, they've expanded several more times to accommodate even more airlines." We looked down upon a room, for lack of a better word, that inhabited dozens of airplanes, a mass assembly line. The vehicles, products, and airplane pieces that surrounded the planes looked like small replicas comparably.

"This plant has been visited by dignitaries- from presidents of the United States to foreign leaders and prime ministers,

Princes, Dukes, even Kings." The admiration in his voice evident, Hazen looked over the factory with pride. The entire day fascinated me and I looked forward to bringing the kids one day. I could envision Josh's eyes as he looked out over this enormous collection of giants. When we finally left, I was growing tired. We had walked most of the way and I realized I was out of shape. Hazen didn't seemed fazed by the exertion.

"So, what did you think of it all," Hazen asked as he slipped his arm around my shoulders once we were back in the limousine.

"Oh my gosh, it's amazing. How could anyone ever describe that to someone who hadn't seen it?" I liked the warmth of his embrace as we snuggled in the back of the car. He beamed with satisfaction as I reiterated, in detail, everything I had loved about it.

"Would you like a drink?" he asked as he rose up and opened a compartment on the side of the limo to expose a bar. I nodded as I continued to talk. He poured a glass of wine for each of us and leaned back, handing mine to me. I had not realized I was so thirsty until he handed me the glass. Without thinking, I downed it. He poured another and gave me a miniature bottle of water from the bar. I drank both quickly as I continued telling him how much I had enjoyed the day.

"Hazen, you live such a wonderful life. I am envious in so many ways. I am so glad you haven't had to endure some of the terrible things I've had to live through." I was opening up to him more now. It seemed odd to me because I had a hard time opening up to anyone. He handed me another glass of wine and another water. I sat the water in the cup holder and drank the wine as I rattled on. "I've never been very ambitious or at least not since I got pregnant with Katie in high school. My mother was very self-centered. Between her selfishness and my mistake, I got started on the wrong foot and couldn't seem to catch a break since."

I was rambling now and, even though I somehow realized it, I could not stop myself. I took another swallow of my wine. It was so very tasty. "You know, I have no idea where my mother even lives now? I guess I could look her up, but why? I mean, she never cared for me. She really wanted to move far away from me. She doesn't even know I have a son. Can you believe that?" I handed my empty glass back to Hazen for a refill.

"Sweetheart, why don't you drink some water?" he suggested. I picked up the water and took a sip.

"I don't care anyway. I mean, even if she did know, she wouldn't do anything differently. I miss my father. He left when I was little. Did I ever tell you that?" I stopped to look at his face for an answer. Then I got up myself and poured another glass of wine. When I sat back down next to Hazen, I took another sip of wine. "Yeah, he left me with that evil woman. I guess I don't blame him for leaving but I wish he had taken me with him instead of leaving me with her. His entire family was so nice. I wonder where they all are today." I was talking more to myself now than Hazen. His silence finally caught my attention and I looked at him directly. He had the most compassionate countenance as he looked at me.

"Abriella, I am so sorry you had to go through all of that," he spoke softly as he brushed my cheek with the back of his hand. The love in his eyes, the tenderness of his touch, and the sincerity in his voice made me feel so safe. I leaned into him and kissed him and he kissed me back. After only a moment though, he pushed me back. "Careful sweetheart." I wanted him badly but I turned and drank the rest of my wine. I lay my head on his shoulder. He was so strong, so physically solid, not like the fashionably skinny men but like a warrior from the Viking days. I admired that he was as mentally powerful as he was physically strong. Yet, at times, I almost wished he were not so that we could go further.

"What are you thinking, love," he turned my head to look at him again. I loved the way he spoke to me. It did make me feel loved and I had never felt that in my life. Even Seth, as nice as he was when we dated, was never affectionate with words or gestures. I was almost thirty-years-old and I had never felt this much love from another human being in my life, not like this, not from a man. I had not realized what I was missing and now that I did, I was not sure if I could ever live without it.

"I'm thinking that I love you," I answered honestly. I probably should not have said that but I did not care. I did love him and I should not have to hold that inside of myself. He leaned down and kissed me, kissed me as he had never kissed me. He pulled my body so close to his that I felt the wonderful crush of his hard chest against mine. His arm was around my shoulders holding me close to him and I couldn't have escaped if I had wanted to, but of course, I didn't. His free hand held my face to his and his tongue explored mine without any reservation. I was intoxicated, not only with the wine but with his presence. He seemed everywhere, around me, beside me, above me. I smelt his musky cologne and my head reeled with anticipation. I raised my arm and wrapped it around his neck to pull him closer to me. His hand left my face and began to explore my body, first only my back and side as he stroked me up and down. After only a minute, his hand slipped over my breast. The sensation that aroused within me felt more like an unquenchable craving, like a drug. Even in my hazy thoughts, I realized that this was the passion that I had missed in sex, the same one I had read about and known was missing but could never seem to find. With every fiber of my being, I wanted this man. I wanted him in every way, as my lover, as my friend, as my husband, as the father to my children.

"Abriella," he cried out as if in pain, "we have to stop this!"

"No," I returned and pulled his mouth back to mine to quiet him. He returned my kiss with fervor that he had not shown yet. He began to pull my blouse up and I immediately caught on and started to unbutton his shirt. Somehow, deep inside, I felt a little guilty. I knew we had decided to wait before we went further. I should not always put the sole responsibility of enforcing that decision on him. I told myself to stop thinking. "Shut up" I said.

"What?" Hazen asked me and I realized I had said it aloud.

"Nothing," I kissed him again. I pulled his shirttail from his pants and ran my hand over his large chest. The muscles under my palm bulged like a prizefighter. He truly felt like a statue. I instinctively began to kiss his neck and stroke his chest. A low, throaty moan came from inside of him and it acted as an aphrodisiac to my senses. I pushed him back on the seat and pulled his shirt away to give me full view of this picturesque man.

"Abriella, no, we shouldn't," I shut him up with a kiss. I did not need both of us thinking. Just as I turned towards him and lifted myself above him with every intention of sitting in his lap, the car began to slow down. "No, Abriella!" he said more forcibly. He seemed suddenly sober and gently but forcefully sat me back on my seat, quickly buttoning up his shirt and then fixing my blouse. I sat stunned, unsure of what had just happened to change everything so suddenly. One moment we were so engrossed in one another that I did not even remember we were in a car. The next moment the driver was opening our door for our exit. The cold air hit me instantly and I realized my mistake. I stepped out of the car as instructed with the drivers help. The cold wind whipped like a tornado and I realized I had left my coat in the vehicle. I turned back to retrieve it and Hazen's hand was extended from the back with my coat. I grabbed it quickly, put it on, and then turned to walk with Hazen but he was just getting out of the backseat. He joined me but without putting his coat on. Instead, he held it.

"Aren't you cold?" I asked thinking that he might be used to this type weather.

"Indeed madam but right now my jacket is acting as a shield."

"A shield?" I looked down and saw that he was holding it directly in front of him.

"Yes, a shield. You have put me in quite a compromising state." Realizing too late what he meant, my face turned crimson. "Yes, I see you understand now." He peered down at me with a half smirk, half scold look. "Let's go" he motioned for us to head toward the entrance. We walked swiftly and I burrowed deeply into my jacket. The arctic air chilled me to the bone. I was not used to cold and, after this trip, I felt sure I would not care to get used to this weather.

"Give me just a minute," Hazen said after we were inside.

"Hazen, I'm so sorry," I told him sincerely. My head still felt woozy from the wine but with the abrupt halt of our lovemaking and the arctic blast waking me up I felt almost sober now. "I don't know what came over me." That was only partially true. Without a doubt, I knew that his manliness had intoxicated me and to a lesser degree, I understood that guzzling the wine had not helped my inhibitions. Hazen looked at me from the corner of his eye with skepticism.

"Abriella, you are a complex woman, you go from cold, aloof ice statue to spirited, sexy kitten. In all honesty, though, you are sexy in both roles." I wasn't sure how I felt about being called a cold, aloof ice statue. I didn't think I had done anything to deserve that role. After all, I had fallen for him the instant I met him- literally. I did like him calling me sexy, though. Hearing that word come from his mouth stirred my blood once again. I stepped toward him.

"Hold it right there," Hazen barked.

"What?"

"You know exactly what. I'm just regaining my composure from our last escapade." We began our way to the elevator. "Abriella, I need your help." He said to me once we were in the elevator and he had hit the correct button.

"With what?" I would do anything for him.

"With trying to keep us chaste." Oh, that.

"I told you I was sorry, Hazen."

"I know. I am sorry also. The thing is," he reached over and hit stop on the elevator. I had only seen people do that in the movies and did not even realize it was a real possibility. "The thing is, I really like you, hell, who am I kidding? I am falling in love with you," he stepped toward me and intensely looked at me. I felt like a mouse before a cat. As he got closer, I backed up instinctively. "Abriella, I am a man who has not always lived in a pure manner. My natural instinct is to take a gorgeous woman like you and ravage her." My back hit the wall behind me and I had no choice but to stop. "Four years ago, I would not have left you wanting in that limousine. I would have fulfilled your every desire." He felt menacing but in the sexiest way I could have imagined. He put his arms on the wall behind me on each side of my head. I felt trapped and hoped he would never release me. "Do you understand Abriella?" I nodded. "I am trying to maintain my composure with you, to be a gentleman, to respect and honor you but," he sighed deeply and let out a long slow breath, "you are not helping. You tempt me beyond my control. You appear innocent and then suddenly you're ripping my clothes off. You look at me with such adoration. It is too much for a man to bear alone. Do you understand what I'm trying to say?" I did not care what he was trying to say. I wanted him to kiss me. I leaned forward to initiate what I desired. Just before I reached his lips, he pushed me away.

"Abriella!" Hazen stepped back. "If you have any regard for my sanity at all, please stop teasing me. It has been a long time and I am in great pain right now. I would hate myself if I treated you with disrespect."

"Hazen, I want you. I'm sorry. I didn't mean to cause you pain. What did I do?" I was a little confused. I understood that he wanted me sexually and that he was battling with those desires to keep from hurting me. I respected that. But, pain? "I don't understand. How are you in pain?" He looked at me in a quizzical way.

"You really don't understand, do you? I assumed, since you've been married that you realized what was going on but you don't. You are like an innocent girl in so many ways." His entire demeanor changed from being a little cross with me to looking at me as if I were a fragile, costly doll. He reached over and hit the restart button on the elevator. I was more confused than ever. What had I missed? What did I not understand? I didn't want to expose my ignorance more by asking so we stood, staring at the door until the bell notified us that we had reached our destination.

Throughout dinner and the evening, I felt a little strange, more intimately bound to Hazen and yet, somehow, more distant. I tried to make him laugh several times with success but he seemed absorbed in his thoughts tonight. The kids' interaction with him seemed more significant. He appeared to be more careful, more observant of each of us. By the end of the evening, I decided that I must have offended him beyond repair. He must have decided that either I was not worth all this drama or I was beneath him because of my blatant inability to resist him. Did he think I was a loose woman? I hoped not, surely not.

Whatever he was thinking, it was obviously interfering with his relationship with the kids and me. I wasn't sure if I should confront him or pretend like everything was normal. By the end of the night, I was feeling self-conscious and fearful. Part of me wanted to escape and get to the safety of my home. Part of me wanted to run away with him, although I got the feeling that he no longer wanted to run away with me. Maybe he had just clicked, like Joe. I had done something that had made him realize I was unworthy, no longer worth the effort it took to be with me.

"Good night," Hazen said before I took the kids to our bedroom- no pet names, no gentle gesture, no goodnight kiss. Unfortunately, I had been right. Whatever had changed for us was done. There was nothing else I could do to reverse it. I had made a fool of myself. I had acted like a tramp for one minute out of pure desire for this man who affected every cell in my body and mind. Was I forever going to be punished? I got the kids in bed, barely paying attention to the book I read to quiet them. They fell asleep quickly and I slipped to the bathroom to cry without disturbing them.

Once there, I lost it. I had not cried in so long that the dam seemed to have broken. I bawled into the tissue trying to soften my whimpers so as not to wake the kids. The catharsis felt good. I was just beginning to calm when there was a shy knock on the door.

"Abriella?" Hazen practically whispered. "Are you alright?" Oh, no, I would have rather it been one of the kids that I could quickly put back to sleep. I didn't want Hazen to see me this way. I looked in the mirror and was horrified to see my hair a mess and my face red and splotchy.

"I'm fine. Go back to bed," I tried to convince him.

"What's wrong?"

"Nothing, I'm fine." It was quiet for a minute and I was just beginning to think that he had gone back to bed. My heart sank.

"Abriella, I need to make sure you're alright. Can you just let me come in?"

"No, Hazen, I'm fine. Go back to bed," my voice cracked and I realized that I was still crying.

"Abriella, I'm coming in," he said as the doorknob turned.

"No," I said too late. He stood before me with a horrified look on his face.

"What? Abriella, are you okay?" he was by my side instantly with his arms around me pulling me to his chest. "What's wrong, my sweet?" Oh, now he has pet names for me, eh? "Tell me." I found my resolve and pushed him away. I didn't want his sympathy. If he didn't want me then I wanted nothing to do with him. "Abriella, what is it?" He looked me straight in the eyes. How could he not see that he had caused this pain? I had exposed my vulnerable side and he had rejected it. It seemed I always had to be tough. If I ever dared to need anyone, I lost them, my father, my mother, my high school lover, my husband, even Joe, although we never had gotten to this point, and now the ultimate betrayal- Hazen, the man with whom I had fallen in love. I resolved never to let anyone in my life again. If I were intent on being alone then, by God, I would not let anyone get in to hurt me again. Hazen may not have understood all I was thinking but he certainly saw a change come over me. It startled him and he literally took an abrupt step back.

"Abriella, are you angry with me?" No! I thought. I just hate you. "What have I done?"

"You know," I said quietly.

"Is this about this afternoon?" I just looked at him then turned to leave him standing in the bathroom. "Come here.

We're going to get this straight right now." He took me by the arm, not exactly forcefully but not gently either. He led me, or I should say pulled me because I resisted a little all the way to the living area. He sat me on the couch and sat beside me.

"Now, you are not speaking to help me figure out what the hell is causing you to cry so I may be a little off here but feel free to set me straight if I veer from the point." He seemed awfully stern. "This afternoon in the car, I wanted you in every way. If that car had not stopped when it did, we would have consummated our relationship right there in that limousine, a few years ago, no problem." He talked in a stern way I had not heard from him.

"Abriella, I had women coming and going and none mattered to me in a permanent way. It took me long enough but I realized that people who operate with no self-control, no discipline, never live in a way that is fulfilling. My heart, and my mind, is forever changed. I can't just *take* a woman," he said this in a spiteful way, "and not worry about the consequences of that union. There is more at stake here than my, or your, personal sexual needs. We have to live for a higher cause. We must respect one another at all times. Abriella," he paused and took a deep breath.

"Without a single doubt in my mind, I love you." He let that sink into my head. "I am in this for the long-haul. I have fallen in love with you, your kids, your life. I don't want to jeopardize that for a quick roll-in-the-hay in the back seat of a car." A mental image of Lonnie taking me in the backseat of his car came to my mind. He had not cared about me, had not worried about the consequences of that union. I looked at Hazen now, waiting for me to respond and knew that he truly loved me.

"I didn't know," I finally managed to say, "I thought you didn't want me. I thought I had displeased you." The vulnerability of the truth made me begin to cry again. He pulled me close to him and cradled me snuggly.

"Abriella, you could never displease me. In fact, the opposite was true; you pleased me too well." His calm speech washed over me. "I only want to preserve our integrity. I may have backed off a little too much to regain a balance but I am and will always be here for you." My tears stopped and I felt truly serene.

"I just thought, because you seemed so distant at dinner and you didn't even call me a pet name like you always do and," Hazen laughed a quiet laugh.

"My dear, I didn't realize that you even noticed that." Noticed that? I lived for that. "I promise you no ill feelings were intended." We held each other for several minutes without either feeling the need to talk. "I think it would be a good idea if we could come up with a way to communicate with one another so that I don't hurt your feelings again. I know, realistically, that you will be hurt and cry again sometime before you grow old and die but *I* most certainly do not want to be the reason for such pain again." He continued to hold me and I felt more loved than ever.

"Hazen," I finally broke the silence, "I want us to have a word, like a safe word or something, where if we begin to go too far again that either of us can say it and we will both make an effort to stop and take a break. I don't want to cause you pain either."

"That's an excellent idea, my love. What would you like it to be?" I thought for a moment.

"I don't know, maybe our name?"

"No, sweetheart, if you call out my name while kissing me, it would only inflame me more."

"Well, we can think about what the word should be. I guess we're not going to need it tonight, right?" I asked, half-wishing we would. Hazen chuckled and brushed the hair from the side of my face.

"One day, Abriella, I will make love to you. We will ignore all safe words and only speak of what we want. I will have you all to myself and will explore every inch of your beautiful body. I will claim you as my own for the world to know that you are off limits. I will pleasure you in ways that I think you have never experienced." Boy, how I wish that day was today. "Can I ask you something?"

"Of course, you can ask me anything," I responded quickly.

"How is it that you were married and have two children and yet, you are so inexperienced?" How had he known?

"My marriage to Seth wasn't exactly traditional, and neither was my relationship with Katie's father."

"Tell me about it." His request felt so innocent and yet, I felt so ashamed. I did not want to tell him all the details of my ugly past. I was afraid his love for me would not be strong enough yet to weather that truth.

"I will, one day," I echoed the same idea that he had stated about our lovemaking. "I can't right now. I'm sorry." I bowed my head.

"Abriella, your past will not change the way I feel about you but I will wait. When you feel secure enough in my love to tell me, I will be here." We held each other for a while longer, neither feeling that anything we had to say was necessary for now.

~ 19 ~

At The Cusp

The next week flew so quickly that the kids and I both felt exhausted on the flight home. We had stayed in Seattle for another day then traveled north to explore the vast farm that housed several hundred cattle and pigs. To the east of that were several hundred acres that grew staples such as wheat, barley, beans, and lentils. At each location, Hazen gave us the VIP treatment with home-cooked meals on the farm and experiencing the most posh restaurants in the big cities. Even one of Hazen's friends, Alex, met us for dinner while we were in Washington. I knew somehow that his approval was important to Hazen. It was one of the best dinners we enjoyed on our trip.

Hazen's father had called several times planning to meet us at various locations. Ultimately, he decided that he did not feel up to meeting anyone right now. Hazen explained that he was taking the loss of his grandfather very hard. I understood and was even a little relieved that I didn't have to meet him yet.

Once home, Hazen told me he was going to return to Colorado and spend some time with his father. He was worried about him. I was secretly glad, not that I wanted him to go but I knew the next few weeks would be insane with the court date forthcoming. Hazen's departure was difficult for us all, even the kids. We had not been apart for nine days now and getting back to our routine seemed as foreign to me as did traveling with

Hazen had ten days ago. We had managed to avert needing a safe word for the rest of our travels. We both consciously made an effort to avoid being alone altogether. That seemed to work well. It was not a solution that would work permanently but for the duration of this week, it had kept us at a safe distance.

When I returned to work that Monday, realization hit quickly. My desk had paperwork piled on every corner. My voice mail was filled to capacity. By the end of the day, all I wanted was to hear Hazen's voice. He had called only briefly to let me know he had arrived in Colorado. I did not want to interrupt his time with his father but I desperately wanted to talk to him.

"Hello beautiful," he answered when I called him, "miss me already?"

"I missed you before you reached your car yesterday," I purred. "How's your dad?"

"He'll be alright. I think he's coming to terms with it but we'll both miss my granddad." We talked for over an hour and I finally told Hazen that we must go. I felt guilty taking him away from his dad after I had kept him to myself all week. "I'll call you tomorrow, all right?" he said just before we hung up. I slept hard that night. I had been so busy catching up with work that I had not called Mr. Morgan about the court date. Rick and I only talked briefly about work. Tomorrow, I knew, I must face the inevitable dark moment of preparing to battle Seth.

"Things are cranking up," Mr. Morgan updated me as I sat across from him in the same conference room that I was beginning to hate. "Seth has attained a court order for all your records from your checking account to your employment record."

"How can that be?" I asked incredulously.

"It's not unusual. I've done the same to him." Everything was getting very nasty very quickly, I felt with so much hate toward Seth, the judicial system, and even my own attorney. This may all be routine to him but it was turning my world upside down. My personal information was none of Seth's business. I had nothing to hide but the fact that he could impose upon my personal information made me feel raped all over again.

"What does he have to gain from knowing how I spend my money or what I make at work?" I asked him curtly.

"To be honest, all that information is pertinent to his case. He is claiming that you can't afford to take care of the boy properly. Everything he's found so far proves otherwise. You're careful with your money, manage it well. Your employment record shows you make good money, not what he is accustomed to but then, that is not necessary to care for a child. I suppose that with the discovery period over, Seth may even back down. He'll realize his initial claim is unfounded." Yeah, right! I wanted to scream at him that he had been giving me false confidence since the first day I met him. If Mr. Morgan was supposed to be the best at what he did, I felt I would surely hate to see the worst.

After my meeting with Mr. Morgan, I tried to focus on work. Hazen and I talked daily on the phone and at times into the night. My lack of sleep was beginning to get to me and my coffee consumption at work increased to keep the cobwebs out of my head.

Valentine's Day fell on a Thursday and I was feeling down because Hazen was not here with me. I finally have a boyfriend on Valentine's Day and I do not get to see him, I thought. Several of the girls at the office received flowers. Therese received a dozen red roses from Joe. Every time a delivery came, I grew excited that maybe Hazen would surprise me. Yet, inevitably, all the deliveries went to others in the office. That afternoon at four, my phone rang.

"Happy Valentine's Day, my love," Hazen's sexy deep voice soothed my jealousy, "how is your day going?" I did not want him to know I was disappointed that I had not received flowers so I tried to be nonchalant.

"Just busy, how about yours?" I turned the tables.

"Busy, as well," I could tell he was smiling through the phone.

"What have you been doing?" I asked pointedly. My door opened just then and I looked up to give whoever was entering a dirty look. I didn't want my time with Hazen interrupted. Hazen stood there on his phone with three dozen roses, one dozen was red and the others were multicolored with light and dark pinks, whites, lavenders, yellows, even blue. I had never seen an assortment of beauty in one place in my life.

"Oh my gosh," I said into the phone as if Hazen were not standing in front of me. Then I put the phone down and ran to him, jumping into his arms and almost crushing the roses before he had time to move them out of our way. He hugged me tightly for a few minutes.

"Sweetheart, it's only been a week since I saw you but I could not stay away any longer, especially given this occasion. I hope you don't mind the surprise visit." I could not speak. I was overwhelmed with love for this man. At last, we pulled apart and sat at the table to catch up. I wanted to tell him about the court date in two weeks but I definitely did not want to spoil this day. After all, I surmised, I would be divorced soon anyways. As we walked through the office, the looks of interest and curiosity were obvious. I had never dated anyone since these people had known me. Even people who wondered about Joe and me never saw us show any affection to warrant the rumors. Hazen was openly showing his love for me to everyone, aside from the astonishing display of roses I carried, his hand remained on my back or elbow or holding my hand or his fingers would twist my hair as we conversed to the others. Without a doubt, everyone would have new, more interesting, gossip to talk about tomorrow around the coffee maker.

"Do you know why I bought you three dozen roses," Hazen asked when we finally had a moment alone. I presumed because he could but I wasn't about to say that so I just shook my head. "The red ones are for you, professing my love for you. The multicolored ones are a dozen each for your two children that I am falling equally in love with each day." I felt I should pinch myself to see if I was dreaming but the fragrance of the roses was too intense for it to be a dream.

When Rick saw that Hazen had flown in for Valentine's Day, he told me I could take off early. Tracy called about an hour later and suggested they keep the kids so Hazen and I could go to dinner. I was ecstatic. Once we dropped off the kids, Hazen pulled over at a vacant parking lot.

"Abriella, I need to ask you something. If you don't want to or don't think we can handle it, I can change plans but," he hesitated and I could see the struggle beneath his façade of manly exterior, "I didn't make reservations in time for us to go to a really nice place. I definitely want to treat you like a queen tonight so, I was thinking, if you are not offended," he stopped again.

"Hazen, we don't have to go out at all. I'm just glad you're here." I was not lying although I had to admit to myself that I was slightly disappointed. "We can grab a pizza and go back to my place if you want."

"Abriella, come on. You don't seriously think I would do that, do you? I would fly us to New York before I would do that, although the reservations would probably be even more difficult to get there." He was rambling a little now and I knew it was not like him to be unsure of what he wanted to say. I placed my hand over his.

"Hazen, what is it? What are you trying to ask me?"

"You seem to know me so well already, Abriella. I have had a feast prepared in my condo. I'd like to enjoy a quiet gourmet dinner with you." My eyes lit up yet he went on. "But I am not going to take a chance of us making a mistake so I must have your word that you will behave and that, if I end up getting carried away, that you will help me. I've missed you too much and I'm afraid that if we are alone, I will be tempted to ravish you until morning." Oh, he asked a lot of a girl! I was not sure if I could muster the self-restraint to stop us if we went too far but I wanted the chance to find out and, frankly, was not too concerned with the consequences if I couldn't.

"Hazen, I can't stay until morning, as you well know, and I don't know if I can promise to stop. I hope you don't think me a loose woman by saying that. I haven't been with anyone in years but you have a crazy effect on me."

"Well, then we will go to a neighborhood restaurant. I am not taking any chances." What? No!

"Hazen, surely we can keep things in that department to a minimum so we can enjoy the feast you've ordered."

"Can we? I want to rip your clothes off right here in the car!" I figured I owed him one since he had been the strong one so far, so I agreed to be the whistle-blower tonight. He reluctantly headed toward his condominium. On the way, he told me all about how his father seemed to be getting slowly better and had insisted that Hazen buy a condominium in Atlanta since he would spend so much time here. He said his father was anxious to meet the kids and me. I was surprised he would tell his dad about the kids before he had even met me.

"You are silly to think it matters," Hazen scolded lightly.

"It matters to more people than you'd think," I added.

"Not to a real man, Abriella." We rode in silence then and he held my hand the whole way. He pulled onto west Paces Ferry Road and I knew instantly that it would be very expensive. Sure enough, he pulled right up to St. Regis, where he had stayed when he was here last.

"I thought you bought one," I inquired, "I didn't know they sold these units."

"Yeah," he began his low-key voice which I learned by now meant something very expensive was about to be revealed. "The Residences at St. Regis are actually located atop the hotel. They had fifty-three private residences that sold. The only one big enough for sale right now was a four bedroom so I figured it was a sign."

"A sign? Why in the world would you need a four bedroom?" He looked at me just as we pulled up and waited for the valet to let us out. Once we were in the elevator, he continued his story.

"Abriella, I don't want to scare you away. I know you've been married before but I haven't. Frankly, I pretty much gave up on the whole eternal love thing, at least until I met you. You are the whole package- beautiful, smart, funny, innocent, mature, and ambitious. You're everything I didn't think existed any longer. I know we just met, and I'm trying to make my mind slow down, but at the same time, I'm thinking ahead. If we continue to move in this direction, we'll have a place to stay while we are in the city." What? What did he mean by 'continue in the same direction'? I was full of questions but we were already on his floor. The hall was wide and his unit was almost at the end. When we entered, the aroma of delicious food hit me.

"Hola, Rosa, estamos aquí," Hazen called. I loved it when Hazen spoke to his employees in their native tongue, even if I did not have a clue what they were saying.

"Hola," a tiny lady called back to us, "Estoy en la cocina." Her voice had a heavy Spanish accent and she appeared around the corner just as Hazen hung our jackets up.

"She says she is in the kitchen" he translated for me.

"Abriella, you remember Rosa from Mi Paz, don't you?" Of course I did. Her bounty of meals had made a lasting impression upon me for the two days we stayed there. I was confused though as to why she was here. Did she travel with him? Hazen read my thoughts. "When I couldn't get the reservations I wanted, I had Rosa fly here to prepare a fabulous meal for us." Of course he did! I could not believe he was willing to go to a local restaurant after having gone to so much trouble to have Rosa flown in and prepare a meal for us here.

As Rosa put the finishing touches on dinner, Hazen showed me the apartment. It was an open plan with white floors throughout the living areas and white carpet in the bedrooms. I wondered how long they would remain white with kids. The soft teal walls in the kitchen and tones of creams and browns elsewhere gave it a very distinct charm. When we had completed our tour, Hazen took us to the dining room. It was majestic compared to the rest of the condominium with white columns separating it from the living area. Judges panels surrounded the room with what looked like accentuated white textured leather within each. The table, although large, was set on one end with fine china, candles, and a bucket of champagne at the corner for easy access.

Once we sat, Rosa began to bring in dish after dish. The meal was seven courses beginning with an Amuse Bouche shrimp salad shooter that had two shrimp atop a gorgeous glass and a cucumber slice on the side. Hazen poured our wine, a light Moscato from his vineyard at Mi Paz. Next she brought, a smoked trout baguette appetizer served in an odd shaped dish with a curved angle. I was thankful for her description of each course as she served it because I felt very ignorant at the moment. After the appetizer, she brought martini glasses with only a handful of arugula greens, a sliced fresh pear, and topped with Asiago cheese and a simple olive oil dressing. There was a breadstick swizzle placed to look like a straw coming from the glass. After we completed this, Rosa brought a warm Carrot Ginger Honey soup. I was thankful for the small portions so that I did not fill up. Rosa kept our water glasses full and I could not help but wonder if she was following instructions from Hazen to keep us from filling up on wine.

After we had finished our fourth course, she brought a tiny glass with two miniature balls of tart lime sorbet with a sprig of basil on top. This, she explained, was the palate cleanser before her main course. I was giddy with anticipation to see what she had prepared. I could not imagine anything being better than what we had already experienced. Hazen topped off our wine glasses as we waited for her return with the entree. After only moments, Rosa entered with our two plates. Each had three lamb chops with the bones tied together at the top with a green onion. They were crusted with thyme, oregano, rosemary, and parsley then topped with toasted hazelnuts. Rich Hoisin and plum sauces were drizzled over each chop and a small ceramic spoon with more sauce lay on the opposite side of the plate. Fresh green beans tossed with toasted pine nuts and a sculptured potato rose with a tomato garnish completed the masterpiece.

I was completely full and hoped we were finished with our meal when Rosa brought two square plates to our table with a chocolate mousse cake. That is what she called it; however, it included two layers of chocolate cake sandwiched between a layer of chocolate mousse. Raspberry sauce lay on four corners of our white plates and four small puddles of crème anglaise beside each of those. The cake/mousse presentation was in the middle of it. Stripes of fudgy, rich chocolate sauce crisscrossed the plate around the centerpiece of cake. I could have easily taken a picture of her food art and blown it up to hang in my office. It was not a huge portion but very rich and she served coffee to go with it.

Rosa served the entire dinner leisurely. Hazen and I talked and shared some of each of our lives. He told me about his mother's passing and how his father and mother were always very much in love. He told me about his summers at the winery and traveling extensively. I told him about my father leaving and how, that one decision had changed the course of my life. I told him how I had always wanted to go to college and how I admired Kayla for trying so hard. Also, the struggles she faced with trying to raise the money for college and worrying about providing for her mother and Gabby.

"That is unfortunate. Perhaps she can find a scholarship for young people in positions just like hers." Hazen seemed truly concerned and it warmed my heart that he could possibly care about a friend of mine he had not even met yet.

"She says she has met with the counselor at her alma mater regarding scholarships at UGA. I guess she was not able to secure one. I have no idea why. She is one of the smartest people I know. In fact, I doubt I would be sitting here with you today if not for her advice."

Once we were finished with Rosa's phenomenal display of culinary art, we went out on the terrace. We had only been there a few minutes when I asked Hazen if Rosa would like to join us.

"My sweet love, she has gone," he responded as if he need not state the obvious.

"Gone? Where?" Hazen laughed gently.

"She is probably close to the airport by now and flying home to be with her family."

"Oh, Hazen, I feel terrible that she flew all the way here to make dinner for us. We could have made other arrangements. She must be exhausted after all that work."

"Abriella, I offered for her family to come here but she said she would rather fly home afterwards. In addition, I compensated her well, so stop feeling guilty about everything. She enjoys cooking, especially the gourmet meals like she created tonight. I think her and, uh, everyone who knows me well is hoping I will settle down. She would be willing to go to China to make a meal if she thought it would help. They all really liked you very much." I relaxed then. As we sat on the terrace, enjoying the magnificent view and holding hands, I felt so content. I could not imagine anything I had done in my life to deserve this man and the love he gave so freely.

"Abriella, I have a gift for you," he said sheepishly.

"Hazen, you've already done too much, flying here to be with me, the roses, dinner. I don't need another thing." I was not being humble; I was being honest. I could not think of another thing I could possibly want.

"All the same, I want you to have this," he handed me a tiny, beautifully wrapped box. When I saw the size of the box, I sincerely hoped it was earrings because, as much as I knew I was in love with him, I recognized that it was too soon for a proposal. I took the box slowly, leery of its contents.

"Hazen," I said after I got the wrap off and was about to open the box, "I'm…"

"Just open it. It's not what you think," he added. I opened the box and there was a gorgeous ring, clearly not intended to be an engagement ring as it had a huge light blue stone in the middle and diamonds surrounding it. I knew without a doubt it had to be expensive.

"Oh Hazen, I can't," I was speechless.

"Oh, yes you can," he said as he took the box from me and took my left hand, slipping the ring onto my finger. "Abriella, I truly feel it is too soon to propose to you but, well, I know in my heart that you are the lady for whom I've searched the whole world over. This ring is a, well, at the risk of sounding juvenile, sort of a promise ring. Will you accept it?" I could not speak. I nodded my head and fell into his arms. We sat on the terrace for a long while enjoying getting to know each other without the distractions of kids, work, or waiters. It was a magical evening.

It was getting late and I did not want to put Rick and Tracy out.

"Hazen, as much as I want to spend time with you, I probably need to go get the kids." Hazen smiled a wicked smile.

"Don't hit me but I sort of asked Rick and Tracy if they could keep them over night."

"You what?"

"Abriella, I have to go back tomorrow and I wanted to spend every minute with you that I could. They were excited, the kids especially. Katie loved keeping a secret from you." Hazen laughed as he looked into the dark sky and I wondered what he was remembering.

"What about the cat? Sparks will starve!"

"I put extra food out for him when you weren't looking, relax."

"Hazen, I can't spend the night. You asked me to be strong and there is no way I can sleep close to you and not," uh, oh, I had almost gone too far, "well, you know." Hazen burst into laughter. "I know you said I am funny but I really did not see what you find so amusing."

"My dear, you have a way of putting things that makes it sound so high school." He leaned forward then and got very close to my face. "Make love, sweetheart, you can say the words, that part is allowed." His smirk was so impish, even for him and I smiled.

"I'm sorry. It is just, I guess, I have never really had an intimate relationship with a man, not really. It's sometimes hard for me to be mature when talking about it." Hazen came closer to me and kissed me lightly but then backed up.

"My dear, you never have to be embarrassed by your lack of experience. I find it endearing." I opened my mouth to rebuttal but he leaned in and kissed me deeply. All conversation ceased then. He began to caress my neck as he kissed me. Then he stroked my hair. His kisses felt so natural and we both began to relax. I moaned and melted into his arms. He reached under me and lifted me up.

"What are you doing?" I asked as he took me into the condominium.

"Would you rather I seduce you on the terrace?" Oh, no, no, no, no, no, no. If he took me to his bedroom, I could not be held accountable for my response.

"Hazen, no, please don't take me to your bedroom if you expect me to behave." He stopped midstride and looked at me intensely.

"I'll tell you what," he began as he continued walking, "I'll keep my pants on and you promise you won't try to take them off. Nothing can go too far if my pants are on, right?" I was not too sure of that and I was not sure I could keep a promise not to encourage him but I nodded my head anyways. He laid me on the bed and I expected him to lie beside me but he pulled his shirt from his trousers. I lay looking up at him with nothing but admiration for the striking man standing over me. He looked down at me with such intensity that I blushed. It seemed to me that he was being somewhat reckless tonight considering it was his idea to go slowly. "I want you, Abriella." My stomach lurched and a strange clinching groped my insides.

I reached my hand up to pull him down and he pushed his shoes off quickly as he came down upon me. He kissed me, slowly and deeply, for several minutes before he slid his hand underneath me and raised me up on the bed until my head lay squarely upon the pillow beneath me.

"Hazen," I moaned. He kissed my neck, shoulders, and décolleté. My body screamed with a raw need I had never felt before. He kissed me all over and, after a few minutes, he started unbuttoning my dress.

"No, Hazen, I'll lose it," I told him.

"I'm alright for now, Abriella. I want to show you something." That is exactly what I was afraid of, I thought. "Trust me." I did trust him. He had shown me he was capable of being strong when I was not. He had respected me like no other man I had known. I relaxed and he continued his mission, artfully exploring my body. He slid his hand up my dress and to the top of my leg. I squirmed with anguish. He found my secret place, the place no man had ever bothered to find and I withered as he took me to a place no man had ever taken me. We had not made love but I had never felt so close to another human being in my life. He turned my body around easily laying beneath me and pulling my head upon his bare chest. I lay in his arms, speechless, still feeling the sensation of waves that had riddled my body.

"Are you okay?" he whispered.

"I guess." I felt so vulnerable. I was not even sure what had just happened. I had not known until a few minutes ago that my body was capable of such feelings. My eyes stung with tears and I was not even sure why. His hand caressed my hair and I could hear and feel his heart beating against my face. The peace between us filled the room. When I finally began to float back to Earth, I realized that I should probably reciprocate. I felt embarrassed because I knew my naïveté would not compare to his expertise but I began to kiss his neck and stroke his chest. Then I reached up and began to kiss him as he had kissed me.

"Abriella, what are you doing?" he groaned quietly.

"I want to make you feel good, too."

"No, my love, you can't do that."

"I know I'm not as experienced as you but I'd like to try."

"No, you misunderstand what I'm trying to say. I mean, you cannot do that tonight. I was strong making you feel good but if you start with me, I may not be able to restrain from claiming you as my own." Challenge accepted, I thought. I stroked his chest and let my fingers wander down to where his pants began. He moaned. I continued to love him, as he had loved me. I kissed his chest and caressed his arms. I let my nails travel the length of his girth. I squeezed his biceps just to see if they were real.

Hazen suddenly became enlivened and he took control, pulling me easily on top of him. I tried not to imagine what our position would mean if we had both been unclothed yet I began to move naturally without his instructions of what to do. This ignited him and, before I realized it, he had flipped us. Now he was on top of me holding up his weight with one hand and unbuttoning his pants with the other. I realized immediately that things were about to get beyond my control.

~ 20 ~

Bitter Truths

I did not want to stop him but knew that this time it was up to me.

"Hazen, no," I heard myself say. I had to be strong. I had promised him. "You wanted us to wait, remember?" Then, because we had never come up with a safe word, I said, "safe word". It was silly but it did stop him. He froze and looked at me. I felt terrible. I had started only to make him feel good but then he took charge and I knew if I didn't stop him we would regret it later. The intensity of his stare rattled me but almost immediately, his demeanor changed.

"Oh Abriella, I am so very sorry," he said as he jumped up from the bed.

"It's okay," I tried to console him as he sat on the side of the bed. "It was my fault. I underestimated you."

"Just give me a minute," he leaned over and bowed his head in his hands and then got up and went to the bathroom. A moment later, I heard the shower running. I knew beyond any doubt that I loved Hazen. I did not want to do anything that would cause us to feel differently about where we were right now. I sat on the bed and imagined being in the shower with him.

Saying, "good bye" to Hazen the next day was more difficult than I had imagined. It was so strange to me that we had become so close in such a short period of time. He promised that he would try to wrap up things with his father and then he was coming back to Atlanta to spend time with the kids and me.

Another week went by and Mr. Morgan called me back into his office, presumably to prepare for the hearing the following week.

"Brie, I'm afraid I have bad news for you." I swallowed hard and the nausea that swept me was overpowering. "Seth and his attorney have opted for a full jury trial. The date for it is set for March fifteenth." He paused and I swallowed the vomit that threatened me.

"Why would he do that? He must feel confident of winning to do that." I surmised to myself.

"I'm not sure. To be honest, I'm quite surprised." I bet you are.

"What do we do?" I asked. "I can't lose my son!" I was feeling hysterical.

"You're not going to lose him," he sounded confident, "not on my watch."

"Mr. Morgan, in all due respect, you have assured me from the beginning that this case would never end up where it is. How am I to put confidence in your prediction when none have come about so far?" Mr. Morgan looked at me sternly then breathed a deep breath.

"Brie, don't phase out on me now. Yes, they have played hardball worse than I estimated but that does not change the big picture. We can turn this around but you're going to have to trust me. We have to do something drastic."

"What do you mean?"

"The tape we have of you and Judge Miller's conversation- we need to use it. The only way we can is if you claim, under oath, that you intentionally called Rick to have a witness to that conversation. It will be admissible then. It will be the smoking gun that will send Seth, Judge Miller, and Seth's attorney back to their corner. You will be able to write your own ticket." I thought of it. I had already decided and communicated to Mr. Morgan that I would not stoop to unethical, illegal means to win. Now my back was against the wall. Was I willing to take a chance on losing my only son on a technicality?

"I, um, I don't know," I stammered. Mr. Morgan seemed relieved.

"Think about it, Brie. Everything happens for a reason. Maybe that entire incident happened for this very purpose. Maybe this is your redeeming ace in the hole." I was growing tired of Mr. Morgan's clichés. I was too fazed to work. There was only two hours left of the workday so I decided not to return to work. I really wanted to talk to someone. I wanted to talk to Hazen but I had never gotten around to even telling him that I was not legally divorced so I did not want to start with asking for advice to get the divorce. I could talk with Rick but his short answers would not suffice me right now. Tracy may be able to shed some light but somehow she did not seem to be the one I needed either. Annie Mae, she was who I needed right now. She was the mother figure that I craved. As soon as I thought of her, I turned my car around and headed south.

"Lawd, chille, who is dis comin' in ma shop?" Annie Mae's huge smile and broad arms took me in. Her hug felt so real, so heart-felt. I knew I had made the right decision. "Looky here, everybody!" I didn't know anyone in the shop today and their curious looks instantly brought back memories.

"Are you busy?" I asked knowing I should have called first.

"I got one more lady comin' in but I'll let Martha take her. Have you met Martha?" I shook my head. "Well, this here's Martha." I nodded to Martha.

"Where's Kayla?"

"She left early today."

"I sure wish she was here." I said. It seemed like I always missed her.

"Come on," Annie Mae motioned, "I can see you gots somethin' on yo mind." We went back through the store and I talked to Ezekiel and Poppa for a brief minute. I thought Annie Mae was taking me to the little lunchroom we had frequented many times but she went to her house upstairs. Once we got in, she kicked her shoes off and sat down, propping them up on a footstool.

"Lawd, chille, Annie Mae gettin' too old for this. Ma feet hurt sa bad every night that I've cut back on my people. That Martha is slow as Christmas, she is. I gots ta think 'bout getting' another girl soon." It worried me that Annie Mae said this because it was not like her ever to complain. She did look older somehow. I had just seen her a few weeks ago. Maybe I had not looked at her. "So, what's up with you?" I caught Annie Mae up on everything with Seth, leaving nothing out.

"What should I do, Annie Mae?" I asked. Annie Mae gave me a look and I wasn't sure if it had been so long since I'd seen her that I didn't understand it or if I didn't want to admit that I did.

"Chille, you sho can git yoself in a mess, cain't ya?"

"I guess that's my expertise, Annie Mae. That's why I have you." I smiled.

"Well, chille, if'n you askin' me ta tell you that there's sometimes a right time ta do the wrong thang than I guess you askin' the wrong person. You knowed I ain't gone tell ya that." So that was it, wasn't it? It was just that simple. Hadn't I already known that? "But," she hesitated, "there is always a way ta do the right thang about a wrong situation." I was not following her and she knew it. "If I'm understandin' ya, tha tape would be good if'n you'd done it 'tentionally, right?" I nodded affirmation. "Then why cain't you git a tape that is intentional?"

"Annie Mae that would be almost impossible. It's a fluke that it happened the once."

"I don't believe that." I had forgotten how assertive she could be. "I believe that all thangs happen for a reason, even if we don't always know what that reason is. Nobody says you cain't use that tape, outside a court, ta git the reaction you is wantin' from that judge, or Seth for that matter. Why cain't ya use what was laid in yo lap to git what ya need?" It was ingenious, except for the fact that I really did not want to have a confrontation with Seth or Judge Miller. It was a workable plan.

"Annie Mae, you are a genius!" I screamed. For the first time I could ever remember, I scared Annie Mae.

"Lawd, Chille, you tryin' ta scare me ta death?" she laughed. "An' why's you only come round when you gots bad news? Cain't ya ever bring me somethin' good?"

"Well, actually, I do have some good news," that was an understatement. "I met a man." I stuck my hand out to show her the ring Hazen had gotten me for Valentine's Day. That was all I had to say and Annie Mae drilled me with a thousand questions. I told her how we met, how rich he is, how respectful he is to me, and how much he loves the kids. I even told her about his insistence that we wait before getting more intimate, a fact that she seemed to appreciate.

"He sound perfect, chille. When do I git ta meet him?" I could not imagine Hazen and Annie Mae together but hoped that one day it may be possible. They were each so important in my life. "He sound like a good Christian man. Do he know God?" she asked. Funny, of all the things Hazen and I had talked about, I had never asked about his relationship with God.

"I've never asked him Annie Mae," I answered. I had gotten out of the habit of going to church since we had left this neighborhood. I tried a few but never really felt at home. One thing led to another and time passed without my ever having found a church home.

"Well, you needs ta find out, although he sounds like he may be a bit more Christ-like than you be actin'," sometimes I hated her honesty. "Don't be temptin' a man beyond what he can take. The good Lord says he won't tempt a man more than he can take and if'n you keep insistin' on it, he may just take that man an' give 'im ta somebody that'll behave herself." The thought of God giving Hazen to anyone else pained me. I was embarrassed but rightfully so, I surmised.

"Well, we agreed to help each other by using a safe word to stop if it got too steamy," I added, a little proud of myself for thinking of the idea. I was not about to tell her we had already used it once.

"A safe word?" Annie Mae burst out, "You mean like them folks that start gittin' too rough with each other in tha bedroom?" She cackled as if that was the funniest thing she had ever heard.

"Well, it's better than going too far, don't you think?" Honestly, her nerve sometimes.

"Chille, tha safe word is, 'stop'! Heaven and Earth, you white folks complicate everythang," she was laughing outrageously now. When she put it like that it sounded a little silly, but still, it had worked.

"Heaven and Earth, huh?" I responded to her mockery, trying to keep it light. "Tell me about Kayla," I asked her, partly to change the subject and partly out of genuine concern.

"She doin' alright, she is. She keepin' her head in tha game, that's all. She a little discouraged 'cause thangs is goin' sa slow gettin' in tha big college. Why don't ya go see her? Ya got time, don't ya?" I looked at my watch and saw that I did have about thirty minutes left. It would be good to catch up with Kayla. "I needs ta lay down for a minute 'fore I fix supper. You go on ahead." We hugged good-bye and I headed to Kayla's house. I hadn't been there in over a year and it all seemed so foreign now.

"Oh my goodness, girl, come on in," Kayla was so excited to see me. Her house had not changed a bit. She got me a soda and we sat at the kitchen table to catch up. I told her the brief version of Seth's ordeal and I told her about Hazen. Then she caught me up with her life.

"Girl, I'm about to go crazy with this situation. I'm trying to get into graduate school but it's harder than I imagined. My mother said I need to take off work this summer to relax before the fall if I get into graduate school. But, honestly, there is no way I can afford to do that. I'm so off track now, I feel like I'll be in school forever."

"Off track? Kayla, you are way ahead of schedule. I am so proud of you!" She had grown up. She no longer resembled the young, shy girl I had met so long ago. She was poised, well spoken, and more determined than ever.

"Yeah, but girl, it's getting harder. I'm getting older and I want so bad to get my mother and Gabby out of this neighborhood. Do you know that we've been broken into twice this past year?"

"Oh no, that's scary." I agreed.

"Yeah, things just seem to keep getting worse."

"I tried to get Annie Mae and Poppa to leave. They have the means, or at least they would if they sold the store and all. They were stead-fast that they weren't budging."

"Well, I'm not married to this neighborhood. I worry so much about Gabby. She's getting older and it's only a matter of time before she starts noticing boys. They're already noticing her."

" Maybe when you start grad school, y'all could move."

"My momma is so stubborn. I could probably talk her into it if I could assure her that our needs would be met but she's not really capable of holding down a full-time job. She's been through too much. She's not all there, if you know what I mean."

"No, I'm sorry, Kayla. I've never noticed anything wrong with her."

"Yeah, I get that. She seems fine to those who don't see her on a regular basis but she's got fibromyalgia and stays in a lot of pain all the time. That gets her down and she gets depressed. She worries too much, too. Sometimes, I think she worries herself sick. She's tried to work several times but it keeps landing her back in bed. I finally told her not to worry. I'll take care of them. She gets assistance here with rent and groceries but rent would be way more if we moved. I really need to get my education behind me so I can take care of them." I hadn't realized that Kayla had so much pressure on her all these years. Her family seemed the most ideal of most I had met here. I had to leave to get the kids so Kayla and I said our, 'good-byes' and promised to stay in touch, a promise that we both made every time we saw each other. Realistically, both our lives were so full that neither of us had excess time to cultivate relationships well.

It was a Friday afternoon and a beautiful day. I missed Hazen terribly. I picked up the kids and decided to get a pizza on the way home. It had been an exhausting day and cooking was the last activity I wanted to do. Just as I was about to put the kids in bed, there was a knock at the door. I froze. No one ever showed up to see me, especially unexpectedly.

"Stay here," I told the kids as I went to get the door. I looked through the peek-hole and it was Hazen! I flew open the door and jumped into his arms. The kids ran to his side and hugged his legs as I hugged his neck. Finally, we released him.

"Oh my gosh, I'm so glad you're back," I admitted. "I really need you here tonight. It's been a crazy day and I missed you so much." I decided right then and there that tonight would be the night I would spill my guts about Seth. I did not want another day to go by without him knowing the whole truth. It would be a perfect time to explain everything with no holiday, schedule, or reason not to tell him. He picked Josh and Katie both up, one in each arm easily and gave them a proper hug. They both talked insatiably about their week, Katie telling him about her show-and-tell at school where she presented the stuffed souvenir horse Hazen had bought her to commemorate her horse-riding experience. Josh told him about taking his model airplane to school, although he had not actually done so. Hazen listened intently as they filled his mind with their activities and yet, he seemed slightly distant or reserved toward them. At long last, we all sat back down. Hazen seemed to act a little weird to me, although I could not put my finger on what was wrong. When I tried to hold his hand as we watched television, he got up and went to the bathroom. When he returned, he got a drink and held it in the hand I was holding. I almost felt like he was trying to avoid me.

It seemed like much more than a week since we had seen him. It took cajoling for fifteen minutes and Hazen agreeing to read their book before I could get them back in bed. Finally, Hazen and I were alone.

"I thought of a safe word for us," I said teasingly, yet secretly hoping we would need it in a few minutes and wanting to warm him up before I talked to him.

"Brie, we need to talk," he was serious and I knew instantly that something was definitely wrong. "To be honest, I came to say, 'good-by' to you and the kids." My heart skipped a beat and my head rushed with blood. Had I heard him right?

"What do you mean?" I asked. Hazen looked down and I thought I saw him wipe a tear but he may have just scratched his eye.

"I know, Brie. Did you think that I would not find out? Did you think that it wouldn't matter to me?" He raised his voice slightly in a way that scared me, not because he seemed angry or belligerent, but because he seemed deeply hurt, terminally wounded. I knew, I could not admit it to myself, but deep down, I knew what he meant. I did not dare speak. "Since I first met you, I have been honest with you in all things. I've asked nothing from you but the same." He looked up at me then and the resolve in his face was undeniable. I had lost him. "Why didn't you tell me you were still married, Brie?

"Hazen, it's not like that."

"Then you deny it?"

"Well, I am kind of married but,"

"Brie, you either are or you are not. You cannot be kind of married any more than you can be kind of pregnant. You told me that Seth is your ex-husband, inferring that you are divorced. Now I find out that you are not."

"It's not that simple, Hazen, let me explain," my voice sounded panicky and my eyes stung with tears.

"Yes, you want to explain now; even when I specifically asked you about it, you evaded my question and led me to believe you were a free woman." He looked down at his hands and sighed deeply. "Okay, please explain. Tell me how it is that you are still married and yet told me you were divorced." My throat constricted. My mind went blank. I opened my mouth several times but nothing could come out. We stared at one another for a moment. I began to panic. A moment or two went by, time seemed to stand still, and yet, I could not find the words to express the complete picture of all life had thrown at me these past four years. Alas, Hazen spoke again, "I guess your silence says it all. Abriella, I do not operate like that. If there is anything you've learned about me it should be that I try to conduct myself honorably." He stood up and I knew my time was limited.

"No! Please, I'm madly in love with you." I pleaded.

"Brie," he looked at me calmly now and I knew it was too late. I should have told him from the beginning. I should have explained while I had a chance. How had he found out? "I don't want to come between you and your husband. If there is a chance you two can work it out, then that would be best," he grimaced when he said this. "Besides, I can't trust you any longer. I'm sorry." I stood paralyzed and trying to make sense of his words. My face flushed hot and I broke into a sweat. I opened my mouth to speak but words still failed me. I felt I was going into shock. All I could do was to look into his eyes, but instead of the love I had witnessed there, I saw a deep and mortally wounded man.

He turned and walked out of my door.

~21~

Aftermath of Integrity

"So what you're proposing is setting Seth up?" Mr. Morgan asked. I nodded. Speech had been lost since Hazen walked out of my door a week ago. I was in a stupor, not fully numb and yet not fully alive. I had decided to take Annie Mae's advice and conduct myself ethically, or at least legally, refusing to lie about the tape in court but instead using it in private to get what I needed. "You know you only have two weeks to implement it." I nodded. "So what is your plan?" Mr. Morgan asked. His countenance changed and his mouth fell open as I told him.

I was depressed, that was an understatement. The grief I felt threatened to overtake me at any moment. I had not felt this way since the night I almost overdosed on pills. I knew beyond any doubt that I would probably do something stupid if not for my kids. When I finally found words to explain to him my predicament, I tried, fruitlessly, to call Hazen. It always went straight to his voice mail as if he kept his phone off at all times now. I didn't leave a message. I tried to continue my life despite the gaping hole in my core. I had only known Hazen a short time, yet I truly felt changed forever.

I solicited Rick's help with my plan regarding Seth. He was reluctant to get involved at first but when I told him how high the stakes were, that I could lose Josh, and then pulled the, 'Hazen left me' card, he finally conceded. I would bide my time. I arranged my life in a way that would insure that Seth would seek me out again. I knew it was only a matter of time and I desperately hoped that time would come before our court date only two weeks away.

In so many ways, I did not care. If not for the extreme price of losing my son, I would not care if Seth used the legal system to abuse me again. I was literally at the point where, I would never inflict it myself, but I would not care if I died. How could I have gone from feeling so happy with my life just a few short months ago to entanglement in this web with Seth and desperately in love with the last Boy Scout on Earth?

To my surprise, Hazen told Rick to keep me on his books but I had to go through Rick if I needed information from him. Other than that, I continued to have full access to his information and all businesses. How could he trust me with his entire fortune and not trust my heart? A huge part of me did not want to continue working for him. I felt spiteful and hurt. Yet a small part of me kept thinking that maybe, just maybe our worlds would come together because of it. So, I continued to give all I had in me although that was much less at the moment.

"Rick, can't you talk to him?" I finally asked Rick after I was getting nowhere calling Hazen.

"Brie, I tried but he just cut me off. I did not want to get involved in this but I really felt he needed to know the truth. I do not know how he obtained his information but he seems adamant that he knew the whole story. He seems to think that you and Seth were happily married until he showed up. I told him you and Seth were estranged but he seemed to think he was in the way of you and Seth working things out. I guess, from his perspective, he is doing the honorable thing." How could he doubt me so terribly? How could he think my integrity meant nothing at all to me, that I could lie about something so important? But I had lied, hadn't I? I continually reminded myself that I had bigger problems right now. I had to stay focused on my plan or I would lose my son. Oddly, after that first night Hazen left, I hadn't cried any more. I just walked around in a stupor.

I spent the next few weeks appealing to the side of Seth that I knew still existed, his rescuer side. At least I hoped I had not misread that part of him. So far my plan had not worked. I had pretended to be broken down on his way to work, standing by my car with the hood up as if something were wrong. He rode past only looking and turning away. I had taken the bus three days in a row feeling as if he must somehow know. I truly felt he was following me, or having me followed. Nothing came of it. I called the police to my apartment one night with a false claim that I thought someone was breaking in but to no avail. What finally succeeded in getting Seth to me would, not only devastate me but, change my world as I had known it.

It was the Saturday before the week of our trial date and I could not help but mope around the apartment all day wondering constantly where Hazen was or who may be with him. The kids insisted we play on the playground. I wanted nothing more than to lie in bed all day but that was impossible. After lunch, I finally agreed, deciding that they could play while I sat on the bench while they played. I sat in a half daze watching them and yet playing the rewind of my short life with Hazen on the big screen in my mind. We had been at the park a little over an hour when I heard Katie scream.

"Josh! Mom!" I was at their side seconds later. Josh lay on the ground unconscious. I fell before him and lifted his lifeless body. His head was bleeding. I grabbed my phone and called emergency services. People crowded around. I was frightened beyond belief and felt helpless to save my son.

"What happened?" I finally managed to ask Katie.

"I'm not sure. He was climbing up the jungle gym and I was on the swing. I told him to get down but then he fell. I only looked away for a minute." She was crying wildly.

"Katie, this is not your fault." It was mine. It was my responsibility to watch him, not Katie's. The ambulance arrived just as Josh regained consciousness. He woke up screaming, which scared me all over again and then he vomited. I felt this could not be a good sign. The paramedics evaluated him and loaded him in the ambulance. Their methodical urgency scared me even more.

"He needs to be checked out by a doctor since he was knocked unconscious," they informed me. "You can ride with him in the back but your little girl must stay." As much as I wanted to be with Josh, I knew I could not leave Katie all alone at the apartment.

"No, we'll follow you," I said frantically hoping I would be able to drive. I had Katie call Rick and Tracy once we were in the car, not trusting my ability to talk on the phone and drive at the moment.

"They're coming to the hospital. Should I call Hazen?" Katie asked after she hung up with them. I had avoided telling the kids that we had broken up. The realization of it hurt me too bad to deal with my pain and theirs. I decided I would bide my time.

"No," I said automatically. The short ride to the hospital pricked my nerves and when we finally arrived, Katie and I sprinted across the lawn from the parking lot to the emergency room entrance. Josh was slightly calmer than when we had left him but when he saw me, he began again to cry. "I'm here sweetie," I tried to console him although I was on the verge of a breakdown myself. Josh was taken right back and I went with him. Katie had to wait in the waiting room. My heart was breaking for them both.

It took almost an hour but the doctor finally ordered an MRI based on Josh's responses to his evaluation. He would not give me any diagnosis or even comfort that Josh would be fine. When they took Josh back for the test, I went to the waiting room to check on Katie. Rick, Tracy, Annie Mae, Poppa, and Ezekiel were waiting with her. When I saw them, I felt relieved. After I hugged everyone, I told them Josh was getting an MRI done. Tracy kept touching my arm or shoulder as I spoke assuring me that she was here for me.

"It gone be alright, missy you'll see," Annie Mae assured me.

"How did you even know?" I asked.

"Katie called me, nearly scared me ta death." I looked at Katie and she waved my phone up as if it were a white flag. I hadn't even realized she still had it.

"Smart thinking, girl," I assured her as I hugged her again. She gave me the phone and I put it in my pocket. "Well, I'm going to go on back so I'll be there when he returns. I'll let you all know what they find. Annie Mae, thank y'all so much for coming." I knew Katie felt better with them here and I no longer worried about her being in the waiting room alone. When I got back to the emergency room, I pulled the curtain for privacy. Seeing all the other hurting people around me only frayed my nerves more. A few minutes went by. Out of shear boredom and trying to occupy my mind, I started looking through my phone. I looked at the call log to see whom else Katie had called. I froze as I stared at the last name on the list- Hazen. The call lasted for over two minutes, so I felt she had probably talked to him, but how? Every time I had called, it went into his voice mail. I stood up to go ask her but just then the orderlies pulled Josh back into the room. He appeared calmer than I expected much to my relief. I hugged him and assured him he was fine. It took another hour before the doctor came in to give me results.

"Ms. Taylor, Josh has sustained a grade three concussion. His brain is not swelling but we will keep him for the night for observation. If he continues to progress we'll release him in the morning."

"Can I stay with him?"

"Of course," he answered. He then looked Josh over thoroughly again, made some notes on Josh's file, and said he would be checking in with me throughout the evening. After letting everyone in the waiting room know that they were transferring Josh to a room, I asked Rick and Tracy if Katie could stay with them for the night. Once we made all the plans and I assured Katie that Josh was fine, I returned to Josh.

About an hour later, they finally took us to a hospital room. It was a semi-private room but the other bed was empty. I was glad. I pulled his curtain around us like a small cocoon. He fell asleep as I sang to him. Only a few minutes later, Josh's door opened. I fully expected the doctor or maybe a nurse. The curtain ripped back and I was astonished as I stared at Seth.

"You have got to be the stupidest imbecile on the face of the planet," he said with trepidation. I reached in my pocket and hit recall, not sure who exactly I was calling.

"Seth, you shouldn't be here," I spoke more loudly than necessary hoping that my voice would be recorded somewhere or that someone would be witness to whatever was about to transpire.

"And why not? That is my son laying there that you almost killed." He leaned forward to look me in the eye, "You are the worst mistake I ever made in my life, Brie. Since the first time I saw you I knew you were an idiot but I underestimated you. You are worse than an idiot. Did you really think that I ever loved you? You were a pawn in my plan. I needed you to be the smoke screen for the world, our stupid upside-down world that cannot accept me for who I am. There, I said it, are you happy," he was getting irate, "I am gay. I can't tell the world that, can't admit it to my father with his bigot ways. But, yes, since you caught me, I'll admit to you that I love Jeffrey. My plan would have worked out perfectly too if you had just been content with diamonds and vacations but, no, not Miss I-Need-Love, not you, you wanted it all. Now, the only good thing about you is that you gave me a son. And I *will* take him. I underestimated your stupidity once but rest assured I will use it against you now to get my son."

Just then, I remembered the tape in my purse. I had kept it with me with anticipation that Seth would show up but none of my plans had worked. I reached for my purse now and pulled out the tape recorder.

"Speaking of underestimating me, Seth, I have something here from your boyfriend that you need to hear."

"What are you talking about?" he spat angrily. It frightened me to do this in front of Josh but the medicine they had given him had him sleeping for now, oblivious to the storm around him.

"Listen," I hit play.

"What is the meaning of this?" he spat as Judge Miller's voice berated me on the tape. I didn't answer. I wanted him to hear the entire conversation. The tape continued only crackling once.

"I am the only judge you will see regarding this case. I have the authority to see to it that I will oversee your divorce case as well and insure that Seth will have the sympathy of a jury, if need be, to assure his wishes are fulfilled. You may think you know all the details because you witnessed Seth and I in a compromising position; however, our history goes back much further than his façade of a relationship with you. I told Seth not to marry you, that it would only complicate the matter but people were beginning to talk so he felt a marriage to a

simpleton like you would be ideal. Admittedly, it did seem ideal for a few years. You were more a slave than wife. Then you had to make trouble by pushing your way into his life. If you had just looked the other way, you would still be married to him, enjoying his money, and wouldn't have to resort to such extreme measures to take his money. Honestly, a baby? I don't even know how you worked that out. Now, you've got Seth thinking he wants a relationship with a son he thought he would never have. Well, I'm neither a simpleton like you nor a sentimental fool like Seth. I will not be blackmailed by the likes of you."

I never looked away from Seth as he listened aghast to a conversation he had only heard one side of before now and had no idea was recorded. He was hurt, I could tell, by some of Judge Miller's words. I was not going to squander away this opportunity with sympathy for him.

"So, you see, I have it all on tape." I clicked the tape off. "If you continue to blackmail me, stalk me, follow me, or abuse me, I will have them play this in court." I spoke with such assurance that I almost believed my bluff.

"You can't! A tape is not admissible in court." He barked.

"Oh yes it is as long as I was aware of it and I assure you, I planned it to the word, even getting your secret lover to spill his guts." I met his stare equally. He leaned toward me as if to scare me but I did not flinch.

"Brie, I swear to God, I will kill you if you ever share this with anyone."

"Seth, I feel sorry for you. You live a secret life. You have no real connection with any other human being. You have no real honest relationship with anyone. I never knew what that meant until recently. Now that I do know, I truly feel sorry for you. Rest assured, my sympathy for your pathetic life will not intervene with me fighting you to the death over the custody of my son. He deserves a mother and father who have *his* best interests at heart not to be used for some revenge plan. I haven't even seen you in years. You didn't even know Josh existed until a few months ago. I *fled from you* in the middle of the night almost four years ago because you raped me. During those years, I grew up. I can now take care of myself, my children, and my life. Neither you nor the likes of your counsel will ever intimidate me again. If you can treat me with the respect that I deserve and be the father to Josh that he deserves, then you can be in his life, to the degree that I see fit. If not, well," I lifted up the tape player and my phone, "then I guess these two possessions will have to come to light."

Seth's awareness that I had Judge Miller's confession as well as his own confession gave me the upper hand. He stared at me in disbelief.

"Ah, you think you've found true love, eh? Well, all it took was one phone call to your boyfriend and he left you!" It was now my turn to be stunned and my face showed it. "That's right! *I called Mr. Bigshot!* I told him we were in love before he came along, that we were working things out before he showed up. I told him the honorable thing for him to do would be to leave immediately. And you know, it wouldn't have been as easy to manipulate him except, apparently, you hadn't even told him about our little situation. So blame yourself for losing him. You may have some damning evidence but I will insure you will *never be* happy again if you use it." I sat in the chair behind me, too hurt to fight any more. So Seth had won.

"You have not seen the end of me, bitch," he said and he turned and walked out of the room. I gripped the chair beneath me, breathing deeply, and finally allowing the stress of the confrontation to expel from my soul. I sobbed. I could not breathe. Part of me felt such a sense of relief. It was obvious that Seth felt trapped and had to walk away from a fight that he was ill prepared to win. I had won the first victory in this long war while at the same time realizing that I would never win the war. Seth's menacing last threat seemed almost empty now. Although I knew he meant them, I also knew that he would risk almost anything to keep me quiet. He had lied to Hazen. I understood now why Hazen was so adamant that he knew the truth. Seth's skill of manipulation was unbeatable. Seth had said that if I used these tapes I would never be happy. I knew in my heart that I had no choice. If that meant I would never have Hazen, or happiness, then I would have to learn to live with it but I could not live without my son.

"Oh dear God, thank you for the courage to face that monster after all these years," I prayed aloud, "Thank you for helping me to be stronger than I ever felt possible. Thank you for sending Hazen into my life to show me what real love feels like." I cried harder just thinking about Hazen. "But mostly, thank you for keeping my son safe on that playground today. Please help me to be a better person." I spoke from the heart. It was the first real prayer I could remember praying for a while. Then I remembered my phone was still going. I looked to see whom I had called. My phone showed Hazen's name.

"Hello?" I hoped beyond hope that he did not answer. "Hello? Hazen, are you there?" No answer. I sniffed, trying to gain my composure. "I'm sorry I called you. I didn't mean to. Seth came into Josh's hospital room and I hit redial on my phone so I would have a witness if he hurt me. I didn't know that Katie had called you last. But," I began to cry again, "if you don't mind, can you please keep this recording?" I whimpered like a hurt dog now feeling the separation from Hazen more than I had since he closed my door that final time. "I may need it in court. You can just give it to Rick so you don't have to see me." A deep sob caught in my chest at the thought of Hazen never wanting to see me again. "I'm sorry, Hazen. I'm sorry you had to hear all that. I didn't mean to involve you in this. I never meant to hurt you. I hope you can forgive me one day. You deserve to be loved." My voice trailed off as I thought of anyone else loving Hazen. It hurt too much to imagine. I hung up.

~22~

Drum Roll, Please

The next day, the doctor released Josh from the hospital. He appeared to be completely unaffected by the fall. I was so very thankful. I told Rick about Seth showing up and my dialing Hazen because he was the last number dialed in my phone. Rick said he would let me know if Hazen contacted him. I also asked Katie if she had talked to Hazen. She had not, she said, but had left him a message asking him to come home. It made me sad that Hazen had not yet responded to either message. I could only assume that he really did not care and that in his mind we were completely finished. How could he not at least call to check on Josh? I said a prayer that he would at least care enough to get me a copy of his voice mail for court.

On Sunday, after we got home from the hospital, Josh, Katie, and I lay around the house watching movies and reading books. I was exhausted- mentally, physically, and spiritually exhausted. All I wanted to do was relax and enjoy my children. Tracy had made a wonderful homemade dinner for us and brought it when she brought Katie home around lunchtime. It seemed that this would be a lazy day; one we all desperately needed.

On Monday, my heart ached. I had finally resigned to the fact that Hazen would not contact us. If he had not called to check on Josh, at the very least, then he was truly finished with us. I knew that as long as I kept my cell phone number, I would subconsciously wait for him to call me. I stopped by my phone carrier at lunch and had them change my phone number. I figured this way I would not keep looking at my phone and feeling disappointed when Hazen did not call. If he truly wanted to contact me, he knew my number at work. I admitted to myself though, that it was unlikely to happen.

Tuesday came and went. I heard no word from Hazen and no word from Seth. Mr. Morgan felt that if we could get a copy of the conversation, the hospital scene was a great change of events and, as usual, assured me that this case was increasingly moving in my favor. I was not convinced.

Wednesday afternoon, just after lunch, I was in my office when the phone rang. It was Mr. Morgan.

"We need to prepare for court tomorrow," he stated matter-of-factly. "Have you received a copy of that tape?"

"No," I replied. We decided I would come after lunch so we would have the afternoon to prepare. When I arrived, I felt sick to my stomach. I had not eaten much since Hazen walked out and my clothes were beginning to hang on me. I had not eaten anything yet today.

"Now Brie, despite the lack of evidence, we will go into court confident that the accusations alone will damage Seth's character" Mr. Morgan got right down to business. "His only two accusations, that you are unfit and that you cannot afford to care for the child, both will be easily dismissed." He dredged on for a long while and I barely heard his arguments as he went through what he proposed would transpire in the courtroom.

"Mr. Morgan," his secretary stepped into the room, "a special delivery package has arrived for you."

"Can you sign for it, please," he responded without even looking at her.

"No, sir, I'm sorry. It requires your signature only."

"Very well, I'll be right back," he told me as he walked from the room stooped over. I sat in the conference room, alone, numb and feeling frozen in time. I do not know how much time passed but it seemed a good while.

"Brie," Mr. Morgan talked quietly as he reentered at last, "we have a development. Come with me please." What was going on? I grabbed my purse and followed him to another conference room, which I had never seen. Mr. Morgan's secretary was setting up something in the corner on some electronic equipment. "Guess what came in?" he asked me. I gave him a blank stare, not willing to play his guessing games. "Your salvation."

I stood, not understanding about what he was talking. "Your conversation with Seth," he explained. Oh! "Have a seat." I sat and he sat beside me. "I just listened to it in its entirety. Not only do you have his full confession but, because you played Judge Miller's tape within this tape, you also have Miller's confession." He chuckled as if something was funny.

"Wait! How did you get this?"

"Someone dropped it off."

"Who?" I was frantic. Was Hazen here? I would run to him and tell him everything I had not been able to articulate to him that fateful night. I stood up ready as soon as I got the word. Mr. Morgan looked at me strangely.

"A carrier dropped it off. What's wrong?" My heart fell. I sat back down. I knew somehow, deep down, that I should just be glad that Hazen had gotten me the tape but I could not help it, my heart hurt so badly to think that after hearing all he heard when he listened to the tape that he still would not come to me immediately. So that really was it. We really were over. I ran from the room and barely made it to the restroom before I threw-up.

When I was finally able to return, Mr. Morgan got me some cold water. His assurance that this was a good thing did not make me feel better. Yes, logically I knew I should be happy and, I was for the ability to build a stronger court case, but my heart, oh, my heart had never hurt so badly in my life. We listened to the tape in its entirety. Once it was completed, Mr. Morgan cut off the recording and turned to me.

"Brie, we could probably use this tape to avoid court but, if you want my opinion, I think we should go on to court. Let's use this tape to bury those bastards for what they've tried to do to you." I did not care. I could not even answer him. All this time, I had wanted to avoid court at almost all costs. Now, I just did not care. Let them rip me apart for all I cared. No doubt, I would keep my son now. Beyond that, I did not care what happened to me. I simply nodded, still unable to speak.

"Okay then. I'll meet you right here at nine tomorrow morning. We'll go to the courthouse together." I was barely coherent enough to understand. I probably should not have driven but there was no other way home. I went home and lay in bed, still numb and yet feeling a deep pain I had never felt. I did not get the kids from their childcare until the last minute. We went through the drive through and got hamburgers for the kids' dinner and I had Katie read to Josh before bedtime. I took a sleeping pill to get to sleep.

The next morning, my head ached from the nightmares I had endured all night. I dressed quickly, hardly taking the time to fix my hair, even though I somehow knew that I should try to look presentable for court. Once the kids were at their schools, I drove to Mr. Morgan's office. He reviewed again all he had suggested yesterday about our agenda for the day. He explained that today would only be a hearing to determine whether Seth would attain a jury trial. The actual trial would have to be reset and a jury chosen. Normally, I would have felt irate that we would be postponed again. Today I felt nothing.

I rode with him to court. To my surprise, Rick and Tracy were there. Tracy hugged me as we entered. Mr. Morgan and I sat at the tables up front just as I had seen on television. Finally, Seth entered with his attorney, a man I vaguely remembered from our circle of friends many years ago. They sat opposite us and were both dressed impeccably. I regretted not taking more time to look presentable. After our initial staring at one another, we did not look at each other again. The clerk stood up, droned on about the proceedings, and called our case. We all stood as the judge entered. I looked up just as Judge Miller took the stand. My heart began to beat more heavily.

Because I was suing Seth for divorce, Mr. Morgan began his case by stating that Seth and I had endured a love-less marriage. He continued for several minutes giving examples of Seth's neglect. How he would show that my leaving was, not only warranted, but also necessary for my safety.

Then Seth's attorney, whose name I remembered was Chance Lassiter, spoke of Seth's generous treatment of my "illegitimate" daughter and me, how he had showered us with gifts, and how ungrateful we had been. Then he explained how I had snuck out in the night for no reason and without explanation or warning. I knew I should be listening, probably even taking notes, but I just could not get my mind to wrap around what was happening until Mr. Morgan asked Seth to take the stand.

I was suddenly nervous. Mr. Morgan asked Seth several questions, drilled him, in fact, about the intricate moments of our life together. Seth made us sound like Ken and Barbie and was so convincing that I begin to think that maybe I had a misguided sense of reality. Maybe I was so disoriented that I had misconstrued Seth's actions. If it had not been for the visuals I had seen personally, I would have lost all faith in my ability to perceive what had happened between Seth and me. Mr. Morgan asked Seth questions for some time. Seth never lost his cool, cordially answering all his questions. I was surprised that Mr. Morgan did not move to have our case changed to another judge or that he did not ask Seth about any of the circumstances we had discussed at his office the day before. Then Chance stood and began his line of questioning.

"Mr. Taylor, you've told the court how you generously bought gifts, vacations, etc for, not only your wife but also her illegitimate daughter." They were pissing me off the way they kept referring to Katie. "What was your motivation for such benevolence?"

"I truly loved them," he responded without missing a beat.

"And what was your reaction when you awoke on the morning of July fourteenth and found she had abandoned you?" Chance asked. Seth looked down at his hands and began to get teary.

"I was devastated," he sniffed. "I frantically looked about the room for a note. She left everything- her car, her phone, everything and I had no way of finding her." Wow! He was good. I began to worry that maybe we had underestimated him after all.

"And what did you think when you finally received the phone call days later that she had fled to Spain?" What? Now they were really going too far. I had never made a phone call! How could they prove that?

"Well, at first I was relieved; you know that they were safe. She said she needed some time to think. I didn't understand why she was upset but I told her to take all the time she needed."

"Did she call any more after that?" Chance asked.

"No. I never heard from her again. The authorities informed me that she had been in an accident in Spain. They said she had been killed." Seth put his face in his hands and his shoulders shook as if he were bawling.

"Take your time, Mr. Taylor. I know this is difficult for you." Chance told Seth. I looked at Mr. Morgan to stop this sham but he immediately placed his hand on mine and patted it. I was getting very nervous. I knew Seth was a scoundrel but even I did not imagine the depth he would stoop. Seth finally continued.

"Of course, I got on the next plane and went to Spain, hoping it was all a misunderstanding. By the time I got there, the authorities said they had cremated her and sent Katie to her grandmothers at Brie's request. There was nothing else I could do."

"I see. So, years later, when you saw Mrs. Taylor eating casually as if nothing had ever happened, what was your reaction?" Seth wiped his faux tears and looked at me for the first time since he first entered the courtroom.

"I tried to chase her. I wanted to know what had really happened in Spain. Had she even gone to Spain or had she paid someone off to tell me those lies?" He was seriously ruffling my feathers now and Mr. Morgan kept his hand on mine to keep me in my seat. I even began to wonder if Seth had somehow managed to pay off Mr. Morgan to insure his victory.

"And were you able to confront her?"

"No, she ran, literally ran from me and hid." Seth looked rebuffed. The proceedings continued like this- Chance baiting Seth's answers and Seth delivering his practiced drama. I could not understand why Mr. Morgan was allowing it to continue. I hoped that he was not believing all these stories and thinking that I was the one who had lied. I hoped again that Seth had not paid for his loyalty.

"Then after you discovered her whereabouts, did you try to talk to her?" Chance continued.

"Yes, I was shocked to see her on a date at the country club. I did not want to approach her there but knew I may never get another chance. She managed to avoid me that night by getting her date to come between us. I wanted to tell him what had happened but I didn't have the chance until she walked away. Then, all I had time to tell him was that I still loved her." What? I was beginning to understand Joe's actions now.

"What did you see that night that changed your feelings about her?"

"I saw my son. She had given birth to my son, who she must have known she was pregnant with when she left me. I had begged her for us to have a baby for years but she never wanted one. When I found out I had a son, I knew I could never trust her again and yet, I also knew I had to find her so I could know him."

"Did you ever have another chance to talk to her?"

"Yes, I went to her work place but her boss prevented it. Then, out of desperation, I even showed up at my son's nursery. We did talk and I even gave her a ride, or tried to give her a ride, to work since she did not own a car, but she became belligerent. She began screaming at me in the car, accusing me of raping her, and lying. It was as if she had completely convinced herself of this, this, other life. She insisted I pull over and let her out. I tried to get her to let me take her on to work but she was getting physical while I was driving so I pulled over and let her out." On and on it went. Lie after lie for almost two hours.

At last, Judge Miller asked if Mr. Morgan would like to cross-exam Seth. Mr. Morgan stood up and walked up to Seth, still seated in the witness stand.

"Mr. Taylor, you say that your wife was missing for several days before she phoned you from Spain, is that right?"

"Yes, two or three."

"Did you report her missing with the police?"

"No, she had run off for a few days before so I just assumed this was another one of her escapades."

"I see, even though she didn't take her car, her phone, her jewelry, or really any of her personal belongings."

"Uh, yes, that's right."

"How much time was there between the moment you were notified of Mrs. Taylor's death and when you flew to Spain?"

"Uh, well, um, I don't remember."

"Give us an estimate. Was it hours? Days? Weeks?"

"No, no, not weeks, um, I think I left the next day."

"Now, Mr. Taylor, you said when you arrived in Spain that you talked with authorities there and found that, not only had she been cremated, but also her daughter had been returned to the states to her grandmother whom they had not spoken with for many years. Is that right?"

"Well, yes, apparently they said she had not died instantly so she had given them instructions before she died to take care of Katie."

"I see. And then you obtained a death certificate for her and returned to the United States to file that certificate?"

"Yes, that's right."

"How long did you stay in Spain, Mr. Taylor?"

"Um, a month, I believe."

"So you stayed in Spain alone for a month after you learned of her death?"

"Yes, well, a friend went with me, you know, to console me."

"What was the friend's name who went with you?"

"J.T. Mulligan."

"No further questions, your honor." What? That was all Mr. Morgan was going to say? I was furious. I had a million questions.

Then Mr. Morgan called me to the stand. I was furious that I had to sit this close to Judge Miller and pretend to have respect for this courtroom. After the bailiff swore me in, Mr. Morgan proceeded to go over the night's events that led up to my leaving Seth. I answered honestly and thoroughly. I was surprised that Mr. Morgan didn't ask me questions about the fight that led to my departure but figured he must be leading up to it. I was surprised when he turned the floor over to Chance.

"So, Mrs. Taylor," he was using a stern voice with me and I wondered what he thought he knew about our marriage. "Are you telling the court that you *fled* Mr. Taylor's house in the middle of the night? That you took several modes of transportation across town, ended up at the Battered Women's Shelter, lived on government assistance for years, was surprised by your pregnancy, and then moved back to North Atlanta, smack in the area where you *knew* Seth would eventually see you and yet, you *never* had *one* ulterior motive?"

"Yes, that's right."

"Didn't you, in fact, instigate the fight, hoping to get pregnant because you and Seth had not been getting along and you didn't want your gravy train to dry up?"

"Objection, counsel is badgering the witness."

"I'm going to let the question stand," Judge Miller replied. Why was Mr. Morgan not getting Judge Miller off this case? It was obvious to me that he was not going to rule in our favor regardless of the testimonies. "Miss Taylor, you are instructed to answer the question," he added haughtily.

"I did instigate the fight but never imagined he would rape me. I was more floored than anyone when I found out I was pregnant months later and if I had gotten pregnant on purpose to continue on his gravy train, then I would not have left without anything to survive." I could tell by the expression on Chance's face that I had answered well. He was trying to think of another question.

"Mrs. Taylor, isn't that exactly what this trial is about? You are trying to get more money out of your husband."

"I'm not asking for any more than the law allows for child-support."

"No further questions, your Honor." Mr. Morgan stood up then and I waited for him to cross-examine me but he did not. In fact, he directed the court.

"Your Honor, I would like to ask for your recuse on this case" Mr. Morgan directed Judge Miller but the courtroom erupted with loud conversation. I had no idea what a recuse meant but I could tell from Judge Miller's reaction that it was not good.

"On what grounds, counsel?" Judge Miller asked sternly.

"Your Honor, I have evidence that would render you biased on this case. I respectfully ask for your recuse." Mr. Morgan repeated calmly. I thought I now understood that recuse must have something to do with his stepping down because of his involvement with Seth.

"In my chambers, counsel. Both of you," he demanded. Both Mr. Morgan and Mr. Lassiter stood and followed Judge Miller into his chambers. I sat, wondering what I was supposed to do, and embarrassed that I did not fully understand what was happening. I could feel Seth staring at me in my peripheral vision but I stared at the clock on the wall that seemed to tick the minutes off more slowly than seemed possible. I could not bear to look Seth's way, afraid of his knowing disapproval. Did he know what was going on behind that door? Was he worried in the least that I had called his bluff? Fifteen minutes passed and I could stand it no longer. I turned in my seat to assure myself that Rick and Tracy were still there. They were, sitting almost right behind me. Rick returned my blank stare but Tracy winked at me to give me the assurance I desired. I turned back forward in my seat. Ten more minutes went by and finally, the door to Judge Miller's chamber opened and the three resumed their seats. After everyone in the court sat back down, Judge Miller began a small, disgruntled speech.

"After pondering the evidence, I award Counsel Morgan a recuse. This case will resume tomorrow morning under Judge Travis." Judge Miller slammed his gavel, stood, and walked out of the courtroom before the court even had enough time to stand for him. I looked to Mr. Morgan with anticipation, fully expecting an answer. I opened my mouth to ask but he cut me off before I began.

"At my office, my dear," he said. After hugging Tracy and telling Rick I would be at the office as soon as I could, Mr. Morgan and I rode back to his office. Thankfully, he began to explain in the car. "Brie, I know you are quite frustrated with today's proceedings but you need to learn to trust me." I was ashamed of the thoughts I had of him earlier in court. He was right, of course. I had a hard time trusting anyone. "Today I saw that, not only is Seth going to conjure up lies, but this case will be all the more simple because of them." He went on to add how easy it will be to produce evidence to counter most of Seth's testimony, such as the phone calls he claimed, which did not exist. I was once again relieved after talking to Mr. Morgan. Once he went over the new angle he was taking, to hang Seth with the rope fed to him today, I felt more confident than ever that we would succeed.

"Ok, dear, I'll see you in the morning, same time, okay?" I nodded to him as I turned to go to my car. "And, Brie, tomorrow I want you to dress for success. We have a new judge to impress." He smiled as he said this but I was a little embarrassed that I had not taken more time today to look presentable. The rest of the day went by like a whirlwind. For once, I was thankful I had a full desk to keep me busy. That night, I made sure we had a light and healthy dinner and were all tucked in bed early. I wanted to get as much rest as possible to start the next day out well.

~23~

The Big Climax

As court reconvened the next morning, I was amazed at the difference in how I felt. For one, I was confident in myself and how I looked, more than that, my expectation of the day was higher. I surmised the new judge as we stood when he entered. He was older than Judge Miller and for some reason that gave me a sense of peace. This judge, Judge Travis, appeared like a thinner, more tired Santa Clause. To my surprise, Mr. Morgan called me to the stand first.

"Miss Taylor, yesterday you testified that you fled Mr. Taylor's house after he had raped you. Can you tell the court the reason why you felt that that experience was a rape given the fact that you two were married and living together at the time?" I thought about what Mr. Morgan and I had discussed in his office and I knew he wanted me to explain that Seth and I did not enjoy a 'normal' sex life and that the rape experience was anything but lovemaking. Therefore, I proceeded to explain in painful detail, the reason why that fateful night was not a typical romp for a married couple. I was somewhat embarrassed by having to explain this to strangers and could not imagine how difficult this must be for a woman to do if she had been raped by a stranger.

"I see," Mr. Morgan continued, "and, in the five years you were living with Mr. Taylor as his wife, did you feel that you two had a healthy love life and relationship together?" I explained to the court how my relationship with Seth did not seem normal to me given our lack of intimacy, friendship, or even trust.

"Mr. Taylor said in his testimony yesterday that you had left many times before; hence, making your disappearance unsurprising. Is that so, Miss Taylor?"

"No," I answered, "I had never left Seth, not even for one night."

"When was the last time you and Mr. Taylor had sex prior to the night you fled the house?"

"Objection," Mr. Lassiter jumped up making me jerk, "This questioning is irrelevant to the case of child support."

"Your Honor," Mr. Morgan addressed Judge Travis, "Mr. Taylor testified that Mrs. Taylor knew she was pregnant when she fled from their home, I am merely trying to establish if that was a possibility."

"Overruled," Judge Travis spat.

"Thank you, your Honor," then Mr. Morgan looked at me.

"Um, I don't remember, probably almost a year." I answered honestly.

"Did you have sex with anyone else during the time of your marriage to Mr. Taylor?"

"No, of course not," I was shocked that Mr. Morgan would ask me that question.

"So you are telling us that because you got pregnant that night, the very night you fled your own home, there is no way you could have known you were pregnant prior to leaving, is that right?"

"Yes, that's right."

"How many times did Mr. Taylor, oh let me make sure I get this word right," Mr. Morgan looked at his notes on his table then turned back to me, "beg for a baby while you and he were together?"

"Never."

"What was his position on having more children?"

"I have no idea. We never discussed having more children."

"You are saying that in five years of marriage, you and your husband never had one conversation about having a baby of your own?"

"That's right."

"Have you ever been to Spain?"

"No."

"Your Honor, I'd like to present Exhibit A. This is Mr. Taylor's phone records for said period. There are no phone calls to or from Spain during the time mentioned." He handed the bailiff a piece of paper and then turned back to me.

"Did you make arrangements with anyone in Spain to fake your death, or report your death, or in any other way presume to make Mr. Taylor think that you had died?"

"No."

"Your Honor I'd like to present as Exhibit B. This is a sworn testimony from the clerk in Madrid, Spain where the alleged accident took place that no such accident involving my client was recorded."

"Where does your mother reside?" He turned back to me.

"I have no idea, in Texas somewhere. We do not communicate."

"Your Honor, I'd like to present Exhibit C. This is a sworn statement from my client's mother stating that, in fact, she has neither communicated with my client nor heard any information regarding her death or her need to take custody of her granddaughter." I was dumfounded. Mr. Morgan had found and talked to my mother? How could she know I was going through all this and not contact me?

"When you saw Mr. Taylor in the restaurant, why did you flee from him?"

"I was scared."

"Go on, what were you scared of, Mrs. Taylor." I knew all this questioning was necessary but it was literally draining me of all the energy and hopeful confidence that I had shown up with today.

"I was scared of him."

"Please explain. Had he ever hit you before?"

"Yes, the night he raped me. He had also threatened me."

"Is there anyone who may have witnessed or heard the events of that night?"

"Yes," I hesitated to bring up George. He was a terrific butler and I felt sure that Seth would dismiss him if he found out he had any knowledge of that night.

"Who would that be?"

"I don't want to say."

"Mrs. Taylor, a witness has already come forth voluntarily to collaborate your testimony. We simply need you to state the truth." Every twist and turn was confusing me and Mr. Morgan continued to put me in a precarious position. I knew my back was against the wall. I had no choice.

"George Moncrieff." It literally pained me to have to drag him into this. He had been my only friend for all the years I was married to Seth.

"Let the record show that this is the same George Moncrieff on our witness list," he stated to no one in particular. Then he turned back to me, "Mrs. Taylor, do you know the J. T. Mulligan that Mr. Taylor says accompanied him to Spain?"

"Yes. He was one of Seth's best friends when we were married."

"Let the record show that this is the same J. T. Mulligan on our witness list, as well," he added again to no one in particular.

"Let's jump to when you accepted a ride with Mr. Taylor to work. He says your behavior became belligerent. How would you describe the events of that morning?" I went on to explain that morning and how I had fallen for Seth's charm once again only to be frightened by his behavior changes.

"Mrs. Taylor, how long has it been since you and Mr. Taylor lived together as man and wife?"

"Almost four years."

"So for four years, you have single-handedly raised two children without any financial assistance from Mr. Taylor, is that correct?"

"Yes."

"Yet, now you are asking for assistance. Why have you not already asked for the child support expected by law? Why now?"

"I was too scared to face him. I decided I would rather struggle rather than have to face him. Then, once he found me and knew I had a son, well, I knew, I knew that he would not leave it alone so I figured I might as well get help."

"No more questions, your Honor." Mr. Morgan walked back to his table and Judge Travis asked Mr. Lassiter to cross-examine me.

"Um, I have no questions at this time."

"You may call your next witness," Judge Travis addressed Mr. Morgan. I was not sure if I should step down now or wait until the court dismissed me.

"Your Honor, I would like to call Hazen Thatcher to the stand."

What? I looked up from the witness stand to see Hazen walk into the court. He was dressed more professionally than I had ever seen him with a suit that looked as if it were custom made to fit his physique. He walked confidently, unfazed, directly up to me as I sat transfixed in the witness box, my legs unable to budge.

"Miss Taylor, you are to step down" Judge Travis stated. I was not sure if my legs would hold me. I could not take my eyes off Hazen and he intensely returned the stare. I finally stood up but my legs buckled and Hazen reached out, supporting me until I could step down. I wanted to fall into his arms. I wanted to tell him not to listen to their lies. I wanted to run from the courtroom and never turn around. I made it to the table just as the bailiff swore in Hazen. Mr. Morgan patted my hand and stood up.

"Mr. Thatcher, can you tell the court the nature of your relationship with Mrs. Taylor?" Mr. Morgan stated. I wished they would stop calling me that.

"Yes, until recently, she and I dated," Hazen avoided my look. My heart broke to hear him reiterate our short relationship status.

"And how long have you known Mrs. Taylor?"

"About three months now." They went on to establish that I worked for Rick who was handling all of Hazen's accounts.

"Have you and Mrs. Taylor ever had sex?"

"No."

"No? Yet you've been together exclusively for almost three months now?"

"We agreed in the beginning to abstain because we respected one another too much and my personal hopes were to make her my wife as soon as she would have me."

"But you said you two dated until recently. Can you explain what changed in your relationship to make you have second thoughts about making her your wife?"

"Yes, well, Mr. Taylor called me one evening, exactly twenty-four days ago, on February twenty-first." Hazen looked directly at Seth as if he could spit in his face. "He told me that they were still married, that, in fact until very recently he and she were *happily* married. He told me that I had intervened in his plan to woo her back to him."

"I see. And he told you this exactly twenty-four days ago?"

"Yes. That's right." Mr. Morgan laughed a falsetto laugh.

"You seem awefully sure of the number of days, Mr. Thatcher. How is it that you remember that so precisely?"

"My world fell apart with that one phone conversation. I went to her apartment that very night, told her and her children good-by, and left that same night for the Soviet Union. I have been there since, that is until my arrival here, this morning."

"Mr. Thatcher, what were the circumstances that took you to the Soviet Union?"

"I left to escape my pain, to get as far away from Abriella as I could. I didn't want to come between a man and his wife, even though I was in love with her."

"So what brought you back?" Mr. Morgan asked. I was frozen; looking at this stately man that I loved and having him this close yet unable to jump into his arms. Hazen turned from Mr. Morgan and looked directly at me. It was the first eye contact we had since he looked at me as he walked into the courtroom.

"I received a voice mail approximately two weeks ago. After listening to it, I knew I had been duped by Mr. Taylor."

"Objection, Your Honor," Mr. Lassiter shouted.

"Overruled!"

"Your Honor, I would like to present exhibit C. This is a copy of the voice mail that Mr. Thatcher received. He gave the small tape to the bailiff and returned to the stand. "Your Honor, because of the sensitive nature of the information contained on the tape, my client asks, out of respect for all parties involved, that Your Honor listen to it privately or in a closed session."

"Very well, bailiff, clear the court."

"Objection, Your Honor," Mr. Lassiter shouted again.

"Overruled."

The next few minutes were a blur as the bailiff cleared the courtroom and another person brought in a tape recorder. Everything happened flawlessly as if orchestrated. Once the court reconvened, I looked around and saw only the judge, the two attorneys, Seth, and Hazen. It dawned on me at that moment that, everyone in this room was fully aware of all the circumstances except the judge and possibly Seth's attorney. We were about to hear the testimony that would, not only implicate Seth of all the lies he had spewed, but also Judge Miller who had been asked to step down from this court for this very reason. I looked over at Seth, incredulous that he would not intervene to stop the proceedings before I irreversibly damaged his reputation. Seth was looking back at me just as stumped that I would go through with it. He leaned toward Mr. Lassiter and they appeared to be arguing.

"Your Honor," Mr. Lassiter tried again to stop the tape before the bailiff played it. "This tape was not presented to my client before today. We feel that it may sway the proceedings in a way that would keep justice from being served. We move that this tape be stricken from the case due to no prior awareness of such."

"Your Honor, Mr. Taylor is fully aware of this tape and its contents. I did not have the original tape in hand until this morning when Mr. Thatcher came to my office with it." What? Hazen had already been to Mr. Morgan's office this morning? I guess the "original tape" part was true since we had actually received a copy.

"Overruled." Judge Travis stated and turned to the bailiff. "Are you ready?"

"One minute, sir," the bailiff looked stressed trying to prepare the evidence. My heart began to beat wildly. Did I really want to destroy Seth? I pulled Mr. Morgan's arm to get his attention. I was not sure how much power I had to stop this but I felt I must.

"Your Honor, my client would like to give Mr. Taylor a chance to settle this out of court before this tape plays, if that is acceptable." The judge looked at me and I met his gaze. I did not like Seth, certainly, I was scared of him, but I never intended to ruin him. If he would only be reasonable, I would let this circus end.

"Very well, Mr. Lassiter, would you like to convene with your client?"

"Yes, Your Honor." Chance leaned toward Seth and they whispered for several minutes. "Your Honor, my client would like to withdraw his custody request and offer joint custody on the condition that the tape and any copies are given directly to him. Also, my client would like to pay Mrs. Taylor restitution for child support since Joshua's birth." Chance looked satisfied with himself as if he had won the case.

"Mr. Morgan, your client's answer." Mr. Morgan did not even ask me.

"Your Honor, my client asks that instead of joint custody she be given sole custody with Mr. Taylor receiving visiting rights that they can agree upon. She respectfully requests that Mr. Taylor pay all her legal fees. Additionally, Mr. Taylor should be responsible for any medical, dental, orthodontic, or psychiatric fees for their son. In addition, a $100,000 arrears be paid within the month along with $50,000 above and beyond the mandated child support each year be placed into a college fund for the child or for any expense my client sees necessary as the child grows. She would like a life insurance policy of one million dollars for Seth Taylor with Joshua Jessie Taylor as the beneficiary." Judge Travis' eyebrows raised as Mr. Morgan went on asking that Seth meet all these demands, none of which

I was aware that Mr. Morgan would claim. When he finally completed his list with satisfaction, he sat next to me. I leaned over to him and whispered that I did not want all of that, that, in fact, I did not want anything from Seth. Mr. Morgan shushed me.

"Mr. Lassiter, what is your client's response?" Judge Travis addressed them. They whispered amongst themselves for only a moment.

"Your Honor, my client accepts these terms." What? I could not believe my ears.

"My, but I am curious as to what is on that tape," Judge Travis almost chuckled. "Very well, then. Need I ask if there are any more questions for Mr. Thatcher?" I had almost forgotten that Hazen was still on the witness stand.

"No, Your Honor," both attorneys stated.

"You may step down, young man," Judge Travis directed him. "This court is hereby adjourned." Then he slammed his gavel down with a smack. I looked at Mr. Morgan who seemed surprised despite his awareness of his plan. Then I looked at Hazen, just stepping down from the witness stand. Our eyes met.

His testimony had been the key to our success. We did not even have to play the horrid tape or call other witnesses. As I looked at him, I wanted to run and jump into his arms but I was not sure. Perhaps he had had a belly-full of my drama and me. My eyes began to swell with tears as we starred at one another. I stood up even though my legs felt like jelly. Hazen walked slowly toward me and never took his eyes off me. Mr. Morgan stepped out of the way.

"Abriella, I came as soon as I could," Hazen began with a gentle voice as if not to scare me. "I was in Siberia. Once I received your voice mail, I led the pack back to civilization but it took a week." He was talking to me as if he was scared I would erupt at any moment. "My love, can you ever forgive me for not believing in you?" Can I forgive him?

"Can you forgive me for not telling you the truth up front?" I asked weakly, scared what his answer would be when I reminded him that I had been the one untruthful. We both nodded our heads and, before I realized what had happened, I ran and jumped into his arms.

~ 24 ~

The Promise

I felt drained from the mental exertion of the day but I knew we had to go out and celebrate. I had carried this burden for almost five years now and, for the first time I could remember, felt completely and truly liberated. Hazen had suggested we all go out to dinner, including Rick and Tracy. He even asked Mr. Morgan although he declined.

"Sure, we'll join you. How about Canoe?" Rick asked.

"Canoe?" I had heard of it, of course. It was a gorgeous place located on the banks of the Chattahoochee River. It was different from the typical skyline view places that people frequented when they wanted to splurge. Their reputation was that of exquisite food and a superb selection of wines, over five hundred, if I had heard correctly

"Alright, sounds great. What time do they open?"

"I believe five-thirty. I'll call for reservations. Is six-thirty alright with you?" I looked at my watch. That would give me enough time to get the kids.

"Oh, sure, yes, six-thirty is fine."

"What do you want to do until then?" Hazen asked me as we walked to his car.

"Well, I need to get my car from Mr. Morgan's office and then I'll have to take it home. I'd like to change clothes, too." He reached for my door but instead pulled me up to him and held me tightly. The unexpected gesture forced my body to relax and as I inhaled, his manly scent intoxicated every nerve in my body. We held each other for several minutes, neither wanting to let the other go. It had been almost a month of heartache and anxiety for us both. Feeling him in my arms was the only way I could convince myself I was not dreaming.

"Don't be mad at me but, can we leave your car for now? I'll have someone come and pick it up but I just can't let you go," he whispered in my ear.

"That would be divine." I exhaled. When we finally got into his car, the emotional release of the day began to hit me. I had to fight back the tears just looking at him.

"What are you thinking, my lady?"

"That I must be dreaming, that I'm gonna wake up and I'll be all alone in my bed, that I don't deserve you." Hazen gazed at me and took my hand in his, squeezing it a little too tightly.

"Ouch," I stammered.

"Just letting you know you're not dreaming," he laughed. As he drove toward my house, he explained that he had taken an extended Siberian dogsledding and camping trip. He had not gotten any of my calls until he finally reached the village of Listvyanka. He explained that this remote village was at one time the site of both the premier Russian research facility and a classified resort maintained by the Federal Security Service. Because of its unique use, communication was possible through satellite services that were not available for many miles around. When he heard, first Katie's and then my message, he said he was frantic to return. Albeit, the only way to get back to a large enough city for air transportation was by dog sled, just as he had gone.

"Abriella, I have never been so anxious to get anywhere in my life. I tried to call you back but your number has changed. Then I called Rick. He gave me Mr. Morgan's phone number and told me what was going on. My biggest fear was that I wouldn't be here for you and then, that you would not forgive me." The thought of holding Hazen's decision to leave against him seemed ludicrous to me, given the circumstances.

"Hazen, I changed my phone number because every time it would ring or bing, I would hope it was you."

"Next time, I speak of such preposterous plans as leaving, you have my permission to tie me down and make me listen. The only thing I don't understand is why you didn't explain once I asked you."

"I couldn't speak, Hazen. All I could think about was that I had lost you forever. I was numb. And what is this talk of 'next time'?"

"No, my love, there will not be a next time."

I figured it would take about twenty minutes to get to the restaurant so we had a while before we had to get the kids and go.

"As much as I want to keep you to myself, I know the kids will be surprised beyond words to see you also. Can we pick them up before we head home to change clothes?"

"Of course," he smiled with a giddy anticipation. Katie squealed with delight and literally jumped into Hazen's strong arms. If she had jumped into my arms that forcefully, it would have knocked me down but Hazen did not even budge. Josh shone with animation when he saw Hazen and Hazen picked him up and swung him around in the air.

"I have an idea," Hazen said once we were all in his car. "Why don't we stop at the mall and get new clothes for tonight?'

"Oh, Hazen, that's not necessary." I said.

"Please, please," Katie pleaded. I knew I was out-voted. We stopped at Lenox mall. I had not frequented it since I left Seth. It felt incredibly wonderful to walk down the mall. The kids were fascinated with all the beautiful stores and displays. It felt good to feel human again. We went into Neiman Marcus. Katie saw a little dress there she liked but when I saw the price tag we left and went to Macy's despite Hazen insisting it was not too much. I bought Josh an outfit that made him appear suddenly grown up. It was khaki pants and a long-sleeve shirt with a warm sweater vest over it. Katie easily found another dress she liked and I changed them both in the dressing room and started toward the car.

"Momma, aren't you going to get something, too?" Katie asked. She was remarkably thoughtful for a preteen.

"No, baby, we probably need to get going. I'm fine." I really did want something new but decided against looking. We headed back toward the car but it seemed to me that Katie and Hazen kept lagging behind causing Josh and I to have to wait on them every few yards. I stopped when I heard Katie squeal.

"Oh, Mommy! You have to get this!" She was touching a beautiful dress. It was a burgundy color and made from thin, soft sweater material. The front was daringly low-cut. I did not think I would be comfortable in it.

"No, Katie, that's beautiful but," but what? It is too sexy for me?

"Just try it on, mommy. We got new clothes and you need something new, too."

"I agree," Hazen prompted. "Here. I'll watch the kids while you slip this on." He gave me a sweet but determined look.

It was all the temptation I needed. I slipped the dress on and the transformation, which overtook me in the mirror, was stunning. I knew instantly that that dress was going with me. Then I looked at the price tag.

"Oh my, Katie, you sure do have expensive tastes."

"Mom! You have to get that!" She could be such a little drama queen sometimes. I was uncomfortable spending so much on one dress but it was delectable. I decided I would splurge just this once.

"May I get it for you?" Hazen asked when we were on the way to check out.

"No, Hazen, I've got it." I did not want him to think I was trying to take advantage.

"My dear lady," he stopped me and turned my shoulders to look him straight on, "You are the most independent, stubborn lady I have ever met. I know you can get it but I was asking if you would do me the honor of allowing me to buy you a small gift. Call it a peace offering if that makes you feel better." His words brought a flashback to my mind of my telling Kayla that my life goal was to become self-reliant. Hazen describing me as 'the most independent woman he'd ever met' made me realize that I have reached my goal. I passed the dress into his waiting hands.

When we finally all got back into the car, I realized that we were now running very late. I tried to call Rick but he didn't answer. He was probably already there. I felt terrible that I had pushed him to go earlier and now I would be late.

When we drove up, the kids and I looked at the beautiful restaurant in awe. From the outside, Canoe was lit up like a carousel at the fair. The lush landscaping gave a quaint effect and it was nestled amongst so many trees. It was truly a marvelous site. I was glad that Rick had suggested it. We parked and strutted in our new clothes toward the door stopping to take in a flower here and an herb there. The lawn invited us to sit on one of the strategically located park benches but I prompted the kids to get in. I hoped that Rick and Tracy had not been waiting too long.

The maître d' greeted us kindly. Before I could tell her our reservation name, she asked us to follow her. Yes, Rick had probably told her to be on the lookout for us. She took us on the backside of the restaurant that overlooked the Chattahoochee River. When we entered the large room, I saw Rick and Tracy at the far end of it. As we walked, I noticed thousands of flowers covered the room. It must have costs a fortune to place fresh flowers in such a room this time of year. The fragrance that filled it made me inhale deeply with delight.

"I'm so sorry we are late," I began before we even sat down, "You know, you can't give a woman extra money and not expect her to go shopping." We all laughed. Hazen helped me with our coats and Tracy sat Josh next to her while Katie sat between Josh and me. This left Hazen and Rick beside one another.

"You're fine," Tracy said, "perfect really. We had time for a drink before dinner. Dear, I am so happy for you. How exciting to have all this fuss behind you."

"Yes! So Rick told you all about Seth surrendering?" I asked her.

"Yes, but I'm dying of curiosity to find out exactly how all this," she waved her hand over Hazen and I as if we were on display, "came about." I was a little embarrassed. Hazen had given me the gist of his story and I did not feel comfortable talking about our problems in front of Rick and Tracy.

"Thank you for asking, Tracy. I would like the chance to explain it to everyone. You see," Hazen automatically began, "well, let me start from the beginning. Seth called me and told me that he and Abriella were married, that she had left in a huff after they had argued. He made it sound like I had broken up their marriage." Hearing this made me furious all over again. "He told me that she would deny his information. He said that her story was that they had not been together in years but that they had, in fact, been happily married for a long time. I thought Abriella was possibly some misguided, bored housewife who was only out for a fling even though she didn't fit that caste."

"But that's not," I started to say. Hazen put his finger over my lips. My heart beat harder. Hazen held my gaze but I could see Tracy smiling in my peripheral vision.

"I was devastated," Hazen was talking directly to me now. "I left that very night for Siberia. I didn't think I could stand to be on the same half of the world as you if I couldn't be with you. I arrived the next evening in the middle of the night. That next morning I commissioned a dog sled safari for three weeks. Wearing myself out was the only way I could clear my mind of you. Instead of helping me to overcome my feelings for you, the vast wilderness mirrored the emptiness I felt at my core. I hoped it would go away so I rode on. A week into this journey, I decided that I could not keep going. The further away from you I traveled, the weaker I got." He looked at me for a moment in silence.

"A Siberian run takes great stamina and strength. I felt my strength was all gone. I wanted nothing but to get back to you. So I had the guide turn our route to go towards the little village I told you about. I planned to call you from there but knew that would be wrong. I knew I must rest a day or so and then head back here to tell you in person that I loved you. I had decided that, ethical or not, I was coming to beg you to have me. I knew in my heart you couldn't possibly be happily married to him and share all you did with me. Plus, the kids! The kids had said nothing of Seth, nothing of their father. Seth's story didn't add up in my mind. Your apartment, Rick never mentioning Seth, everything, and nothing made sense anymore. I was coming back here to get to the bottom of it and see if there was any way to woo you back to me." Everyone at the table was eerily quiet and I felt that Hazen and I were all alone.

"When I got to the village, I found Katie's voice mail and yours. I was stunned. What a fool I had been. I immediately began my course back, now regenerated with a strength from some source that had left me when I thought we were over. If I had not already decided to go to that village, I would not have received your message in time to get here. As it was, I charted a flight but the winter storm delayed our departure. I have just arrived this very morning and went directly to court."

"But you didn't call. I waited for you to call."

"I did call, my love, I called over and over as soon as I got to Moscow Tuesday morning but you had changed your number, remember?" Oh, yeah. The intimacy of the moment hung in the air and even the kids sat transfixed.

"You made promises to me," I confessed. It had been in my mind but I had not admitted to him that I was hurt. "You assured me you would always be there for me and then, the first problem arose, and," I could not make myself say it. He had left me.

"I know, I know, sweetheart." He looked down at his hands embracing mine. "I know. I do. I am so very sorry. I let you down. I hurt you." Then he looked up to meet my eyes. "Abriella, I've never allowed anyone into my heart, my world, as I did you. It scared me. Then I find that you are a married woman! Married! It sent me into a tailspin. I know you put me on a pedestal as if I am superhuman but I am just a man. I misjudged you based on false information. I listened to the wrong person. I will always trust you from now on- forever. If you will have me, please, I will make it up to you. I will spend the rest of my life rebuilding that trust that I broke when I left. Will you have me, Abriella? Will you give me that chance?" I looked around the table at Tracy who seemed to be holding her breath. The kids were both smiling as if they understood somehow better than I did. Rick even had a smirk on his face, understanding the outcome before I spoke it.

"Yes," I whispered looking back at Hazen. I leaned forward and put my arms around his neck. His hands immediately slipped around my back and he had me in his arms lifting me up as he stood. He squeezed me so tightly that I could not breathe but I did not care. I could not believe it! Hazen did love me and he was back into my life just as quickly as he had left. What a glorious day this was turning out to be. When he finally released me, my eyes stung with tears. Even though they were tears of joy, I bowed my head to avoid him seeing me. He lifted my chin tenderly and I saw that his eyes were also wet.

"Well, why don't we have a toast, to Abriella and Hazen?" ick announced.

"One more thing," Hazen cut him off. He reached into his east pocket, but it seemed there was nothing in his hand. He took y hand and slipped on a cluster of rubies and diamonds. "Now, efore you say, 'no', let me just tell you that this is not an ngagement ring." I breathed a sigh of relief. As much as I loved m and would have most definitely said, 'yes' if he had asked me marry him, I knew it would be foolish. We needed time, to build the trust, to get to know one another, to insure our long-me happiness.

"But," he continued, "This is a promise ring, unlike the ther. I promise never to betray you again. I promise always to eat you with respect. I promise to take care of you all the days of y life."

"Sure sounds like a proposal to me," Rick boasted. Tracy it him gently on the arm and shushed him.

"Yes, well, if all goes as I hope and intend an engagement ng will be forthcoming." Hazen smiled.

"Isn't this all so very romantic, dear?" Tracy said to no one n particular. "All these flowers and now a beautiful ring."

"Flowers? You mean," I looked around at the massive ouquets that filled the entire room.

"Yes," Tracy was beaming, "He called numerous flower shops to get this room filled at the last minute." Rick gave Tracy a warning glance and patted her hand in her lap as if to quiet her.

"I wanted the evening to be perfect," Hazen said shyly, embarrassed by his chivalrous act.

"It would have been perfect just because you are here but this," I motioned around the room taking it all in again, "this is over-the-top. You didn't have to,"

"Yes, I did," he reached over and kissed me on the cheek, "it is the least I could do." The server came up slowly as if to insure we were finished with all the grand gestures and schemes.

"Mr. Thatcher, would you like a bottle of our best Champaign?" she asked Hazen. Did they know him here?

"Actually, I'd like two of your best bottles of our Napa Estate Select."

"Two bottles, sir?" she seemed unsure. Hazen nodded politely. "Um, yes, sir." She turned and walked away. I picked up the wine list casually and began to look for what he had ordered. I did not see it.

"It's not on the menu, sweetheart," Hazen whispered in my ear as Rick, Tracy, and the kids all began to talk.

"Oh, no, I wasn't," I was about to lie, "Okay, I was." Hazen smiled.

"I don't ever want you to worry about the costs of anything. By the way, you look good enough to eat tonight. New dress?" He winked teasingly and his eyes took me in. I was suddenly self-conscious of my low neckline. I put my hand up to cover the top of my breasts. Hazen took my hand in his, "please, I deserve to be punished for what I did to you. Go ahead, continue to tease me." He smiled a wicked smile and kissed the back of my hand. I could not stop looking at the gorgeous ring he had given me. I knew it must have been ridiculously expensive.

"Hazen, you spent too much," I was feeling guilty that he t he should have to go to great lengths to apologize to me. I ›uld have fallen in his arms with a simple, "I'm back".

"I would have gotten more but time was limited. As it was, ɛ snow storm that kept me from reaching Moscow, and bsequently from leaving Moscow, found me near the Republic of ıkutia." I looked puzzled. "It's on the far-eastern side, on the rimeter of the Arctic Circle." I still did not understand but he emed proud so I beamed back at him. "When we are ready for a oper engagement, we will travel to India or Africa and pick out a amond that suits you then have it set in the setting of your oice."

"Hazen, I'm not used to," he cut me off again.

"Well, you're just going to have to get used to it. I have no tentions of ever letting you get away again." He smiled so veetly and reached over to kiss me lightly again.

The entire evening was the most elegant I had ever .perienced. Our meals were incredibly exquisite, from the grilled east of Long Island duckling to the cocoa-crusted Cervena :nison. The dishes were unique and delicious. Rick and Hazen :ted as if they had known each other for years, which of course, ey had, but I did not think of them as being very close until night. Tracy kept peering at Hazen and smiling at me. After our eal, Hazen insisted on an assortment of desserts. Our server 'ought Earl Grey infused Crème Brulee with lemon zest ortbread, chocolate "mole" mouse with bittersweet flatbread and lapeno jam, and a blueberry-almond pie with lemon curd and veet thyme sauce. The kids most liked the popcorn ice cream ındae with Canoe's Cracker Jack and the chocolate grotto, salted ıramel pretzel dust. We sat around the table for an hour after we ad eaten enjoying the camaraderie and trying to breathe again.

Once Katie finished eating, she slid off her chair and sat in :azen's lap. Everyone seemed so naturally gelled. Josh grew jealous and had to sit on Hazen's other knee. Rick and Hazen talked business a little and everything in between. Tracy and I whispered about the wonderful turn of events that had all transpired in one day. The end of the evening did not disappoint either.

I wanted desperately to have a minute alone with him so I asked him to stay so I could get the kids in bed. As if no time had passed at all, he began to help me get them in bed making sure they brushed their teeth and reading them a story. Josh was already asleep before Hazen finished the story and Katie was not far behind. I was not sure if Hazen had insisted on the story for their sake or his own. He truly seemed to miss them.

At long last, we were alone. I made coffee for us, not wanting to chance our misbehavior again with more wine. We sat on the front porch for a while but it began to get chilly. On the couch, Hazen held me until I warmed up. We caught up on our lives since we had last seen each other. I told him about Annie Mae and Poppa, no longer worried about hiding my secret past. I told him the entire story since high school. I told him about how I intended to help Kayla get her family away from there. I held nothing back and it felt like a homecoming of sort. Hazen shared his story with me as well.

"I won't lie to you, Abriella; I was a hellion for many years. It drove a spike between my father and me. We have only come back to terms these past four or five years that I have acted like a dutiful son. My biggest regret is that my mother did not live to see the new me, or to meet you. She wanted grandkids so badly. I wanted nothing of the sort." It hurt me to think of Hazen not wanting children.

"You seem so, I don't know, acclimated to children. You are a natural father. It surprises me to find out that was not your desire."

"Yes, well, you did not know me then. I traveled the world tasting of its menu, if I can put it delicately, and not having a care

r my future, much less being responsible for anyone else's." He
oked down, then away, and finally back at me. "I had a brother,
der than me, who was the perfect son. He made excellent grades
school. Everyone expected him to succeed to my father's throne.
was my fault that he died." I was stunned. I began to shake my
ad, denying that it was possible that this superhero could be
pable of any such crime. Hazen pulled his arm away from
ound me and leaned forward, folding his hands in front of him. "I
d been gone for four years. I hadn't talked to anyone, not even to
eck in. I felt that they, my mother and father, had all they needed
my brother."

"Then, one day, my father calls out of the blue and asks me to
turn home. My brother was getting married and, apart from them
pecting me in the ceremony, they would need me to fill the gap
f the workload. I went home and all was well for a season.
owever, I grew anxious after a while. I managed to stifle my
elings but one day, my brother, Jared was his name, well, we had
big fight. I wanted to travel again and his wife wanted to start a
mily. We didn't have the labyrinth of officers in place then like
e do now. I was needed. Selfishly, I left. That very night, Jared
as in an accident and died. He was headed home after doing
me paperwork at the office and it was late, very late. He fell
sleep at the wheel." My eyes overflowed with tears and my heart
th empathy for Hazen and his entire family. I leaned forward to
omfort him. He looked visibly shaken. He began to tremble and I
lt powerless to stop the pain that came from him.

"I came home for the funeral but, um, I just, um, I couldn't," his
oice shook with emotion, "so I left shortly afterward. I did stay in
uch better after that but," his voice trailed off.

"Hazen, you mustn't blame yourself." I tried to console.

"No, I know. That's what everyone, even my father, has said
ut, you know, if I had just stayed to help he may have been home
vith his wife." I could not imagine the grief he must still feel and I

knew that no words would properly help him so I just held him. After a few minutes, he regained his composure and continued his story.

"I was never quite the hellion after that but went on a spiritual quest instead. My dad called for me to come home a little over a year later because my mother was dying. The doctors say it was cancer but I truly believe she died from grief." He leaned back, pulled me with him into the soft couch, and held me close to his chest. I could hear his heart beating wildly and I held him tightly to try to stop the pain. "I finally stepped up to the plate after that to take my share of the responsibility. I still travel but always kept a finger on the pulse of my dad's life. We've made great strides and are quite friendly now. I suppose with my grandfather gone, that will only get better. I am all he has left." Hazen let out a huge breath.

"I didn't mean to overload you," he said as he looked at me finally.

"No, I'm glad you shared all that," I answered honestly. I had put him in a bracket by himself- not human, but a perfect angel-like immortal. I realized now that his maturity and wisdom had come by great peril. It helped me now that I knew his story to see him as a flesh-and-blood man. It helped me to accept his ability to love me.

"So, my dear, if you will still have me," he forged a laugh, "I have a history. I have sown my wild oats. I have grown to be a man who takes his responsibilities seriously." He turned to look into my eyes and brushed back my hair. "I am ready, no, eager to be a man worthy of love, worthy of your love, and your children. I am ready to have more children as well when you're ready." He smiled when he said this but I could see that he was intent on that course. "Will you have me, Abriella? Will you marry me?" I knew he did not mean anytime soon. He had explained that well enough at dinner tonight and on Valentine's Day. It made it easier to ıse him.

"You'll have to ask my Poppa first," I laughed.

"Great idea!" He said loudly. "Shall we go now?"

"Hazen, it's the middle of the night," I looked outside and saw ıt it was actually light.

"No, my dear, it is six-thirty in the morning!" What? Had we ılly sat up all night talking? I had thought I was tired when we ːived home last night and yet, under his spell, I had enjoyed the tire night talking to him.

"Abriella, you are such a strong woman."

"Me? No, you are the strong one, Hazen."

"You have overcome so many misfortunes, catastrophes, and ıexpected obstacles. I believe it was Carl von Clausewitz who id, 'Courage, above all things, is the first quality of a warrior'. ɔu have exemplified courage in all things. I will be honored to be ur husband."

I was fascinated that this man, with all his striking good looks, ımense wealth, and oozing charm would even look twice at me. ɔ imagine actually being his wife dumbfounded my imagination. ad I any idea that our world was about to change, I would have ːld him captive in our little haven forever.

~ 25 ~

Crash

"I came to bring you something," I smiled as I handed Annie Mae a check for a thousand dollars.

"Lawd, what's this?" her eyes grew bigger.

"A token of my appreciation for all you and Poppa have done for me. I got a big check from Seth and it's the first of many to come." I felt so proud to be able to share my fortune with her. I always had plans to pay them back but that day never seemed to come. Now my conscience was clear.

"Chill, I don't want yo money," she handed the check back to me.

"Annie Mae, please, I've always wanted to pay y'all back and never thought I'd ever be able to. Please, take a vacation, go out to dinner, or buy yourself something nice." The pleading in my voice must have gotten to her because she slowly conceded. It made her uncomfortable, I knew, but she was just going to have to get used to people loving her because now that I could, I planned to help my chosen family meet their needs. She slipped the check into her apron with the tips she would collect throughout the day.

"So whut's goin' on?" she eyed me skeptically, "Sumpthin' wrong?" A few weeks had gone by since the court date and Seth had sent the money on which he had agreed. Hazen and I were inseparable. During the day, he would frequently go with me to the office allowing me to show him the plan as I lay it out for his empire. Almost every day, he would leave early, pick up the kids for me, and meet me at my place. The few weekends that had come and gone since our reunion, Hazen, the kids, and I had enjoyed the activities around Atlanta.

The first weekend we went to the Body Exhibit and the Dinosaur museum, which were in the same building. Then we walked the quaint shops surrounding them. The next weekend, we celebrated Josh's birthday by visiting the Coca-Cola museum and The Atlanta Aquarium, which were side by side to each other. That night we had a little ice cream party for a few of his day care friends at the local parlor.

The kids began to blossom before my eyes. Josh, especially, started talking more and clung to Hazen as if he were his biological son. It seemed strange to me that Josh would grow up with no recollection of all Katie and I had lived through. He would not remember what it had been like not to have a father. For that, I felt blessed. I could not help but wonder how he and Hazen's relationship would evolve as Seth began to seek visitation. Ironically, I had not heard from Seth or his attorney yet about Seth's right to see his son. I wondered if Seth had decided against it.

Hazen talked frequently of our proposed marriage now and he was making plans for the kids and me to spend their school's Spring break in Colorado with his dad. He seemed anxious for us to move forward. Of course, my heart wanted that as well, especially when we enjoyed our stolen kisses and few intimate moments. Hazen and I shared a passion that I could only imagine would grow stronger as each day passed and I worried that we would not last long enough to keep the integrity that was so important to us both.

"You know Hazen, the man I told you about?" I told Annie Mae as I visited with her after delivering their taxes in person. It was an excuse to see them again but one that Rick did not seem to mind.

"Yeah, chille, I ain't met 'im yet but I hope to one day," she sounded so maternal.

"Well, I'm in love with him, Annie Mae. There's no doubt in my mind. He's perfect, handsome, smart, caring, kind, and loves the kids." I smiled. "We talk of getting married but, I'm afraid. What if I don't know him- as I thought I knew Seth but didn't? What if we don't make it either? I just couldn't face losing him. I'm all out of courage for this lifetime. I know it sounds crazy, but in so many ways, it takes more courage to trust and love Hazen than it did to face Seth."

"Chille, it shouldn't take no courage to be with the ones we love. You was courageous when you went up against Seth and his trickery. You was courageous when you came here wid nuttin' but the clothes on yo back and yo baby's hand tremblin' in yours. You got the courage of a warrior, chille, but, I say it again, it ought not take courage to tell a man like you just described ta me that you love 'im. I 'spect he's waitin' on you ta decide you wants him for life."

"I do, Annie Mae," I burst with enthusiasm now. "I love him more than I ever thought it was possible to love another human being, except my own kids."

"Chille, you beam when you talk 'bout him. I knowed you love 'im. But if ya feel like ya need more time, then jus' wait till you be sure. What's the hurry? Just enjoy the courtin'."

"You're right, Annie Mae, but sometimes I just want to jump right in and start our life together." We talked for a while longer and then I knew I needed to get the kids. On the way to my car, I asked Annie Mae how Kayla was doing.

"Awe, chille, didn't she call ya? Oh, yeah, she said she tried to but yo number musta changed." I made a mental note to call her immediately and give her my new number.

"Why? What's wrong?"

"Chille, ain't nuthin' wrong. That high-falutin' college she was wantin' ta go to sent her a letter sayin' she could come git her degree for free! HA! Can you believe it?"

"What? How is that possible? I thought she had exhausted all means trying to get in on a scholarship." I couldn't wait to talk to Kayla and find out all the details.

"I don' know, chille. All I knows is she's plannin' on goin' this summer. She an' the whole family movin' ta Athens."

"That's wonderful!" I had a million questions to ask her and called her as soon as I got on the road.

"Kayla! Annie Mae tells me that you got a scholarship after all. I thought you had given up for this year."

"Girl, I had. I was as surprised as anybody. I got this letter out of the blue saying that I would receive a full scholarship that covers tuition, books, everything."

"Oh my gosh, Kayla! I am so happy for you."

"Yeah, apparently this is a new scholarship recently set up for underprivileged minorities wanting to go to grad school. I hadn't even applied for it! The benevolent donor had named me to receive the first one. I have no idea how anyone like that would know about me." I was beginning to think that I might know someone who knew about her and was willing to help.

"That's fantastic. Annie Mae said your mom and Gabby are moving with you. How did that come about? Are you getting a job in Athens to support them?"

"No, girl, that is all included in the scholarship! It covers room and board for me and any family who is dependent upon me. This is a dream come true! We're packing now and moving in a few weeks." I was breathless and overjoyed for her. I felt that Hazen had definitely created this scholarship for Kayla and kept it anonymous. Well, I resolved, he may not have wanted credit for it but I would certainly thank him anyway.

As I drove back to North Atlanta, thinking about Hazen's new role in my life, I made a decision. I wanted Hazen to meet Poppa and Annie Mae. We talked of it many times but stayed so busy on the weekends that we never got around to it.

"I'd love to meet them," Hazen said after I proposed the idea. "Shall we go to them or should I send a car for them?" It was a good question. I wanted them to be comfortable. While I couldn't imagine Hazen in their neighborhood, I knew that they would probably feel more comfortable there. I called Annie Mae the next day and asked her how they would like to proceed.

"You mean, he's willin' ta send a car ta fetch us?" She sounded animated.

"Annie Mae, we could pick you up. If we came in the limo, we would all fit easily in the back but if that makes you uncomfortable, we can come there. Are there any restaurants there or would you rather cook?"

"Oh, no chille. Annie Mae be gittin' mighty tired these days. I'd just as soon we eat out, s'long as the place gots some *real* food." I knew she inferred that she did not want the vegetarian cuisine that Katie and I enjoyed.

"Alright then, why don't we go this Saturday? We'll pick you up at four and I'll make reservations around five."

Everyone grew very excited as the weekend came. The kids were giddy about being able to ride in the limousine again. Katie was exuberant to see Poppa, Annie Mae, and especially Ezekiel.

On Friday afternoon, just before I was about to leave, my phone rang.

"Hello, Brie," Seth spoke coldly. My heart froze.

"Seth, hi," I stammered.

"I would like to get my son this weekend."

"Uh, this weekend? To be honest, we have big plans for tomorrow afternoon."

"Big plans, eh? I suppose you'll have big plans next time I call also."

"No, Seth. It's not like that. You'll need to give me more notice. Seth," I hesitated to talk to him about what was troubling me but I knew it was an inevitable conversation, "I've been thinking and, well, I feel like the first few times you meet with Josh that we should transition him so that he comes to know you before I just drop him off to spend the day with you."

"Brie, you cannot dictate how I see my son."

"Well, Seth, I am trying to be nice but, yes, to be honest, I can. I want Josh to know you but, right now, he has no idea who you are. I don't feel comfortable just sending him off with you until I know he is relaxed with you." There was a long silence but I waited for Seth to process this new information patiently.

"Very well then. Next weekend, why don't we all go to my lake cabin together? We could go boating, maybe cook out, I don't know, swim in the pool if it's warm enough." I was stunned. I knew it would probably not be warm enough to swim and I had no desire to spend the entire day with Seth.

"Uh, I don't know, Seth." I stalled to think.

"I'll bring Tiffany and you can bring Hazen if you wish." That did make me feel somewhat better. "Tiffany wants to meet my son anyway, seeing how she will be his step-mother." I got a knot in my throat that threatened to choke me. The thought of Josh having a stepmother made me apprehensive. Seth must have noticed my delayed response so he continued.

"Brie, I know you think I'm a monster. I'm not. I never thought I'd have a son. I want to be in his life."

"Okay," I couldn't believe my ears. Would Hazen even be willing to do this?

Saturday afternoon, Hazen picked us up in the limo and we all excitedly traveled across the city to Poppa's and Annie Mae's home. I was also nervous. This experience would make the stories I had told Hazen about me real and I was not sure if he would be able to handle that. When we drove up, we realized there was not really a good place to park a limo so the driver parked directly in front of the store on the street.

"Why don't I jump out and get them," I said, "Hazen, you stay here with the kids."

"Abriella, I'd like to meet them properly," he added. So Hazen, the kids, and I all went into the store. Poppa and Ezekiel were sitting by the old pot-bellied stove near the back.

"Hey, Poppa!" I exclaimed. I realized I sounded a little more animated than usual and chalked it up to my nervousness.

"Hey, baby," Poppa returned the exclamation as he rose from his rocking chair. Ezekiel and Poppa were dressed in their Sunday best and I was proud that they felt the occasion was that special. "Momma'll be down in a minute," he added. "She's goin' through her entire closet tryin' to look presentable." Ezekiel had already greeted Katie as Poppa and I met.

"Poppa, this is Hazen Thatcher. Hazen, this is Jessie Copeland, otherwise affectionately known as Poppa." My nerves immediately calmed as the two men shook hands and fell into an easy conversation. Hazen asked many questions about the store and complimented Poppa and Annie Mae for their entrepreneurship. I soon knew they did not need me here so I excused myself to go help Annie Mae.

"Oh, chille, I'm sa glad you come up," Annie Mae seemed frazzled and I had never seen her so.

"Annie Mae, what's wrong?"

"Chille, I shoulda gone shoppin' ta git a new outfit for tonight. I got nothin' presentable."

"Annie Mae, you look stunning!" I gave her my honest opinion. I had seen her dressed up many times at church and on holidays but, except for the tired wrinkles around her eyes, she looked fabulous. The dress she had on was a bright yellow but with a small print of colorful flowers. The small print seemed to tone down her weight somewhat or either she had lost some weight.

"I think I'll wear this one," she said as she took a deep green, long-sleeved dress out of the closet.

"Annie Mae, no. You'll burn up in those long sleeves. It's April. You know how hot natured you are," I encouraged. "I love the yellow dress you have on. Have you lost weight or is that the dress?"

"Oh, no, chille. Now you just tryin' ta flatter me. I'm as nervous as a chille on tha first day a school."

"Annie Mae," I spoke gently as I put my hands on each of her arms to get her full attention. "You look fantastic! Seriously! Why are you so nervous? I've never seen you like this."

"Chille, I don' know. I guess I never met a rich man before. I don' know how ta dress, or act, or nuthin'."

"Annie Mae, come down and meet him. He is just like anyone else. Besides, he is going to be in your life permanently. He will love you."

"Maybe that's it," she sounded more exasperated than before I tried to sooth her, "I think I be worried he won't like me and I knowed he gone be my son-in-law. He'll be the only son-in-law I'll ever have and, and," she looked like she was about to lose it.

"Ok, that's it. Let's go." I grabbed her hand and pulled her toward the door to go downstairs.

"No! Chille! I ain't got ma jewelry on yet!" She easily pulled from my loose grip and put clip-on earrings and her wedding band on. "Okay, I'm as ready as I'll ever be." We walked down the stairs and Poppa and Hazen still sat in the rocking chairs where I had left them. Poppa whistled as Annie Mae approached them.

"Well you look just as purty as the day I married ya," Poppa said, no doubt trying to relax Annie Mae. It worked.

"Oh, you stop your nonsense, Poppa, and in front of company, too." She blushed a little but slid towards him as he stood up and put his arm around her shoulders.

"Hazen, this is my Annie Mae. Annie Mae, this is my Hazen." They both smiled at my possessive introduction. Annie Mae put her hand out as if to shake his hand but Hazen reached in and hugged her neck. I knew right away that Annie Mae was hooked.

"It is so nice to meet you, finally," Hazen told her, "Abriella has told me so much about you and how you helped her."

"Well, she exaggerates about that, I think," Annie Mae stated, "We didn't do nuttin' we wuddn't supposed ta do as good Christians."

"Well," Hazen laughed, "that may be true but there are far fewer Christians who do what they are supposed to do so, again, I must thank you." Annie Mae liked this response and after a few more minutes of chatting, I suggested we leave.

"I'd like to see the cottage, if that's possible," Hazen surprised me as we walked toward the front of the store.

"Oh, no," I started to tell him that it was occupied with a tenant but Annie Mae cut me off.

"We can do that. Old man Weaver died last week. I just finished cleanin' and polishin' it yesterday." I was excited to see it but apprehensive what Hazen would think of my previous living quarters. We all walked down the path, between the store and the house beside it, toward the small cottage in the back. Nothing had changed. The path still had occasional broken step stones and the grass was still sparse. As we stepped up on the tiny front porch, nostalgia overcame me. Katie ran enthusiastically to her old bedroom, which was now a plain beige.

"Momma," Katie shouted, "they painted over my elephant! I wish I had gotten a picture of it." She pouted briefly. We looked around, which only took a minute because of its size.

"Look, Josh," I pointed to the bathtub, "this is the very place where you were born." He looked at the tub and then at me in disbelief.

"You mean, I came out of that spigot?" Josh asked sincerely amazed. Everyone burst into a loud laughter.

"No, baby, mommy lay in the tub for you to be born." I could tell he was a little hurt that we were laughing, so I added, "we aren't laughing at you. That was just an astute observation for such a young boy." That seemed to appease him somewhat. After a few more minutes, and a few questions from Hazen, we finally made our way to the limo.

As we traveled toward downtown Atlanta, a middle-ground that Hazen thought would be perfect, the conversation in the limo was nonstop with everyone trying to talk over everyone else.

"Where we eatin', chille?" Annie Mae addressed Hazen. He smiled at her pet name for everyone as if it was reserved for him alone.

"Well, Abriella said you liked southern cuisine so I did some research and found that Fat Matt's is a local favorite. They're known for their bar-b-que ribs and they have a blue's band that plays every night, I think." I marveled at Hazen's ability to hone in on sources that I was unfamiliar with even though I had lived here my entire life.

"Oh, that sounds nice," Annie Mae said to Hazen. "He sho' got a sexy voice, don' he?" She said to me as she leaned closer as if to tell me a secret but her voice was much too loud and everyone heard. Hazen smiled again. The ride went quickly and

Annie Mae obviously felt comfortable soon after we left their house. Ezekiel found the limo fascinating and I couldn't help but smile as Katie acted like the professional showing him all the gadgets hidden in the back, like the wet bar. Once we arrived and sat down, Annie Mae began oohing and aweing over the menu.

"This all look good," she announced, "Poppa, we may hafta come back here again someday." He smiled his knowing smile that they probably would not but shook his head in agreement. The service was excellent and our food arrived quickly. Some ordered ribs, others chicken, and still others a pork sandwich. Because Annie Mae could not select a side, Hazen told the waiter to bring one of each of them. The table looked like Poppa and Annie Mae's table on Thanksgiving Day with "Rum" baked beans, potato salad, Coleslaw, Brunswick stew, mac n cheese, collard greens, and even roasted peanuts and potato chips. Everything tasted as good as it looked.

Once we were finished with our plates, Poppa asked Annie Mae if she would like to dance.

"Awe now, Poppa, you knowed I cain't dance," she replied, embarrassed.

"Come and dance with me," he insisted, standing and holding out his hand for her. I could tell that, despite her embarrassment, she wanted to so I prompted her to go.

"Come kids," Hazen joined, "let's all go dance." The kids jumped at the chance and we all proceeded to the small dance floor.

"You are so precious," I told Hazen when I finally had a second to lean forward and whisper in his ear. He smiled. The dancing continued for several songs.

"I gotta sit, Poppa," Annie Mae finally announced. We all followed them back to the table where two whole pies, one sweet potato and one pecan, awaited us. I sliced each pie and served everyone a small piece of each. As the night wore down, I looked around the table and realized I had never been this happy in my life. I knew that I would never find a man more suited to my life, more respectful of my plight, or more loving to my children and me. I swelled with love for this man that God had brought into my life.

On the way home, the conversation was quieter and more subdued.

"Well, I do believe the rum in those baked beans made me a little dizzy," Annie Mae joked. "An' they musta got ta Poppa, too. I ain't seen him sa frisky since I met 'im." We all laughed and Poppa blushed. As we grew closer to their house, a grey cloud appeared to overshadow the evening. Things were drawing to a close. We said our farewells and everyone appeared genuinely happy with the outcome of the evening. My heart hurt as the limo drove away, leaving people dear to my heart behind.

"You love them, don't you?" Hazen asked as he watched me. I nodded. "I certainly see why." It was an evening I would savor because our lives were about to take a drastic change.

It became increasingly difficult to let Hazen go each night. He was such a big part of our lives. I continued to question if I could completely trust him or if I should wait until I found his fatal flaw so that I could run away. I did not want to find a flaw, yet my mind kept badgering me that there must be something wrong with him for him to be in love with me. The next week flew by and as Saturday drew nearer, my nerves fraying began to get the best of me. Hazen appeared unaffected by spending the day with my ex and I wished I could be as calm as he remained. Katie was a little apprehensive also and asked if she could stay with Rick and his grandkids. Tracy agreed that was fine and I felt a small amount of relief as well, knowing I at least would not have to worry about Seth's behavior towards her.

Saturday morning, Seth called and gave Hazen directions how to get to the lake house. It was as if we customarily gathered on a regular basis. We arrived at the lake house at two o'clock as decided. I could not help but be envious of Tiffany. She was only a few years, maybe five, younger than I and yet, she was stunningly beautiful. Her body, not yet rearranged from bearing a child, made her look like a bathing suit model. Her hair shone and her nails immaculate. All the old insecurities of the past came up my throat threatening to choke the breath out of me. I felt like a cabbage patch doll beside a Barbie. Her demeanor, though polite, let me know that she hated me. I felt nothing but pity for her. I knew that she had no idea what she was getting into and that I was powerless to help her.

Hazen and Seth shook hands when they greeted as if they were old friends. I guess, men are able to detach from a situation in order to continue. The courtroom scenario seemed years gone by to them and yet it stung fresh in my mind. Seth suggested we all take a boat ride. Josh was excited and Seth took extra care to insure he fastened Josh's life preserver. Once we were out on the water, Seth asked Josh if he would like to drive the boat. Josh jumped enthusiastically and Seth had him sit on his lap, monitoring and instructing him as if it were a driving lesson. Hazen and I sat around the plush leather seats surrounding the port side while Tiffany sat on the starboard. She did not seem to take any interest in Josh, as Seth had suggested. She moved to the massive front of the boat where a large flat area served as a bed, rubbing oil on herself, and finally lay out gathering the sunrays and sipping her wine.

After thirty minutes or so, I began to relax. Hazen, always attentive to my moods, encouraged me to sunbathe as well. I decided I may as well get to know Tiffany so proceeded to lay beside her, self-conscious as I was that sitting side-by-side to a model only accentuated my flaws.

"So, how is the wedding planning going?" I tried to sound chipper with a girlfriend slang I vaguely remembered. She did not look up or glance my way but answered in monotone.

"Well, we had to postpone it, as you may know. We weren't sure if the divorce would go through in time for our April wedding." I heard the hurt and anger in her voice. I understood it. She blamed me. I had no answer so lay silently, unsure of what other topic we could discuss.

"Why don't we go to that island there for a little swim break?" Seth hollered above the noise of the motor. Everyone nodded in agreement except Tiffany, who continued to ignore her surroundings. We docked, swam in the lake for a bit, and enjoyed a small snack from the picnic basket that Seth had brought. I wanted to ask about George and decided this would be my best opportunity.

"Everything looks delicious. Did George prepare this?" I asked Seth directly. He looked miffed for only a split second and then answered curtly.

"No, George retired." Retired? I seriously doubted it.

"Ah, good for him. Where did he settle?" I wanted to find out where he lived. If he still wanted or needed to work, I would have Hazen find him a job.

"I've no idea, Brie." I felt that he probably did but he understood why I was asking. That was okay. I would find him on my own. The awkwardness of the conversation finally lifted as we swam. Hazen and I kept a polite distance from Seth as he interacted with Josh. Josh responded to Seth's doting with giggles and hugs.

"It's getting late. Let's head back to the house. The staff should have dinner prepared by the time we get there." Seth announced again. We obediently dried off with towels and reentered the boat. From the position of the sun, I figured it must be about five o'clock. I felt weary from the emotionally uncomfortable day. I was thankful that Hazen had agreed to join me. Seth, although pleasant, controlled our time. I was thankful that Hazen did not have the alpha-dog syndrome that would have begun an even tenser day.

Josh was getting tired but Seth enticed him to sit with him again to drive the boat. I had abstained from the wine that Seth brought but began to think that maybe one glass would relax my nerves. Tiffany had consumed several glasses, probably half a bottle and seemed content to ignore everyone else and for us to ignore her. I somehow felt that Seth would blame me for her and me not hitting it off but I could not find the inclination to care. So, I sat beside Hazen and sipped on a glass of wine. As we rode, the lull of hitting the waves began to relax me and I lay my head on Hazen's shoulder. The next thing I knew, I was flying in the air. For a second, I thought I was dreaming. Then I saw it.

As if in slow motion, I saw Tiffany go forward, Hazen tried to grab my arm but I was out of reach. Seth still had Josh in his arms but they were higher in the air than any of the rest of us. The boat appeared above me and as I fell into the water, I tried desperately to dive deeper to avoid it landing on me. I did not make it.

The impact of the boat slammed my left leg and I knew instantly that my foot was broken. I frantically tried to swim deeper to avoid the boat but it, now inverted, began to sink holding me hostage beneath its keel. I could feel the pressure of it pushing me deeper. I had not gotten a good breath before I dived, having only just woken up from dozing. I knew my air supply was minimal at best and the throbbing in my foot was somehow interrupting my ability to think clearly.

Was this to be how I would die? Would Seth now attain full custody of Josh? Josh! As soon as I thought his name, my maternal instincts gave me a new strength to fight the presence of the boat pushing me down and ignore my pain. I looked up and saw Hazen in the murky water beside me. He was trying with all his strength to push the boat off me but without avail. Were we both to die in this dark water? We looked at one another, only inches apart now. He came toward me and, as if we understood somehow that this was our last moment together, he drew near to kiss me. I had no air left. Even if Hazen were somehow able to lift me miraculously from under the sinking boat, I would not make it to the surface. I motioned for Hazen to swim on, to get to the surface, to save himself. He ignored my frantic waving. I felt dizzy now, light somehow. I knew he would not leave me until he saw it was too late. The thought of him perishing because of me brought a fresh grief I had not fully felt at the loss of my own life. I knew what I must do.

I accepted my plight. I pushed myself toward him, accepting that my last breath would be while kissing him. Then he would let me go and save himself. He reached for me, understanding somehow that I wanted a kiss and eager to grant me one last wish.

Our lips met. My last tiny breath of air was gone. Then Hazen, rather than return my kiss, began to push his own breath into my mouth. At first, I was relieved to feel my lungs fill with air. Yet, just as quickly, I realized his plan all along was to surrender his own last breath to save me. I tried to pull away, not wanting to steal his final breath. Not able to beat the thought of living without him. He pulled me closer and continued pressing his precious breath into me until my lungs were full. I knew I had no choice now. I would make it to the surface but I would get help and return for him. At the very moment I thought this, Hazen pushed me with a strong force toward the side of the boat. Then he grabbed something on the boat for leverage. He placed his feet against my back and pushed me with a powerful force, freeing me from the confines of the boat. I turned around to help free him, refusing to believe that we both could not come out of this alive. I looked toward the top and realized we were much deeper than I had known. I looked back at him, painfully aware that he had given his life to save me. I knew he would not want me to stay and perish as well. I swam toward the surface, determined to survive. With my painful foot, it was impossible to swim quickly and I worried that I still would not make it before I ran out of air. As I managed to get closer to the surface, I turned looking back to see how far the boat had sunk. There was no trace of it. Yet I could see something in the water.

The figure was Hazen facing me but at a depth that was hard to make out. I was ecstatic. He had gotten free from the watery grave. Then, I saw the blank stare on his face as his body began to sink.

~ 26 ~

A Life Without Hazen

I barely made it to the surface before gasping for more breath. I tried to scream for someone, anyone, to help Hazen. I looked around, frantically splashing in the water and somehow aware that my eyes stung with salt and my foot throbbed terribly. I took another deep breath and finally managed to scream.

"Over here," I heard a woman scream back at me. I turned in the water and saw Tiffany on the shore some distance from me. She was sitting beside Josh.

"Hazen!" was all I could get out, hoping that she would somehow understand the entire story by the mention of his name. "Help!" I added without even realizing my words. She motioned for me to swim toward her. I was not going to leave Hazen. I must dive and try to save him.

Just then, a loud splash hit the water right behind me. I turned quickly and saw Seth had Hazen in a chokehold. He immediately began to swim toward the shore. As if rehearsed, I followed. Hazen was unconscious but not blue, which I could only hope was a good sign. Seth stopped every so many feet and breathed fresh air into his lungs. I grew hopeful every time I saw Hazen's chest rise although I knew it was only Seth's breath forcing it. Panic kept threatening to overtake me as I tried desperately to keep up with them.

At last, we reached the embankment. Tiffany instructed Josh to stay put away from the edge and she jumped in the water once we were close, helping Seth pull Hazen onto the sand. I dragged myself up to him. Tiffany began CPR expertly while Seth caught his breath. I began to pray as I gasped for more air. After only a moment, Hazen began to choke and gasp. I burst into tears, reaching for him to hold him. Tiffany pushed me away with her hand and Seth turned Hazen on his side.

"I had some other boaters call for help," Tiffany told Seth.

"Good," he responded.

"They should be here any moment." Hazen continued to cough and gasp. I looked up, saw Josh about twenty feet away from us, alone and frightened. I motioned for him to join us since I could not walk to him. He jumped up and ran toward me, crying uncontrollably. Once the paramedics arrived, the rest of us stood away giving them ample room to work on Hazen. I was still frightened but felt secure that he would be all right. Once they secured Hazen on the gurney, the one with the blond hair came and looked at my leg and foot.

"Your leg appears only bruised but your foot is definitely broken," he stated matter-of-factly. They wrapped my lower leg, ankle, and foot and told me to sit there until they got Hazen in the ambulance. The paramedics put Hazen in the ambulance and Seth turned to me.

"I'll take care of Josh. Call me when you get home and I'll bring him to you." He offered.

"I don't know if I'll get home tonight," I added. I looked at Josh held securely in Seth's arms and I knew he would be safe with Seth. Seth had saved Hazen's life. He would not hurt his son. "Will you bring him to me?" I asked Seth. I hugged Josh tightly, not wanting to let him go.

"Josh, are you okay staying with Seth, I mean daddy, while mommy goes to the hospital?" I hoped.

"It's ok, mommy," he said, calm now. "I'll take care of him and Tiffany." I smiled and hugged him tightly then let him return to Seth.

"Ok, I'll call you later, then," I looked at Seth as the paramedics placed me in the front seat, "oh, and Seth, thank you." My eyes began to sting with fresh tears and I could not finish the unspoken words to complete my sentence.

"It's alright, Brie. He'll probably be fine. Now, go." I did not like the way he said, "probably". I felt Hazen was secure now. Seth closed my door and we sped off.

I called Rick on the way to the hospital thanks to Tiffany pushing my purse and cell phone into my arms at the last minute. I told Rick not to come because I knew Hazen and I would both need treatment for some time and yet, they met us at the ER door before the beeping of the ambulance finished backing toward the entrance.

"I told you to wait. There's no sense in everyone having to wait up here," I admonished him.

"Nonsense, dear," Tracy took over.

"Mom, are you and Hazen okay?" Katie sounded panicky.

"Yes, we'll be fine," I tried to sound confident. The paramedics took Hazen in before me and I sat, waiting for someone to fetch a wheel chair. Rick, Tracy, and Katie stayed with me until someone finally came.

Once inside, personnel took me to one curtained room and I had no idea where they took Hazen. I kept asking nurses, technicians x-raying my foot, and finally the tech who cast it, yet no one gave me information. My doctor came to brief me on the care and follow-up for my broken foot. He offered me pain medication but I refused. I must stay fully aware so I could see to Hazen.

"Doctor, please help me. The ambulance brought Hazen Thatcher in with me. He almost drowned. I am frantic to find out how he is doing."

"Are you his wife?" I looked at him, tears welling up again, knowing that my answer would shut me out of the information I needed so desperately. "You know we are not supposed to give personal information unless you are family."

"We are engaged," I stretched the truth. The doctor looked around, stepped closer to my bedside, and spoke lowly.

"He's in intensive care, stable for now." What? Intensive care?

"But, why?' My mind raced trying to think of why he would need care. He had awoken on the sand. He had coughed, spit water, vomited a little, and even gasped a breath on his own.

"My dear, sometimes, depending on the length under the water and so forth, there can be damage. The first 24 hours will tell how he will recover." The look on my face told him I was petrified. "This is more a precaution than anything else, I'm sure," he added quickly. "A Pulmonary specialist is treating him. I wish I could tell you more. I'm sorry." Did he wish he could tell me more? Or was he scared to tell me more?

"Thank you. Will I be able to see him?"

"I'm sorry." He told me before he walked away. I knew that if I did not have this cast on, I would hop off the table and go directly to intensive care. There would not be enough security to keep me from finding him. The nurse finally finished my exit papers and wheeled me to the ER waiting room where Rick, Tracy, and Katie waited.

"How's Hazen?" Rick asked immediately. I told him all I knew. "I called his father. He's flying in but, even with a private plane, he won't be here for hours."

“I hate he’s all alone. I need to know his condition, Rick. He saved my life.”

“Hold on,” Rick said. He walked away from us as he pulled his cell phone out of his pocket. I turned to Tracy who still had her arm around me. Katie appeared calm and I was thankful she had not been with us today. I had a million unanswered questions for Seth. I did not even know what had happened. My entire demeanor towards Seth and Tiffany changed. I owed them so much and if Hazen lived, I owed them much more. Rick stepped back into our circle then.

“Dr. Mortimer is not working but he’s going to call the ER doctor in charge and see if there is any way you can get to Hazen. It’s a long shot so don’t get your hopes up but keep your fingers crossed. He’ll call me back in a bit.” I had to sit down. I still felt drained. We all sat in silence. I kept thinking of how the day had gone badly so quickly. It could have gone worse. Hazen and I could both be dead. Hazen had saved my life- literally giving me his last breath. If I ever felt sure of anything in my life it was that he loved me- enough to give his life for me. If he lived through this, I promised myself I would marry him. Perhaps a long courtship is necessary at times but after this day, I knew I did not want to put off committing my life to Hazen for another day.

“Ms. Taylor?” A nurse called from the door. I stood immediately, unsure why she was calling me. Has Hazen died? How could I live my life without Hazen? He changed me. Before I met him I was content; he had changed all that. I knew I could never be complete without him. I could never be fulfilled if he was gone.

“This way,” she said when I reached her. I followed her down the hall, up the elevator, through a large waiting area, and down another hall. Once we reached the double doors, she hit a buzzer and the doors opened. She walked too quickly for me to keep up with my crutches and she had to wait for a moment for me to catch up. The rooms here were different from the others throughout the hospital. Each room surrounded a nurse's station and were separated from it by a large glass wall. She walked up to room 214, hit another buzzer, and stepped aside. She waved her hand for me to proceed.

"Your brother's in here," she said as she walked away. I turned to see Hazen, laid in the bed with tubes beeping at all angles. I hobbled slowly to him. He was unconscious. I propped my crutches against the wall and sat beside him. Hoping he could hear me, I proceeded to take his hand in mine and talk to him quietly.

"Hazen, its Abriella," the fear began to choke me but I swallowed it back down. I had to be the strong one now. "I'm here for you." The only response was the swishing noise of his heart monitor and the monotone beeping of another machine. I squeezed his hand hoping he may be able to squeeze back even if he could not speak.

"Hazen, I love you. I'm sorry I've been stubborn about marrying but, if the proposal still stands, the answer is yes." I sniffed. "Dear Jesus, please save this man. He does not deserve to die this way. Heal him. Touch him. Help him, I pray." Was God still here? I felt that He was. I leaned over the bedside and lay my head on Hazen's hand, afraid to put too much weight any were else. He had always appeared so stong, so virile, and capable. It was surreal that water could bring him to this.

"Hazen, you saved my life. I didn't even have a chance to thank you. You have to come back so I can thank you." No response. "Hazen, you're so strong and wise. Tell me what to do. Can you hear me?" What could I do to reach him? He was the greatest man I had ever met. He had rescued me in so many ways. Then I knew. I knew that if he was going to find the strength to come back to me, he would need a great motivator.

"I need you, my darling. I need you to show me you hear me. I need you to love me for the rest of my life. I need you to teach me how to love as you do. I need you here to protect me from life. Do you hear me, Hazen?" Still no response. I lay my head down again. This time, I openly wept. I begged God to save him. I cried for a while, trying to find the catharsis yet none came. The grief of losing Hazen hit me fresh with each breath I tried to get.

"God, please, take me! Hazen deserves to live his life fully. His family needs him. His father is still grieving over his father's death and if he loses Hazen now, he, he…" I could not even imagine what his father's response would be.

"It would be hard but he would survive," a deep voice said.

"God?" I looked up.

"No, I'm Hazen's father." His voice came from behind me and startled me. I turned around to see a tall, stout man before me. He looked just like Hazen but older- distinguished, strong, and capable. Before I realized what had come over me, I hobbled to him. Maybe because he looked and sounded so much like Hazen, but without reservation, I fell into his waiting arms as he met me half way. He held me tightly and calmed me with his soothing shushes. I cried for only a moment when I realized I did not even know this man.

"I'm, I'm so sorry," I said as I tried to back away.

"No, my dear, you're fine," he spoke more quietly. He helped me back to my chair beside Hazen and he walked around me, standing closer to Hazen's side. Neither of us spoke for a few minutes. Then he broke the silence.

"I have a confession to make to you my dear," he began after a few minutes silence. "When Hazen told me about you- that you were a single mother keeping his books who had been on welfare, I made a presumption about you. From what I just witnessed, I know I was wrong. I hope you can forgive me."

What? I did not understand. I looked up at him questioningly. "You see, many women have tried to get Hazen's fortune. I assumed you were as they. I'm sorry. I see now that you truly love him." Oh, understanding dawned on me. I wondered if that was why he had not flown to meet me.

"It's okay," I sniffed, still trying to get a hold on my emotions. "I can see why you would think that." I was not sure how else to respond, "but Mr. Thatcher?" I hesitated. I was not sure how to tell him this.

"Yes, dear, what is it?"

"Hazen saved my life. He was free from the boat. He only swam under it to save me. He gave me his last breath." I began to weep openly now. "He wouldn't be here if he had just swam to the shore. This is *my entire fault…*" I choked on the last words. "Will you ever be able to forgive me that?" He patted my shoulder and ran his hand up and down my back to sooth me. I kept my head hung down, too humiliated to look at him.

"I know what he did, dear. Don't blame yourself. Hazen has always had a mind of his own. He obviously loves you very much but it would be just like him to do this for a stranger, as well." He squeezed my shoulder to calmed me.

"Mr. Thatcher, a life without Hazen would not be worth living to me now that I've known his love." He did not respond.

"I understand, my dear," he spoke quietly. I knew he was thinking of his wife and son who had preceded him in death.

I put my hand in Hazen's again and held it with both of my own. My tears spilt over his hand and I realized I was probably squeezing him too tightly. I let my grip loose a little. Then I felt it. It was slight but unmistakable. Hazen squeezed my hand in return.

~ 27 ~

Afterwards

A week passed since the accident. Hazen's father stayed to offer support and help with arrangements. He transported Hazen to a rehabilitation center where he would regain his strength and receive the medical care he needed to recover fully. The doctors at the hospital appeared glad to see him go. The fuss that Mr. Thatcher and I bestowed on Hazen disrupted their routine and our myriad questions kept them on their toes.

"I'm fine, my darling," Hazen told me after I asked him half-dozen times could I get him anything. This would be the first night he would be alone. Well, not alone really. There were dozens of doctors, nurses, techs, and therapists.

"Promise me you'll get well quickly," I pleaded.

"I promise. I will do everything the therapists tell me and even practice between my sessions." He was smiling at me as if only trying to appease me.

"Good. No, wait," I thought again, "Maybe you shouldn't overdo it, you know. I'll go ask if you should do more exercises between your sessions." I got up to leave his room but he stopped me, laughing.

"No, sweetheart, I can ask them tomorrow. Go home! Get some rest!" He grabbed my hand and pulled me onto the bed with him. I looked at his contented face and suddenly filled with gratitude. The doctors expected him to make a full recovery. His youth, physical condition, and stamina were all in his favor.

I would be eternally grateful he was in my life. He pulled me to his chest and I melted against him like chocolate on a hot summer day. He kissed me deeply and his hands cradled my face, not willing for me to pull away. I was not trying to pull away. I wanted him more than ever.

"Eh, hum," we heard a deep voice at the door behind us and immediately pulled apart.

"Hi, dad," Hazen smiled sheepishly. I jumped out of the bed and tried, fruitlessly, to straighten my hair and shirt as if we were in high school. I looked down and blushed.

"I would say, 'you kids need to get a room' but I guess you have one, huh?" he laughed. His resemblance to Hazen was remarkable. He aged well and had the sophisticated grace of a self-made man. We had shared many conversations in the past week, some serious and others whimsically hysterical. He had a wonderful sense of humor and I loved him already.

"Hi, Carl," I spoke shyly.

"So, one more week and then you're outa here, huh?" he addressed Hazen.

"Why don't I let you men talk. I've got to get the kids anyway." I kissed Hazen good-bye and hugged Carl. He placed a gentle kiss on my cheek as he always did now. "I'll see you tomorrow," I told Hazen just before I closed the door. It was easier to leave Hazen now that I knew he would be fine. The first time I had left him in the hospital, I cried all the way to Rick's car. That first 24 hours proved to be one of the worst in my life. The pulmonary specialist did not believe in giving false hope. Hazen had been under water for several minutes. If he had not been as young, strong, and healthy as he was, he would not have made it.

Seth explained later that he had hit a huge rock, only slightly protruding from the surface of the lake. He held onto Josh and managed to pass him to Tiffany who swam with him to shore. Seth returned to help us. He saw us embrace, when I thought we were going to kiss, and then saw me swim to the surface. He immediately dived deeper to retrieve Hazen. Apparently, he and Tiffany were both lifeguard trained. Their quick response and training had saved Hazen's life.

Regardless of whatever difficulties Seth and I had endured, I would be forever in his debt. Oddly, the situation changed our relationship. Seth had even visited Hazen once in the hospital. I wasn't present when he came but Hazen said they had a nice talk.

"Can we go see Hazen, now?" the kids both asked when we got home.

"Well, not today. Let's let him get settled in but tomorrow when I get you from school, I'll take you to see him. How about we make him some get-well cards?" This ignited them and kept them busy until I was able to finish dinner.

"Hi," Seth called late that night, "have you got a minute?" His voice sounded strangely comfortable as if we were friends. I did not particularly want to be friends with Seth or Tiffany but, I had to admit, it was better than the reverse.

"Uh, sure."

"I need to talk to someone. I know you're going to think this is crazy but I thought of you." Yes! That did sound crazy to me. What in the world did he want?

"Okay," I added hesitantly.

"The thing is, um, Tiffany and I broke off our engagement." I was shocked.

"Oh, Seth, I don't know what you want me to say. I am so sorry. Are you okay?"

"Yeah, it was my idea, actually."

"Well, then, is she okay?"

"Yeah, she will be. She is a very strong woman. The thing is, well, here's the reason I needed to talk to you; I have tried to be happy. I've tried to live a normal life. Brie, you know what I am. As much as I hate myself, I can't help it." I was stunned. Was he telling me he was coming out of the closet? I did not know what to say.

"When I saw you and Hazen together, that day, it made me realize how happy two people could be when they're open to express their love to one another. You have no idea how hard it is to hide who you are." He stopped for a minute and because I still could not think of one good thing to say, I remained silent. "The thing is, if I could be, well, you know, open, I think I could have a chance at that kind of happiness."

"With Judge Miller?" I interjected involuntarily.

"No, actually, we broke up after all the mess," he sounded dejected. I knew exactly what mess of which he referred. "No, I mean a real relationship." I was glad he did not linger on Judge Miller. For some reason, I hated him worse than I hated Seth. I think deep down, I knew that Seth was a good man. He had been vindictive and mean because he had been miserable living a lie and untrue to himself; whereas, Judge Miller was a corrupt person.

"Well, Seth, I'm sure you've given this a lot of thought. If this is what you want, what's holding you back?" I knew the answer- his family, particularly his father.

"Yeah, well, you know dad. He'll disown me. It's this society. Everyone's so screwed up." His frustration was taking over.

"Seth, screw society. You know, there are much more important issues with which people need to concern themselves than with whom you sleep. There are wars, starving children, hurting teenagers, suicidal veterans, the list goes on."

"Brie?"

"Yeah."

"I'm sorry. I'm sorry I put you through all I did. I was just,"

"Seth, you don't have to explain. I understand. You were miserable. It's impossible to be happy and treat others kindly when you're miserable."

"Wow! When did you get so wise?"

"I've always been wise, Seth. You just didn't see it," I teased him playfully to lighten the mood. He laughed with me. "Well, I need to get in the bed. I want to go see Hazen first thing after dropping the kids off. Are you getting Josh this weekend?" Seth had been picking Josh up almost daily for me since the accident to help me out.

"I'm not sure. I guess that might depend on how my coming-out goes." I felt sorry for him. It must be terrible to have to worry that the very family who is supposed to love you may turn their backs on you when they learn you are not what they thought.

"Well, I'll say a prayer that it goes well. Just let me know about Josh when you can."

"That seems odd, doesn't it? To say a prayer for me that my coming-out goes well?"

"Well, Seth, loving one another was the greatest command that Christ gave us. If we can't love, then, to me, we are not fully realizing our spiritual selves."

"Huh, maybe I may go with you to your church sometime if that's how they feel." I did not have the heart to tell him that I was not sure where my church would be.

"That'd be great," I told him. "Hey Seth, while we're are talking, can I ask you a favor?"

"Uh, I guess," he didn't sound too sure.

"Hazen is going to need extra help for a while," I exaggerated, "Do you happen to know if George is working for anyone or how to get in touch with him?"

"Uh, well, actually he's been gone since right after I announced you died. I heard he went to work at some restaurant but couldn't keep up so he quit. I have his old number if you want it. He may still have it."

"That'd be great!" I sounded a little too exuberant. He had me hold a minute while he looked up George's cell number.

After we hung up, I did say a prayer for him.

"Hi, beautiful," Hazen's voice was like a medicinal balm to my spirit. He understood I could not stay with him every night. I had the kids to take care of and get in bed. So, each night he would call me from his hospital and now, from rehab. We talked on the phone until either became too tired to continue the conversation.

When I finally went to sleep that night, I lay thinking over how far I had come, how much I had grown, and how blessed I felt. I wonder, I thought, what my life would have been like if I had stayed with Seth. If we had fought that night and, instead of leaving, I had stayed and then found out I was pregnant. I would have never had the gumption to leave Seth then. I would have stayed with him, lived miserably, and never have found the blissfulness that surrounded me now. That one decision I made had created a ripple effect for which I was grateful. I would have never met Annie Mae, Poppa, Ezekiel, or Hazen. Kayla may have grown frustrated and never finished school without Hazen's help. With George aging, I knew he could not handle an arduous job and I planned to hire him to help Hazen. I felt I could returned the favor to George that he had graciously bestowed upon me for so many years. I drifted to sleep with a smile on my face realizing that despite the traumatic years that had molded me into who I am today I liked myself now. I admired the woman I had become. While I would never have chosen the path, I appreciated the outcome.

A few weeks went by and my life began to settle into a wonderful routine. Hazen was gaining strength quickly and I was back at work. Rick, always the gentleman, had allowed me off work until Hazen was able to get home and take care of himself. Hazen approved of my hiring George to be his butler and take care of him once he was home but I wanted to be there for Hazen, too. With Hazen's health fully restored now, we were inseparable. Plus, getting reacquainted with George was priceless. George had taken a few years to travel, visiting relatives and had met someone. He and his partner, Marty, enjoyed their life but George was restless and jumped at the chance to be Hazen's butler in Atlanta. He would keep the place nice in Hazen's absence and, when Hazen was in town, he would prepare meals, shop, clean, etc for him. It was the perfect arrangement for us all.

"Hey Brie, can you come into my office for a minute?" Rick asked my first week back at work.

"Sup?" I asked as I entered his office.

"Sit down." That sounded serious. "Carl and I had lunch the other day." We all felt very connected to Hazen's dad now and were on a first name basis. "He made a proposal to me."

"Really? I thought Hazen was supposed to propose to me," I always tended to be sarcastic when conversations got heavy. Rick just looked at me.

"He feels that you alone will not be able to handle the transition you're talking of undertaking for his business. I agreed." I could not believe it. I knew I was under experienced and had, in fact, told Hazen that at some point I would need to pull in some help but to take the whole account away from me? It stung and I tried to pretend I was mature enough not to let it bother me.

"I see," I managed to get out without betraying my true feelings.

"The thing is, he recognizes you have a gift. He loves your ideas so far. One thing that's got him thinking is that he already employs many accountants all over the United States. After talking to him at length, he sees the wisdom in creating a central agency that takes care of everything in house." I was totally lost now. I had no idea where Rick was going with this. I assumed he was trying to let me down easy and I opened my mouth to tell him not to worry about me. After all, with the support I was getting from Seth, I did not need to work really. I loved my work and did not intend to quit. Loosing Hazen's account hurt me more on a personal level than on a monetary one. Rick held up his hand to stop my interruption.

"Carl feels and, like I mentioned, I agree that this is bigger job than one person can do alone. He has proposed opening a new office, employing enough accountants to manage the various business in one location, and he's asked me if he could steal you away to oversee that office. He's proposed to make you his CFO." What? Surely, I had not heard correctly. "Now before you jump at the chance, I need to tell you that Carl wants you to travel to all the businesses on a regular basis to keep your finger on their pulses, so to speak. Of course, I reminded him of the kids. He said he had no problem hiring full-time teachers to accompany you out of town in order to home-school the kids if you wish. The schedule wouldn't be constant. In fact, I suggested doing most of the travel in the summertime while the kids are out of school. The bottom line is the job is yours if you want it but it would be a change in lifestyle."

I was speechless. On the surface, it sounded ideal. Yet, did I really want to uproot my kids, change my routine life, and become an executive? Rick looked at me expectantly.

"Rick, I don't know what to say. I don't even know if I'm capable, I mean, that's a lot of responsibility." A million thoughts scrambled in my head. "I think I'd like to talk with Hazen about it."

"Of course. He's in no hurry."

"What about you?" It wasn't as if Rick couldn't run the place without me but, but, but what?

"Well, Carl originally asked if I'd be willing to take on the responsibility in house. I had to decline. I have too many other clients that have been loyal to me for too many years. His businesses alone would be a full-time endeavor. He is going to give a financial compensation package for stealing you away from me though."

"A compensation package?"

"Yeah, well, I told him how I rely on you heavily. It's already been difficult doing without you since you're on his accounts full-time. I was already looking into hiring another assistant to replace you, seeing how involved his businesses would be long term."

"You were already going to replace me?"

"Brie," Rick softened his voice when he heard the hurt in mine. "Surely, you realized that this was going to be a permanent promotion for you if you did a good job." No, I had not. "Look, talk to Hazen. Think about it. Take your time. You may want to talk to Carl, as well."

"Of course." I stood up to leave and just as I put my hand on the door handle Rick spoke again.

"This is a good opportunity for you Brie. Don't screw it up by overanalyzing it." I nodded and walked away.

"Does that upset you?" Hazen asked me when I told him his father's proposal.

"No, not upset me really but," I hesitated, "Hazen, is he offering this to me because of our relationship or because he really thinks I am capable?" There, I had said it.

"Oh, no, no, no, sweetie," he was at my side immediately and cupped my face with his hands, "Trust me, my dad is very adamant about business. He would never put you, or anyone, in charge of his empire unless he trusted them. He mentioned it to me first and I told him I thought it was a splendid idea. After all, you will be my wife soon and we might as well get our monies worth out of you." He laughed loudly at his joke.

"Ha! There's no engagement ring on this finger, Mr. Thatcher!" I joked back.

"Well, we'll just have to change that then. Do you want to go to Africa next week?"

"What?"

"I told you when the time came to get your ring, I want us to go pick out the diamond of your choice from the best mines in the world."

"You're crazy! That's absurd!"

"Why?"

"Do you have any idea how much a trip like that would cost? I would be quite content with an American diamond from any jewelry store on any corner."

"Oh, so now that you're holding the purse strings of the company, you're going to cut down my expenses?" He was still laughing. I walked into the room to check that the kids were still sleeping from all of his loud laughter. They were. When I came back, Hazen was sitting on the couch. He patted the seat beside himself. I sat obediently.

"Abriella, you say you would be happy with any diamond from any store but," he looked down and began to doodle imaginary lines on the back of my hand, "I think you are anything but ordinary. Any diamond from any story is *not* going on my wife's hand." I saw then that this meant a lot to him. He had been raised differently than I had been. I was important to him and the way he showed that was by making sure I had the best. Anything less would be an insult to his manhood.

"It's ok. When you're ready, I'll accompany you to Africa and we will pick out the prettiest diamond on the entire continent." He looked up at me then and smiled the biggest smile I had ever seen on him. "*But*, prettiest does *not* necessarily mean the biggest! Okay?" Hazen smiled and I was not sure exactly what that meant.

A few days later, I called Carl and asked for a meeting. He suggested that Hazen and I fly up to Colorado for the weekend with the kids. It sounded like a great idea so Hazen and I made arrangements.

"The kids are so excited," I told Hazen the night before we left, "they're having a hard time going to sleep."

"Me, too," he added. "Abriella, I need to talk to you."

"Please don't give me bad news."

"No, not at all. I was thinking, the kids will be out of school in what, two more weeks?" I nodded. "I'd like for us to go on a safari to Africa. I'd like to ask my dad to come along, too."

"Hazen, that sounds like an awesome trip but, I don't know," I was racking my brain trying to find one good reason to say, 'no'. "How long would you want to stay?"

"Well, I was thinking while we are there, we could check on the charities I set up. I could have some supplies shipped over while we're there and oversee their use. Maybe we could even work on some other needs that need to be met there, like some more orphanages and schools."

"So, how long would all that take?"

"Okay, here's the deal," he took a deep breath, "if we could stay the summer, I could really help a lot more. It's just too difficult to manage from such a great distance."

"The whole summer?" I exclaimed, astonished.

"Why not?"

"Well, first of all, if I'm going to help your dad, I'll need to meet with the accountants, and set up an office somewhere, and," my head was getting dizzy from thinking of all that needed to be done.

"Abriella, that's going to be a long process. Dad has been doing business this way for generations. I don't think one more summer will shut him down. Besides, with our portable office, you can do anything anywhere in the world that you could do here." He had a good point. "I was thinking while we're in Africa, we could find that perfect diamond for you, too." My heart was racing. "You know, we've been very good about keeping our distance from one another but once we tie the knot, I could ravish your body without hesitation or reservation." He had a twinkle in his eyes that I had not seen in a while and it instantly affected me.

"Okay," I whispered.

"Okay?" he repeated.

"Okay!" I said louder.

"We're going to Africa!" Katie screamed from the bedroom.

~ 28 ~

African Dreams: A New Era

We arrived in Africa the second week of summer. Since Hazen and I had discussed taking the trip, a million details had to be completed. The weekend in Colorado with Carl had been glorious. Hazen and I found it increasingly more difficult to restrain from ripping one another's clothes off. Hazen had even suggested we get married before we went to Africa. I almost said, 'yes' but knew that I would feel we had sold-out. I had never had the whole package wedding and fairy-tale ending. I wanted it all.

Our entourage would grow exponentially. Poppa, Annie Mae, and Ezekiel were to join us mid-summer for two weeks, at Hazen's expense. They could not turn down the opportunity of a lifetime. It felt, for once, that I really had the family I had craved for so many years. Seth reluctantly agreed that Josh's experience would be monumental. He did make me promise to Skype him at least weekly so that he and Josh could continue to build their relationship. Even Sparks, Katie's cat, seemed to be taking the travel in stride, only meowing for more attention when he occasionally had to stay in his kennel for extended periods.

We went to Cape Town, the second-most populous city in South Africa, for a few days. Hazen insisted we take the first day to visit several diamond dealers he knew in the area. He wanted to surprise me with the ring, he said, so he had me pick out five different stones that I loved. He was to choose from those and have it set once we returned to the United States.

With that settled and Hazen happy, he and Carl set out to show us the beautiful coastline. We visited Table Mountain. It is a flat-topped mountain, which boasts a view overlooking the city of Cape Town. There was an entire National Park with days' worth of activities to keep us all busy and exhausted. The ocean was crystal clear and gorgeous so we charted a yacht for a few days to explore up the coast. It was a phenomenal ship with large staterooms and a private crew.

The kids behaved magnificently and Carl watched them several times so that Hazen and I could slip in a few hours here and there. Both the kids adored Carl and, without me prompting, began to call him Popps. Carl loved the nickname. He finally had the grandkids that had eluded him for so many years.

As Hazen and I swam in the seas, he told me that sharks are particularly plenteous off the coast of Africa. We did not swim long.

We took the kids to Two Oceans Aquarium, which is the largest aquarium in South Africa. It had more than 300 marine species and the displays were some of the most impressive I could imagine.

Hazen taught me how to handle making travel arrangements so that I could aptly handle future plans for business and our family. He also introduced me to their mobile office, which went with them anywhere they traveled. It was complete with several computers, printers, and basic office supplies. It enabled them, and now me, to do any work necessary while abroad.

After a week of fun, we traveled north to Zimbabwe. Hazen insisted we fly, stating that the travel on land was demanding and often unsafe. For once, I did not argue. The difference between these two countries so close in proximity was frightening. The striking difference between the two destinations, so close in proximity yet so different in every other way, made me reflect on Atlanta. This was how I felt when I arrived in Annie Mae's neighborhood. How could two places be so close and yet one is starving while the other flourishes?

"Zimbabwe is one of the poorest countries in Africa," Hazen explained as we made our way from the makeshift airport to the camp where we would stay. "It has the lowest life expectancy in the entire world. Men live only to about age thirty-seven. Women only thirty-four."

"Oh my goodness, that's terrible," I exclaimed. "Why?"

"Well, the HIV and AIDS endemic wipes out populations and has also caused a great strain on the economy. In fact, the 2013 statistics ranked Zimbabwe last at number 184 of the world's poorest countries."

"Oh Hazen, this is terrible. Do you think the kids should see this?" I worried aloud.

"Abriella, we just spent ten days enjoying the best that life has to offer. The balance will be good for them. They need to see that life isn't only pleasurable but that many people are in dire need."

"Yes, but Hazen, this abject poverty is disturbing, even to me, I don't know if," I was profoundly affected seeing the people around me. Hazen saw my feelings and stopped me.

"My beautiful lady, I know that you spent several years in south Atlanta thinking you were surrounded by danger and poverty. Here you will see what that truly looks like. South Atlanta will look like an ice cream shop comparably. I promise you that your children will be safe here. I also promise that they will be better adults because of having witnessed this extreme poverty and done something to ease these people's pain." I looked deep into his eyes and I saw what he meant. He was wealthy beyond anything I had ever seen and yet he had a heart for people who hurt, hungered, and were in great need like no one I had ever met in my life. If my children could grow up to be like him, then I was on board for his plan.

"Okay, Hazen, I trust you," I told him.

"I won't let you down, my love." He leaned down and kissed me and despite being surrounded by famine, disease, and filth, I felt secure.

We stayed in Zimbabwe for about six days, helping where we could, delivering supplies to the med clinic, and restoring hope in people that we would likely never see alive again. I was amazed at how the children reacted.

Katie particularly took a keen interest in wanting to help. She washed the small children, prepared and delivered meals, and even helped some in the medic area. I could see her changing before my eyes. She had always been very mature for her age. She had always shown a warm heart for those in need. However, now I saw in her a transition from wanting to help others to a need to make a difference.

Josh, although only four, seemed to understand that these children he played with were more fragile than he. He would help the ones who were weaker to join in their dances and he taught them a few games, such as duck-duck-goose. Yes, I had to agree, Hazen had been correct in his assessment that this experience would balance their idea of life. I knew now that my children would grow up with the best that money could buy-good schools, vacations, and experiences like this trip. I understood Hazen's determination to make sure that they should also experience the worst that life presented. They would be in the position to make a difference. Hazen wanted to insure that they did.

The next few weeks passed quickly. We went on a safari that started at the Makgadikgadi Pans National Park, the home to 30,000 zebra and wildebeest. Next we flew to Camp Moremi where we saw lions, leopards, cheetahs, and a wild dog. Lastly we went to Chobe Game Lode, the only lodge in Chobe National Park and saw their massive elephant population. The thrills of being in the middle of this gorgeous continent excited me to no end.

"Hazen," I began demurely one afternoon, "You were right." He smiled.

"Oh? About what in particular?"

"Everything- this trip, the kids seeing this, everything. But, especially about us getting married. I wish we *had* gotten married before we left the states. I want so much to be in your arms every night rather than going to my bed alone." He raised up immediately from the comfortable lounge chair from which he had been relaxing before I spoke. Before I realized it, he had me in his arms, his face only inches from mine.

"My darling, if you mean that, I will arrange for us to marry in Africa. We could have a traditional African ceremony here and if you want, we could have an American service upon our return."

"Oh, Hazen! That would be amazing!" Could I believe my ears? "But, wouldn't that be too much?"

"Don't be silly, Abriella. If you wanted a ceremony on every continent on Earth, I would arrange it."

"Now who's being silly?" I asked. Hazen brushed my jawline with his fingertips.

"I hope you're not angry. You are so precious to me but, I, well," he stammered. Then he reached in his pocket, pulled out a ring, and slid it on my left ring finger. "I went ahead and had the stone set. I guess I was hoping you would decide you couldn't wait until we returned to the states to reap all the rewards of being my wife." He smiled a wicked smile and I knew exactly what he meant. The ring was stunning. The five-carat Alexandrite beamed with a reddish hue for the moment, although I knew from Hazen teaching me that it is a color-changing gemstone. Its hue will shift depending on the light of which it is exposed. Bringing out the color of the Alexandrite were dozens of diamonds, not only surrounding it but also gracing the entirety of the band. Hazen had told me he would only buy the best-crafted diamonds so I knew that this ring must be in excess of $100,000.

"Hazen, I don't know what to say," I stammered. "This isn't one of the stones I picked out." I could not stop starring at my hand and this magnificent piece of jewelry.

"I know, my love," he took a deep breath, "Don't be mad but, well, I took your tastes in advisement but I *knew* that you would not pick out the quality stone that I felt truly exemplifies our love. This Alexandrite is one of only a hand-full like it in the world. Not that you are one of a hand-full of women; you are unique but I didn't think you would like a ten-carat stone, which would have better shown the way I feel about you." I shook my head in agreement. "The Hearts of Fire diamonds that complete the ring were my idea, you know, to make the Alexandrite even more beautiful. I love this stone for us because, just as it changes hues, our love will change over the years; although both will only go up in value."

I looked up from the ring then and Hazen's face glowed with pride. I would never tell him that I thought this symbolic token of our love was too much. He loved me. He felt I somehow deserved this so I would keep my opinions forever silent.

"Hazen, it's the most gorgeous ring I've ever seen in my life." I grabbed him and hugged him tightly. We sat there for a few minutes enjoying the moment. Then I pushed away from him and took him into my arms, kissing him as passionately as I had ever felt. He returned my kiss, pressing deeply toward me and I returned his movements, inflaming our insatiable appetites. I groaned beneath his strength and his right hand began to pull me closer, caressing my back and then my front, cupping my breast. As if something took over between us, we both begin to move in a way we had never dared before, pulling each other closer although there was barely a hair's breadth between us already.

In a last effort of bravado, I decided to put myself in a position of controlling the situation, hoping I would be able to stop us if I needed. I somehow knew that I had better take control before Hazen grew too strong, so I turned and faced him, straddling him beneath me.

Our lips had not stopped trying to quench their thirsts yet. I held his face in my hands as he had done to me so many times and pulled him to me as my fingers laced through his hair. I pulled the band out that held his hair back and ran my fingers down the length of his hair.

He moaned deeply and lifted me easily up in the air with his hands on my hips. I thought he was going to set me aside but instead he sat me back down on him, having adjusted my stance to make himself more comfortable. I could feel him- this man who wanted me. Every nerve in me screamed to be satisfied. My thoughts tried to intervene but in my heart, there was no need to stop. We were to be married quickly now. I had never wanted anything anymore than I wanted him at this moment. This last thought was my undoing.

"Hazen, I love you," I managed when I pushed away slightly. "Take me. Take me now, my darling." I wanted him to know that I did not need to wait any longer. I was ready.

"Oh, Abriella," his breath was more husky than usual and his deep longing evident. "I want you, my love, I do but," I cut off his protest with a kiss and began to move upon him in a way that I knew would make him forget his senses, forget his scruples, and make me his. It worked. Hazen began to grasp me as if he would tear me apart. He ripped open the front of my blouse, sending buttons flying across the room. Then he cupped both my breasts and pulled them to his mouth. My heart raced as never before. We were about to consummate our relationship. Would we have any regrets?

"Hazen, are you sure? I don't want you to regret this later." I tried to speak and yet my voice came out a whisper.

"It's too late, my love, I must have you now." I agreed by pulling him closer to my décolleté, hoping he would never stop. He stood then, realizing that we could not do this on the lounge of the living area of our quarters. We needed privacy. He carried me, still straddled around him, toward his bedroom.

When we walked by the window, we both instinctively looked out and saw the kids swimming at the pool with Carl. Katie happened to see us and waved.

"Mom, Dad, come join us," she shouted. I looked at Hazen, his face aglow at her declaration. He sat me down with one quick thump.

"Did she just call me 'dad'?" he asked.

"Yes," I answered. Then Hazen looked at me. I knew before he spoke that our longing would have to wait until our nuptials.

"Abriella, we can't, if not for the preservation of our own respect then for theirs." I breathed a deep sigh.

"Agreed," I told him although my brain was the only part of my body that agreed with him. "But, Hazen, we had better get married quickly." We went then to our prospective bedrooms and changed into our swimsuits. My blouse discarded in the trash.

So it was to be. Hazen and I would marry in a traditional African ceremony and, if I chose, we could still have my dream wedding upon our return, although I felt in my heart that this ceremony would be more true to my heart.

After our passion cooled, we decided to wait until Poppa, Annie Mae, and Ezekiel arrived mid-summer. It would mean the world to them to be a part of it. I would have Poppa walk me down the aisle and give me away.

As we planned our wedding from the mobile office, we continued our exploration up to Egypt. Over the course of a week, we saw the Giza Necropolis, which includes the Great Pyramids, the sculpture of the Great Sphinx, and many other sites. Because it is located on the outskirts of Cairo, we stayed there and enjoyed many amenities and foods. We also visited the ancient Nile River. Surrounded by all this ancient knowledge my heart stirred with the unbelief that anyone could see these sites and not believe that God had not created them. It seemed to me that it took more faith to think that this all came about so beautifully by accident.

Alas, Poppa, Annie Mae, and Ezekiel joined us. When they arrived, they were exhausted so Hazen arranged for servants to cater to them with relaxation treatments and nourishing foods for a few days until the jet lag finally wore away. We took them to see the Great Pyramids and shopping at the local markets in the cool of the day. Annie Mae helped a little with the wedding arrangements, suggesting that we keep it as close to African tradition as possible.

"Annie Mae, what kind of wedding did you and Poppa have?" I asked one day as we worked on finding the ideal location.

"Oh, chille, we didn't have no big weddin'. We got married at tha church but back then we didn't have no money. My aunt made tha cake. It was nice, though." Her eyes wandered to the day she said her vows to the man with whom she would spend her life.

"I have a great idea," I said with a sudden epiphany, "You and Poppa will repeat your vows here. We'll have a double-wedding!" The idea excited me so much that I jumped up from my chair, suddenly overtaken with a new and somehow more important determination than planning my own wedding.

"No, chille, this is your day," Annie Mae began protesting.

"Annie Mae, this is going to happen. Just accept it and be happy." After a few more minutes of arguing, she finally conceded to allow me to include them.

"Oh, honey chille, I'm nervous already!" she exclaimed. We laughed together and it truly felt like I had spent the day with my mother. I decided that maybe sometimes our biological families are not the families with which we were born to live our lives. Maybe, if our own families were incapable of loving us, we were intended to be a part of a family of our own choosing.

Poppa had asked specifically to visit Elmina Castle, located on the coast of Ghana. Since Poppa rarely asked for anything, I was curious why this was important to him.

"Brie, I have no proof but the story that's been passed down for generations in my family is that my African ancestor was one of the 30,000 slaves a year who passed through the 'Door of No Return'. That's the portal through which slaves boarded the ships that would take them across the Atlantic known as the Middle Passage." He paused to get his breath and I could not help but notice he seemed older than I had ever seen him.

"Elmina Castle was built in 1482, not for slave-trading but for gold trade. It had some fancy suites at top for the Europeans and slave dungeons below. Them cells sometimes held 200 people at a time, without enough space to even lie down. Lots of tha slaves was lost due to malaria and yellow fever."

"Poppa," I lay my hand over his to soften what I was about to ask, "do you still harbor resentment towards whites for enslaving your ancestors?" Poppa used his other hand to cover mine and patted me paternally.

"No, baby. It wasn't only whites. Most folks don't realize this but it only takes a little searchin' to know that African rulers, merchants, and middlemen was as much helpin' tha slave trade as was the white travelers, if not more. You see, many Africans also took part in vicimizin' their own kind. Precolonial empires like Dahomey and Ashanti grew rich by trading their fellow Africans."

"Wow! Poppa, I've never heard this. How do you know so much about all this?" I envisioned him sitting as a little boy around his father and grandfather's laps as they told him stories they had heard growing up.

"Well, baby," he chuckled slightly, "I love ta read. I like history tha most so, naturally, I had a keen interest in the history of my own people." The years I had spent with Annie Mae and Poppa, I never really gotten to know them. I realized now that they had their own lives, their own problems, and even their own history. This new knowledge made me both appreciative that they had taken me in, and made me feel more an outsider from their world.

So, we traveled to Ghana and visited the infamous castle. It was not a castle in the sense that one thinks of a majestic castle. In fact, it looked like it had been only common at the height of its popularity. Today, it was a tourist attraction and looked more befittingly like ruins. It was an emotional day for Poppa and Annie Mae. I felt uncomfortable there, with them. I felt I had interrupted their time. I was surprised at the end of the day when Annie Mae announced that they would like to renew their vows right here, at this castle that had probably housed their ancestors.

"Annie Mae, if that's what you want, we'll do it but I don't want to have my wedding here. I feel a deep resentment toward this place. Frankly, I'm surprised you don't," I told her when we were alone.

"Chille, I see yo problem. You feel like, I don' know, you somehow responsible for slavery. Don't feel that a way. I have no idea if yo ancestors had anything ta do with mine but that was all too long ago for us ta worry 'bout it. What the devil meant for bad, God turned inta good. I hate that my people had ta suffer such cruelty but there ain't nothin' you or me can do ta change history. I hope this don' come out tha wrong way, but I'd a never met my Jessie, or had the life I have in the U.S., or even been able to raise my 'Zekiel if we wuden't where we are. I'm not sayin' it ta sound selfish but, I look around an' I see these here people dyin' and starvin'. I guess I'm just selfish enough ta be thankful I live where I do."

"Annie Mae, that was very eloquent but, I still, well, I just don't want to get married in a place with this history."

"That's okay, too, chille. Me and Poppa wanna renew our vows here, where our ancestors went from their old life ta their new one. It's a way of us honorin' them." That made sense to me and I appreciated that she felt comfortable talking with me about such delicate matters and allowing us to choose our own wedding sites.

The next day, we rushed to prepare for the ceremony that would take place that evening. Poppa and Annie Mae chose their traditions carefully. They especially wanted to "jump the broom". This tradition of jumping over an ornamental broom as public declaration of love and commitment to one another, started by slaves whose masters did not allow them to marry. In this way, the slaves made their own traditions that were honored among themselves. Poppa and Annie Mae would take the broom home as a memento of this occasion, just as the slaves hung their wedding brooms on their walls.

At the conclusion of their ceremony, they also had a libation ceremony where they poured Holy water onto the ground as they recited prayers to honor their ancestors. It was a sunset wedding and perfectly situated over the bay.

After the ceremony, the people of the area joined in as we had a huge party, celebrating Poppa and Annie Mae. Ezekiel could not stop smiling the entire day. I felt so honored to be a part of this important moment in their life.

Within the week, we arrived at our wedding destination-the Benguerra Island in Mozambique. The islands that fill the sea are surrounded by clear, turquoise water and are filled with whales, dolphins, and dugong. Our group would lodge on one of the private islands of the Azura Retreats on Benguerra Island. After another day's plans were complete, our wedding day followed on the next day's sunset. We had arranged for a luau-style party to ensue after the ceremony.

To get to the island, helicopters took us across the Bazaruto Archipelago on a ten-minute ride. The views are amongst the most gorgeous in the world. Awaiting us on the beach, actually nestled in the water, was a white table and white chairs with an array of fresh tropical fruit. Once we settled in our quarters, magnificent hut-looking structures, the staff catered to our every whim. Our honeymoon suite had hardwood floors, a huge king-sized bed with mosquito nets surrounding it, and one wall that was only a window so that the view of the beach and ocean felt as if we were outdoors. Indeed, the window could slide back so that the room was completely open to the beach.

Annie Mae, Poppa, and Hazen took the kids and Ezekiel to the swimming pool. The staff, run by a woman named Chinaka, began to work on me as if I had never dressed myself. They massaged, polished, waxed, and painted me until I barely recognized myself in the mirror.

As sunset approached, Chinaka informed me that Hazen and the others were all ready. The ceremony would begin in a few minutes. My nerves were on edge. Was I excited? Scared?

"Could you have Annie Mae come to me, please?" I asked her. She nodded and motioned to one of her assistants to fetch her. Then she guided me to slip on my wedding dress. Just as she fastened the last hooks, Annie Mae came in.

"Oh, chille. You the pretties' thang I ever did see," she said with awe. "I knowed when I first saw you that you'd clean up good but lawd have mercy." Her eyes were misty and having her here settled my nerves somewhat.

"Annie Mae, thank you for coming. I don't know what's wrong with me. I feel so nervous. Am I doing the right thing?" She looked at me, stunned, I guessed, that I had any doubt.

"Chille, only you can answer that but I'll tell ya right now if yo heart is tellin' ya to stop, then you'd best stop."

"Every fiber of my being wants Hazen, in every way. I love him beyond words but, but, I'm so scared that I'm only living another fantasy that will turn to a nightmare." I begin to sniff. Annie Mae made her way closer to me. Then she put her arms around me and hugged me, a rare show of affection for her.

"Chille, I told ya long time ago to always follow your heart. Sounds like your hearts tellin' ya ta run down that aisle and join tha man at the end of it that loves ya. Sounds ta me like you been thinkin' too much again." She was right, again. My mind raced day and night trying to find the negative emotions that would spoil my elation of this day. I loved Hazen.

"An' I'll just go on ahead an' say it, chille. If you ain't gonna marry that man, I'll go stand in yo place," she burst out laughing at her own joke. Her ploy worked; I smiled. I looked at the Chinaka, patiently waiting with a tissue to repair my eyes. I nodded that I was ready.

"I'll tell Poppa ta come and get ya," Annie Mae said as she kissed me on the cheek and left.

"My lady," Chinaka spoke with a strong accent, "may I speak plainly?" I wondered if I really had time but nodded.

"My name means, 'God decides'. I have found that, although we think we are much in charge of our lives, God will use our circumstances to create His will in our lives. Sometimes, we may go off path but if we surrender to Him, He directs our path. I see your man. He is a good man and does much work for our people. He is a man of God. I am not a prophet but, at times, I do see. I know that you and he will make a difference in this world together." Then she bowed and slid backwards away from me. I was speechless. God decides. I most certainly felt His presence in my life. Was it possible that He had decided that Hazen would be my mate for life?

"You look beautiful," Poppa said as he held out his arm to escort me to the beach. His voice was like a warm liquid pouring over me and I joined him at the door. We walked the short distance to the beach where the sun lay on the crest of the horizon. I looked up to see all the people I loved most in the world. Hazen faced me at the end of the aisle and beyond him, a school of dolphins jumped joyously.

Acknowledgments

I would like to thank my dear friend, Rosella Hall, who graciously offered to be my editor. You scanned tirelessly even while we enjoyed the beach. Your particular expertise is priceless to me.

I must extend my gratitude to friends who offered your time to help insure my book launch for *The Tapestry of A. Taylor* was a huge success: Rosella Hall, Judy Wise, Elaine & Mark Lupo, and Melanie Evans. I will always treasure your dedication.

A huge thanks to Covenant Woods Retirement Community for their contribution to my success thus far. You hosted my first book launch party with much fanfare. It was a day I will cherish for the rest of my life.

A big thank you to my son, Kyle, who continues to make sure my lack of ability does not compromise my book covers. With your drive to perfection, I have no doubt you will achieve huge success in life.

Again, and always, I must thank my parents, James & Elsie Carlisle, who believed in me when no one else did, who solidly supported me in every way, and whose love sustained me for many years now. You know my heart, and love me anyway-thank you.

Lastly, but most importantly, I must thank Jesus Christ, my Savior. He has steered me through dark days, held me through living nightmares, and prepared a table before me for which I could only dream of prior to writing. Most significantly, He died for me on a cross before I knew of His existence. If you are not already acquainted with Him, please read John 3:16:

"For God so loved the world that He gave His only begotten son that whosoever should not perish but have everlasting life." IE: whosoever = you

About the Author

Kathleen C. Mitchell completed her B.A. in English Language d Literature at Columbus State University after a long and luous journey, which spanned almost 20 years. Her termination to complete her education is a testament of its portance to her.

Kathleen draws her ideas from her varied past in several reers, as a single-mother for many years, and the interesting ople she has known throughout her life. She currently resides th her husband and children in Columbus, Georgia. Although joying her career of choice as a Mother and more recently as a ına, she aspires to create stories that both entertain and inspire aders to live confidently and to never to give up on their dream.

The Tapestry Series began Kathleen's writing career. She may be contacted at MitchellManuscripts@gmail.com, Amazon.com/author/KCMitchell, Facebook.com/authorKCMitchell, or KCMitchell.webs.com.